Sin Virus

Joe Torosian

ISBN: 9798776121814

"A man who strays from the path of understanding comes to rest in the company of the dead." --**Proverbs 21:16**

"In came Miss Progress in her black dress look at the mess, she is a killer."—**The Avett Brothers**

"Don't you understand what I'm trying to say? Can't you feel the fear that I'm feeling today? If the button is pushed, there's no running away There'll be no one to save with the world in a grave Take a look around you boy, it's bound to scare you, boy."—**Barry McGuire**

JOAB
(1)

"Blades before bullets," Joab Finch said. "Blades before bullets."

Since the advent of the gun, this had never been a problem. But now there weren't enough bullets to go around. Eighteen months after The Tilt, there were enough bullets to keep a rough form of society functioning, some industrial plants going, and vague retentions of older ways. But there weren't enough bullets to shoot without consideration of tomorrow. And since tomorrow always came, it meant there weren't enough bullets to stop the dead from coming.

And the dead always came.

"I shouldn't have to keep saying that," Joab reminded the men. Middle-aged with stringy black hair caught in a tail, he was long and lean even before fast-food options vanished. "Keep your shotguns slung. Let's try not to draw every devil on the mountain."

Crazy Chang and Anspach, stationed north on Highway 19, radioed the 40-passenger Ford bus was on its way down. Considering the blind turns, tight corners, fallen rocks, and deceased automobiles, this was no easy deal.

1

The passengers were likely young, hungry, or infected, or their leaders wouldn't have risked so much. Kids may have been immune to the virus, but not its consequences. And no one left a safe place for an uncertain outcome in the flatlands below.

"We want to get to them before the army does," Joab said from the shallow turnout. "If the bus approaches while we're here, keep those shotguns slung, and don't run." His delivery was careful to make them understand what he wanted. "We don't want them thinking we're bandits. They've had contact and are expecting escort. They'll see right away we aren't that escort."

Buffering the highway, on both sides, was foliage and trees as green as they ever were. The sounds of bugs brushing wings and wind coursing through canyons were the same as they ever were. It was grey, cold, and reminded Joab of campus life when he attended Whidbey College in San Diego. The most unpleasant things to consider then were student debt and climate change. Now, thanks to The Tilt and the return of the dead, those were warm memories. Like a great evening with friends in a coffee shop.

"The guys are in place down the road to tip us when the army gets close," said Drew, a former seminary student and Joab's unofficial lieutenant.

"Who?"

"Hiram and Frank."

"Those guys?" Joab let go of a grin. "Can they stop talking long enough to notice anything?"

"Also, I sent Troy back to camp. That ankle he turned on the way didn't get any better. He can walk, but if things get stormy, I'd hate to make him run."

"That's fine, I didn't want a married guy out here," Joab said, studying both directions from the middle of the road. Green camouflaged pants and boots covered his lower half. A green tee-shirt with a long sleeve gray thermal beneath garbed his torso. "So we have eleven. Keep track of that number. I don't want anyone getting lost."

"There were quite a few devils in the woods," Drew said.

"A little busier than usual, huh? They smell us, they must, right?"

"It seems," Drew said. "The guys did a good job of keeping quiet, but I think, with winter over, they're starting to break out of the smaller villages."

"Cumberland probably, Big Sky?"

"Big Sky's no small village," Drew said.

"Maybe a resort? What was the total number last time we were able to get online?"

"Population?" Drew said, looking up to consider the math involved. "Counting the 39,000 in Sky Porch alone, and Big Sky, and all the surrounding towns; the number was over 70,000 in residence in these mountains. And we have no idea how many got stranded up here when it started."

"Everything's thawing," Joab said.

The advantage of being in the city was you couldn't forget what was going on. Burned out cars, boarded up homes, debris, abandoned suitcases and backpacks, broken glass, bodies, body parts, and bones were everywhere. Dried splatterings of blood—now deeper crimson than fresh red—painted walls and fences. Above all else, there was the persistent stench of death. The cities were full hell.

The mountains, though, could still be as tranquil as a bay before a tsunami. It quickly lulled the senses to sleep with its cooler weather, brooks, and tall trees. All beautiful, yet falsely reassuring at the same time. As the swirl of the breeze brought the scent of pines, it also carried bouquets of dead flesh.

After taking his turn in the rafters of the Bradbury Church and hearing his colleagues and friends below being devoured, Joab knew the mountains were better.

"Where do you want me?" Drew said.

"Keep Hiram and Frank in close contact, and the rest of you watch everything above us. My goal is to drive that bus right into camp. But if it gets testy, we're going to have to walk them in. Have Crazy Chang and Anspach make their way back after the bus passes them. I'll meet them at the edge of the Utility Road."

Clarity was not lacking. When thoughts came about butting out and the people in the bus not being their concern, clarity stepped in and showed the way. For Joab, there was no wait and see because hesitancy got people killed. They had to intervene.

Larry and Noel's presence had changed the game and made this action mandatory. They provided the direction and produced results. Best yet, they gave everyone a reason to believe better days were down the timeline. The miracles they were accomplishing were comparable only to the story of their arrival.

With previous boundaries marking life and death gone, that arrival, fantastic and unimaginable, was wholly plausible. It wasn't a leap for Joab to believe Larry and Noel's story. And it was made easier because of his reconciliation with the one who made the impossible possible.

"Hiram, Frank...how does it look?" he said, touching the prehistoric headset with a thin wire trailing to the radio clipped on his waist. **"Anything?"**

"Hiram took out a devil..." Frank said. **"...We're going to go down the road a bit more. There's a better perch for us to see around the bend."**

"Be sure you stay out of sight..." he said. **"...We don't want those soldiers spooked."**

"Affirmative..." Frank said.

"When you confirm what's coming, just get back to camp via the back trail. I don't want anyone becoming fast-food out here."

"Affirmative."

"You can just say 'yes,' Frank," Joab said. **"We're not soldiers and save the debates about Star Wars versus Battlestar Galactica for camp. The woods are storming, so watch your backs."**

"Affirmative."

"You want me to stay with you?" Drew said.

Joab, still in the center of the road, stared south. The military would come that way, and he knew what was coming from the north. The weekend retreat that never ended—a bus of young people worn out from hiding for the last 18 months and hoping for hope.

"Thanks, but no," he said. "I need you to keep me a perimeter up on the western side of the road. They're going to think I'm a bad guy, to begin with, and I don't want any devils getting through to increase the stress."

"I was thinking about the army," Drew said, gesturing his shotgun in their expected direction. "You might need help with them."

"The good news is the army isn't here for us. The bad news is what they're coming to do and what they may find." Knowing what they were likely to find provided Joab with even better clarity.

Low hanging branches and bushes rustled down the embankment on the eastern side of the highway. There hadn't been a gust of wind, so they knew it was a devil. In the flatlands, they were called monsters, ghouls, and mostly just the dead. But devil had become the terminology over the past year for the people at camp.

They went to the edge and took a glance. The devil snarled at them and began the difficult climb. Joab put an arm out to hold Drew back.

"Let it ride," he said. "If it makes it up, I'll drop it."

"So why do you think the army's coming?"

Joab, who didn't feel middle-aged or near as smart as he once thought, smiled at Drew. When the world was still conventional, and his hair was shorter, the desire to comfort and make people feel at peace didn't run through him the way it did now.

Both knew the army was coming to prevent infection. Anybody bit, deeply scratched, or sick with fever was assumed to have the virus and remedied. And the best remedy for the virus was a 5.56 round to the back of the ear.

Joab had championed a culture that dictated well-staged displays of compassion. He helped create acts that—by appearance—helped impoverished and marginalized minorities. But by design, the intent was to generate emotions, foster guilt, and seize a moral high ground. Seldom did his efforts ever meet anyone's day-to-day needs and never their spiritual vacancies.

The new compassion was the dark work of the military. Dispose of the infected and suspected infected without regard to age or backstory. Lift morale, and sustain the narrative that things were getting better.

"Whatever was working for this group near Sky Porch has stopped," he answered. "The only reason for heading to the flatlands, San Quintana, or San Bernardino is because they have to. Someone's bit or they're out of food, and they decided to make a run."

Drew cast his eyes north. "It shouldn't be like this."

"We've had that talk, and we'll keep having it until we die," Joab said. "Go on. I've got this. You take care of all that." He pointed at the trees and brush covering the slope. "Try to keep things in hand. I don't want any gunfire, but I also don't want a mob of devils rolling down while I'm talking."

Joab motioned for the young man to go. The perimeter was critical. Whatever shape the sure to be exhausted leaders were in, they needed to meet him without the anxiety of attacking devils.

The devil, currently attempting to climb the eastern embankment, poked his head up to the highway for a moment before sliding back down the damp dirt.

There weren't enough bullets, and unlike others boiling with rage, he'd wait for it to get to the top. Prudence was key to staying alive. It also forced him to contend with all his reflexive regret.

The sound of the Ford engine reached him. Brushing a hand over his head and capturing escaped strands, he reset his ponytail and wiped at his beard. He pondered about the differences he could have made if he hadn't been so educated.

So dang smart, so dang marvelous…Wendy, how did you know?

When the bus rounded the bend and came into sight, it was lumbering like a running back with a torn ACL. The engine knock was enough to wake anything in the throes of hibernation. Joab began waving and issuing a crafted smile.

If they decided to drive through him, he'd take out the tires with the shotgun. What it could lead to didn't matter because he understood what he was saving them from. A little bit of fear was better than certain death.

The off-white bus slowed, the brakes screeched as it stopped, and its frame rocked on old shocks. Through the windshield, behind the bearded driver, heads popped up. Frightened eyes glued onto Joab, waiting for his move.

He walked from the rust-pocked protruding nose to the passenger entry. He rested shotgun, pistol, and machete on the ground. If his men were doing any work in the woods, he prayed it was with a blade.

"Look," he projected his voice through the glass of the folding door. "No bites." He raised the sleeves of his thermal on both arms. "No bites. No needle marks." He pulled on the collar around his neck to show his untouched skin and then lifted the thermal to expose his midsection and back. "No fever, no drugs, I just want to help."

"We're going to the city," the driver said through the closed door. "We radioed in. They're coming to meet us."

"How many infected onboard?"

"That's none of your business."

A familiar bellowing cry came from the inside. The sound of what Larry called the Sin Virus was burning through a female. The driver bent his head in exhaustion.

"Let me help you!" Joab spoke with hands up, palms open, and no big gestures. "I can take you to a safe place, a place with a cure."

Eyes locked on him from behind the windows. Talk of a cure got two reactions. First, it generated hope. The second was the inevitable disappointment. A thriving commerce of secret treatments and organic remedies emerged with the virus's onset and added to the despair when they failed.

"There's no cure!" The driver yelled through the glass.

"Then what are you going down the hill for? If you know there's no cure, then you know what they'll do. They're going to kill anyone infected. They're going to kill anyone that has a bite or a scratch. They're going to kill anyone with the flu—even children. You've had access to a radio. You must know that."

The driver glanced to the passenger section and back with pursed lips. Someone Joab couldn't see was challenging him. Another howl of agony erupted, and the man looked like he was being squeezed.

"They will not reason with you down there," Joab said. "Their sole mission is to keep the infection from spreading. I've seen soldiers shoot on suspicion of infection. I'm begging, let me help you."

"What's it to you?"

"It's nothing to me," he answered. "But, it could be everything to you."

The discussion continued inside the bus. Joab smiled at sad faces pressed against the windows.

"There's nothing you can do for us," the driver said. "We're going."

"There's no help for you down there. I know you've got people about to turn, or you wouldn't be going down the mountain. The army will kill them!" Joab made a gun gesture to his temple to illustrate. "Reason this out, friend. There aren't enough resources left for them to send somebody to escort you down. They're only coming to keep the sick from protected areas."

A loud wail spiked through the conversation. A petite blonde woman with a narrow face stepped into the stairwell. Under the right circumstances of a shower, makeup, nourishment, she might have been considered attractive. As it was, all she had was her end of the world look—stern and borderline emaciated. It was evident to Joab this woman had given up meals and gone without to help others.

"They told us thieves were robbing people and leaving them stranded. And that they would lie about having a cure," she said.

"I could have shot your tires out. Your bus has about another fifty miles left in its engine; I don't want to steal it. And I'm not holding a gun on you now. I'm telling you I can take you to a place that can heal your infected."

The driver shook his head again but with less conviction. The woman put a hand on his arm to stop. "Our seven-year-old daughter was bit. Can you heal her?"

"Children are immune to infection," Joab said. "You've figured that out, but down this mountain, they'll still shoot her. There's no testing going on, no research; they just want to eliminate risk."

"You're asking us to trust," she said. "That's a lot."

"I know," Joab said. "It is a lot. But NORM is taking every measure to keep order in the flatlands."

Discussion started again. He heard their voices slug off each other. Certain the army wasn't much further away, he considered using his gun as the decider when it appeared the woman won the debate.

"They don't make exceptions."

The wind blew the aroma of pine punctuated with the after-scent of the dead. Devils were close.

The folding door collapsed, she beckoned Joab in.

"You can hold my guns," he said. The tiny woman quickly came off the bus, took the pistol off the ground, and gestured for him to go inside. Walking the aisle, Joab took in the group. Teenagers, thin, hair long, looking hopeless, stared back void the natural confidence youth provided.

"We have two that are infected," the woman said. "Jessica's 19, she's in the most pain. Aaron's 18, he was bit on the shoulder late yesterday. The fever hit him hard this morning."

Moving closer, he got a better look. Aaron, quiet, was wrapped in a blanket with his back to the window. Further back, with no one else near her, was Jessica. Wisely, they hadn't put her between anyone and the door.

"Is this your daughter?" A little girl with big round eyes stared back at him.

"Yes."

"When was she bitten?"

"Loren was bit a week ago," the woman said. "Move closer to Angie, honey, let this man by." The little girl slid back into the teenager's arms.

"And she has no fever," Joab said in an assuring voice. "You knew that, or you wouldn't have waited a week. But the soldiers will only factor that she's been bit."

"You've seen them shoot people without a fever?"

"I have," Joab said. "Suspicion of infection is all the cause they need."

"We've been on this mountain since it started," she said. "Three of our people have died. A volunteer and two of our teens." She cleared her throat of emotion, and her speech level sharpened. "We lasted as long as we could, but we have nothing left."

"My name's Joab."

"I'm Heather," she pointed to the driver, "Owen's my husband."

"Youth Pastors?"

"Yes."

"I did some youth pastoring myself," Joab said. "You've done a good job, both of you, but now you need to let me help you."

The couple traded looks. Heather gave the nod.

The sound of a shotgun came. Heads swiveled to see where it came from. A moment later, a second and a third fired in succession.

"My men, guarding the perimeter," he said and then touched his earpiece. **"Drew, you hear me?"**

"Go ahead."

"Send Duran back here...I want him to ride with these folks into camp."

"You really have a cure?" Heather said. "How's that possible?"

"We really have a cure. Otherwise, I wouldn't have stopped you. We don't have enough bullets to be bad guys, nor an oversupply of food to bring more people in, but we have a cure, and we have a safe camp."

Owen and Heather were a generation of leaders Joab helped shape. And this was the youth group they were responsible for.

Ping.

Reflexive regret—he didn't know what else to call it—pinged at him. It didn't hit like a fist to the gut or come as a lump in the throat. Occasionally, it came as a single tear welling in his eye. Predominantly it pinged in the manner of a servant being beckoned by the thumping of a hanging metal dish. Faithful as a good servant, it always arrived to remind of what he'd once been.

"I'm sure it's been hard for all of you," he told them. "But we will save your friends, and we will give our lives to protect you."

Heather handed him back his gun. The teenagers, scared when Joab came on the bus, relaxed as he returned down the aisle and went back outside. Owen followed, and he knew why. He'd stepped into another man's house and turned his wife's opinion against him in front of the kids—bad move.

"You're Joab Finch?" Owen said.

"I am."

"My wife and I both read *Justice Before Jesus* in seminary," he said.

"I'm sorry," Joab said. "If I could give you your money back, I would."

Ping.

"A cure?" Owen said, his voice low so as not to be heard on the bus. "I admired your work before, but I know a liar. Everything's gone, no vaccine is out there, the country's in shambles, and no one has a cure, but you? How convenient."

"I get it," Joab said. "After all, what's dangerous-looking about me? Guy stops you on a mountain road looking the way I do with a shotgun? Speaking of my shotgun, pick it up. Keep it as long as you stay with us."

"Don't patronize me," Owen said. "I'm not some clod who volunteers on weekends. Protecting this group is my job." He snatched the weapon.

"I complimented you, and be careful—it's loaded."

"No, you patted me on the head like a little boy thinking it would make me blindly trust you because you used to be somebody. That's why you're giving me this right now." He gestured with the gun.

"Do you know how to use it?"

"Yes," Owen said, "I know how to use it."

"Remember, red is dead."

Joab wanted to put a hand on Owen's shoulder to convey sincerity but knew it wouldn't be received. "You kept your group safe, and I want to hear all about it back at camp. But right now, we need you to get this bus going in the other direction because the army's coming with a bullet to the head kind of cure. And all your begging

15

and pleading won't prevent them from capping your daughter. God's my witness, I know this to be true."

"I've learned not to trust anyone."

"Owen get back on the bus," Heather said. "Let's go."

"I'm a firm believer in not trusting anyone," Joab said. "But right now, listen to your wife. Get on the bus and get it turned around."

Duran, 22, appeared on the western embankment and hustled down.

"If you have a cure, why aren't you taking it down into the city?" Owen said, his expression showing contempt.

Joab looked south, down the road, then back without a smile. "Because they don't want to have anything to do with it."

Duran arrived. "Jefe?"

"Yeah, Derek Duran," Joab said, "this is Owen. His wife Heather is on the bus with their youth group. I want you to get these folks to camp." Then to Owen. "Use the turnout and go less than a half-mile back. Duran will have you turn left on an old utility road. It won't look big enough for the bus, but it is. It will lead you right into The Garden."

"The Garden?" Owen said.

"It's the name of our camp," Duran said. "It's a name we gave it, so the army wouldn't be able to track us."

"Give me your shotgun," Joab said to Duran. "I'll give it back to you at camp. Now go."

They began the process of turning the bus around as Frank's voice came into his ear. Joab looked at Owen behind the wheel and spun his finger in the air to indicate he needed to pick up the pace. The youth pastor handled the bus well. Carefully he turned it about and got the nose pointed back in the direction it came.

"Joab, we've got a jeep about a mile from your spot. Two soldiers with M-4s and a minister," Frank said.

"One of those guys, huh?"

"Affirmative."

"No one else?"

"Just the jeep."

"Get yourselves back to The Garden."

"Affirmative."

The bus spat black exhaust from its tailpipe and began the short trek to the Utility Road. When it was gone, Joab turned the other way.

Only three?

He wondered what they would have done if the bus driver, in this case, Owen, had been infected. Two soldiers in a jeep with a 'spiritual' counselor was not an escort. It was triage.

Joab ordered Drew and the rest of the men to clear out. He thought about going with them but knew the jeep would keep searching for the bus.

"Anspach...Chang...?"

"Go ahead, Jefe," Anspach said.

"Wait for me on the Utility Road, but off the highway. If you hear another vehicle after the bus. Just take off for camp..."

"Got it."

An open vehicle, especially in the mountains, was nothing to be exploring in for long. Not wanting the soldiers to come to any harm, he waited.

Distrust of the military felt odd. Most knew those serving were quality, but the soldiers were being put through a meatgrinder. Either follow orders or risk discharge. There was also talk of threats that their families would be moved off base.

When ordered to shoot the living—man, woman, child—they shot with no allowance for ethical or moral considerations. It was how the soldier kept their family safe. It wasn't what they volunteered for but what the army and government had become.

Ministers, the individuals in white collars—not necessarily associated with Roman Catholicism or high church—were the new NORM-appointed political officers. Their mission, labeled as morale and encouragement at the outset, rapidly morphed into an ecumenical rat squad.

The clanking of the bus's engine faded, and the sounds of the forest returned. His men moving back to The Garden would draw off any devils closing in. Alone, he heard in the trees above him, birds moving station to station, and the metallic hum of insect wings rubbing together. The forest was like a giant theater, a stage

that remained as players and props came and went from one
production to the next.

*"If only we could grasp all that the wood of the stage felt and
saw."* A theater teacher at Whidbey told him years before. *"If only
our eyes could see all that has been walked into it over the
decades. What would its personality be? Would we not long for its
thoughts?"*

Snapshots came of hikers, scholars, campers, and hunters in their
times and how they must have felt these things in this exact spot.
Like his on stage in Whidbey's Little Theater, their moments
seemed the most important of moments only to flicker, fade and
sleep.

"Into the vale of years," he whispered the quote from Othello.
"Into the vale of years. She's gone. I am abused. And my relief
must be to loathe her."

Ping.

The tugging of brush joined the chirping. A footfall slipped in
among the orchestra of bugs. To the left, Joab saw the devil had
made it to the road from the eastern embankment. The new player
on this part of the stage had a face the color of a bluish-green dye.
Yellow eyes bulging, the deliberate stagger to its walk testified the
virus had had its way some months before.

It came, with damaged crumbling teeth, attempting to growl a
sound it may have been able to produce at one time. Instead, the
old man it had once been only hissed air. This devil was speedily
deteriorating in a demanding environment. Its clothing was in
muddied shards. A fraying lanyard hung from its neck, and Joab
snagged it.

"Lee Barnes, Colgate, Colorado…You came to ski and never went home."

Dead men told no tales, but these days a dead man—who was now a devil—told Joab a lot about Lee Barnes's spiritual condition when he died.

"Implore your Highness' pardon, and set forth a deep repentance." Joab pumped the 12-gauge chambering a round. "That's Macbeth, Lee." He leveled the barrel. "Nothing in his life became him like the leaving it." He squeezed the trigger. The devil's head blew back into the ravine it had worked so hard to get out of. The carcass sank to its knees, then to the shoulder of the road.

"I should have studied Shakespeare."

Stepping around the former tent of Lee Barnes, he peered into the rocks, bushes, trees, tall weeds, and grass. There was movement in two different places. Joab waited to see if it could have been a deer or something indigenous to the forest. What he saw was the bald scalp of a man and the matted, dirty gray head of a woman. If they had been working in another direction, it changed when they heard the shot. In better health than Lee Barnes, the male growled at him and began, with the woman, the difficult task of climbing to the road.

He knew he should have used the machete strapped over his shoulder. But with the bus gone and the soldiers coming, it didn't hurt to have a few devils downed or otherwise hovering to make the conversation short.

The bald devil eyed him and became more agitated.

"When you get up here, we'll talk about your friend, Lee. For the record, much of this is my fault."

Ping.

The two devils were too old to have been his, but they still delivered the same feeling. Regret pinged like a nagging harpy. "It really is my fault."

Joab moved back to the middle of the highway and saw the jeep. He raised a hand and showcased his pleasant expression for the three spinning toward him. It was a risk, he knew, but he did have faith in what remained. These weren't mere soldiers, they were American soldiers, not Russians or Europeans. They wouldn't drop him like a devil. They'd hear him out—to an extent—and then drop him.

The jeep, acknowledging his wave, slowed to a stop.

The two soldiers were a mystery, but he did know the man in the white-collar. He also knew the man was an idiot. Joab didn't always view the Minister as an idiot but reflecting over the last 18 months, he'd learned Kevin Montanez, like himself, had been incredibly dim.

"Pastor Joab Finch!" said the clergyman hopping out of the passenger seat to greet him. "Scholar, theologian, all-around muckraker of churches and denominations. You old mother…" He capped Joab's bio with a forceful obscenity before giving him an embrace.

Pulling back, the Minister smiled. "Brother, I am so happy and relieved to see you at the head of this business today."

"Pastor Kevin Montanez," Joab said. "It's been a long time. I thought you were working up north, preaching the whole social stew of justice and leading special committees for the governor." He touched the plastic clergy collar wrapped around the base of his neck. Montanez had neither been a Roman Catholic nor Orthodox in his career. For the most part, like Joab, he'd been an enemy of anything resembling the old school church. "What's this?"

"All for the cause, brother," he said. "All for the cause. It's Minister Kevin now."

"What happened to the frumpy looking seminary radical? Did you have a come to Jesus moment?"

"In my own way, yeah, I did," he said. "How about you? You'd sooner quit a job than stay between the lines. How in the world did you end up here?"

"The world ended," Joab said, keeping an eye on the soldiers.

"Yeah," Minister Kevin reached high with his hands and stretched. "It didn't exactly go the way LaHaye said it would, thank god."

Both soldiers carried M-4s at the ready. The younger one turned his back to the jeep and remained by the steering wheel. The veteran stepped around and gestured to Lee Barnes. "You had some action," he said. "Has it been busy?"

"A little," Joab answered. "Area's running hot with all of these vehicles passing through."

"Man, I didn't know you were up here," Minister Kevin said. "You ought to be down in San Quintana. We could use you." The soldier circled the two of them, studying the terrain. "This is Sergeant Bricklander. That's Private Flores over there."

Flores turned halfway and gave a nod.

"Where's the bus and the group with it?" Bricklander asked. "I see the tire tracks."

"There with us now," Joab said. "They're safe."

"They've already been here?" Flores said with evident relief.

"Joab, they contacted us for help," Minister Kevin said. "We can keep them safe."

"Can I ask a question?" Joab said, and no one indicated he couldn't. "Who was going to drive the bus?"

"The driver," Minister Kevin said.

"I'm curious because if the bus driver was bit, were you going to let him go to the flatlands and then cap him?"

"Joab, we came to help them," Minister Kevin said.

"They were expecting an escort. Two soldiers and a burned-out youth pastor is hardly that."

"What can you do?"

"We can cure them."

"Come on, Joab," Minister Kevin said, "be practical. There's nothing to argue here. It's settled. Let's get to know each other again."

"Practical?" Joab grinned at his old co-worker. He preferred to think of Kevin as more co-worker than friend. "Back when we were crusading, the last thing any of us wanted to be was practical. Practical meant being part of the machine, and the machine wasn't working for anyone. Don't you remember, we were the generation that was going to lead the world back to Christ—not necessarily Jesus, but Christ?"

"Well, when the world ended, I got practical."

"So practical, you're ready to give the order to shoot the infected on that bus?" Joab's sarcasm—a skill he perfected going through the ranks of ministry—was always his best tool when someone else had authority. "So practical, you won't make any consideration for someone bitten but exhibiting no sign of fever?"

"Brother, what are you going to do with them? Live like dogs out here in the sticks and use tree leaves for toilet paper? The rest of those kids will at least have a chance to have a life down in the city."

"And the ones bitten or look like they may have bitten, you have the soldiers kill?"

"Hey," Bricklander said. "You two can have your talk, but keep us out of it."

"How many times can a United States soldier follow an order he knows is wrong?" Joab said, drawing a glare from the sergeant. "I don't believe you're a killer. The only negative I see is listening to my old co-worker here."

"How can you kill what's already dead, Joab?" Minister Kevin said. "If anybody's bitten, you know they're as good as dead."

"Not necessarily."

In a different season of ministry, Joab and Kevin agreed on everything except how many questions were needed to wear down the white Christian leadership of a local congregation. Their well crafted and carefully masked passion was to crush those opposing them. It was all about using one salvo of ambiguous truth after another to diminish the foundations of faith. To create doubt in the Bible, overturn accepted theology, alter the view of Christ, question the motivations of the Spirit, and inflict incriminations of racism, sexism, and privilege to shame opponents into intellectual retreat. The polite and pliable term for this in a classroom was; deconstruction.

With full conviction, this was Joab's—and his comrades—way of being Christ to others. No one inside the church was a brother or sister until they were like-minded in highlighting American Christianity's failures and cultural inequities. Mocking "White American Christianity" at every turn sold well on college campuses, seminaries, and in progressive churches where it had gained footing.

It was cool, it was now, and tasted delicious but proved hollow when the Sin Virus came.

"Come on, Joab, there's no cure."

"You need to use that radio in your ear and get them turned around," Bricklander said.

"Or what?" he said.

"Or you're going to have a problem. I didn't come up here for nothing."

"You want to start a fight right here, Sergeant? Any firing is going to draw every devil in the neighborhood."

Joab knew a tough dude when he saw one. Bricklander's hair was a combo of salt and pepper. His face, discolored either by the sun or too many beers, was scarred.

"Devil?" Private Flores turned to them.

"Monster," Minister Kevin inserted. "Ghoul, the dead."

"Trouble with the word, devil?" Joab said

"Great, let's make things even more complicated," Minister Kevin said. "It's plague; it's not good versus evil; it's not judgment from God. It's just plague. Influenza, polio, smallpox, AIDS. It's just another terrible plague that produces a more frightening result. As we evolve, so do our struggles."

"You mean like new levels, new devils?"

"Cute."

"The situation," Joab said to Bricklander, "with all respect, is the group has infected people. You'd be putting bullets in the heads of two teens and a little girl because you don't have a cure. We do."

"You do not have a cure," Minister Kevin insisted. "You start talking that cure business, Joab, and it gets real tricky. Because you're going to try to bring God into a secular situation. Not everyone believes the same thing. It screws with morale and drives doubt. There is no cure."

"And what's the skin off your butt if we don't cure them or we get overrun? There were 70,000 souls in residence in these mountains when this began. Do a few dozen more make a difference?"

The mention of 70,000 in residence caused Private Flores to shift uneasily.

"My thinking is this," Bricklander said, "with all due respect, I'm not going to risk more lives to come back here again. Some of those other kids on that bus might like a roof over their head and warm meals. So get them turned around, or you're coming to San Quintana with us."

"I'm not alone, Sergeant."

"And that means?"

Joab shrugged and looked at Minister Kevin. "So, there are no more differences?"

Minister Kevin exhaled, paused, and adjusted his tone. "Our disagreements were no more than Catholics, Wesleyans, and Calvinists have had for centuries that purists turned into war. Don't ever say I have no belief in God. We're just loving people and not letting the distractions divide anymore. There's a greater good happening. The kind of good you used to believe in, Joab. Spiritual people realize there's more than just the cross and a few magic words."

"That crucifixion, resurrection, and atonement stuff does get in the way of being practical."

"The Joab I worked with saw things my way."

"That Joab is dead," he said.

Bricklander coughed to get back into the conversation. "Get in the jeep. We're taking you with us."

"I'm not leaving the mountain," Joab said.

"I'm arresting you," Bricklander said. "We're going to go down the hill, and you'll give us directions to your camp."

"I told you, I'm not alone," Joab emphasized again, knowing how the soldiers felt about untrained citizens with guns. Eyes shifted to the woods around them. "My men will defend me because we're in the right."

"I never knew you to be so self-righteous," Minister Kevin said.

"Please," Joab said. "You and I were the definition of self-righteous."

"I'm not going to let the sergeant arrest you," Minister Kevin said. "We're going to leave you here to die. If any of your people make it off this mountain and aren't infected, we're going to take care of them."

"I'll tell you what," Joab said. "Come to the camp, and see for yourself. You can bring a radio with you, and when you see it all, you can call in the camp's exact location."

The offer put a brake on the tension. Minister Kevin and Bricklander exchanged looks. It made Joab feel better since he had no men in the woods to prevent his arrest. He felt no ping for the Rahab-like rationalization.

"You'd do that? You'd take me to the camp and let me call in its location?"

"How long have we known each other? I may not be down with your theology anymore, but we have a history. And there's something at my camp the rest of the world needs to see."

"You trust him?" Bricklander said.

"We've known each other for over twenty years," Minister Kevin said. "We've worked camps and causes all over this state."

"All I want you to do is witness the cure," Joab said. "And be honest when you report back."

"I'll go with this deal," Bricklander said. "I want you to have a cure, I really do. I like the idea of this ending easily. But, if I have to put my men at risk to come back for you or this whore in a collar, I'm going to be angry."

"Whore?" Minister Kevin said.

"That's what all of you are," Bricklander said, giving the Minister a small green radio with a rigid plastic antenna swiveled down.

"I'm sure he calls us as he sees us," Joab said. "And the last thing I want is trouble with American soldiers."

"I won't be able to get a team back here until tomorrow," Bricklander said, climbing into the passenger seat. Flores eagerly got behind the wheel and cranked the motor. "So you're gonna be stuck."

"I'll bunk with Joab tonight," Minister Kevin said. "You good with that?"

"As long as you don't talk in your sleep about Glenda."

The jeep turned and drove away.

"You don't mind if we stand here for a few," Joab said. They were shoulder to shoulder in the middle of the highway. "I know you, but I don't know them, and I have people to protect."

"It's okay; this is going to be a good thing."

"It is."

"Glenda, wow, I haven't thought about her in years," Minister Kevin reminisced. "Now that was a good looking girl."

"What happened to her?" Joab said.

"She didn't like men."

"Men, or you?"

"Men."

"What are you really doing with this collar?" Joab said. "What happened to the progressive, socialist clinging to his Seattle grunge look?"

"It's a crisis, and if all I have to do to bring everyone together is wear a costume, so be it. It's a uniform we've all put on. Monks, Mormons, Muslims, Seeks, Buddhists, you name it."

"That's wild."

"That's it, though. We don't do much in the traditional sense," Minister Kevin said. "We don't do any old school salvation services, and no one's asking us for that. Our presence just has a calming effect, and the collar is something everyone recognizes. It indicates the government's here for all who have a need. So we all go along because it inspires."

"Everyone?"

"Everyone, except holdouts like you," he said, smiling. "You all set?"

The jeep was long gone, the churning of the motor growing further away. "Let's wait a moment."

"No problem, I can stand to stretch a little. It was a long ride, and that jeep ain't built for my old bones." Minister Kevin flexed back his shoulders to loosen his muscles. "I imagine you don't get much news up here."

"A little from the radio, a little from stragglers," Joab said, slinging his shotgun. "I did hear about Europe."

"England's holding out, barely, and Poland seems to be doing all right. The rest of Europe, well, forget about it. Our government's in control. It's just difficult getting people convinced. We're working hard to make them see things are getting better."

"Are they?"

"We're Americans were used to traveling, hopping on a plane, and eating out. That's a tough change." The Minister looked up the embankment behind Joab and then turned east to where the devil lay on the road's shoulder. "And none of that stuff's coming back, at least not for a long time. But some of the things we've been working on all our professional lives are happening. There's a level of tolerance now that's never been there before. We're consuming less, learning to share, not harming the environment--it's kind of beautiful. An even playing field for everyone, finally."

"How Utopic," Joab said.

"Close, it's still tough for minorities, though. The majority of them were in the cities, and they took the hardest hits. They couldn't get out."

"Privilege strikes again," Joab said.

"That's more on the money than you might want to think. DC's going to be issuing directives, through NORM, to commandeer the resources of corporations and our wealthiest people. To keep balance and ensure a permanent diverse representation, the election structure will definitely be changed."

"Everyone's going to go along with that?"

"Of course not, but we'll convince them it's in the national interest to keep everything on track in the struggle to get back to normal." He laughed.

"Is normal ever going to happen?"

"No, not a chance. This plague's provided the opportunity to change the world for good."

Joab yawned and took another look at Minister Kevin Montanez. Hispanic last name wrapped in lily-white skin and capped with receding blonde hair. Enchilada on the label, cheeseburger on the inside, he was the iconic California hybrid. Hip, cool, happening, and intersecting with multiple cultures. A perfect blending allowing him to be a little bit of this and a little bit of that. And the credibility to claim offense at any perceived, imagined, or unintentional slight.

"We were stressing about coming up here last night, Bricklander, especially. I'll tell you, he looks like a tough guy, but he's about out of gas."

"A lot of mileage?"

"A lot," Minister Kevin said, moving closer to the edge of the road. "Where's the camp?"

"Did they send you out here for the people on the bus or the sergeant?"

"Partly," Minister Kevin said, trying to study something through the dense growth of trees. "Partly for the bus, but mostly to help Bricklander do his job. Oh, I see them now. This is an active area. Where are they coming from?"

"So you're like the old KGB officer. You make sure everyone follows the game plan, or else."

Minister Kevin laughed. "I guess you can say that. All I would have done is share what went on. If he didn't follow through, I'd remind him of the consequences and put him on report."

"Then what would happen?"

"If he didn't shoot? I'd explain his situation. Ultimately we'd threaten him with discharge and his family's removal from the base they're on." He looked downslope as more noise came in the brush. "Are these monsters coming all the way down from Sky Porch?"

Joab's left hand went to the machete strapped over his shoulder. In one sweep, he pulled and brought it across the back of the minister's legs. With blood waterfalling down his trousers, he reached for his thighs and shuffled around.

"Joab!" he gasped

Swinging again, Joab struck into his shoulder. The blade lodged, and blood leaped onto his black coat. The minister gave a hard wince at the pain but didn't scream.

"You're the infection I have to control," Joab said, wrenching the machete back out of the muscle and bone. He kicked a boot into Montanez's chest and sent him down the embankment.

Falling, Minister Kevin began to scream as the devils welcomed him.

"Nothing in his life became him like the leaving it," Joab said before taking a long breath and sheathing his weapon.

There was no ping.

LARRY
(1)

Larry Garrison was reading his Bible in the nearly empty dining hall.

"Don't you know that you yourselves are God's temple and that God's spirit lives in you? If anyone destroys God's temple, God will destroy him; for God's temple is sacred...."

It wasn't too long ago Larry looked at his Bible like an untouched erector set. Anything was possible, everything was available, but you had to figure out how to put the whole thing together. The instructions, in microscopic (usually German) print, were torture to read.

Connect Apostle A with Prophet B while securing coupling to prevent judgment.

And it never worked for him until Sunday night, September 30th. Since then, the scriptures rose off the page in 3D fashion.

"...and you are that temple."

"Mr. Garrison! Mr. Garrison!" Cora, ten with no parents, called to him. "They need you!" she stopped, caught a breath, "a bus just came in!"

"Tell them I'll be right there." He moved a plastic spoon to the page his Bible was open to and went outside.

I can't be Mr. Garrison. I don't want to be Mr. Garrison.

The specifics regarding Larry's age were shaky when dates came into consideration. He was positive he didn't look like his dad. That Mr. Garrison had little hair and a gut hanging avalanche-like over his waist.

He watched the bus bounce and ride over the grass to the center of camp before stopping. Noel Sedaka, followed by a combination of ladies, moved to greet it.

Joab's group walked in from the Utility Road, some heading to their bunks in the large tent they dubbed "Mandalay," some to the dining hall. Wheeler, the most popular of the security team, was mobbed by the kids. "I'm sorry, guys, I'm sorry. I couldn't get anything this time," he said with a big smile as they pressed around him. "Let me put my stuff away, and we'll play catch down in the meadow." The boys cheered.

"Will Chang come?" They asked.

"I be in!" Chang said. "And I'll be bringing all my moves." The kids tried to tackle him as he raced away.

Larry didn't see Joab, but no one had to worry about him. If the news was good or grim, the chief defender of The Garden was always present and providing options.

Today the good news was the bus. A fluke, likely providence, allowed them to hear the radio transmission the day before. The stress--even before gaining the trust of the people inside--was getting it to stop.

Duran opened the door. "Noel, two have bites, and they're hurting pretty bad."

"Only two?" she said.

"Just two," a small blonde woman said. "Everyone else is okay."

"Okay," Noel said, gesturing to the easy-ups set out by the trees. "Let's get everyone over to the tents."

Larry arrived and picked up the smell of body odor and the very distinct scent of the virus doing its excruciating work.

"Have the rest of them come out," he said. "Deb, Liz, Kelly, can you get the others checked and situated? Let's also get them something to eat."

The students unloaded, and the women went to work.

"Come on in," Noel said with cheer. "Glad you're here. We're going to take care of you."

"I know how we look," Larry said as they passed, clinging to their backpacks and dirty clothes. If not for being washed and better fed, he and Noel appeared young enough to be coming off the bus with them. "We'll tell you everything about this place later."

"So glad you're here," Noel said.

Duran's radio squelched, he put a hand to his ear. "Joab just made it back to camp. Says he's going to Mandalay and will see you in a bit."

Though always confident of Joab, Larry still exhaled, "Good."

"I'm Heather," the short blonde woman introduced herself.

"Hi Heather, I'm Larry, and this is Noel."

"Nice to meet you," Noel said. "We're going to take care of the two on the bus right now."

The bearded driver, shotgun in hand, stepped off the stairwell. "Who's in charge?" He demanded with eyes passing over them. "Who am I meeting with? Where's Joab?"

"This is my husband, Owen."

Noel gave Larry a knowing glance. It was an acknowledgment they were about to go down a familiar road.

"You're looking at the people in charge," Larry said. "It's us."

"What?"

"We're the ones in charge."

"Oh, my god," Owen said. "Is this a joke? Teenagers are running this camp?"

"Really?" Duran said. "You want to start this now? It's your people that are dying. Let them do what they do."

A loud cry came from inside the bus.

"Get out of the way," Larry said. His tone came with authority, and Owen could only glare as he cleared from the entrance.

"What are we doing here, Heather?" he said.

"Good god, Owen," she said, following Larry and Noel. "Give it a rest."

The smell was worse inside. Larry led the way to the back. A girl, face fading into pale ash, shivered through a clenched jaw. Voice gone, eyes bulging, her expression pleading for help.

"What are you going to do?" Owen said.

Larry ignored him.

Across the aisle was another teenager. He sat against the window, a blanket wrapped around his shoulders. He pointed a shaking hand at the girl. "First," he quivered, "help Jessica first."

"How long ago were they bitten?" Noel said to Heather.

"She was bit two days ago, Aaron late yesterday. Is it too…"

"No," Larry cut her off. "It doesn't matter." Deliberately, he smiled at her, knowing he'd sounded rude. "It doesn't matter at all."

"What are you going to do?" Owen asked, but they continued to ignore him.

Larry straightened Jessica in her seat and sat next to her as she groaned. Noel went to the bench behind and put hands on the girl's shoulders.

Heather and Owen moved closer, but Larry put a hand up for them to come no further.

"Hold on for a second," he said, and Owen's face lit with anger. "Jessica…Noel and I are going to pray for you." A tear came into his eye as he took in her condition.

How he felt empathy, even sympathy, for people he'd never met before was and wasn't a mystery. It wasn't who Larry had been, but the prayer to give God control built into him who he was now. The calling, the Christian life, was a constant, involuntary compulsion to care—to have everything taking place in the lives of others matter. He wasn't the first, and he wouldn't be the last to live this life, but it would be nice if it took a few hours off to go fishing every once in a while. Because God's spirit was always pressing.

"Jesus loves you, Jessica," he said. A surge of tears came out of her eyes, and she twitched in her seat. "He loves you." She began to tremor.

"Stop, stop…" A weak voice came from the girl.

"Oh, god! Look at her eyes, Owen!" Heather said, and her husband put a hand around her waist and another over his open mouth. "We've known her since she was twelve. She…" More tears. "Her eyes are yellow!"

"Lord," Larry prayed. "Jessica's your creation." The girl's body lunged violently forward then back. Larry put a hand under her chin to keep it from smashing into the seat in front of her. Noel held tightly to her shoulders as she convulsed. "In the name and the blood of Jesus Christ, your son, heal her."

"I know you!" she said through clenched teeth. "I know you!"

Jessica's body shook, her mouth loosened, gasps of dry heaves wrenched out of her. Foam seeped from her lips as she began a long, humming sigh. It filled their ears, and in wave-like motions, muscles started flexing, loosening, keening off the rigors of death. She let go of a crying sound that better fit a teenage girl.

"Finish, Lord!" Noel prayed as more tremors shook Jessica's body. "Finish! Death no power! Demon no power! Jesus, Jesus, Jesus, only Jesus!"

"No," came from her mouth in a husky male tone. "No! I won't! I won't go! I won't go until you're all dead and with us!"

The window to the right blew out as the bus rocked. Owen and Heather stumbled back as Jessica screamed like someone coming out of deep water and gulping for air. Drawing in a deep breath, she opened her eyes.

"I'm alive!" The teenager leaped up and raised her hands high. "I'm alive!" Tears poured out of her, "oh god, oh god, oh god... I'm alive, I'm alive."

Larry sat back and tilted his head upward. Jessica reached for Owen and Heather, and they took her.

"You okay?" Noel asked.

"Yeah," he said, taking a deep breath. "You?" He touched her forehead. "I think you got cut."

Noel fingered the spot and felt a dab of blood. "I'll live."

Others often asked what it felt like to heal someone from the virus. In his finite thinking, Larry could only describe it as a rush of the Holy Spirit through his body. As irrational as feeling a breeze when there was no avenue for it to arrive by. Peace when there should be no peace.

"You're gonna need to rest after this," Noel said, patting his shoulder.

"I'm good," he cracked a grin, "I'm better than good."

"Owen," Heather said, holding Jessica's face in her small hands and running thumbs over her cheeks. "They healed her!" Jessica's skin had returned to color, and her eyes back to bright blue.

"Thank you!" Jessica said, grabbing back for Larry and reaching to put a hand on Noel. "Thank you!"

"How…?" Owen started and then stopped as if he didn't want to hear the answer.

Larry looked at Owen, knowing this was something few had seen over the last 18 months. "Joab must have told you; we know the cure."

Untying himself from Jessica, he handed her back to Heather. "We're gonna talk later, I promise," Larry said. "Right now, we've got to take care of Aaron."

"I was dead, Heather," Jessica cried. "I could see myself sinking in darkness…It was like I was drowning. I was screaming, I could see you, but you couldn't hear me. I was begging for help, and you didn't know."

Aaron sat up on the bench. Larry took the window, and Noel slid in from the aisle.

"I don't know what to say," Aaron said.

"Did I ask Jessica a question?" Aaron shook his head. "No, I didn't. And I'm not going to ask you a question. All I'm going to do is let the Holy Spirit demonstrate the power of how much you are loved."

A smile emerged, painfully, to the young man's face. "I could use some of what Jessica got." Aaron wasn't as far gone. He had pain, he had fever, but could still communicate.

"You're about to get some of what Jessica got, but after, Aaron, who God is and where you place him in your life will be up to you," Larry said. "Do you understand?" He looked at Jessica, "That goes for you as well," and then back to Aaron. "What you are about to receive is an amazing gift, but the gift of salvation is up to you. I can lay hands, pray, and heal you, but I cannot save you spiritually. That's between you and the Lord."

"I want salvation," he said, tears streaking. "I want to live. I want this..." he searched for words.

"This what?" Noel asked.

"There's this doom in my heart all the time." Now tears flowed in currents. "It feels like being buried in the dark where no one will find me. I want it gone."

"Then let's go big, Aaron," Noel said. "Let's do this right."

"Aaron, do you know the story of the paralytic?" Aaron didn't answer, and Larry continued. "It's okay. It's sort of new to me too. But these friends of a paralyzed man can't get to Jesus while he's teaching in this house. Instead, they cut a hole in the roof and lower him down to where Jesus was."

As he was sharing, Larry sensed a feeling of discomfort come over Owen. He didn't see anything out of the corner of his eye or hear him move. But an unseen, spiritual clunk had passed out of the youth pastor's disposition and into the space they were all occupying.

"The Lord's impressed and tells the paralytic his sins are forgiven, but this creates a problem. The friends brought him to Jesus to physically heal him, but when Jesus saw this man, he saw his physical condition second. What he saw, first, was the sin in the man's life, the sin separating him from God, and took care of that."

Larry knew Owen's eyes were pressing. He was likely a solid family man, a caring minister, but how could Aaron not know this story from the New Testament? Again, it confirmed to Larry what Joab had been sharing about the spiritual condition of this world.

"God's going to heal you today, Aaron," Larry said. "Right now, but what he sees first is the condition of your heart, not this bite and fever destroying your physical body."

"I understand," Aaron said.

"It's okay if you don't understand all of it, but do you understand God loves you?"

"Yes," Aaron said.

"That he's already paid for you with his blood?"

"Yes."

"And you saw what worked through Noel and me in regards to Jessica's healing?"

"I did."

"That power is God. He loves you, and he wants you."

"Are you ready to accept Christ's forgiveness?" Noel said.

The same words, a year and a half before, had been put to him and Noel.

"Are you ready to accept Christ into your life and accept his forgiveness of your sins?"

Like an unexpected attack on a fortified base, Larry's defenses fell that Sunday night (September 30th). After hearing the words audibly, he heard them again in his spirit. He had no counter-attack, no way of keeping the Lord at arm's length, and no will to prevent a swift voyage to the altar. If his feet touched the carpet, he didn't know. He didn't remember standing but only arriving at a full altar—a full altar with a slot perfectly reserved for him to kneel at and pray.

"I can't live this way anymore," Aaron said.

If asked to lift the bus at this moment, Larry was confident he could have done it. The fatigue he felt before was gone. The stagnant air was overcome by a mountain breeze coursing through with no smell of death.

Aaron uttered the prayer. Standard, on point, but without the practiced sound of somebody partaking in a responsive reading. It was real, it was sincere, his body didn't shake but passively accepted.

A year and a half on the mountain, with his youth pastor, how can this only be happening now?

"Lord, we rejoice," Noel prayed aloud. "We praise you!"

As Noel prayed, Larry sensed three things with eyes closed and heart in agreement with everything his partner shared. First, her words were simple but eloquent. The second was the feel of an electric-like current transferring through both of them into Aaron. And then there was the third.

With his eyes still closed, the spirit confirmed this was something Owen either didn't understand or refused to accept. The minister—as most ministers were, according to Joab—didn't see things the way they did.

"Lord, we ask your touch from side to side and head to toe for Aaron," Noel prayed. "Heal him by the gracious blood of your son...."

A shaking worked through Aaron's body, and he put his hands on the seat in front of him. As if suffering through a muscle spasm, his jaw hung open.

"... You've told us to gather in prayer and ask. We are asking. We are asking you to move, cleanse this body and restore it. All the glory goes to you...."

According to the calendar, Noel's birthday was two months after Larry's. Her voice, however, sounded deeper. As if affected by

45

years of pain, years of learning what it took to live this life they were forwarding in. Women at 19 usually had beauty, perhaps sweetness, but seldom the depth or warmth a mother twenty years older had.

Again, the bus rocked, and a draft of foul odor shot from Aaron and out the door with less violence than occurred with Jessica.

"…In the name of King Jesus, we pray."

Aaron's face flushed red. His eyes lit, and his expression sharpened like someone coming out of the shower and hitting a cold room. Discarding the blanket, he held up his hands and flexed them.

"I thought I was dead," he said as laughter began escaping him. "I thought I was dead, and I'm alive!"

"You were," Noel said. "In more ways than one, I guess we all were." She lifted the yellow sleeve of her blouse above her shoulder and revealed a scarred section of mangled flesh. Then she looked at Owen and Heather. "Why don't you guys get cleaned up, get some food, and a place to sleep. We'll meet after in the dining hall to talk."

BRICKLANDER
(1)

"…All our days as a country, as a people, we have fought the good fight, and we have prevailed. We've witnessed the collapse of empires, but we have survived. In this current crisis, we've known hardship as we have never known it before. We've experienced the pain of seeing a loved one turn into something we never believed possible. And we have survived as other nations have disappeared. This speaks to the

resolve instilled in us as Americans. Keep faith, keep working, keep believing, dawn is coming, and like I learned in Sunday School as a boy growing up, joy comes in the morning. God Bless you, and God Bless the United States of America."

The national anthem began to play.

Captain Reggie Torres, his feet on the desk, pointed a remote to the other side of the office and shut off the radio. "I don't know how many times we have to hear this thing before they think we got it."

The nation saw or heard the President give this speech one year after the virus arrived in America. Half a year later, it replayed when the power came on in the morning, shut off in the evening, and at various times in between.

"It's the new Gettysburg Address," Bricklander said. "Stars and Stripes."

First Sergeant Jeff Bricklander updated Torres about the interaction on the mountain and talk of a cure. Both were familiar with the last report about a small ranch compound in Kansas claiming a cure. No mention was made of an offer for the group to stand down. The report only read they were cultists, and three attack helicopters, fully armed, smoked them with hellfire.

A quick response and resolution, but the plains of Kansas were more accessible than a nest of communities tucked within the mountain ranges of California's Inland Empire.

"We should make them an offer," Bricklander said. "I don't think they're dangerous. Stupid, but not dangerous."

"When Minister Kevin checks in, we'll put the location in a file and torch it if we ever get the chance," Torres said, sipping from a glass of sun tea.

"Which means never," Bricklander said.

Torres raised the tea in agreement.

The National Office of Resource Management—NORM—made those calls. With everything of importance—fuel, food, ammo— limited, the loons on the mountain could rot for all NORM cared.

Resources the country needed now and later were always the determinate. The dead didn't eat food left on the shelves of a grocery store. The dead didn't pick fruit from a tree, waste gasoline to power vehicles or generators. The dead didn't scrounge for extra ammunition. The living did, and every time they got their hands on something, it became one less resource for NORM to manage.

"You know," Bricklander said, "there are at least a half dozen little towns in those mountains besides Big Sky and Sky Porch at the top. That camp could be the forward base we've been looking for. A place to choke the dead before they get to the flatlands."

"And we'll let the kooks in residence handle it," Torres said, putting his feet down and turning over a map on the desk. "NORM hasn't finished building the retaining wall that's supposed to go around San Quintana. So before we settle on a forward base, I'd like to get a few nights' sleep with a completed wall. And I can guarantee that's what they're going to be complaining about at the town hall tonight."

"It would be nice," Bricklander said. "But, you know, NORM."

"Yeah, he's a bastard."

In the 20th century, San Quintana had been a destination for families to pick apples, drink cider, and enjoy the best autumn had to offer in Southern California. But by the 21st. Century the realtors had come in, started selling lots, and building homes.

And then the world ended.

Resting on Highway 19, San Quintana now served as a buffer between the ghouls on the mountain and the Inland Empire itself. Its population of 3,000—down from 7,000—enjoyed a protection most suburban areas didn't. Seeing its importance, NORM placed Captain Torres and his company, consisting of three battered platoons, 122 live bodies, in the community.

The wall, six-feet high, was begun and finished south and west, but the east side was still hanging in the wind. And to the north, only shadow stood in the way of Sky Porch and the other mountain communities.

"Wall, or not," Bricklander said, pulling his chair closer to the other side of the desk. "If the cork gets popped at Sky Porch, nothing's going to stop the dead if they decide to come down."

"So we leave those folks up there to do our work for us," Torres said. "Beyond that, we just have to hope things keep getting better."

"Are they getting better?"

"You expect me to say anything that isn't Stars and Stripes?"

Bricklander and Torres understood. They first heard NORM's mission statement eleven months before. **"Things are getting better!"** started every newscast. Nearly every written report in the media repeated the same, **"Things are getting better!"**

It sounded good, it was uplifting, but close to a year, later it was hard to see. Reports came about cities won back, but those in uniform knew the truth. The advance on Los Angeles reached the San Gabriel Valley but stoned at the Arroyo Seco. In the Civil War, few places were as scary as Shiloh and the Wilderness. In World War Two, it was Omaha Beach, in Korea, the Chosin Reservoir, and in Vietnam, it was Khe-Sanh. In the war with the dead, no place evoked chills amongst the troops like the carnage of the Arroyo Seco.

"How many should I take when Minister Kevin calls in tomorrow?" Bricklander said.

"Nobody," Torres said. "Minister Kevin can stay up there until Jesus comes back. We're not budging until NORM tells us to get him. If he calls, say we're waiting on NORM. He's a whore, and the longer he's gone, the better it is for all of us. Now, tell me about the highway."

"Funny," Bricklander said. "The fella we met up there, this Joab guy? He feels the same way we do about the ministers."

"Well, that'll discourage Minister Tim. He's certain they're all beloved. Highway?"

"Look at it," Bricklander said. "It's nothing we didn't already know. If the dead guys leave the mountain, they land here."

"And take all of the IE."

Currently, San Quintana wasn't dealing with large mobs of dead. The concern was about the dead trekking down with winter over. Meeting the bus had been most of the reason for the drive this morning, but also to study the shape of the highway.

"It's surprisingly clear," Bricklander said. "We saw fewer cars on the side of the road than expected. A few rocks had rolled in, but it's open. And I can only assume if that bus made it to the point where we met this guy Joab, then the highway, at least up to Sky Porch, is passable. When they contacted us, did they specify if they were in Sky Porch or near it?"

"They didn't," Torres said. "We've seen the drone video. I don't think a bus could get out of Sky Porch. The bridge over the dam would have to be passable, and I don't think a bunch of kids riding a church bus would be able to open it."

"I wouldn't think so."

"Cumberland?"

"Maybe," Bricklander said, "but that's a village, not a town. A 100, 150 people living there tops. I'm thinking one of the resorts."

"No matter, NORM's asking for a choke point somewhere on the highway."

"I'm no engineer," Bricklander said, "but it's going to take a heck of a lot of ordnance to bring part of the mountain down on the road. And that's just the main access. Look at the map, look right there at Wintercrest, Mountain Road 37 empties into the flatlands. Orchards and groves, and that large open area in front of the old church, right there." He tapped a finger.

"What about barricading one of those switchbacks?"

"You could, but the problem is there are other roads between the communities. You could put up a barricade and have a squad man it, but they'd most likely get cut off at some point. Even if we thought a spot was secure, it could change in an instant."

Torres studied the map.

Bricklander continued. "I know we speculate about how well those things see at night, but I don't need an egghead from NORM to tell me they smell us because they do."

San Quintana was secure, but the dead did pop up. Either straggling in from the east or breaking out from within the city itself. Power shut down at night, and people didn't come out much. However, the days of cringing behind locked doors and fortifying homes were over. Many went into San Bernardino and Riverside for work. Some worked in San Quintana. The rest lived off what NORM provided.

"The best thing for us now is that old church," Bricklander said. "Argue for that spot. It's got a lot of killing ground and no surprises. We could build a bulwark around it and use a platoon to man it."

"You realize what's left of our company isn't much larger than a full platoon," Torres said. He was a college graduate, enlisted to pay his debt, saw action, and then returned to private life. When the virus put an end to his marketing career, it was back to a desperate military.

"I know," Bricklander continued, "but it's in a good spot. It's about a mile from when you come off the mountain. The orchards are to the west, and there's a lot of open space north and to the east. We could use Claymores and all the stuff NORM's pulling out of mothballs and put up a pretty good fight."

"Show me again." Torres leaned forward, and Bricklander pointed.

"Right there…If given a chance, meaning we get reinforced and properly supplied, we can turn that church into the Alamo."

"We lost at the Alamo," Torres said.

"We?" Bricklander said.

"I'm Tex-Mex. I like my guns and walls." Torres popped a pen and made notes. "You on or off this afternoon?"

"Off," Bricklander said. "It's my rotation. I got a session with the family."

"A call from the Old Dominion."

"That's right, ever been?"

Torres shook his head. "I hear parts of it are beautiful."

"It's all beautiful."

"*Up men and to your posts, and don't forget that today you are from old Virginia,*" Torres muttered. "I'm going to make the recommendation for the church, with a further recommendation of trying to blast the mountainside coming out of Sky Porch. Might as well reach big."

"NORM or not, I think we've farted around long enough and need to get eyes further out on 19—especially with no wall in San Quintana." Bricklander stretched and picked up his hat. "Are we good?"

"We're good."

"I'm going to rack out before I see the family."

"You might want to shave before your kids see you," Torres said as Bricklander moved toward the door. "You look awful."

"Stars and Stripes."

"Brick, wait a second," Torres said. "There's something else."

"What?"

"I have to ask…"

"…What?"

"Are you alright?"

The debriefing was the purpose of the meeting, but Bricklander felt a tightening in his torso because he knew what was coming next. According to the latest evaluation by NORM's Ministers, Torres had to know if his first sergeant was tip-top between the ears.

"I do my job."

"When we told you about the bus last night, you didn't handle it well."

He didn't. His crap filter, otherwise known as the face he showed the public, was worn out. He couldn't mask it anymore. When they told him about the bus, he dropped several curse words and indicated he wouldn't follow through with what NORM required or what Minister Kevin ordered.

Rosa and his three daughters were three thousand miles away, but he knew they'd hear the sound of his rifle if he shot another teen. No one was more relieved at not seeing the bus than him.

"I wasn't happy about it," he said.

"Brick, I can't lose you," Torres said. "Those whores…"

"…Minister Kevin…"

"… That's right, and Minister Tim, carry a lot of weight up top--they all do. If he puts you on report for being unwilling to dispatch the infected, they'll pull you. Hell, they might even discharge you. I know that doesn't sound too bad right now, but you don't want to go back to Virginia unemployed and your family put off base before you get there. We know how it works these days."

How much chest-candy covered his dress uniform? More than he could describe. But none of it would keep his family on base or earn him the benefit of the doubt because NORM was a bastard.

"It's a great feeling when you kill someone that straps a vest of dynamite on a kid," Bricklander said. "I cannot describe the satisfaction it gave me to have them surrender, press the barrel of my gun against their forehead and pull the trigger. I don't dream about it, I don't stress about it, and sometimes when I think about death, I think capping terrorists like that will be the thing that gets me through the pearly gates. But the sad sacks up top still wanted us fired at before answering back. The evil being done made no difference. They had to have due process. They had to have their rights observed when we knew what they were."

Sunlight came through the window.

"Now, I'm not even required to check to see if it's a deep scratch, cut, or a dog bite. They want me to kill Americans--even children. I've done that on orders from Minister Kevin and Minister Tim. And because they have leverage with my family, they're going to force me to do it again. And it's going to haunt me until I'm forced to eat a bullet."

"You know this army stuff doesn't mean anything to me. I'm only preaching Stars and Stripes to pay the bills and keep my family safe," Torres said. "But if not taking the shot puts my children in jeopardy, then I'm taking the shot. I'll live with it later, and so will you. We have kids, we have family, and we don't get a choice. I'm your friend, so I'm telling you, as a friend, if one of those whores tells you to cap somebody, you cap them. Your family's needs are more important than your self-esteem. Our personal happiness," Torres glanced at the daylight and shook his head, "got canceled a long time ago."

"How about if I shot a Minister?"

"Shoot a Minister, and I'll get you two months vacation in Virginia," Torres said with a chuckle. "Just tell me you get me, Brick."

"I get you."

"Tell me you ain't going to go Elvis on me or lose it between the ears."

"I'm not leaving," Bricklander said but made no promise regarding the thoughts running between his ears.

NOEL
(1)

Noel Sedaka was setting paper plates and bags of chips out for lunch in the dining hall. Pitchers of thin lemonade were already on the tables. Karla and Beth were in the kitchen, putting together sandwiches and cutting them in half.

In her early forties, Karla gave the impression she'd be interested if the right person showed up. Beth, very open about being 62, said her days of romance were over. Her 26-year old special needs daughter, Tammy, and son Jeremy—nicknamed "Wolfman" by Joab—were all that mattered. Both were widows of the virus.

Tammy, unable to speak, sat in a wheelchair near the unlit stone fireplace with eyes wide and mouth drooling. No one knew why the occasional smile traveled across her face but assumed a memory was firing in what remained of her brain.

"The best part of her is with the Lord," Beth said to anyone who asked. "And we got to keep the best of her to love."

Larry came in, said hello to Tammy, hugged her, and took a seat. Noel, replaced by Kelly, went to meet him.

There was minimal complaining at The Garden. Noel never heard a gripe about what she did or didn't do. When grumbling came, Larry took the brunt of it. They were co-leaders, but it didn't always work that way. All frustrations, reactions, and demands began with Larry and then Noel. Seldom did anything start with Noel and then progress to Larry.

Some of the ladies cared about this, but Noel didn't. And why, in the wake of everything going on, anyone cared amazed her. She was delighted with Larry being the nail absorbing all the hammering of complaint.

"What's the signal for me to come over and end the meeting if it goes bad?" Karla said to the two of them sitting by the double doors. "I've spent two minutes with that Owen guy. I don't like him or the way he talks to his wife."

"You want to kick his butt for us, Karla?" Noel joked.

"I don't know if I could," she said before setting down a pitcher of water. "But I bet Beth could."

"If Beth went toe-to-toe with Joab, I'd put my money on Beth," Larry said. Karla winked and went back to the kitchen. "Cool or not cool?" he asked Noel.

"Karla?"

"No, Owen. We know Karla's cool."

Larry was facing the entrance. Noel, across from him, could see Tammy by the fireplace staring at another corner of the room.

"Not cool," Noel said, her eyes back on him. "I think we're going to need Joab's help. Heather will come around. I think she's already there. Moms are funny about kids being healthy. And those two on the bus are healthy now."

"What do you think Heather saw today?"

"Easy," she said. "We risked lives to get their bus here. We welcomed them. Then right before her eyes, the Lord healed two of her students. As Crazy Chang would say, 'She be in.'"

"Nice vocabulary."

"Yeah, I'm sure Miss Tanney would expect better," Noel said. "If I thought she was still around, I'd send her an apology."

April Tanney had been their Senior English teacher at El Monte High School.

"So why doesn't Owen get it?" Larry said, his tone indicating he had a theory.

"I can answer two ways because I'm a brilliant 19-year-old with a broad vocabulary," she said. "He's either a moron or too smart."

"Or a lethal combination of both?"

"He'd be a lot cooler if he grew up listening to the Steve Miller Band," Noel said.

"Space cowboy or a gangster of love?"

"In our day?" she smiled and pretended to think. "He'd be the midnight toker telling us it's a seed-bearing plant."

Larry's voice dropped to old school FM level. "Dude, it's of the earth. God wouldn't give it to us if he didn't want us to smoke it, man."

"Good business for you, though," she said.

"Kept me in with the hip crowd," he said. "Would you believe me if I told you I never smoked it?"

"Now? Yes. Then? No."

"And, now, it's all legal," he said, an ironic smile emerging. "I could've been a pro."

When they returned to the Free Wesleyan Alliance Church in Arcadia, 18 months before, they were shocked by what Pastor Chip told them—then horrified as the world melted down. Later, Joab filled the gaps on where the church went off the rails. They came to understand the primary differences between what they accepted as their theology versus what the church currently believed.

It was another strange part of the equation for Noel. When she and Larry needed wisdom, it came, and it was still coming. They understood things 19-year olds usually didn't. They had to understand because they couldn't share their burdens. There were helpers, great people handling the day-to-day, but the weight of leadership sat on them.

"I think it was good you showed your scar," Larry said. "I know you're not a fan of it."

"It's alright," Noel said. "If it healed without leaving a scar, it wouldn't be much use."

Noel was bitten on the top of her shoulder when the Arcadia Church came under attack. The healed wound--a whole set of bumps and lumps—testified to the immunity belonging to believers.

It also happened before a bite, or deep scratch, was declared fatal and an instant death sentence.

"You know there are things I can say to you that I'll never say to anyone else," Larry said. "But..." He looked beyond her through a screen window. The camp was lining up for lunch. "I'm tired of defending our age to every new person who comes to The Garden. There are times I just want to pop someone like Owen." He leaned back from the table. "And I wasn't even one of those guys in school. I was barely a step above geeks like Darren Bradford."

"Small potatoes," she said. "I see it in the opposite. I think our age humbles people like Owen and Joab. It's another reason why God has us here. When we're obedient, and God works through us, I feel strong. And I think it's a demonstration of God's—hold on, a big word here—sovereignty."

Larry grinned. "And clarity?"

"As Joab would say, 'Clarity, amigo.' God's in control."

"We had no idea what we were praying for on that Sunday night." His expression was half happy, half sad.

"Obedience."

"Obedience sucks."

"Really? We've got an entire camp listening, not because we're cool. But because we've been obedient. Obedience is the currency of faith."

"Wow, listen to you," he said. "I know it doesn't suck, but it still feels like a spaceship picked us up and dropped us off somewhere. A year and a half ago, I got up feeling better than I'd ever felt before. I had the best morning of my life, and then...."

His eyes fell to the table, and she could tell he was playing at the edges of what he really wanted to talk about. If they were back in El Monte, Noel would have thought Larry was building to some big romantic question. At The Garden, it was something else.

Another layer of the veil between them was zero interest in each other. Larry wasn't ugly. She just didn't find him attractive. A nice guy, nicer than her brother, but he was as unattractive as a brother.

The lack of kismet was apparent to Beth. When the ladies began delving into the realm of matchmaking, she said, *"You and Larry are brother and sister. I knew it when I first laid eyes on the two of you…But you and Drew…"*

Noel wasn't ready to go there and kept focused on Larry. "Spit it out before lunch starts."

"I don't want to get super serious."

"Then, just be serious."

"Okay, do you ever feel like you've been robbed?" The dining hall doors opened. "Not in a bad way, but, you know, when I say things and the words come out of my mouth. Like praying for Aaron on the bus."

"I don't understand."

Larry adjusted himself in his seat and leaned closer. "I feel like we never earned those words. I don't have an education. We don't have a gray hair between us."

"That's God's problem," Noel said, grateful they could talk like this because each had moments when things felt weird. "We agreed to be obedient and to let him do the rest. And he's doing it, Larry."

"I'm not doubting. You know, I'm not doubting, right?"

"I know you're not doubting. But think about this," she said as benches filled, "why would someone like Joab ever listen or submit to us? This guy has a doctorate in something, and a master's in something else, and he humbles himself to us? If that's not God, I don't know what is."

"I wish I had some experience or memories, so I could better understand what I'm talking about." Stopping, he stood as others sat within listening distance. He scanned the dining hall. "I think Heather and Owen must have got sidetracked."

Noel came around to him. She pulled at the front of his shirt. "We'll talk more."

"Yeah, okay," he said, but Noel wouldn't let him go. She knew there was more, and his next sentence confirmed it. "I'm not over it, Noel. I dreamt about her again last night."

"It's a distraction, Larry," she said. "As sweet as the dream and Denise Hemingway might be, you have to fight through it."

JOAB
(2)

Back in camp, Joab's first stop was Mandalay. The sizable tent, set up on the southwest side of The Garden behind the cabins and below a hill, was the home of the security team. A place where sleep was harder to come by than laughter and cringe-worthy discussions.

His bunk was begging him to stay, but he knew he needed to get caught up with what was going on. Keeping the .44 with a 4-inch barrel at the back of his waistband, Joab stored his gear and Duran's shotgun. Since they were never off the clock, he and the security team were always armed.

The morning clouds were gone when Joab exited and rejoined the day. By appearance, it was beautiful and a reminder of God's grace.

Formerly the Boy Scout campground called Camp Goodspeed, The Garden's isolation was its best feature. Without telephone and power lines, and only accessible by an ancient fire road, Goodspeed became too challenging to maintain and was shuttered. But with intact structures, water wells, and being minus a caretaker or affiliation, it became the perfect refuge after The Tilt.

Joab spent two weeks at Goodspeed early in his ministry, but it had faded from memory. He'd been to dozens of camps, with their unique quirks in his career, but Goodspeed was less than an afterthought when the virus landed.

While in the rafters of the Bradbury Church—as devils dined, and the smell of death rose—a lever clicked, and the Boy Scout camp returned to memory. Knowing it had been closed, it became his goal after escaping Bradbury. Later, providence doubled down when he collided with Larry and Noel.

Providence then tripled when they came across a Ford F150 abandoned off the side of the highway. In its bed were cases of Remington 870 12-gauge shotguns. In its seats were full cases of shells. Joab guessed they had been stolen once, stolen again, and then lost after an attack by the dead.

The first few weeks at Goodspeed, five adults turned. They'd been previously bitten, kept it concealed, died in their sleep, and went on a rampage after re-animating. Everyone coming into camp, soon renamed "The Garden," was now checked.

Since then, there had been only three perimeter breaches. The last occurring ten months before, but still, everyone remained on their toes. With nothing taken for granted and around-the-clock security, folks were always careful.

If his math was correct, the new additions pushed The Garden's population to 187. For now, they were fine, but they'd have to start scouting further out for supplies. The hope was always to find the abandoned home of some well-prepared American waiting for an earthquake, war, or Rapture. They'd struck gold a few times, but that kind of search was dangerous.

There were devils in the woods and devils locked behind doors by departed family members. There was also a high probability of coming into an area defended by others ready to shoot anything disturbing a bush or tree branch.

Before The Tilt, Joab thought God was preparing him for some transcendent moment. Looking back, he knew that was impossible. With speaking days over, tangible things were now Joab's responsibility as a glorified fetch boy. Whatever his background had been before—and it was considerable—all spiritual matters were forfeit to Larry and Noel's leadership.

"The spiritual axis of the world has tilted." Larry preached a year before. *"I'm not saying I've learned this by revelation or vision, but it seems to make sense. Spiritually, the church lost its way and went off track, and the Sin Virus spilled in. It's our job to right it. To right, The Tilt."*

Larry and Noel's presence shed light on things he refused to see before. They reinvigorated a passion and comprehension for the Virgin Birth, the Resurrection, blood atonement, and Trinity. They were the agents the Holy Spirit used to bring him back after everything he believed and advocated for had been proved wrong by the virus.

Ping.

There could have been a worse penance for his old patterns, but God spared him. Joab embraced it and felt gratitude. He didn't think many like him got an opportunity to clean up the evil they propagated. So maxed-out servanthood with zero adulation was his desire.

Heading for the dining hall, he saw Owen, Heather, and their little girl standing alone near the three oaks. Radar or oversized ears weren't necessary. Owen's body language showed he wasn't adjusting. The little girl, with a fresh bandage on her arm, hugged her father around the waist. Mom and Dad's discussion died when Joab approached.

"Forgive me for being rude," he said, squatting down to his knees. "But I didn't introduce myself to your little girl. What's your name?"

"Loren," she said, slipping back behind her father.

"Hi, my name's Joab. Can I give you something, Loren?" He glanced at her parents, who gave tacit approval. "I always give one of these to everyone who comes to camp named Loren." He held out a chocolate bar. The little girl smiled but didn't move. "I wouldn't take it from a creepy old guy like me, either. Here, I'm going to give it to your mom." He handed it to Heather. "She can give it to you after lunch."

Loren gave him a nod and a face full of dimples before he stood back up. "Did you get situated, okay? I heard Larry and Noel took care of your people."

"Good as new," Heather said. "I don't know how, exactly, but we can't thank you enough."

Owen wasted no words, "I don't feel comfortable here."

"Do you, Heather?" Joab asked. She returned a nod. "So there's the problem. Did you talk to Larry and Noel yet?"

"Didn't get a chance too," Owen said. "Not sure if I want to."

"We can talk if you want," Joab said. "But we probably don't want to do it in front of this pretty little girl. I'm guessing she's anxious to get to that chocolate bar."

The charm attempt fell incomplete. The family didn't budge or offer a grin. Joab was unsure if they wanted him to move on or stay. His seeing eyes may have been middle-aged, but his ministry eyes were old and old eyes saw everything. It was always the old eyes that saw something out of place in a service. It was old eyes that picked up on inappropriate dress, questionable actions, or veiled passive-aggressive insults. And the old eyes of a pastor could see the mileage built up in another.

"Would you like me to get Larry and Noel? Or do you want me to share with you?"

"You'll do," Owen said. "I don't think the kids have anything to say that I want to hear."

"Great, I'll be straight with you as well," Joab said. "Are you ticked off because the world sucks right now or because you feel like you're not in charge of your group anymore?"

"What?" Owen's head shook in offense. "All I care about is the safety of my family and my group."

"Hey, it happens. A lot of people get that way, and the truth is, while you're in this camp, you're not completely in charge. It's a hard adjustment."

"Not completely in charge?" Owen said. "What am I in charge of?"

"Then it is the hangup?"

"For starters, yes. Tell me what's under my control?" Owen said. "You've got the guns and the manpower. What am I in charge of?" He drew a breath. "Can we leave anytime we want?"

"Anytime you want," Joab said in a very pandering tone. "We've designed a perimeter here to keep the bad guys out, not hold the stupid in. We're hoping you'll stay. There'll be concern about you leading the authorities to us from down below, but no one's going to make you stay. No one's going to make you or your wife do anything you don't want to do."

"What if we don't believe the way you believe?"

Joab had been waiting for it, knew it was coming, and it landed. Even after seeing his people healed, Owen still couldn't cope. Maturity moved Joab beyond the desire to laugh in the youth pastor's face and effort in keeping the dialogue open.

"Okay," Joab said, and Owen postured as if to prepare for a physical punch back. "I can speak to you as Joab, head of security who led a group of young men to the highway to save you, folks. Or," he held up the palms of his hands, "I can be the Joab who walked in your shoes and traded out everything for the wisdom of man. I can relate with the fool you are because I was a fool myself."

"Fool?" Owen's cockiness, dormant while behind the bus's wheel, was flexing and wide awake. "Speak for yourself. I don't consider myself a fool. I've kept my group safe for over a year."

"Larry and Noel laid hands on your people, right?" Joab said, looking at Heather, who confirmed with another nod. The breeze blew strands of hair across her white face. "What happened?"

Owen hesitated.

"Come on, it's not a hard question, smart guy." Joab felt Owen's eyes penetrate him, looking for a way to take to cap the discussion. He pushed. "Come on, seminary grad, say it. Everything in you wishes it was by Beelzebub or some fundamentalist alchemy that your two were healed. But you know that's not true. So tell the truth about what you saw."

Owen chewed his lip and seemed on the verge of responding but didn't.

"You saw something your crappy theology doesn't allow you to believe in, and you realize you're not only wrong now but that you've been wrong for a long, long time. I know because I've been there."

"No!"

"Then answer me!" Joab's voice rose to meet Owen's, "what did you see?"

"I saw two young people healed in Jesus' name," Heather said, catching a stern expression from her husband. Loren reached out for her mom. "Owen, get over it, or don't get over it, but we're not leaving. Thank you, Joab." She took her daughter and went inside the dining hall.

Owen started walking to the bus, and Joab put a hand on him. "Real quick, kid, before you storm off, hear this. You're a minister, and I was a minister, and I believed one set of rules before The Tilt

—that means before things changed—and now I believe something else after The Tilt. I was you, but this changed me. It gave me clarity."

"I believe what I was taught," Owen said with less bravado, Heather's walk away deflating him. "And whatever you mean by The Tilt doesn't change that."

"The Tilt is what Larry tagged this as," Joab said. "The world appears largely the same, but it's not the same. Not destroyed, but tilted spiritually, and this Sin Virus has come in."

"I can't accept that."

"We were taught the same thing and taught it to others. I'm also captured in print, with 55,000 words--a book you read--confirming my stupidity." He felt a hunger pain rumble in his stomach. He'd eaten nothing since breakfast. The breeze, hopeful in effect, continued across the grounds. "I was a good man. I was doing good work."

Ping.

"You familiar with Pasadena, Owen?"

"I went to seminary in Pasadena," he said.

"Me too. Great city," Joab went on. "It's a perfect combo of wealth, poverty, the Rose Parade, Old Town, aristocracy, and gang violence. I worked there for years, helping the oppressed and disadvantaged. In my church, we fed people, gave them clothes, taught them computer skills, job skills, social skills, showed them how to access government agencies. It was great work. We pointed out things on the ballots for the community to vote and advocate for. We fought with the people to overcome oppression, genderism, racism, and even biblicism. In front of a thousand people at the FWA church in Bradbury, I renounced my white privilege to great applause. I spoke that we should lean on the truths Intersectionality teaches us. It was all so powerful in words but absolutely powerless when the virus hit."

"My faith's strong," Owen countered.

"But what's it built on?"

"The goodness of people."

"When the virus hit," Joab continued, "we had several compassionate ministry centers in different parts of the city. They were overrun, first by people looking for refuge, then by devils at the doors, and finally by those inside our walls. They kept coming, and, finally, a couple of vans with workers, kids, and myself made it to the Bradbury Church. But several, already bitten, turned, and things fell apart."

"So what? You're not saying anything that didn't happen to millions of others," Owen said. "You got overrun? The whole country's overrun. We were trapped up here when this started. I saw three of my people die."

"We made our last stand inside the sanctuary. When the doors began to break and the stained glass busted in, we prayed for the cops to come, the National Guard, for anybody to help us. Four of us made it through a backstage door. Angela, our compassionate ministries director, a woman who put everything into helping the poor and the oppressed…" Joab swallowed, "…she got bit. And this godly woman, by appearance, ended up turning and killing the other two before I pushed her from the rafters to the sanctuary below."

"I'm sorry," Owen said, "but none of this is unique."

"You don't understand what I'm getting at. We believed we were Christians doing God's work. We were such good Christians we didn't pray for his help and protection--we prayed for cops and guns. We didn't pray for the Holy Spirit. We didn't pray for spiritual protection. We saw the dead coming back to life, and we thought the answer was in the physical. Because the supernatural had been conditioned out of us and was just too impossible to believe in."

Joab knew he was in the present with Owen, but describing his time in the Bradbury sanctuary transported him back. Fear tickled every pore of his skin at the recall. The long hot days in darkness came with the sound of devils feeding below. Their presence working on his resolve to hang on.

"I spent three days in the rafters of that church listening to devils eat and search for more food. I'd doze into sleep, and the shrieks of colleagues found hiding would wake me. It was dark, I was alone, and it became clearer and clearer that all my work for justice, all my work for the oppressed, hadn't saved anybody. In terms of eternity, I changed no lives. I might have moved a few people from one tax structure to another, from a lousy neighborhood to a less lousy one. But I led no one to the Lord. I, and those I worked with, just used them as cover to feed our vanity and feel very good about ourselves. Clarity came, and I knew I didn't have a clue about the God I spent a lifetime using to high-road others into guilt and shame."

"I kept my youth group alive for 18 months," Owen said. "I'm not going to let you judge me."

"But you had to come here for them to experience the blood of Jesus," Joab said. "You're a youth pastor, and you were with those teens this whole time. How did they become infected when believers can't be infected?"

"You are so arrogant! So egotistical to believe you know all there is to know about God."

"You ever drop a devil?"

Owen stared at him.

"Ever have to drop one of your students? Ever have one of them come at you and see the infection right in front of you and realize you didn't have a theological answer at the ready? It's one thing to have a gun or a blade, but we both know there's something in the spiritual realm happening when dead walk the earth. The theology I was taught and, in turn, taught others didn't save them, couldn't save them. I prepared them for nothing but the next election. As we demonstrated it, kingdom living was just another way of teaching them salvation by works." He took a breath, waiting for a ping to come. "I was real big on works, bagging on white people, and the American church. That was my thing. Salvation? Sin? Nope, but I sure did get a lot of churches to take down the American flag."

The joyful sounds of people talking over a meal came from the dining hall. The world was all madness and death, but the people inside the dining hall had found something to let them casually converse and gently laugh. It was a perfect paradox.

Ping.

"Owen, we've both made this mistake. We bought into a lie of good deeds and the false bravado that we could change lives by marching, resisting, and compromising. We were so desperate to appear open-minded and seeker-friendly that we thought we could just keep the red letters and blow off the rest of scripture. We trusted so much in our righteousness—you trusted so much in your righteousness—that you couldn't believe the healing you saw on your bus today."

BRICKLANDER
(2)

The beeping wristwatch opened Bricklander's eyes, and he was unsure if it was morning or evening. The uninterrupted sleep had taken him far away.

Feet to the floor, rubbing his face, excitement came over him. Bricklander left the classroom/barracks for the bathroom. Working the razor made him wish he'd trimmed his hair. After practicing a smile and smoothing both eyebrows, he left for the TOC—Tactical Operation Center—in the school's former administration building. His video link was scheduled for 2:45. If missed, he'd have to wait another month.

Jogging across the playground, he passed swings, a Jungle Jim, and painted lines for kickball. Everything else tagging it as a school was gone. It was Camp Braggs, now and into the foreseeable future.

He came through the door.

"I was getting worried, Sergeant," First Lieutenant Gayle Holsopple said with a gesture to the clock on the wall. In her forties and entirely gray, she was in perfect shape and subject to all the talk that went with it. "I'd hate for you to miss your call."

Beyond looks, Holsopple had everyone's respect after holding her own in the Arroyo Seco. She had Third Platoon, which consisted of

27 breathing souls. They held down TOC and much of the logistics around Braggs.

He followed her to the converted walk-in closet the soldiers used to talk with their families. It was a nice touch by Holsopple. Family connections were infrequent enough, but to have the once a month chat shared with everyone else coming in and out of the office could be brutal. When soldiers cried, they wanted to cry alone. Bricklander was no different.

Gliding past her, he took a seat at a small desk, slipped on the headset, and adjusted the mouthpiece.

"You're the last one today. The link can go down any time after 2:55," Holsopple said. "If you're lucky, it will last until 3:30. I have no control from this end, so don't take any frustrations out on Third Platoon. It's all up to NORM, and, it's been established, he's a bastard."

"Stars and Stripes," he said, feeling his heart race.

"Come out when you're ready." Which meant when he stopped crying. She left, and he clicked the mouse over the icon.

"Rosa!" he said, "Oh baby, you look beautiful!"

Had a month passed? It felt like years and seconds, all at the same time. He put a hand to the screen to touch her face and long hair. The image, three thousand miles away, began wringing out tears.

"Jeff," Rosa smiled and cried with him.

"Where are the kids? Are the kids with you? Are they okay? You okay?"

"Daddy!" Three daughters sprang from all sides of his wife into view. "We love you, Daddy!" They said in a chorus.

"Oh, I love you too." Bricklander battled the boulder manifesting in his throat. The time was too precious and too short to waste weeping. "I love you all so much."

"We love you!"

The basics came quickly with a hundred things to talk about and mere minutes to do it in.

"Okay," he cleared his throat. "We don't have a lot of time."

"Jeff, are you being safe? Is your area safe?"

"Yes, yes," he said. "It's getting better." No statistics were available to prove the statement's truth, but he was no longer firing his weapon every day. So there was some validity to the lie. "Things are starting to turn. How about you? Are they keeping you safe?"

"Yes, it's good," she said, but her fake smile wasn't as convincing as his. "It's getting better here, too."

They exchanged a silence for the smallest of moments, indicating they both knew they were speaking for the sake of NORM, who was likely eavesdropping.

"Daddy!" Marcia jumped in her mother's lap. She was seven years old and the middle sister. "They said we're going to play soccer this summer! Are you going to come?"

"Oh baby, I want to, I want to come, I'll try." A military career and its experiences kept him from making a foolish promise.

Margie, his three-year-old, replaced Marcia. "I love you." Rosa coached her. "I miss you." She kissed the monitor. "I have to go color." She barely knew him. Due to deployments, his life with Margie was measured in months.

Tears, impossible to dam, came.

"Are you crying, Dad?" Shelby said, getting in front of the camera.

"Just a little beautiful," he said. "I miss you all so much. Are you being safe?"

"We miss you too, Dad." Shelby was twelve. "Things are good. Sergeant Harper told me to say hi. He says you used to be in the same platoon together."

"We were--tell him the same for me." He remembered Harper. Good guy but a bit of a dork who always fell butt-forward into opportunity. "I love you, Applesauce."

Shelby, giggling at the nickname he gave her long before, blew him a kiss and slid out of the seat. Rosa came back in front of the camera. Marcia and Margie were arguing about something in the background.

"Jeff?"

"I want to see you," he said. "There's talk about leaves coming, but I'd have to find my own transport to Virginia."

"Travel's hard," she said.

"NORM's a bastard," he let slip.

They both stared at each other, and he knew he had shortened their time.

"Are you being careful?" she said and then looked in another direction as a voice in the room spoke. "I only have a minute."

"I'm being careful," he said, knowing a mention of an open jeep ride into the mountains would flare her anger.

"Jeff, I'm so sad. I miss you so much." She paused and put a hand to her head. "You remember us. Before being all Stars and Stripes, you think about us first."

"I do, Rosa, I always do…."

The words stopped again, they shared a long gaze, she smiled, "You're really turning gray…."

The picture went dark.

Bricklander waited, hoping the screen would light up again. It didn't, and he had to accept what he got. He was Stars and Stripes, so he put his faith in fellow soldiers to protect his family. They'd do their job, he'd do his, and they'd be together sooner rather than later. He had to believe that. America was still America, and Stars and Stripes gave hope.

Holsopple, leaning over another lady in uniform, Sergeant Myers, didn't look his way when he came out. "Washroom's down the hall," she said. Everyone got sent down the hall after family time to splash water on their face.

He went into the center of the office structure. When it was still a school, this was the attendance and administration office. In the back was the nurse's station. A floor above a former science class served as living quarters for Third Platoon. The roof above was used for observation.

The water-cooled his emotions.

"You remember us."

Last night, the mountain trip this morning, knowing they would run into a bus full of young people, how could he not have thought of his family? How could he have not thought of his children if forced to put another young person down?

"Thank God for Joab," he said to his reflection in the mirror.

Coming back, Holsopple tossed him the cap he'd left by the computer. "You better not get caught without a lid."

"Thank you, LT," he said.

"Stars and Stripes," she said, eyes remaining with Sergeant Myers.

"Stars and Stripes."

The cap was necessary because every little thing helped keep order. It kept them focused. Stars and Stripes reminded them they were United States soldiers. If the military held it together, the citizenry would as well. It was all about the flag, baseball, football, apple pie, and America always being America.

Outside, he fastened the cap, looked left, and then right. Technically he was off duty until this evening—the perk of going into a hot zone. He turned left underneath the concourse, went past the building he was just in, and came to the open grass at the school's front.

The grass was beautiful and almost Virginia green.

Three soldiers were standing by the main gate. A ghoul, reaching at them through the wrought iron fence, brought back what stood in the way of Bricklander getting home. From a safe distance, the soldiers were waiting for orders before taking it down.

When there was no urgency, everyone had learned the slower pace was the safer pace. The monster might have been alone, or it may have splintered off from a group. It was rare in San Quintana for a swarm to be in the town's perimeter. The men observing from the top of the TOC were double-checking the area. When given a clear sign, the soldiers would take action.

"Brick, weren't there any hot chicks on that bus?" Sergeant Tom Lancaster said. "You couldn't bring any of them back?"

"What's going on, Tom?" he said. "Hammer, the thing already."

"Just waiting," Lancaster said. "There wasn't one good looking woman on that mountain? You know how long I've been in dry dock?"

"What about that Red Cross worker?" Bricklander said, looking through the fence for anything coming their way. The pop-ups were a source of frustration in San Quintana. Families knew the loved ones they locked away weren't going to be fixed but couldn't bring themselves to put them down.

And sometimes, they got out.

"That Red Cross babe was three spins."

"Try three and a half," said Private Cruz.

"Come on," Bricklander said, "how can anybody be three spins nowadays?"

"Have you seen these Ministers?" Cruz said as a door opened on the second floor of the TOC. "Speaking of which…."

Minister Tim appeared and came down the steps. A napkin, tucked around his neck, was kicked loose by a breeze and blown away.

"They say the Red Cross is always there when you have a need, Sarge," Private Esposito said to Lancaster.

"And you wonder why you're in dry dock," Bricklander said. "She couldn't have been more than 225."

"Holsopple's sweet looking," Lancaster said.

"You like cougars?" Cruz said.

"She's only a cougar if she's got age on you," Lancaster said. "She ain't older than me."

"Just colder," Bricklander said.

"Iceberg," Lancaster added, then hollered to the men on the observation deck. "How long is this going to take? Look at this thing!" As if on cue, the monster reached a hand further in. It had been a man, relatively young, but the corpse was decaying in long strings that hung off its bones. It had been turned for some time. What remained of its flesh was quickly declining from blueish-green to a rotting black.

It smelled, but at this point, the smell of the dead was familiar enough.

"Holsopple's happening," said Esposito.

"She's no Desert Queen," Lancaster said. "She's hot in Kabul, and she's hot here. I wish I were Mr. Holsopple."

"They've spotted another about to turn the corner," Minister Tim said, joining them. "How's everyone doing today?"

The soldiers nodded, but no one answered. Minister Tim was less liked than Minister Kevin, owing to his 'I'm-smarter-than-all-of-you' personality. They also ceased discussion about the attractiveness of Lieutenant Holsopple. They knew any comment about her was subject to the Minister's opinion and could get recorded in their file.

The second monster arrived at the street corner. Cruz handed Bricklander his weapon and picked up a baseball bat. Any chance to conserve ammunition they took--especially when a Minister was nearby.

"Push him back first, Cruz," Lancaster said. "We'll open the gate."

The private jabbed the barrel end through the fence, and the monster went backward. Lancaster slid the latch and swung the gate. "Now, give him a migraine."

Cruz immediately stepped around and flattened its head. The squash of it produced black streams as the skull caved. Going to the next one on the corner, he re-cocked the bat, unleashed, and it collapsed. Then the soldier dropped his head.

"What's the problem?" Lancaster called, but Cruz didn't respond. "You mind watching the door for a second, Brick?" The sergeant cursed and ran to the corner with Esposito.

Bricklander clicked off M4's safety in anticipation.

"Oh, my," Minister Tim said, standing next to him.

A woman in her twenties came holding her left forearm. Blood was spilling out of it. "Help me, help me..." she cried, "please help me!"

Esposito put a hand to her shoulder to stop her from going further. There was nothing they could do. Many had tried chopping off a limb after a bite, but backyard amputations only resulted in bleed-outs and eventual reanimation.

"Get her name!" Minster Tim yelled. "We'll need her name!"

Lancaster scowled at the Minister and turned to the woman. He spoke, she spoke back. Esposito pulled a roll of gauze from his belt and began rolling it around her forearm.

"Maybe you should go talk to her?" Bricklander suggested. "That's your job, isn't it?"

"What can I do? She's already bit," Minister Tim said. "Have you heard from Minister Kevin yet?" He noticed Esposito applying the gauze. "Oh, what the hell is Esposito doing?"

"No." Bricklander didn't look at him.

"Hopefully, we will soon…Did you get her name!" The minister asked.

Lancaster grudgingly nodded.

"Then what are you waiting for?"

"Maybe we should contact her family?" Bricklander said.

"Please!" she screamed. "Don't kill me! Please! I'll go, I'll just get out of town! Don't!"

"And drag this out further?" he said to Bricklander. "Cruz, for godsakes hit her!"

"Please…Please…" she fell to her knees and begged.

"Use the dam bat, Private Cruz!" Minister Tim said. The soldier hesitated. "Use it, or I'll find someone that will!"

Lancaster took his M9 from its holster and put a round through her head. She flopped back to the sidewalk--arms and legs starred out-- life over.

"Oh that's so sloppy," Minister Tim said. "They wasted gauze and a bullet. When are you people going to understand you have to be smarter about this? The only way this is going to get better is if you follow the protocols in place." He headed back to finish his lunch. "Let me know when you hear from Minister Kevin."

Bricklander focused on Lancaster. *Holster the gun, Tom.*

He was about to race toward his friend when the pistol was holstered.

"Tom?"

Lancaster raised a thumb to indicate he was okay…for now.

NOEL
(2)

From the dining hall porch, Noel watched the men gather by the three trees. She was about to head to the amphitheater for chapel. Her job was to share announcements, encourage with positives from the day, and pray. They'd worship, and after, Larry would bring the message.

As early evening shadows stretched and the sky turned purple, Noel's mind went to the place it always did. Her battle was the same as Larry's, but with someone she saw every day.

Drew.

Drew had a manner Noel couldn't ignore. All his actions were honest. He never brought attention to himself. His words, gestures were never for the benefit of anyone else. Surrounded by thousands or alone, she knew he'd be the same.

A year before, following a chapel, they shared a hug. To Noel, it confirmed their feelings were mutual, but it didn't progress. She held back because he held back. And time passed with no further evidence he felt anything for her, but she knew he did.

Of course, he did.

Despite her past—a past only Larry was somewhat aware of—Noel didn't think about Drew sexually. Thoughts of sex were dark turns down old roads. Roads she never wanted to see again. Lines she had crossed with consequences she couldn't erase. Instead, she thought about the hug and the night they touched hands by a campfire. She thought about the odor of soap he carried after showering. The little expressions his face made when thinking, reading, or listening.

While God had granted wisdom she never studied for, insight never acquired through experience, he kept in place the same fears any teenage girl had. The terror of an infatuation being made public and the mystery of attraction.

Drew, dressed in dark clothing, was with the rest of the men by the trees in the center of camp. He was on security, and it was a good night for it. They expected a full moon. However, beyond positioning themselves in two-man teams around The Garden's outside perimeter, she wasn't sure exactly what they did beyond stopping devils.

"Noel, Noel!" A dozen kids gathered around and interrupted a pending and sure to be sweet daydream. Seeing Loren already running with the group caused Drew to evaporate from thought. "What are we singing tonight?" Alison asked. "Are we going to sing *Pharaoh, Pharaoh*?"

"We've sung it every night this week," she said, beginning the slow walk to chapel. "How about something fresh?"

"But Loren doesn't know it!" Alison said her blond bangs, like a waterfall, covered her forehead. The rest of her face, smudged with dirt, was lit with a sunshine smile. According to the information she gave Joab when he found her, she was nine. She'd been hiding, alone, inside a compost toilet for two days after devils wiped out the camp her parents had made.

"Loren," Noel said, "is everyone treating you nice? Alison, you guys treating her nice?"

Loren nodded. Her smile was small but a big deal considering she was new and had a bandaged bite on her forearm.

"Of course, we are silly. That's why we want to sing *Pharaoh, Pharaoh*," Alison said. "Why are we asking you? We should be asking someone cooler."

"Who's cooler than me?"

Alison pretended to stare into a make-believe camera with a blank face. "Uhhh, Derek Duran? Uhhh, Wolfman…" Everyone, including Loren, laughed. "Uhhh…Joab?"

"Okay, I get it," Noel said.

"Uhhh…Larry?"

"Alright, I'm not cool."

"…Uhhh, Liz?"

"Noel, you said we were going to play baseball this week," Todd said. He was eleven and at The Garden with his parents, Gavin and Candida. An older sister, high school age, didn't make it out of the city. "When are we going to play baseball? I'm tired of soccer. It's for girls."

"No one wants to play a stupid game like baseball, Todd!" Alison said.

"I'll ask Wheeler to help out tomorrow, and we'll play," Noel said. "I like baseball too."

"Hey! You guys giving Noel a hard time?" Joab said, coming from behind and joining them on their way.

"Joab!" The kids screamed and zoomed to him as if he were a magnet.

He scooped Alison up. "Sweetie, you should be taking care of Noel and not letting jokers like Todd and his friends rough her up."

"I just want to play baseball," Todd said in frustration.

"Alison's the one picking on me the most," Noel said.

"Joab! Are you coming to chapel tonight?" Teddy said.

"Where else would I be?"

They moved like a mob, passing the old shed, with the kids clinging to the adults and excited about the evening. Noel didn't know what Joab thought about it, but to her, it was beautiful. Defender, tough guy, whatever the label, the kids were Joab's weakness. To the kids without fathers, he was an anchor. If his time ever came, she guessed, it would happen while trying to protect the kids.

"Are you going to sing *Pharaoh, Pharaoh,* with us?" Teddy asked.

"I'll sing with you, but I'm not doing the motions," he said.

"Oh, you're crazy, Joab!" Alison said. "If you don't do the motions, we're going to make you do all our chores!" The kids cheered. "Or we'll bop you. You see this?" Alison held up a fist. "It has a friend!" She raised a second one. "And they're not as nice as me."

"Alright, alright," he said. "I'll do it. I don't want to meet your crazy friends." The kids cheered again. "But you have to let me talk to Noel right now. So beat it to your seats, or I'll make you do dead bug tonight!"

The kids took off. Todd lingered, a red baseball cap--courtesy of Wheeler--with an Angels logo resting on his head.

"And Todd, I promise, we'll set up a baseball field tomorrow," Joab said. The boy's face beamed, and he took off with the news.

"You're gonna have to tell me sometime what 'dead bug' is," Noel said.

"If everything's cool tonight, I'll show you."

"Do I want to know?"

"Oh, you'll love it," he said.

Joab was a hero. So reliable, so faithful, she feared, at times, of putting more faith in him than in God. And, like a parent, Joab was always looking out for her. He gave reasons why he disapproved of Wolfman, Crazy Chang, or Gonzo being a boyfriend. Often joking, *"If I was your dad and you brought that guy home...."* But he never gave any hint of disapproval regarding Drew.

"You think those kids love me?" she said.

"I'm sure they feel sorry for you," Joab joked. "It's easy to see why they like me. You, on the other hand, are hideous--like some sort of a monster."

"Your kindness encourages me."

They stopped at the steps down to the amphitheater. From a spot just over Joab's shoulder, Noel could see the back of Drew's head as he spoke to the men working security.

"How many have of them do we have now?" Joab said, looking into the crowd.

"Kids?"

"Yeah."

"We have 63 under the age of 13," she said. "But only one, Trinity, under the age of four."

"That's a lot of kids."

"You okay?"

"Yeah," he said, bringing out a smile. "God's got a plan, right?"

"I'm counting on it," Noel said.

"63 kids," he said. "187 people total in camp. That's a lot of food and a lot of people to protect. Some of these folks haven't put a devil down in over a year. And I'm not sure that's a good thing."

"It is a good thing," Noel said. "I know there's more down the road for us, Joab, but, for now, we've made things a little bit normal. Think of Alison; she's got no one but us. I pray she never sees a devil again. I pray she never has to drop someone she knows."

"I don't want to pretend like I'm in charge here, Noel," he said.

"That's getting old."

"I know."

"We're all in charge here," she said.

"No," he answered quickly. "You and Larry are running this show. I serve the Lord by serving you and Larry. But I get a feeling change is coming. I don't know when, but I do know we have to be ready because something's going to happen."

"I try not to think about the future," she said. "Not too much beyond tomorrow, anyway."

"Drew will come around," he said.

"Tell me it's not that obvious?"

"Only to the people that love you," he said and side-hugged her. "Did you get any time with Owen and Heather?"

"Not really," Noel said. "Heather and I talked a little during lunch about chapel but nothing else. They didn't meet with us."

"I spoke to Owen," Joab said.

"And?"

He shook his head, "He's a jackwagon, and I'm qualified to know a jackwagon."

"No clarity?" she said.

"No clarity, amiga," he grinned. "I'm not concerned about him bolting. I think Heather feels safe here, so that forces him to put up with us. But he's holding something back."

"Theologically?"

"No, he's the smartest guy in the room. If he's got some perch to stand on, he's going to stand and let everyone know. A lot of us seminary folk do that around proles like you. But right now, with Owen, it's something else. The Garden's relatively safe considering what's going on in the world."

"So why would he want to leave?" she interjected.

"Exactly," he stared at her. "Why would he want to leave?"

"We should pin him down after chapel," Noel said. Twin anxieties played in her stomach. One, guilt for the distraction she was letting Drew become, and two, the unknown Owen was holding back. "See you after?"

"See you after."

JOAB
(3)

If Big Leon and Big Geoff, currently sitting on the picnic table under the trees, had set there a year ago, it would've drawn the ire of the entire Garden. Both arrived weighing over 300-pounds. Now, along with Kuykendall, the "Big" adjective spoke more to memory than current conditions. The Garden was a tough place to gain weight.

Half of the camp's 30-man security team were scattered on the grass in a semi-circle listening to Drew. There was no protocol, no saluting. Only two, Sandoval and Pena, had military experience. It was all last names or nicknames.

These men were different than their peers. They had an edge other men didn't, and nearly all the teenage boys lacked. They were rough on each other, cruelly ribbed one another, but took none of it personally.

No rule existed that it had to be all men, but there were no women in the group. For the first two months at The Garden, one female— Shawna—had been part of security. She was also the last one killed after slipping into a ravine with Abel Chapman. They were attacked. He survived, she didn't, and no other female had volunteered since.

Joab, as their leader, issued the handles. For Anspach, Wheeler, Hutchinson, Bash, Legaspe, Brewer, Duran, Pena, Hernandez, Chapman, Mason, and Scott, it was last names. There was Mr. Sandoval, over 60, and a Marine Corps veteran, who insisted the "mister" be done away with.

Pure nicknames went to Bird, Crazy Chang, Vegas, Matts, and Wolfman. Wolfman because, as the youngest, he was always on the prowl for a date. Crazy Chang always wanted to do something dangerous. "It's fun!" He'd say. "You got to get your fun-on because there's no more fun in this world. I be in for fun."

Bird, with a 5-2 build, was shaped like a bird and loved to climb. Matthew became Matts because it was quicker to say. Vegas—Joab couldn't remember his real name—was Vegas because of the UNLV sweatshirt he wore the entire first year at The Garden.

The "Bigs" kept their first names: Big Geoff, Big Leon, and Big K., which was short for Kuykendall. Joab enjoyed calling him Kuykendall, so it stuck. For unknown reasons, Jay, Orlando, Hiram, and Frank didn't pick up a unique tag. And Drew was always Drew.

These were the fellows who made their home in Mandalay, where the weak of heart did not dwell. To go along with a cowboy-like spirit, none of them had blood ties at the camp. It made them willing to take risks. If one of them were killed, no one would lose support.

The three married men on security—Gavin, Alan, and Troy—kept their first names. And because they had families, it made Joab reluctant to use them outside The Garden. They lived in the cabins.

Wolfman—his mom, Beth, and sister, Tammy—was the only other with a family connection at The Garden.

"Standard patrol tonight, fellas?" Joab said, coming alongside Drew.

"Standard," Drew answered, "but we want to hit you with something."

"As long as it ain't a dutch oven from Big K., go ahead."

"Nah, it ain't that bad," Hutchinson said. "The Arroyo Seco ain't even that bad."

They laughed.

"Did you notice anything about this morning?" Drew said.

Joab reviewed thoughts, spent a millisecond on Minister Kevin, and recounted the walk back with Anspach and Crazy Chang. There was the devil he shot coming up the embankment, and… "The devils?"

"Quite a few," Drew said. "We're pretty well tucked back in the bush and get one occasionally passing, but we started picking them up immediately. We shot three when you were dealing with the bus, but we took out four more with blades, and by the sound of it, you shot one yourself."

"And there were two more down that same embankment after you left," Joab added.

"Troy dropped another coming back with his bad ankle," Drew said.

"Jefe," Big Leon said from the picnic table. Probably 28, bald, half white, half black, half something else, and now closer to two spins on the scale than three. "They're coming out of the resorts and campsites. All the barricades those little communities had, even Big Sky, have begun to rot."

"Since we're counting," Hiram volunteered from the base of the tree. "We," he gestured to Frank, his friend from high school, "also saw a group of three further back in the woods on the east side of the road. They were far back in the bush, so we let them pass."

"Yeah, they didn't look like Star Wars fans, so we let them go," Frank joked.

"What are you thinking?" Joab asked, ignoring the humor.

"That, that's a lot. A year ago, not so much, but now it's just not ordinary," Drew said. Then he rubbed at his mouth before asking a bigger question. "I want permission to push further out tonight and see what's coming down the road."

"You mean from Sky Porch?"

"Big Sky," Drew said. "Sky Porch is still bottled. and I don't even want to consider the possibility of that nightmare."

"Population, 39,000," Anspach refreshed while leaning against a tree. His hair seemed to be permanently disheveled. He appeared taller now than when they met him. As with everyone else, Joab attributed it to loss of weight. "If Sky Porch is open, there's nothing to discuss."

Orlando, 21 with a 21-year-old's mind, sighed. "That's a lot."

"No kidding," Big Leon said, flashing a crooked grin. "If that's the case, we might as well eat, drink, and be merry for tomorrow we die."

"In which case the devils will eat, drink, and be merry," Kuykendall quipped.

"That's if all of them turned into devils, and if they've broken out," Joab said. "We should keep our focus on Big Sky. We just finished our second full winter up here, and so far, so good."

"Overdue?" Drew suggested.

A moment passed, the sounds of the kids laughing in the distance reached them. Joab could only guess what those sounds meant to the rest, but to him, the children's joy boiled his fear. Everything took a back seat to the kids.

Ping.

"So why don't we park a team on the road?" Kuykendall said. "This way, we'll know where they're coming from."

"I'll meet you there," Hutchinson said, which was his way of saying he had no intention of parking it on the road. A stoner in his youth, he cleaned up his act after his second divorce. "That's asking for trouble."

"Out in the open like that, you'll turn into fast-food, fool," Big Geoff said. Tatted, bearded, Mexican, his home had been Baldwin Park. "I say we protect our camp, Jefe. That's all that matters."

"That's 360 degrees with no walls and nothing protecting your six, Big K.," Wolfman said. "I don't mind scouting and moving, but I'm not interested in parking it on the highway."

"Dude, I wouldn't want to park it with you anywhere," Wheeler quipped.

"Why would you, when you've got Roberta," Wolfman responded, and a round of laughter circled the group.

The joke about Roberta was a perennial in Mandalay that everyone, except Joab, was hip to.

"I don't know," Joab said. Guarding the seldom used Utility Road into camp was one thing; going out to the highway was something else. "I believe those things smell us. It could get dicey out there in the dark."

"It's a tough call we're going to have to make at some point," Bash said. "I might not agree with the highway, but we're going to have to get eyes looking north."

New people in camp, and a promise of security, decided for him.

"Not tonight, guys," Joab said. "Let's secure the perimeter. We just got a bus-load of new people. We told them it's safe here. I want them to feel that way. We'll check things out tomorrow."

"There's a couple of girls in that group that are straight from the candy shop, " Wolfman said.

"And too young for most of us," Big Leon said. "Wolf, you better watch out for that Owen guy."

"Dude, acts like a hard-butt," Hutchinson said. "He makes me sick."

"You want me to kick his butt, Jefe? I'll do it right now," Big Geoff said with his semi-serious look. This meant that even if he were only kidding, he'd do it if Joab gave an okay. "If he's talking trash, I'll straighten him out."

Joab couldn't help but smile. When the world was still the world, his men were misfits. Now, these misfits were the best the world had to offer.

"So standard patrol?" Drew said.

"I think that's best," Joab said, glancing at the trees noticing how the branches were starting to bud again. "Great walking weather, huh?"

"Great walking weather," Drew said.

"We'll start taking patrols out tomorrow to see what we can see and do some scrounging. We're going to need more food."

"Hey," Wheeler spoke, "if I don't go, keep an eye out for some baseball caps. I'm trying to get all these kids caps, and they're getting harder to find."

Cap ministry, Joab thought. *How pure is that?* Without a suggestion, Wheeler came up with the idea to get each kid their own baseball cap. It was a big thing with the boys, and now the girls, thanks to Alison's activism, wanted in.

"Does it have to be baseball? Can it be a football cap?" Hutchinson said.

"Anything, as long as it's not all bloody and disgusting," Wheeler said. "Elias wants a Yankees hat, so keep an eye out for one."

"Can I suggest something else," Kuykendall said, "With the rains done, maybe it's finally time to get to planting and growing some food."

"We don't have anyone with that experience," Bash said. "I don't mind digging, but growing takes some skill. We all weren't like Hutch back in the day."

"Dig deep," Hutchinson said, "drop in a seed or two, flood it with water, and God does the rest."

"Strictly medicinal?" Joab said.

"Of course," Hutchinson said. "But we'll need someone who knows how to roll."

"Well, if it gets to that, I might have somebody that could help," Joab said.

"Joab's got some stories," Crazy Chang said.

"Yeah, and I'm going to keep them to myself," he said, touching his ear to indicate their radios. "Stay in touch, guys."

Drew went to work.

"Alright, we know the routine. Everybody man up, get everything secure before the sun goes down. I'll have Duran secure the interior…."

"…Duran's leading worship tonight," Sandoval said.

"Then Mason, the interior is yours," Drew adjusted. "Adjourned."

"Wait!" Wolfman called out. "Joab, can I ask a question?"

"Wolfman, you can ask me any question you want, but if you want me to score you a date with a girl from that group, then, brother, you're on your own."

"Even Wolfman can't get a date at the end of the world," Big Leon said.

"That's cold," Orlando said. He was a year older than Wolfman but less confident. "I feel you, Wolf."

"Guys, it's something else," Wolfman said, holding up his hands for everyone to listen. "I'm starting to think after a year and a half; we might be the only fresh meat left on the mountain. In the long run, won't we be safer if we go out there and start dropping them? I mean, we're always on defense. Shouldn't we start taking it to them and cutting down their numbers?"

It was rare for Wolfman to offer a thought that didn't have anything to do with a girl. Since arriving at The Garden, his suggestions centered around dance and date nights. They looked at him with shock. Their young man with the raging hormones was growing up.

"I be in," Crazy Chang said. "Let's go get some. Better to go after them than waiting for them to come to us."

It sounded good and a perfect tension reliever. Plus, every devil dropped was one less devil to contend with later. But the moment Joab met Larry and Noel and heard their story, his task was straightforward. Serve the Lord by serving them. It meant he had to ignore the feel-good thing, which was what Wolfman and Crazy Chang wanted to do.

"Clarity, amigos," Joab said. "Guys, I want to. Hear me, I want to, and that day's coming, but right now..." He looked toward the amphitheater for a moment and then back to the group. "Right now, God's called us to protect this camp, and I've spent enough of my life being disobedient."

"Sounds a little dramatic, Jefe," Anspach said.

"Dead people walking around tend to make things dramatic," he said. "Let's keep it tight tonight, and we'll take a peek at what's out there tomorrow."

LARRY
(2)

Larry sat on the bed, staring at his cabin's wood walls, ready to leave for the amphitheater.

He was never bothered before chapel. In an emergency, they never hesitated to get him in the middle of the night or wake him from a nap during the day. But the hour, or so, before preaching, it was as if he had the virus.

He was sure it was Joab's doing.

"It's not about preparation, Larry," Joab would say, *"but about prayer. Study all you want, but it won't mean a thing if you're not prayed up."*

It was about getting through, successfully, something he knew nothing about. There was no training in Larry's background, no seminary, no internship at a big or small church. He didn't spend five to ten years apprenticing as an associate. No one showed him where to start or when to finish. When he did go to church, he seldom paid attention, hoped there wouldn't be an altar call, and prayed his parents wouldn't waste time talking to people in the foyer.

On Sunday, going to church had nothing to do with God, Jesus, or the Great Commission. It was about making it to lunch and getting home before the Rams kicked off.

If they could see me now.

The night Larry surrendered to God was the day he, essentially, got hired. He prayed for his life to matter, for it to mean something, and for a Sunday night and a glorious Monday morning, it was great. The God stuff was easy.

Then, he and Noel opened the closet door.

Up to then, his best skill was knowing how to roll.

"Garrison, can you roll one for us today? I'll give you two bucks."

"Make it three."

The ability to sprinkle leaf into a Zig-Zag and make it functional to inhale wasn't easy. A lot of pricey product was wasted in the trying. So someone with the right touch, like Larry Garrison, became a commodity.

A commodity until that Sunday night when visiting Reverend Joe Hyde opened the altar. Larry had brought the usual distractions with him to the back pew of the Arcadia Church. When the service began, pen, paper, and a rolled-up magazine were at the ready, but from the start, an invisible hand seemed to grab him by the chin and force him to listen.

At the altar, his eyes were watering as a gang of hands pressed in on him for prayer. From a narrow view, on the other side of the sanctuary, he caught a glimpse of Noel and his friend Chip experiencing the same.

Exact words were difficult to remember. They seemed to implant themselves. Everything happened so fast that there was never a settling period—no time to second guess himself or the decision made for Christ. Larry remembered, clearly repenting and clearly surrendering to whatever the Lord wanted him to do. He remembered fresh air racing into his lungs, weight coming off his conscience, and contemplation, for the first time, about the future.

Then, the following day, not long after the first-period bell, the world changed.

Ninety-six hours and some eye blinks later, he was preaching. Studying his Bible and noticing the words rising off the page, he became familiar with Biblical accounts beyond the Sunday School flannel board.

It was his work now. There was no wondering about what field to get into, no career path to pursue through education. He surrendered, and the Lord put him in chains.

Sermon preparation, along with putting out minor personality fires, was the work. Praying over the infected wasn't. Noel agreed with him on that. When they engaged in those things, they both knew they were purely conduits of the Holy Spirit. It would exhaust them. But all it required was obedience.

Gaining knowledge, the nuts and bolts of a Gospel he only pretended to understand growing up, was the long hike up the steep mountain. Much of it was fascinating, but after a while, he wanted to sit down. Often he just wanted to stop thinking.

The clock indicated it was time to go. "Grace, Lord," he said, getting up and tucking his Bible under an arm. "Keep giving me your grace." He went out the door.

Derek Duran's guitar, with voices, came from the amphitheater. There was no audio system in place, and even if there was, they didn't have the fuel to support a microphone. Every drop of fuel they scrounged went to the kitchen.

"My life and my love I leave in your hands, and I'll do everything as your will demands...I know it's not much your gifts to repay, but it's all I can give and all I can say...."

There had been debate in the beginning about outdoor worship and fear of drawing devils or even authorities. A week after getting to Camp Goodspeed, as they sat in the unswept dining hall, Larry and Noel insisted worship was in the Lord's hands. They also said it would be in the amphitheater. Joab said he'd handle security.

In 18 months, nothing but blessing had come from the services.

The camp picked up the chorus.

"I'm yours, Lord...Everything I got, everything I am, everything I'm not...I'm yours, Lord. Try me now and see. See if I can be completely yours."

"Good luck tonight, Preach," Mason said, stationed by the three trees. He was 27 but spoke to Larry with great respect.

"You doing okay? Joab and the fellas treating you right?"

"Big K. never stops talking, and Mandalay smells like used socks, but yeah, I'm doing fine," he said.

"That's Mandalay. I was in there until Joab booted me into my closet over here."

Larry knew there was pain inside Mason. Pain wasn't uncommon, nor was the ability to recognize it special. But only by the Holy Spirit was he able to sense and offer distinct empathy. Everyone had lost someone, and no one moved on from losing a spouse, parent, sibling, or child. It just got stored to the back of the heart, needing only another sadness to reacquaint it with the present.

"You want to hang out a little tomorrow?" Larry asked Mason.

Mason smiled. "I think I'm supposed to help lay a baseball field out for the kids, but if you've got time, that be great."

"Cool," Larry said. "I'll meet you in the morning on the meadow, I'll help with the field, and we'll rap for a bit."

"Great."

"You be careful up here."

"I'm yours, Lord..." The chorus of voices rang.

"Sounds like it's going to be fun down there," Mason said.

"Should be."

"Take my mind..." Duran followed

"Everything I've got..."

"Take my heart..."

"Everything I am..."

"Take my soul..."

"Everything I'm not..."

"Everything, everything..."

"I'm yours, Lord. Everything I got, everything I am, everything I'm not...I'm yours, Lord. Try me now and see. See if I can be completely yours."

The best part of coming into the amphitheater in the middle of worship was no one noticed. They didn't see Larry coming down the stone steps on the left side and sliding next to Noel at the bottom.

Again, worship amazed him. Millions were dead, yet, they were here freely worshiping with joy.

Duran promised to do *Pharaoh, Pharaoh,* tomorrow, and the kids groaned. Then he promised to do it at the end of the service, and they cheered.

"Well, how about if we do it now?" The kids erupted, and two dozen of them came down to the floor of the meeting place.

"Joab! Joab! Joab!" They shouted at The Garden's lead soldier. He shook his head. They kept chanting his name, the adults applauded, and another overwhelming feeling came over Larry.

How did we manage this?

Joab got up from his seat, and joy erupted.

"You didn't," A different voice said, and he didn't argue.

Noel elbowed him in the side and pointed to the girl standing between Alison and Cora getting ready to do the song's motions. "You see that?"

"Who is it?"

"That's Loren," Noel whispered in his ear. "Owen and Heather's daughter."

His eyes met Noel's, and he felt a thump in his heart. "Wow."

"Pharaoh! Pharaoh! Oh, baby, let my people go!" The kids sang and performed the stereotypical ancient Egyptian motions. Joab, two beats behind, was red-faced with embarrassment.

Larry wiped his eyes several times as they sang the song he once knew as *Louie Louie* by the Kingsmen. It felt like the amphitheater was being lifted off the earth and guided to the Lord's throne.

"I got through the Red Sea, and what did I see? I saw Pharaoh's chariots coming after me. I raised my staff, and I cleared my throat, and all of Pharaoh's army did the dead man's float!"

Everyone at The Garden let the worship, and the joy of the children, carry them. It was narcotic-like but cleaner, purer, and, tangibly, truer in effect. He'd heard stories in high school of not so retired hippies mastering the art of mainlining tequila into their bloodstream for a rush. Tonight, they were mainlining God.

"Pharaoh! Pharaoh! Oh, baby, let my people go!"

Duran led them in a series of slower songs before Noel prayed and invited Larry to speak. The history of previous campfires over the decades marked the cement floor. Behind the stage, the hill continued to slope gradually downward. Small brush, prairie grass, and rocks went on for ten yards before hitting a rusty chain-link fence. Inside the fence, a security team was on guard.

They didn't use fire in the evening meetings at The Garden. One, to be responsible about not drawing attention. Two, the fear of what a single spark could do to their hideaway.

The sun had set, and Larry knew he wouldn't preach long. The little kids and teens didn't have it in them to sit through a 45-minute talk, and he didn't have enough life experiences to share for 45-minutes. He'd keep it to a tight 20, maybe 25, if the Lord stepped in.

"What makes you special? Being tall, short, athletic, singing all the notes, driving a car, swinging a bat? What makes you special? Look at yourself, look at your hands, touch your arms, examine your mind. I agree you're special, but what is it that makes you special?"

Noel had gifts of compassion, nurture, and organization, but she didn't know about them before The Tilt. Up to that point, he didn't realize speaking in front of people was his. It took a world shaken —tilted—to find out.

"I'm gonna tell you what makes us special. Are you ready? What makes us special is this moment? If you know Christ, then you know he created this moment and arranged for all of us to be here. I have not preached this message before, but this is the message God gave me to preach even before our new friends arrived on the bus today. This is the message we need to hear tonight, not the guys out on security…but us."

Besides not knowing how the words came, Larry marveled at the ability to press a sermon button in his head and then study how it was being received by the people in the audience. He knew who they were and was able to factor in how it may hit them while continuing to preach.

Karla, sitting next to Debbie, had been a widow for a year. Husband, Deke, had been bitten and executed in the city. She found her way to The Garden after getting lost and driving into the mountains.

There was Beth with her disabled daughter Tammy, who never spoke. There was something special, almost otherworldly, about Tammy. People asked if what they did for the infected could get Tammy out of her wheelchair, but nothing moved him to take action. There was no burn or compulsion to do something like that. His job was to preach the Gospel, lay hands on the infected, and not question the Lord's will.

Liz Cortez, the middle-aged hairstylist, did the grooming in The Garden and never hesitated to set things straight when they steered crooked. Charles Kiln was 74 but in excellent health. He was a constant encourager, persistent in letting everyone know God was in control. His "amens" were always the loudest.

They all had testimonies about who they'd been and how they came to this place. Larry could see fatigue in all their eyes, but it didn't affect how the words came out of him. It didn't affect the tone. Nor did the icy stare from Owen, sitting near the top, change his delivery.

"We all have talents, but they're not our birthright. Our birthright is an eternity with God and the blessings he wants to shower on us. To come into a better relationship with him. The creator of all things wanted a family, and we are that family."

Amid the message, he knew what to take out before it ever came out. He could insert something just arriving in thought, at the right moment, to grab the attention of someone beginning to fade...And the sermon kept running as if on an assembly line.

"It's the Holy Spirit," Joab told him under the three trees late one night. *"You're in a great place right now with God. A place where you know all there is for you to do is trust him. When we get to a place like that, it turns the Spirit loose inside us. Don't worry about it being your message as much as it being about distributing the message God wants shared. What you are required to do is to prepare your soul—and be a clean filter."*

And the sermon kept rolling.

"Salvation, life, our birthright is found in no one else...Neither is joy, neither is peace, and neither is victory! And victory is there for us! Victory in this crisis! Victory in this terrible moment! Make no mistake about this, the church of God will be victorious!"

The "amens" from the crowd were nice, but they didn't detour from the message. They didn't make Larry speak louder or with more speed or more purpose. The sermon kept rolling the way God wanted it to roll; he worked to keep the filter clean by kicking aside any notions that this was by his power.

He'd come to recognize the miracle—for the preacher who, indeed, was called—was to operate at multiple levels during a message. The filter was always in danger of getting clogged. Satan was offering anger at Owen. Denise Hemingway often parachuted into thought to detour him from the selected path. There was the question as to why there'd been no healing for Tammy. Ideas came during the current sermon about using it to build on his next sermon. But he kept them all slotted into their appropriate lanes.

And the sermon continued.

"Our victory will not come with guns, blades, or our wisdom. Those things might be used, but our victory will come from the one who gave us our birthright. From the Son of God, from the power of the Spirit, from our Father in Heaven! And no bite, infection, or election can take that away from us!"

Different voices affirmed.

"Amen."
"Amen."
"Amen."

"You might be thinking, 'Larry, how do you know this?' I know this because I'm in the Word. Because I'm on my knees. Because my hope is not built on the strength of The Garden, the wisdom of Joab, the grace of Noel, or the love of you people. My hope is built on Jesus, Jesus crucified, and praise God, that empty tomb."

The sermon went on, and then came a click, only his ears picked up. It was a very familiar click. The sound came like a gas tank just before it filled. A few more squeezes, a few more selective words, were all that would fit.

Scripture.

"Don't you know that you yourselves are God's temple and that God's Spirit lives in you? If anyone destroys God's temple, God will destroy him; for God's temple is sacred, and you are that temple!"

"Yes!" Charles Kiln shouted. "Amen!"

"And again," he said as if to express irony. "We are immune to this virus. You want something touchable, put that touchable right underneath your reasons for faith. By the blood of Christ, we are immune!"

Larry pointed a hand to Duran, who came with his guitar.

"The altar is open," he said as Duran began to strum. "God bless all of you."

"Well of water ever springing... bread of life, so rich and free. Untold wealth that never faileth my redeemer is to me..." Duran sang slow. It was one of the few songs Larry and Noel were familiar with.

And the citizens of The Garden came. Mostly the young, followed by the adults---previously organized by Noel---to pray for them. Owen and Heather held on to Loren as their group came forward. Larry walked off to the side and didn't see the exchange of expressions between the married couple before Loren came. Heather followed her down.

"Hallelujah, I have found him whom my soul so long has craved. Jesus satisfies my longing through his blood I now am saved." Those familiar with the chorus joined Duran. *"Hallelujah, I have found him whom my soul so long has craved. Jesus satisfies my longing through his blood I now am saved."*

Larry didn't write the sermon for children, nor craft it for adults, but he knew he would get compliments about his ability to reach and touch them all. What they never understood— except for Joab —was he was only a filter.

BRICKLANDER
(3)

A Grunt was expected to go through the door first, be the first target and first casualty, but "Public Relations" was an officer's job. A consistent face telling the people what they needed to hear in terms and tones best received. A round, pear-shaped voice, a youthful look with some mileage, nice hair, strong jaw, and a positive vibe to register hope through evident despair.

In other words, a good-looking liar.

The problem was the company of soldiers assigned to San Quintana didn't have one. Lieutenant Farmer was likable but stumbled over questions. Lieutenant Holsopple was quick, precise, and too cruel. And Lieutenant Carlson was considered, unanimously, by civilians and soldiers alike, to be a douchebag.

The job to encourage fell to Captain Torres. Bricklander, with a face looking like ten seasons of professional football without a helmet, paraded the muscle.

The first sergeant gave citizens the sense they had a man's man in the trenches with them—a battle-scarred veteran who was still vertical. A slashing wound stretching from the bottom of his right earlobe to the middle of his chin was the signature disfigurement.

The still functioning United Methodist Church sat about 100 people in its sanctuary chairs. The carpet and curtains, a matching burgundy, played well for December pageants but was awkward for townhalls in May.

People were there to get answers to their questions about water, power, trash pick up, and new safety guidelines. They came to be encouraged. They wanted to hear things were progressing, even if incrementally, back to what had once been.

An older African-American man raised his hand. "My name's Roy Scandrick, and I want to know how close the army is to taking back Los Angeles?"

From the pulpit, Torres spieled about how some companies and offices had relocated outside of the city. Work was resuming, but the going was slow. The captain then broke down the map: Everything west and directly south of Los Angeles was a swamp of the dead to the ocean. The military detonated northern passes at Pacific Coast Highway and the 14-Freeway. There was a measure of control from Malibu to Ventura. The Agoura Hills before the 101 spilled into Camarillo was a checkpoint. Interstate 5, where it linked with the 210—thanks to geography and focused efforts by the military—was open through the Central Valley, where the agriculture hub was well guarded. Taft was the safe zone, especially after the fire-bombing of Bakersfield. Further north, Fresno was a battleground, but very few dead were leaking south on 99.

From the East, the army had worked its way into Pasadena and pushed to the edge of Arroyo Seco but no further. The 210 Freeway was open while vast swaths of the San Gabriel Valley remained a No Man's Land.

In the Inland Empire, below the mountains, Torres reminded that the army had made a stand. San Quintana was proof of that. They weren't a hundred percent safe; no place was. But, along with San Bernardino and Riverside, though still dangerous, they were functional.

The information seldom changed, but if repeated with different words and sincerity, it smoothed anxieties.

Bricklander sat to the left and behind Torres. He felt he could cut through all of it with a few curses and encouragement about ratting out neighbors hiding the dead in their homes. When these loved ones escaped, they killed and, worse, created panic.

"Of course, we'd like to get power returned to you fully, but we have to build slowly," Torres said.

"My name's James Canto," a college-aged man in the back asked. "Why aren't we using solar?"

"It doesn't work," Torres said, and some catcalls came. "On a small scale, with some of your smaller items, of course, yes…It works. But if you're talking about powering a place like San Quintana, you can forget it. And before you ask, those wind-farms along I-10 are all in disrepair."

An older woman raised her hand and stood. "My name's Ginger Wells. This power getting shut off is not cutting it." Bricklander had seen her before. Looking to be in her late 60s, she gave the impression of being unhappy even before the world ended. "Some of us are working outside San Quintana during the day, but by the time we get back, we're coming into a dark city and dark homes."

"I understand, but those aren't my calls to make. With summer coming, the days are extending. Hopefully, things will get a little bit better. But for now, everything has to be conserved for the bigger cause." Heads nodded, heads shook, there was some applause along with some boos. "Folks, I could lie to you, but I won't. First Sergeant Bricklander and I have seen it with our own eyes; this is Eden compared to the rest of SoCal. You have some good people in your local citizen patrols, Herb, Darren, Nancy, and others lined up in the back there. They do an excellent job escorting folks back into town. I'm sure they could use some more help."

"My name's Dale Lehman. You want us to believe it's all business as usual, but there's risk in everything we do." Lehman was also older but well built with long, receding, gray hair. "Even coming out at night for something like this is a risk."

Some 'amens' were said. Others concurred with nods.

"I'm thinking back to six months ago," Torres said. "How many of you were here six months ago? Do you remember what it was like? It's changed, hasn't it?"

"But you've got weapons, back-up, and a secure base," said a young woman speaking out of turn from her seat. "No one's watching my back."

Torres looked to his notes on the podium, then glanced at Bricklander and smiled.

"I think he's going to have to address the elephant in the room," Minister Tim said, sitting next to him with his shining baldhead and surprising gut.

"Been avoiding it long enough," Bricklander said, getting ready for the onslaught.

Another woman, with a teenage boy sitting next to her, raised a hand. "My name's Maeve Heiser. My husband and parents are dead, and all I have is my son. I've been fortunate enough to get work in San Bernardino..." she paused.

Bricklander thought she was getting ready to cry, but so many were beyond tears.

"...I don't want to sound ungrateful," she continued, and the tears came, "but I don't feel comfortable when I'm outside my house. When I hear a shot go off in the middle of the night or when the lights come back on. I know something's happening. I don't know how you expect me to trust. I mean, I stand guard when my son mows the lawn. This doesn't feel like it's getting better. I wish you'd all stop trying to give us the impression it is and start telling us the truth."

"Yeah!" came from several in the crowd. "Stop the CYA and give us the truth!"

Torres took a breath.

"Have you heard from Minister Kevin yet?" Minister Tim asked in a low voice.

"No," Bricklander said. "I expect tomorrow."

"I'm awful fond of Kevin and the work he does. I've never met someone with such a compassionate heart."

"I agree with Maeve," Roy Scandrick said. "Things change too fast for us to have any peace."

Bricklander nodded at Torres and pretended to listen to Minister Tim.

"It shows the cruelty of our business when someone has to stay with those fundamentalists overnight," Minister Tim sighed. "Those people are sick. Nothing but hate."

"I do appreciate the sharing," Torres said. "This is why we schedule these things. We know the perimeter of this city is not perfect. However, we also know that these monsters do not dig tunnels, pole vault, or parachute in from other neighborhoods. We know these things are attracted to us. Studies are coming back, confirming they can smell us. They seem to be able to see in the dark. Every entry into San Quintana is manned. We keep numbers, and our numbers have gone steadily, if not drastically, down over the last six months..."

He paused to let it sink in.

"…But, our biggest problem, in the community…."

"…Is that you people were supposed to finish that six-foot wall on the north side," said another man cutting Torres off. "I'm Herman Wagner, and my house is right there on the corner where Montview turns back into Highway 19. It was in the original plans when the army placed your company here. NORM said the wall would be the first action taken and the reason why we wouldn't be evacuated."

"Sir," Torres attempted to reassure, but the citizens were having none of it. "That was the priority, but the National Office of Resource Management allocated those resources to the interstates to get our highways open. I have no control over NORM."

"NORM has to make hard calls," Minister Tim whispered. "These people don't understand."

Bricklander knew if he argued against NORM for the right to murder puppies, Minister Tim would say NORM had good reasons to protect those puppies. If NORM killed the puppies, Minister Tim would say they had good reasons for killing the same puppies.

"What happens if the dead come down from the mountains?" Maeve said. "What are we going to do?"

"The mountains remain our priority," Torres said. "Nothing's going to come down and surprise us. But you need to hear this—right now, the bigger problem is the dead that are already here. In many ways, the reason for the unease you have is because each of you knows of a neighbor hiding a dead loved one."

"Whoa! Whoa! Hold it, Captain!" said a tough-looking, well-tatted man. "We know where you're going with that. We're not going to let you come into our houses on a pretext of looking for the dead and then have you confiscate our guns and ammunition."

"Absolutely not!" Another voice echoed.

"You people aren't coming into my house!"

Bricklander knew the next shout would be for them all to go to hell.

"To hell with that!"

Which would be followed by...

"We still have rights!"

Bricklander served in operations taking the army from El Monte into South Pasadena. The areas were void of any people trying to hang on. It was nothing but a bloody, gut drenched graveyard. But that wasn't the case in California's Inland Empire because people never left their homes, never became refugees. Because of this, more than anything else, their sense of being Americans, of having rights, never melted away. They were uncompromising in the wake of things because they were still in their homes. Meanwhile, survivors from Los Angeles County lived in refugee camps off Highway 395 near places like Lone Pine, Bishop, and even a re-opened Manzanar.

"You want it safe," Torres said. "We want it safe, but you're going to have to start taking responsibility because you know you have dead living right next to you. And I don't have the authority to kick in your door."

"Soon," Minister Tim said to Bricklander. The sergeant didn't know what he'd done to earn all of the Minister's comments. He felt disappointed with himself for not putting out a more hateful demeanor. "I'm told NORM's going to suspend all those rights very soon."

"Damn right, you don't," said the tough looking man. "Because you violated that trust when you disarmed those people in Arizona. That's why we'll never give you our guns."

"I'm going to throw a name at you," Torres said. "Kristen Block. Does anyone know Kristen Block?" The crowd went silent. "Does anyone know why Kristen Block's not here tonight?" No response came. Some heads looked down. "Kristen's not here because she was bitten on the arm today by a monster that got out. One of my men had to execute her in front of our base this afternoon."

"I wish he'd use a better term than 'execute,'" Minister Tim muttered.

Ignoring the comment, Bricklander whispered back. "Does NORM expect us to confiscate those weapons?"

"It'll be a priority. We can't have crazy white people running around with guns."

"White people?" Bricklander wondered if Minister Tim saw himself as part of the group he labeled; *Crazy White People.* "All these people don't look white, and they're not going to give up their guns peacefully."

"Trust me, I know white people and how they feel about their guns," Minister Tim said, staring back as if the sergeant had no grasp of the reality. "That's why the military will be sent in."

"To take weapons from Americans defending themselves?"

The minister nodded.

Gun confiscation occurred in Kingman, Arizona. Bricklander knew because the scuttlebutt coming through PNN (the Private News Network) was more reliable than any news service. The National Guard called for everybody to turn in their weapons. The military was lacking supplies. When compliance failed, they took the guns with violence. Things spun out of control. The National Guard bugged out of Kingman and left the population unarmed. Images of the carnage were posted on the internet and seen by the world before being scrubbed by NORM.

Torres raised his voice. "We're trying to protect you! Your neighbors are getting you killed now. Kristen Block was only 25-years old."

"You can protect us without taking our guns!"

A public relations professional would have excused himself. Captain Torres, still with a little civilian inside him, got ticked.

"I don't want your fricking guns!" he yelled back, "but I swear to God if one of my men is killed by something coming out of your house, I'll light you up and burn your home to the ground!"

And that was that.

"If you want a war with San Quintana, we'll go to war!" Tough guy shouted.

"Shut up!" Roy Scandrick said. "Are you crazy?"

"Not crazy enough to let them take our guns!"

Shouts launched all over the sanctuary.

Bricklander stayed in his seat. In the past, his suggestion was to let a few of the dead in, create some chaos, and the citizenry would be thrilled to let them clean house. Until then, they'd continue to believe they were in pre-apocalypse America.

As the debate got louder, he thought of firing his M9 into the air to grab their attention, but this wasn't a movie. Minister Tim would likely reprimand him for wasting a bullet. The report would be sent to NORM, placed in a file, and added to any reason they'd need in the future to discharge him.

Minister Tim looked down at his feet. The white-collar he wore dug into the flesh below his throat.

"Shouldn't you step up and calm things down a bit, Padre?" Bricklander said. It was the second time today he questioned the Minister's job responsibilities. And for the second time, he got the same answer.

"Not my problem," Minister Tim said, shaking his head. "I wouldn't know what to say. Probably best to let them vent. They'll learn the hard way."

LARRY
(3)

Noel set out a water pitcher and cups for the meeting, making Larry think of his mom.

Owen and Heather had joined them, along with Joab, in the dining hall at 10:30. Noel's gesture reminded him of his mom bringing him a slice of cake during a birthday party. He was capable of getting it for himself, but out of love, she brought it to him. Love was Noel's realm, and Larry knew she'd be the one who sanded down the rough patches of this discussion.

"Nice service, Pastor," Heather said, sitting with Owen on her right.

"Thank you." Early on, Larry rejected the Pastor title but came to realize it's what he was. To the citizens of The Garden, he was the Pastor. "I'm glad you're with us."

Heather's eyes cast down, Owen squeezed her hand and looked across the table to Larry and Noel sitting to his right. Joab, to Larry's left, was at the head of the table, near the doors.

"I need to say thank you," Owen said, working hard to sound humble. "Before anything else gets said, you have welcomed us, and I believe your motives are good."

"We want you to feel welcomed," Larry said, sensing, with no acknowledgment of Aaron and Jessica, that the conversation was due for a hard landing.

"I'm having a hard time with your ages. This doesn't make sense. I understand what you're attempting, but I don't see God's hand in the how of it. I know of Joab, and he's qualified; my wife and I are seminary graduates, but I don't understand how God can be working through you. You don't even look like you're out of high school." He stopped, looked at his wife, and continued. "And the other thing is, I don't feel safe here."

"Given what happened on the bus today, why would you say God's not involved?" Larry said.

"Let me put it this way," Owen said in a tone that sounded like his ego had reasserted control. "I understand your theology, but I don't agree with your theology." A smile of condescension issued from his face and moved it side to side. "You essentially did the Sinner's Prayer with Aaron on the bus today. Did that accomplish anything that hadn't already been done?"

"Believers are immune to the virus."

"Are they?" Owen said and then shook his head again. "And this why I don't want to get into all of this. I can see we won't agree, and the bottom line is we just don't feel safe here."

"Then leave," Larry said, feeling Noel's knee knock into his. "If you need to go, go. No one's going to force you to stay. But age or experience cannot allow you to deny what happened on the bus today."

"Just like that? You want us to leave?"

"I don't want you to leave, but if we can't make you understand what's going on, you certainly won't be forced to stay. Your people got healed today, but you're upset about our age and education level? If it helps, I'll be 20 this fall. And if Jesus is Jesus, then I don't entirely get this theological difference between us. Maybe you and Joab can clue Noel and me about what we don't know or what we're doing wrong."

"I've finished seminary. I'm ordained," Owen said. "You can't expect me to take instruction from you or to surrender my thinking."

"Technically, to be straight with you, I didn't finish high school either," Larry said. "But isn't Jesus always Jesus? Does the work of the cross change? Did the resurrection occur? Did the healing on the bus happen? What do we disagree on other than us being too young to know what we know?"

"Your theology is wrong," Owen said, his voice picking up momentum. "I don't think you have a clue about Jesus. And if Joab's decided to absolve himself, it doesn't mean I have to. I won't. Just because you don't talk like you're 19 doesn't mean you're not 19."

Larry leaned across the table, the furnace in his gut beginning to heat. "No, I don't sound like I'm 19, do I?" Noel's knee slammed into him again. "So explain it? Define what's taking place and what took place on the bus?" A few seconds passed. "You can't because there's no faith involved. Test the scriptures about what we're doing here. But I know that could be a problem for you." He peered into Owen as he had seldom peered into anyone else before. By the Spirit, he could see all of the older minister's insecurities. "Because, beyond the red letters, you don't believe in the scriptures."

"I don't buy into the tired theology you're preaching," Owen said. "A system that pushes and unjust substitutionary atonement. A theology taking no account of the church's biases regarding race and socio-economic conditions. It's unclear to me if you're peddling the Jesus you think you know or some concoction of white American Christianity. And there's no debating it because you're not nuanced enough theologically to have that kind of conversation. "

A laugh slipped out of Joab. They turned to him, and he held up a hand in apology. "I'm sorry," he said. "That's my bad."

"You haven't answered how Jessica and Aaron were healed." Larry knew the corner he was pushing Owen into. The youth minister, with flecks of gray starting to pop in his beard, wasn't leaving at all. He couldn't justify taking his family or people back out on the road. "You don't have an answer, do you? I'll tell you what, forget about it, just tell us when you're leaving."

"You know I'm not leaving," he said. "My wife won't go, and some of the teenagers have turned 18. They don't want to leave either."

"Then please stay," Noel jumped into the conversation. "It's been safe here. There's food, shelter, and we're working on the kids' schooling. You can help around camp."

"Perhaps I could teach?" Owen said.

"No," Larry said faster than a fastball hitter could hit a fastball down the middle of the plate. "Maybe some math, some grammar, but nothing spiritual."

"Why not? What are you afraid of?"

"I don't trust you," Larry said. "You're not the only one with doubts here. Personally, I think theologically, you're a menace. We can have long discussions right here or out under the trees. But I wouldn't trust you to speak or teach here. At least not any time soon."

Own let go of his own disdainful laugh. "Ignorance and arrogance, that's a heck of a combination for a teenager preacher."

Heather's hand pulled away from her husband's and went to her forehead in exasperation.

"I understand this," Larry said. "Noel and I wouldn't be here if it weren't for people like you."

"And that's supposed to mean?"

"Believers are immune to the virus, but Aaron and Jessica had to come here for healing."

"What are you saying?"

"You know what I'm saying."

"Can you both maintain?" Noel spoke. "Just back off for a second." She looked at Heather and Owen. "You're staying, excellent. That's all we need to discuss tonight."

"Owen, Heather?" Joab said, and they faced him. "If your group or your child is in danger, I'll be the first to help, so will a lot of people in this camp. We got terrific people here who love the Lord."

"That's great," Owen said, quickly turning away. "I'll keep it in mind."

"Please, look at me, Owen," Joab said, and the minister slowly turned back. "Don't try to shame our people out of good theology to fit your bad theology. And let's be clear on this, if you attempt to teach something directly at odds with what's being taught in this camp and cause division or confusion, I'll kill you. I mean it. It's the teaching you and I espoused, our mentors espoused, that left the church unable to deal with this Sin Virus. The dead are walking, and we think it's because some bug escaped a government lab. The dead are walking, and we equipped no one to see the spiritual side of this. In fact, we worked overtime to take any supernatural view away from them."

With that thud, the remnants of cordiality came to an end. Larry wasn't upset with himself for getting hot. It was as if the Spirit was dragging him into it. But, Joab terrified him by sounding so sincere in his threat to kill Owen.

"Like I said," Noel repeated with more effort. "We don't need to discuss anything more tonight."

"You don't know anything about me," Owen said to Joab.

Joab pressed. "I know Aaron, who's been in your care for 18 months, just met Jesus for the first time today. Jessica wasn't a Christian either. How many people have you led astray with your theology?"

"I don't have to take this!"

"Yeah," Joab said, "you do because we are in this place. And every whiff of this beautiful mountain air carries with it a little bit of death. And that little bit of death reminds us of our failures as ministers of the Gospel."

"Let's leave it and go to bed," Noel said, trying one more time. "We can pick it up fresh, with cooler heads, in the morning."

"He just said he's going to kill me."

"He's not going to kill you," Larry said. "He risked his life to save you today. We're only making clear that we're not going to have spiritual division."

"Why is truth a spiritual division? Even if you are a minority of one, the truth is the truth," Owen said.

"When it's not the truth," Joab said.

"Truth is right in front of our eyes," Owen said. "It's all the injustice around us, and God expects us to act. It's a mighty white camp you have here. By the way, how many minorities do you have? I think I've seen five all day."

"Nice try," Joab knew the routine because it was one he perfected. If the debate gets tricky, change fronts and attack on diversity. "You talked about knowing truth. Give me in scripture a truth we're not sharing here. Give it to me an example where sin is remedied without the blood of Jesus."

"I'm not going to perform for you, Joab. I'm not a biblicist living and dying on the belief that every word in the Bible is some divine, sacred inspiration."

"I was good at quoting the Barths, Bells, Clayborns, Chalkes, Rohrs, and MaClarens too—even Gandhi if it fit. I was brilliant at quoting men and shaming those who quoted scripture."

"All of you are stuck in the past, and you can't see the world for what it is today. You can't see the failures of a western culture that built cathedrals to house God and excluded those who didn't fit a pre-described mold."

"Everything has changed," Larry said, bringing his hands up as if he was holding a small ball. "The earth has gone off its spiritual axis. It tilted, and things, like the Sin Virus, have spilled into our world from another realm. It's as if Ephesians 6 has become a flesh and blood fight. The only antidote is the blood of Christ. This concept of kingdom living instead of kingdom-advancing, this business of 'God being love'—and love only—and the condition of that love being no mention of sin, judgment, or the supernatural is destroying everything. It leaves us defenseless."

"What makes you so pure, Larry?" Owen gunned back. "Where do you come from that makes you so righteous? How come you and a demented few see it but no one else?"

"I have to…" Joab began.

"… I'm sorry, Joab, I have to ask something," Heather cut him off. "Owen and I are both seminary graduates. I was raised one way in the church, taught something different in college, and believed something else in graduate school after going through deconstruction. Now, my mind's reaching back to something I believed when I was a teenager. Something I haven't felt for a very long time."

"What did tonight feel like?" Noel said.

"Like I was a teenager again…," she paused, "…I felt humbled. It was like being away for a long time and coming home."

"Where do you think you've been?" Noel said.

"She's been serving the Lord," Owen asserted. "Serving against 20th-century models of the church that weren't accepting, loving, or inclusive. We fought against it. We fought against groups that equated flag-waving as an act of worship and lived Christianity through the lens of nationalism. We rejected all of that. We loved and accepted people. We don't have to apologize for anything. We don't…"

"…And what good did it do Jessica and Aaron before they came to this place?" Joab interrupted. "I'm not without guilt on this. I'm responsible for everyone I ever led, taught, spoke to, everyone who read my book and articles. My vanity led people into deception, and there isn't a day that it doesn't haunt me."

"Do you know how many hours of ministry we've spent in kitchens downtown?" Owen said. "Clothing the homeless, helping the disenfranchised, loving kids whose parents rejected them because they were gay or trans? Fighting churches that peddled white privilege instead of dispensing with it? The church you model idolizes the flag, leaves people behind, rapes the environment, dishonors immigrants, and does nothing for the widows and orphans."

"But do you lead anybody to Jesus?" Joab said.

"You're incapable of understanding," Owen said.

It didn't feel like they'd leave the dining hall without punches thrown. Larry hoped Noel would step in again.

"Again, did your good works save your people?" Joab said. "Or only make you feel important?"

It wasn't a fair debate, and not even Heather's body language was siding fully with her husband.

"It's archaic and egocentric to propose to know the will of God. Tragically, you judge people that way. Seeing them as saved and unsaved, guilting them with concepts of a Hell that doesn't exist."

"Shut up, Owen," Heather said, wiping her eyes. "I'm so screwed up right now. I can't reason any of this, but I have to know; is this the end of the world? Is Jesus coming? Is there going to be a Rapture?"

Owen dropped his head backward, looking into the darkness of the ceiling. His frustration venting out via a sigh.

"You're asking me if this is the Tribulation and if the Rapture is about to happen?" Larry asked her back.

Heather nodded. "I remember learning about it and how it was just around the corner. I was seven years old the first time I heard my pastor and parents talk about how it could happen any day, but it never did. I got to my twenties, and I just let it go. My husband's right, we've been doing good work, but I have no answers to give our people now and no answers for Loren." She wept, and Noel's hand reached across the table to comfort her. "You were bit, Noel, I saw the scar on the bus. Why didn't you get an infection?"

"I got saved on a Sunday night and was bit two days later," Noel said. "The only constant since this started is children and believers in Christ are immune."

"Then what the hell are we?" Owen said. "What are we?"

"Aaron and Jessica answered that," Joab said.

"Come on, Joab," Noel pleaded. She gave him a look that begged for no more comments. "Please? Can we dial it back?"

Joab leaned back, Owen didn't explode, and Heather regained some composure. "We're good deed doers, Owen," she said.

"We're more than that," he returned.

"Let me answer your first question, Heather," Larry said. "I haven't heard a trumpet sound. We're still here. The scripture says he's going to come, so we shouldn't worry about what we know will happen. But we should concern ourselves about what we need to do."

"The dead are coming back to life. How does the Bible explain that?" she said.

"Because it's not in the Bible, Heather," Owen said. "Because the Bible is filled with subjective symbolism and is flawed. It has beauty and meaning but is flawed when we attempt to make it a final authority."

"The dead are dead, Heather," Noel said. The older woman worrying about her daughter, her husband, the next day, and a million other things, tightened her grip on the younger woman's hand. "They don't talk, they don't reason, they don't remember anything, the virus occupies the old tent."

"I'm so confused."

"Because your theology doesn't afford you to have any hope beyond yourselves," Larry said. Owen's eyes burned at him. "You trained in a theology that diminishes God. A theology where man, and man's wisdom, is the new sacrament."

"I'm done with this!" Owen jumped up. "We're out of here."

"You saw it, Heather," Larry said. "It wasn't good works or positive vibes that saved Jessica and Aaron today. It was the blood of Jesus."

"I'm going," Owen said to his wife. "You can do what you want." He began to head for the doors.

"Not yet, sport," Joab said. "I don't care how you feel right now. You can drive the bus out of here tonight or stay, makes no difference to me, but I have to know something first."

"I thought you knew it all, Joab."

"Why don't you feel safe here?"

"Why should any of us ever feel safe?" Owen said.

"Having a problem with us being leaders is one thing," Noel said in her most soothing fashion. "But you survived up near Sky Porch for a year and a half. You've been here a whole day and haven't seen one devil pass through our grounds or heard a gunshot. Worship ended an hour ago, and we didn't do it in whispers. That should tell you something."

"It tells me nothing," Owen said.

"Why don't you feel safe here?" Joab asked again.

"It started to get dangerous," Heather said. "Really dangerous, that's why we had to get out of Sky Porch."

"So, you were in Sky Porch?" Joab said.

Heather nodded, and the atmosphere in the room changed. Larry could feel icy anxiety rise.

"Why isn't this place safe?" Joab pressed. "And why are you in such a hurry to get out of here?"

"Tell them," Heather said. "Tell them, Owen, or I will."

"Because..." Owen's eyes rotated around the dining hall and rested on them. "...They're coming."

JOAB
(4)

Joab understood.

Too often in ministry, most of a pastor's energy wasn't spent planning an event or sermon but defending every action taken. Awful or wonderful, always in the back of the minister's mind, was a practical, feasible defense for the stink-eyes on a church board, or Retirement Row, that loved finding flaws.

At the moment of hire, a minister's dress, how they cut their hair, the grip of their handshake, and, once in a blue moon, what they believed theologically, needed to be justified. If you were a Calvinist, you were defending yourself to a Wesleyan. If you were a Progressive, you explained you were only following a Wesleyan model.

For Owen to be under the authority of a pair of 19-year-olds was tough. After hearing how "heartfelt," "brilliant," "authentic," and "transformational" your ministry was for so many years, it was inconceivable to have it called into question or require a defense.

"We had to get out," Owen said, sitting back at the table. "We were there for a retreat when everything hit and sheltered in our cabin."

Pasadena had been bad, but a place like Sky Porch, where thousands came every day, was a blood bath. Even if the local population could hide behind its doors, there was an army of devils multiplying by the hour and no place to siphon off once the bridge was blocked.

"We lost one person the first day--Maggie was fourteen." Owen stopped again and extended the painful pause. Joab knew the youth pastor didn't want to cry in front of them. "We were shopping when it started. It was cold, ice was still on the sidewalk, and Maggie slipped. She got overwhelmed. I saw them tear her to pieces, and nobody knew how to stop them then. Some men tried to help, but they got bit."

Heather let her husband catch a breath and picked up the story. "We got everyone else back to the cabin. We passed two of them on the way, but they were feeding. At the cabin, we had food and distance. The local radio station kept broadcasting. The police station got overrun. The city broke into sections, and different groups began fighting not only those things but each other for resources."

"We heard people screaming from the shopping district for hours," Owen said. "When it stopped, we got some things done. There was still power, so I made sure all the lights were out and put the radio in the hallway so it wouldn't be heard outside. We put spare blankets over the windows and barricaded them the best we could."

"Did you think about trying to drive out at the beginning?" Larry asked.

"I did," Owen said, "but two calls came in after we got back to the cabin. My lead pastor at the church told me to stay because it wasn't any better back down the mountain. And Aaron's mom called to say she loved him but not to come to her. So we stayed."

"Was Aaron's mom in danger?" Larry asked.

"She was trapped inside an office building downtown," Heather said.

"We know a little about that," Joab said. "There are several here at camp who had loved ones drive to work and never saw them again."

"The text messages were the worst," Heather said. "Parents sent us, and their kids, messages about where to meet them and that they'd wait for us. Then they started cursing us because we hadn't come down the mountain."

Noel fingered misting eyes and cleared them.

"The texts kept coming for three or four days," Heather said. "Finally, with the power gone, they couldn't recharge the phones anymore."

They shared how Owen began scrounging, first from nearby cabins for food and then hitting different parts of the city distracted by the battles taking place.

"The cabin was above the shopping area." He shook his head. "Things just exploded there. The streets were covered curb to curb in blood. The dead weren't eating the food; they were eating the people. So all the shops, for a while, were well stocked." Wiping at his mouth, he continued. "Then things began to run out, and people in other parts of Sky Porch began coming in. They fought with others, and that drew in more of the dead. There's a supermarket parking lot that looks like a butcher's yard."

As the husband and wife alternated accounts, Joab felt regret. When they met, he praised Owen to appeal to his vanity. In truth, the youth pastor had done a great job protecting his people.

But it was the polluted theology, the lack of faith, bringing this down on all of them. God was Joab's shield now, but not always. Before everything broke down, it was his strength--he was Owen.

Now God had given them all exactly what they wanted—a world protected by their strength, motivated by their goodness.

As the night grew late, they shared about losing others, and when the battles stopped, the terror of devils roaming nearby. Sniffing and searching for new prey because the easy ones were gone.

"Highway 19 was blocked at the bridge. The route through the high desert had been blown by the military," Owen said. "The desert route was too far, even if it was open. We'd have had to travel through the middle of the city to get to it. Those things you call devils, their numbers kept growing."

"How did you get out?" Noel asked as a chill came to the dining hall. She pulled the sleeves of her sweatshirt over her hands. "That bus is no small deal."

"Like this place," Owen said. "There was a service road, probably used by fire trucks, that cut around all of the traffic. I found it, followed it, and came out near the bridge. The bridge itself was relatively clear. We only needed to clear the entrance. The pile-up was just big enough to discourage those things from trying to get through. We rolled several cars down the embankments and a couple more into the water to clear space for the bus. I nearly rolled us into the lake twice, just trying to reach the bridge."

"The dead took notice," Heather said. "They started working our way. That's when Aaron was bit."

Conversation stopped as they digested the story. It was an account similar to others but with the added burden of young people to care for.

"Hey," Larry said. "Don't worry about Aaron. He's healed. Rejoice and forget it ever happened."

Owen was still hesitant to make eye contact.

Joab knew but wanted to hear it to be sure. "So, you drove out…?"

Owen shrugged and looked back up at Larry and Noel. "That bridge is open, and all those dead have a way out now." Then directly to Joab. "Thousands of them."

"Drew, you copy? You there?" Joab said into his radio, his eyes never leaving the table. He forced a smile to let the couple know he wasn't angry.

A moment passed, static came, **"On the Utility Road."**

"How's it looking?"

"Good, real quiet."

"I need you to do something…" Joab felt Noel's eyes focus on him. **"Take two men and take a peek at the highway."**

"Trouble?"

"Yes."

"Soldiers or devils?"

"The bridge at Sky Porch."

The dining hall was silent. If personality and calling followed form, then Larry and Noel were thinking about the next spiritual step. Was the group ready to move out? Did they need more time? Was their work done?

Owen, on cue, was back on defense.

"I had no choice," he said. "Any one of you would have done the same thing."

"Dude," Larry said, sounding deliberately young. "No one's questioning that."

"I had no choice."

"You did," Noel said. "And you chose to save your people. It was the right thing."

If he knew the others' thoughts, Joab wasn't sure if they knew his. Time, he needed time. Leaving The Garden wasn't his call, but if that was the plan, he needed to buy time to delay the devils coming down 19.

"What are you thinking, Joab?" Noel said.

"If we're thinking tactically," he said. "There's no barricade we can put up to keep a hundred, let alone a thousand devils out. Then again, unless drawn, thousands wouldn't come this way down the hill. They'd stay on the highway, hit the flatlands, and addios San Quintana."

"Then we should go now," Owen said.

"I don't make decisions, but…." Joab chewed his bottom lip. "There's something about this place that defies the tactical. Unless you two are hearing different from the Lord, my answer would be for us to stay put until we learn a little more."

"I haven't sensed anything," Larry said, "but I'll pray."

"Maybe it's time for us to share our story, Larry?" Noel said. "Maybe this is the crisis where the sharing of our testimony will build faith?"

"What's the testimony?" Heather said

"I think you're all crazy," Owen said, jumping ahead of his wife. "Well, intentioned, but crazy. Thousands could be coming down. We'll get cut off, and eventually, they'll find us. We've got to go." Then he looked at Heather. "Baby, we've got to go."

Joab's mind, ignoring the turn in the conversation, kept working. At some point, he started talking and was unaware he was broadcasting to the others.

"If devils truly react to odor, The Garden would be at the mercy of the wind. But that doesn't matter because of how the wind hits and works through the canyons and ravines. It changes direction all the time."

"Joab?" Noel said.

"At first, they'd come in trickles, maybe dozens, maybe at worst a hundred at a time on the highway. Right off the bat, I don't see columns of thousands marching out all at once."

"Right, and that's why we should go while the window's still open," Owen said.

"We need time," Joab said. "You two need to pray," he directed to Larry and Noel. "Tomorrow, I'll take a small team out to see if we can spot anything. Perhaps get a jump on their direction."

"Won't they take the highway?" Owen said. "It's right there for them."

"They might, and I hope so," Joab said. "Then again, they might get distracted by a rabbit, squirrel, or something else and turn down one of those smaller roads. I'm concerned about them scattering and coming through the forest above us. Did you just hit the road? Did you stop anywhere near Big Sky or even Cumberland?"

LARRY
(4)

We didn't stop anywhere," Owen said. "I know I put this place in danger. I'm sorry, but..."

"It was inevitable," Larry cut him off. "It's no one's fault. We need to pray because if we're thinking in the tactical, as Joab says, there are 187 us and some with bites unhealed. We're not ready to move."

"Larry," Joab said. "If they come in force from the forest above the camp via Big Sky...?"

"I know."

"There'll be very little we can do."

"There's no bridge blocking the exit from Big Sky," Noel said. "But it's all forest and mountain. That's tough terrain for the devils. We know they usually take the simplest route, and that would be Highway 19."

"But if they do come down from the forest," Owen said, "what do we do? I don't want to fight with you people, but we need to get out of here."

"Your little girl," Larry said, "is not ready to go down the hill. You know what they'll do to her."

"Is that true in all cases, or only what you've heard?" Owen said.

"I've seen it," Joab said, holding a finger to the piece in his ear. "I've seen them shoot young, old, anyone with a bite, or anything looking close to a bite."

"Then what do we do?" Heather said.

"We let them walk-through," Noel said. "We'll close up and go inside for three days. Joab's men will start a fight with them on the highway and lead them away from us." She looked directly at Larry. "We're not ready to leave--you said so. Joab's men can draw them down the mountain and buy us time."

"And it would leave this place wide open," Owen said.

"It would work, but we wouldn't make it back," Joab said. "Good thinking, Noel."

"I'm 19," she said. "I've got no problem writing checks for others to cash."

"Are you just pretending not to see the situation?" Owen said, his agitation returning. "A 187 people locked inside this dining hall and flimsy cabins? There are tens of thousands of them in Sky Porch."

"We can't leave," Larry said. "We have people, including your people and daughter, who have fresh wounds. You do know the escort they sent today was two soldiers and a minister? That's medical triage without a doctor."

"We don't have to go to San Quintana," Owen said. "We can go someplace else."

"On who's roads? The military controls the roads, and NORM controls the military," Noel said. "And the road leaving this part of the mountain has to go straight through San Quintana. I understand what you are saying, but until we get the go-ahead from God, we can't leave."

Joab shook his head for no one to speak. "Drew took down a single devil on the road and waited for more but saw nothing."

"Get them back," Noel said. "It's dangerous out there."

"We're wasting time," Owen said.

"The woods were crawling today with devils," Joab said. "And I don't think they're coming from Sky Porch. It's too soon. We need to find out where the ones we saw today came from."

"We'll cancel everything taking us away from the center of camp and be prepared to hit the dining hall at a moment's notice," Larry said. "I know the kids wanted to play baseball tomorrow. Set it up in the perimeter, outside here; there's plenty of grass. I don't want them on the meadow. It'll be too far to come."

"What are you going to do about chapel?" Heather asked.

"We'll keep doing chapel where we always do it, and when the time comes, we can do it right here," Noel said.

"Have you considered my opening of the bridge was God telling you it's time to go?"

"Loren, Owen," Heather said. "We got to think about Loren. If these people hadn't shown up, they would have killed her today. We're not taking any chances with her."

Joab held up his right hand. Listening, he bent his head. **"No, Drew, pull your guys back to camp. We want everything secure here."** He lifted his head back up. "They're coming in."

"This place is going to get overrun, Heather," Owen said. "Then what will we do?"

"At least we know this place won't shoot Loren, Jessica, or Aaron."

"You've seen a couple of miracles today," Noel said. "Trust us, trust that God has brought you to a special place."

"Joab, why don't you get out there," Larry said. "I'll leave my radio on. Let me know if something breaks." Without hesitation, Joab was out the door.

"I'll get Karla and Debbie up," Noel said. "And make them aware of what we could be facing."

Owen pushed away from the table and stood.

"Wait a second, please," Larry said. "I wanted to get Joab outside doing what he does best. I don't want you and him going at it right now."

"Thank you," Heather said. "I like Joab, I just...I'm too worked up for fighting."

Did he like Owen? No, Larry knew he didn't like Owen. Was Owen a jerk before The Tilt? Most likely. Was he a jerk now? Yeah, but Larry understood the importance of keeping the peace.

"I want to make a few things clear, and I can speak for Noel on this," he started and could see Owen brace himself. "I was harsh in the way I spoke to you at first, and I apologize. And from our hearts, none of us, including Joab, think anything negative about you and that bridge. Whatever happens, I don't want you to struggle with it going forward."

"I'm not."

"Don't lie," Noel said. "And the reason I say that is because if you remain defensive, there's no way we're going to be able to work together."

Owen tried to counter her, but Larry didn't let him.

"You can still do what you think is best for you and your group, but I'm asking you to stay. The Garden's going to be fine."

"How can you say that?" Owen said. "How can you presume to know the will of God? I think our coming, and the opening of the bridge was God's sign."

Heather leaned over the table and dropped head in hands. "The bus Owen, did you see the healing that took place on the bus?"

"What does that have to do with it?"

"The soldiers would have killed our daughter if they found her."

"Just because they say so," Owen said, "doesn't make it true."

"You were on the bus, Owen. You saw it," Heather said as tears streaked down her thin face. "You're my husband, and I love you, but isn't it obvious?"

"And God only works through them?" Owen said.

"Said Miriam and Aaron," Larry said, proud he was able to link Owen's line to a Biblical reference. It was the best part of the meeting as far as he was concerned.

"They've got the market cornered? The rest of us should bow down to them? Maybe it's time for them to take those skills down the hill."

"When God says so," Noel asserted. "We will."

The wheel of frustration with Owen had spun from him to Joab, and now it landed on Noel. She never got angry, at least not in an obvious way. Larry noticed when upset, she cried, worked harder, and delivered quicker responses.

"You'll know them by their fruits," Noel said. "In this place, you've been welcomed, healed, and not condemned, but think us arrogant. And I agree, God got you out of Sky Porch for a purpose. I agree it was to get you to The Garden. But it wasn't to rescue us. It was to rescue your soul. You can't leave because you still need to get saved."

Owen walked out of the dining hall. Noel had cleared the matter.

NOEL
(3)

Noel and Larry's roles were clear at The Garden. He was upfront, she was behind the scenes, Larry was Paul, Noel was Barnabus. Always the road smoother, the bridge builder—except this time. When she said it was God's plan for Owen to get saved, she knew it struck an unguarded flank and concluded the conversation.

"Well, I think that about wraps it up," Larry said, going through the double doors and releasing a short laugh. "You know where to find me."

Heather remained seated and sobbing.

"I apologize for my tone, Heather. I know I hurt both of you, but it's true. There's a veil over Owen's eyes." She touched the woman's shoulder in comfort and walked to the doors. When something was out of place in Noel's soul, she could feel her stomach grind. Now, there was no such indicator.

Owen needed to get saved, and he needed to hear someone say it.

"I don't understand this church," she said, looking through the screen. Joab had men crisscrossing the interior of the camp. The light in Larry's cabin went out. The full moon allowed her to make out Owen leaning his back against the 40 passenger bus. "The night I got saved, there was one thing, Jesus. Only one to serve, Jesus. Only one to be obedient to Jesus. But people here are slaves to everybody and everything except Jesus. How can that be the church?"

When God got Noel, it was a blindside. That Sunday night, she came to church solely to get out of the apartment. Getting away from two rooms, a dirty kitchen, a bathroom with a busted

148

medicine cabinet, and a harping mom was all that mattered. Distance from it all would let her pretend new beginnings were possible, at least until she went home.

Heather continued to sniffle.

"I'm not sorry for what I said." Noel slightly turned the older woman's way. "I'll never be sorry for that."

"I never thought I'd long to live," were the first words she whispered after her altar experience. Later, she learned Chip was alongside her, and Larry was kneeling on the other side of the sanctuary. *"I never thought I'd long to live, but I want to…I want to live!"*

Why would anyone want to live when they felt so worthless? When they meant nothing to no one? Noel thought she mattered to Donny Caheny--he was 19, she was 13 when they started having sex after school at his empty house. He'd grunt, sigh, yawn, and then say she had to go. She was only with Max Venegas once--he was a grade older, and Alex Kalomba twice.

It never got better. Each guy replaced her with someone else. And every feeling was about not being good enough—about being nothing. Alex took her to the clinic to get rid of the baby in the summer of '78, and she was ready to die then.

"I want to die," she remembered repeating the thought. *"I want to die. They lie to you, they lie to you, they lie to you…."*

Noel had never heard the guest speaker, Joe Hyde, preach before, but it was as if he spoke directly to her. When she contemplated Jesus, she thought about what it meant to matter and knew there was a future for her—she couldn't get to the altar fast enough.

Weights that not only held her down but beat at every good feeling she ever had about herself came off.

If she was going to live, she had to get to the altar. Being born again was understood, and her business with God began that night. As she prayed, and others prayed around her, for the first time in a long time, or maybe forever, she longed to live.

Only Jesus restored her. Only Jesus made her like new. Only Jesus saved her. And it was only Jesus she was going to serve.

Why don't these people get that? Why is that a battle?

JOAB
(5)

"What are you thinking, Joab?" Kuykendall said.

He was standing with Crazy Chang, Jay, Mason, and Big Leon by the three trees. Their eyes aimed east to the Utility Road in anxiousness. They all expected the sounds of gunfire, voices screaming in their earpieces, and a brigade of devils to emerge from the night.

Curving south--to the left--of the Utility Road and then west, were the cabins stretching to the dining hall. Behind the cabins was Mandalay. To the Utility Road's right, to the north, was another stretch of smaller cabins ending with Noel and Larry's closets.

"Just thinking what we're all thinking," Joab said. "And maybe a few other things."

"Does it have anything to do with food?" Crazy Chang asked. "Because I'm telling you if it has anything to do with food, I be in.

I don't care what's out there. I'll peddle a bike to Big Sky for half a candy bar."

"I'll take that action," Big Leon said, "something with nuts covered in chocolate. How far are we from the ski resort?"

"Big Leon, you've got the camouflage for night work," Jay said, and the black man smiled. "Those devils won't see you, but white bread like me will turn into fast-food before you can say, 'Hi, my name is Owen, and I'm a douchebag.'"

The group shared a laugh spasm, which Joab found interesting. He hadn't said a word to any of them about Owen.

"Remember," Crazy Chang said. "I was a statistics major, and it would increase our odds if you made the run, Big Leon."

"You guys know I'm more mocha than fully black, right?" Big Leon said. "My mom was white, so how black do I have to be?"

"You could renounce the whiteness, but they'd still smell you," Joab said. "They smell us, they see us in the dark, it makes no matter. So, Chang, you can make that run, but I don't think your odds would be any better than Big Leon's."

"Jefe, have you seen how fast I am?" Chang said and sprinted ten yards in one direction, made a sharp cut in the other, and then turned and raced back to their spot. "I like to see Big Leon do that," he puffed.

"You got some game, dude," Jay said.

"I need game with those kids chasing after me all day," he said.

Joab, in thought, stepped from the group. "Either way, we still have to get eyes on the highway in the morning."

"You want to take a team out at sunrise?" Kuykendall said.

"I do. I want to head north and see what we can see, maybe steal a few candy bars while we're at it."

"I'm with you," Kuykendall said.

"Nothing but love for you, Big K., but I'm taking the fast guys."

Kuykendall and Big Leon, though slimmer, weren't much faster. Joab wanted the track team. "Jay, you up for a hike in the morning?"

"Always."

"Then get back to Mandalay and get some sleep," he said. "We'll take Bird, Wheeler, and Duran and leave before breakfast."

"You're cutting me out of the candy run?" Chang said. "I can scoot, you just saw me."

"Hey, I'm Team Chang, but sometimes you lose focus."

"Where's that coming from?"

Big Leon let out a grunt. "Who was the one that got into the Battlestar Galactica debate with Frank last summer and nearly got a chunk taken out of him on the highway?"

"That could've happened to anybody," Chang said.

"Not to anybody paying attention," Big Leon said. "You nearly became Panda Express."

Chang cracked a smile. "That's actually funny. The "fast-food" expression is getting a bit played. I'll be Panda Express. You can be Roscoe's."

The two men bumped fists.

"What about me?" Jay said.

"What do you got in you?" Big Leon asked.

"A little bit of this and a little bit of that."

"You look like Subway, my brother," Chang said.

"You can always hang with me, Chang," Kuykendall said. "I love talking Galactica."

"I be in."

Joab loved them all. The idea of putting any of them in harm's way made him sad. They were all in their twenties, but they were kids. Even the married guys, Gavin, Alan, and Troy, looked like they still needed parental permission to go out at night.

"Chang, I want you sticking around here because if it gets crazy, I know you're the one who'll get crazy enough to keep our people safe," Joab said. "Plus the kids like you, you might be able to chill them if something happens.

"Whatever you say, Jefe. I roll with you, but am I really the crazy guy at camp?" Chang said.

"We call you 'Crazy Chang,'" Jay said. "Does that give you a hint?"

"I thought it was a term of endearment, and I thought you were going to bed."

They shared a smile. Jay said goodnight and walked off for Mandalay.

"Mason," Joab said. "I'm going to need you to lend Drew a hand. The fast guys are coming with me, but our best fighters will stay right here just in case."

"Do you think they're going to come down 19?" Mason asked.

"I do," he said. "But I don't think the worst will happen to us. The worst is going to happen to San Quintana."

LARRY
(5)

In his cabin, Larry prayed but received nothing new in return.

The standard prayer experience, by his bedside, was the evacuation of pressures, surrender, and clear thinking. What followed was never an audible voice but a line of thought to pursue. This time, though, nothing came, not even the familiar sensations of a breeze across his brow.

He got into bed, got out of bed, prayed some more, and got back into bed.

What emerged from the cob-webbing thoughts were things he'd done in the past and things he could or might do in the future.

Some made sense, some were ridiculous, and all incoherent as a monologue between himself and the cabin's ceiling meandered on.

When God spoke, no other action presented itself. Adrenaline would flow, and there was a breeze—yes, even in a closed room—brushing his face. Tonight a trumpet sounding would have been terrific, and a clear voice even better to give guidance about the things headed their way.

Nothing.

Resting on a sheet, covered by a sleeping bag, Larry drifted into a comfort zone, squeezing and occasionally smelling the green plaid scrunchy in his hand. He gazed at the streams of moonlight spearing through the window. Then—right on time—Denise Hemingway floated in to defend the space she'd owned since the fall of his freshman year.

Hemingway...Hemingway...Hemingway...

It was like candy to think her name and poetry to say it.

How did she get a name like Hemingway?

"Tall," he said to no one. She was tall when he was a freshman and still tall when he spent the morning with her at Arceo Park three years later. "Farrah hair, great dimples, and tons of teeth."

Farrah hair, great dimples, and tons of teeth. They were the lines he repeated to himself for as long as he could remember. Denise Hemingway came to thought, and *Farrah hair, great dimples, and tons of teeth* came in a line behind it.

There had been girls before her. Girls he'd been out with, but no one else was Denise. In the 18 months since arriving in this new but dying world, no one had taken her place. For the most part, he'd been able to keep her memories in storage. But of late, when things were quiet, or when he needed to think, she came like a Dickens ghost to taunt him about what he lost.

"Peach Nectar," he said, naming her perfume.

Her lyrical name, the Peach Nectar smell of her hair, the feeling of the one time they embraced— enslaved him. It was happening more and more and leaving him vulnerable to massive bouts of sadness.

What makes you weak and vulnerable?

Larry squeezed the scrunchy and drew in its perfumed aroma. It never came out of his room. He never left it out in the open but always held it tight at night. It wasn't magic or anything he could slay devils with. But it was the last thing in the world that smelled of Peach Nectar. The last thing in the world keeping Denise Hemingway possible.

NOEL
(4)

A wind came through the camp, shaking the leaves in the oaks. It looked beautiful in the moonlight, smelled beautiful for the most part, but the peace it intended was false. Everyone knew what was prowling out of sight in the woods.

Drew, shotgun slung on his shoulder, stood in the center of camp. From her cabin (left--east--of Larry's), he was a silhouette. Between her and the dining hall were the three oaks rooted on a crown of ground.

She considered going to where he was.

Noel knew she didn't need to justify anything. She and Larry
played at false modesty, but it was ridiculous. They were unique.
Not better, nor more beloved, but they did come to this place with
a clear purpose and a rare set of skills. Toss in Joab's support, and
it made The Garden theirs to command.

Larry remembered a tunnel of lights and brushing fingers with
another boy named Darren Bradford. Noel didn't. She remembered
opening a closet—perhaps a flash—a whoosh, and they were here.
Emotionally, it was painful as Larry lamented over Denise
Hemingway, and she wept over her mother.

Peering between the curtains at Drew, Noel smiled, thinking of her
mom, knowing Wendy Sedaka would've approved.

If he knew the truth would he want someone like me?

Inside the cabin, more like a closet, there were hooks to hang
clothes, a bed beside the door, a pillow, and a sleeping bag. There
were two windows, one looking to the center of camp, and the
other, covered by a towel, looking into the woods. Slipping off her
shoes—Noel wouldn't change out of her clothes tonight—she sat
on the bed. From an angle against the wall, she could see the three
oaks, the decrepit toolshed she repeatedly begged to be torn down,
and the open area of the meadow beyond.

A shadow figure, looking like Mason, met Drew by the trees. Joab
joined them.

The burning hope had always been a full house at Thanksgiving
and Christmas. A home that looked like it was from the right side
of town with falling leaves, a porch, and family. Something to
belong to besides her mom and a garbage apartment. She wanted

something that resembled what she saw during the holiday seasons on television as a kid.

No one would give it to her, not Donny, not Max, and not Alex.

"Why would Drew ever want me?" A tear-streaked, she wiped at it and then knocked her head against the cabin wall.

An hour passed, and sleep was impossible.

Drew, still by the trees, kept his eyes in constant rotation around the camp's interior.

Not long after arriving at The Garden with 16 people, they sat around a rare campfire, talking and dreaming about what might be possible. Joab shared the background of Camp Goodspeed. They spoke about repurposing solar panels to revive the pump to the well. During the discussion, she touched Drew's hand. Their fingers clung to soft dirt between the beach chairs they were sitting in. And as they came up, dirt filtered out before they lowered their hands again. More dirt twined in, and they rose again. No one saw as they kept repeating the act while others talked.

She blushed at the memory.

It was accidental, mindless, but signals flared. Not wanting to expose too much of what she was feeling, Noel gently smiled at him. He smiled back, and the thud of it exploded inside her. Adrenaline transmitted through her body. It felt like a muscle in her face was twitching; there was a burning sensation in her lower back and working up her spine. Her feet tingled.

And that was it.

Since the night by the fire, and the hug a year ago, there had been nothing else. Drew took no action toward her. Sensibility tried to tell Noel to doubt the experience, but his smile was burned on her brain. It happened.

"It was real," she whispered behind her window as she watched him. "I know it was real."

BRICKLANDER
(4)

It was 50 miles from San Quintana to Brackett Air Field in LaVerne. A helicopter could have been there and back in a snap. Pre-virus, helicopters were as abundant in America as burger places with golden arches. Now there weren't enough pilots, mechanics, or fuel. Parts, hard to come by, were cannibalized from other machines. Much was held together by the old duct tape, baling wire, and spit routine.

In the Inland Empire, only three military helicopters were operating. An Apache and two Blackhawks. So today, Bricklander, Lieutenant Farmer, and five others were rolling in a truck to pick up mail, MREs, ammunition, and assorted items.

The official reason was the pickup, but the real purpose was to keep morale above the depression line. By regularly rotating men out of town, they got a chance to stretch their legs, blow some steam, and spend some money.

Brackett Field included a functioning truck stop. A store with ice, soft drinks, snacks, and beer. It had an arcade, showers for purchase, and places to sit and drink coffee. But its best feature was truck drivers—some from around the country--willing to share what they've seen. They were the most accurate source of news.

"Sarge, why am I the only brother making this trip?" Private Doughty said, loading into the back of the truck with Private Crowder. "I always get stuck with white boy Crowder, dogging my moves."

"We've only got five or six brothers combined in San Quintana, and that includes civilians. What do you want me to do?" Bricklander said. "And forget about the women at Brackett. I'm hearing NORM moved them out."

"You serious?" Doughty said. "Who said?"

"Lancaster," Bricklander said. "He said the sex workers were moved out. And you know, Lancaster, if there was anything available, he'd have found it."

"NORM's a bastard," Doughty cursed, taking his seat.

"Stars and Stripes," Bricklander said.

"There are plenty of women in San Quintana. We should have a get-together dance," Crowder said, taking off his cap. With balding red hair and freckles, his only hope was organized socialization.

"Minister Tim suggested the very same thing, but the good people of San Quintana shot it down."

"Texas is better than this," Doughty said. "Sarge, I thought things were getting better?"

"What I heard," Gibson said, climbing in, "is that there was a group of women doing 'business' at Brackett. But more wanted in, including some dudes, so NORM pulled the plug. The ladies are now black market items, and you've got to know someone if you want to exchange goods and services."

"Do we know anyone?" Doughty asked.

"Just Crowder," Gibson joked.

Doughty cursed again. "Crowder, why are you so ugly?"

"Your mom likes me," Crowder responded, and it got no more than an eye roll. Mom jokes just didn't cut it anymore.

The truck's tarp covering was off, and its metal spine exposed. No one liked driving anywhere in the open, but the heavy canvas created too much heat, and the I-10 was secure to the border of East LA. So there was little risk.

"Doughty," Jarvis said, joining them. "Would you go to the Arroyo Seco for a chick?"

"If she was stone cold, you bet," he said, sliding further down. "How bad can The Seco be?"

"You ever heard of Khe Sanh?" Bricklander said. "Ask for duty in the Arroyo Seco, and you'll learn all about Khe-Sanh."

"We're you at Khe Sanh, Sarge?" Doughty said.

"I wasn't even born, but an old-timer clued me."

"What was the Arroyo Seco like?" Crowder said.

"Gibson and I were there," Jarvis said. "It was bad. An absolute cluster--still is. The dead just seemed like they sprouted out of the ground."

"I was in the surge to get back Pasadena," Bricklander said. "We had to fight our way through Baldwin Park, El Monte, and Temple City. They wanted us to draw a line and box in Los Angeles, but that included Highland Park, Eagle Rock, even parts of Glendale. It's dense with the dead. You're constantly surrounded because the population never had a chance to evacuate. Short of a tactical nuke, there's no way we're taking LA back."

Private Barnes got behind the wheel of the truck. Lieutenant Farmer took the passenger seat and knocked on the glass to let them know they were ready to roll.

"Minister Kevin call, yet?" Gibson asked.

"Not yet," Bricklander said. "I have a feeling Minister Kevin's going to be in those woods for a while."

"Stars and Stripes, on that," Gibson said. "That gets my day off to a nice start."

"Amen," Doughty said. "If we can get rid of Fat Minister Tim too, we'll be alright."

The drive on I-10 was a lark and nearly free of traffic. Exits were sealed, save for a few critical off-ramps. What remained of the California Highway Patrol cruised from the Inland Empire to the remains of the 710-Freeway.

Barnes kept the miles-per-hour at the NORM mandated speed of 65. In the open air of the truck, they all felt freedom. Like Americans before the world ended, driving with the top down, sunglasses on. The Californians—Crowder, Barnes, Jarvis—reminisced about rides to the beach and how this felt like one.

Behind dark glasses and closed eyes, Bricklander daydreamed about the Shenandoah and a picnic with the family. Barnes honked at something, but he kept his eyes shut, not wanting to leave what his mind was slowly conjuring from the best memories of his life.

"We should moon them," Crowder said.

"Crowder, you should keep that fuzzy butt of yours under wraps," Jarvis said.

There were colors in Virginia he'd never seen until moving there. Calm breezes carried autumn leaves down and around Rosa's long-running auburn hair. If there was an outer office to heaven, Bricklander reckoned it was the Old Dominion.

A hand beat against the cab. "Catch them! Barnes, catch them!" Crowder shouted.

"Be cool," Jarvis said. "I'm telling you guys don't do it. You hang your butts off the side, and Barnes hits something, you're gonna get launched."

"Sarge, can we moon them?" Crowder asked.

"I'm a non-commissioned officer in the United States Army," Bricklander said. His eyes remained closed and unconcerned about who would be receiving the mooning. "I dropped my drawers when I got inducted. I'm not doing it again."

"That's not a, no," Doughty said.

Bricklander heard another tap on the back of the cab. Barnes accelerated beyond NORM guidelines.

"Now! Do it now!" Crowder yelled.

"Oh, that's nasty," Jarvis said. "Crowder, bro, you need to do something about that red growth."

Laughter filled the truck bed, but in the Shenandoah, where Bricklander's thoughts remained, green grass and groves of trees filled the picture. A waterfall and a swift-moving current running over long-washed rocks issued peace from a distance.

Maybe if I clack my boots together three times and repeat, 'there's no place like the Shenandoah, there's no place like the Shenandoah....'

LARRY
(6)

It was a groggy start.

"Can I get you something, Larry?" Kelly asked, bringing him out of a blur with her gracious smile. "Some hot tea?"

"Will it wake me up?" His father called him 'Loafing Larry' in the morning because Larry could milk putting on his shoes and socks into a career.

"It's not exactly Earl Grey," she said, "nor espresso, but it'll snap you to."

"What's expresso?" he said, rubbing his eyes.

Kelly gave the strange face mothers sometimes put on for their kids.

"What? What did I say?"

"Espresso," she clarified. "Not expresso, espresso."

"Where I come from, you just scooped your coffee into hot water," he said.

"Where you come from? You act as if you've never been to a Starbucks."

The oddities surrounding him and Noel stretched beyond spiritual uniqueness. It surfaced in so many weird ways, from a morning beverage to what was called a *music download—?*

"I need to get tonight's sermon done," he said. "So, I'll take it."

"Coming right up. I'll bring you some scones, too."

"Cones?"

"Poor sheltered boy," Kelly said and headed for the kitchen.

Guilt hit for not being up to see Joab off. Out late, up early, Larry emerged in time to see Wheeler receive a hug from Elias before the group left. He knew a leader needed to demonstrate awareness and appreciation. And he knew he needed to express more gratitude because there'd be no Garden without Joab and his men.

The kids consumed oatmeal and Tang for breakfast as the adults did tasks from trash disposal to inventory and landscaping.

Noel's first words, every morning, were about the shed being put out of its misery. Kept out of convenience, the shed housed tools, toys, and odds and ends. It was on a long list of things to fix, repair, and destroy.

"Every time somebody opens the door, the whole thing shakes," she'd say. *"It's going to come down on someone—you wait."*

Kelly brought his tea. He sipped. It was less than hot, very bland, but it did clear the cloudiness. Combined with the light of day, it helped him forget about Denise Hemingway, who was nocturnal for the most part and usually crept in as the sun went down.

What was he going to preach tonight? Larry flipped pages in his Bible and found where he left off in Galatians. Who had bewitched the Galatians? A better question might have been who had bewitched Owen?

Noel, entering the dining hall, pointed with exaggeration at the tool shed. "It's going to fall on somebody."

By now, the news about Sky Porch had circulated but had not overwhelmed the camp. The Garden continued about its business full of energy. The kids, Battlestar Galactica, and the shed were still the trending topics.

Larry knew moving 187 people wasn't possible, nor was the same 187 able to defend the camp. The only option was to encourage them in their faith. A message would come; it always did. His mind would get working, Joab would return with news and a plan.

Idling through Hebrews, perusing the Faith Chapter, he heard Noel and the ladies clapping hands to commence clean-up. Bodies began scattering. The kids ran to their cabins and chores. Soon they'd gather in circles on the grass and in the amphitheater for school.

Big Leon, Frank, Big Geoff, and Crazy Chang were gathered around a table in the dining hall's east corner. They weren't yelling, but he heard their voices.

"The original Battlestar Galactica was a rip-off of Star Wars."

"Just because it's a reboot doesn't mean it wasn't a rip-off originally."

"It's not a reboot and has nothing to do with Star Wars."

"But the women are better looking. In Star Wars, they're not that hot. Plus, the sequels got really stupid."

The only one who didn't speak was Big Geoff. His eyes locked with Larry's and rolled. Telepathy was not one of Larry's gifts, but he knew Big Geoff was screaming for rescue.

A sleepy-eyed Hiram came into the dining hall with the perpetually disheveled Anspach, who walked by looking for breakfast.

"You and Frank up all night?" Larry asked.

"Yeah, but you wouldn't know it the way those dudes keep talking," Hiram said. "I never knew there could be so many opinions about so many things that don't matter."

"I lived in Mandalay for a while, I know."

"Tell Noel, I'm going to try and take that shed down today."

"Get some food, get some sleep, and a good wind will take care of the shed," Larry said. "If they're too loud in Mandalay, you can crash in my cabin."

"Nah, I'll survive," Hiram said. "Plus, I drool when I sleep, I wouldn't want to soggy up your pillow. Thanks, though. And be sure to tell Noel. I feel better about myself when she's smiling." He moved on.

The screen doors pushed open again. Todd, the boy with the Angels hat, came running in.

"Dude," Larry said. "What's up?"

"Mr. Garrison!" he yelled. "Mr. Garrison! We're going to play baseball today!"

Back home, Larry would have mocked Todd's excitement. Right now, it was one of the best things in his life. He hoped before the day was over, they'd all have faces beaming like Todd's.

"After school, Debbie said, we're going to layout the bases!"

"Awesome, I'll finish my stuff and get out there."

"You gonna play? Because we're going to play a real game. Will Joab play? I want to be on his team."

"How about me?" Crazy Chang called from the corner. "I got game!"

"I'll take you!" Todd shouted back.

"What about me?" Larry said.

"Yeah, I want you on my team too. All of us, we'll beat everybody!" Todd high-fived Larry and raced back.

The Garden's not going to fall.

JOAB
(6)

The overcast morning teased with drizzle, but no rain fell. As Joab and his men walked, every dry moment was appreciated until the sun broke through. The difference between yesterday to the current day was stark. The day before, devils were popping up, shuffling in and out of the woods. Today nothing, not even a squirrel scrounging for nuts, could be seen going north on Highway 19.

"Where do you think they are?" Duran asked in the standard, careful-not-to-draw-attention voice all subscribed to in compromised areas.

Extended from a safe position, the chatter was minimal. A wandering devil in the forest wasn't the concern, but the possibility of a large mob hitting them was something else. A sprint to escape had three outcomes: A dead end, a last stand, or a marathon run for shelter. Duran, Wheeler, Jay, and Bird were fast. But, given his age and a right knee that clicked when waking in the morning, Joab was the weak link.

The plan was to march for an hour, mark the spot, get a sense of any considerable advancement, and return. Packed light, the men carried Remington 870 shotguns and machetes. Each had a sidearm and handheld radios clipped to their belts. The further they went, the weaker the signal back to camp became. Duran made sure at least two of the radios were off at all times to save battery life.

"I don't know," Joab said. "If what we're expecting out of Sky Porch came this far. A few might go off the road, but not all of them."

"What if they all went off the road?" Duran said.

"Then we'd be in a world of hurt," Jay answered. "We want them on the highway, not scattered and coming down above us through Big Sky."

"But if they were on the east side of Highway 19," Wheeler said. "That would detour them away from us."

"And I'd be singing the Hallelujah chorus," Joab said.

"I can't imagine Big K. wanting to be out here," Jay said.

"Big K.'s lost a lot of weight since pizza delivery stopped," Wheeler said, "He's feeling spry."

Everyone liked Kuykendall, and there wasn't anybody at The Garden that didn't want him by their side when the devil hit the fan. But while he'd thinned, he was still big. Big about everything from laughing to eating to just yacking.

"We should all do our jobs as well as Big K.," Joab said.

The opposite of Kuykendall was Bird. The smallest, quickest, and best able to climb anything without a handgrip or toe hold. Gilbert was his first name, his last name—Kwon, Kwok, Kuo?—everyone forgot after Joab labeled him 'Bird.'

"Remember last year when we found the chickens and the ladies cooked them for us?" Jay said, leading to a story they all knew.

They needed to be quiet, but Joab raised no protest. The road was weird this morning, and talking eased anxiety.

"I remember," Wheeler said. "By the time I rotated in, there were some claws and bones to gnaw on."

"Dude, Kuykendall cleared that table like a hurdler," Jay said.

"He apologized," Bird said. "He said he was sorry."

"That's Big K., if he turned into a devil, it's game over," Wheeler said as they stepped through a scattering of fist-sized rocks that had fallen with the melting snow. "My ultimate payback is going to be the day we have cheeseburgers."

"Cheeseburgers?" Joab said. "Man, you're optimistic."

"Lord, lift me up and let me stand," Duran sang. "Put a cheeseburger in my hand. A better taste I've never found--than grilled onions and cheese on juicy ground-round."

"Bro," Jay groaned. "You're killing me."

"I don't know how, I don't know where, but one of these days, we're going to be sitting down with cheeseburgers," Wheeler said. "Even better, Double-Doubles, and I'm going to make sure Big K.'s on patrol, and when he comes in and finds nothing but the smell of grilled onions… I'm gonna dance."

The bends of the road went back and forth. Joab, feeling age in his hips, led them on a large curve to the right before moving left. It exposed an open track heading gradually upward. They'd come to a sweet spot, a clear extended view of the highway with forest spreading to the east.

A pair of cars were on it. The closest, parked next to the mountain, looked intact. The second, further up and on the same side, was half on the road and half off. Only its open trunk remained in the descending lane.

"Nice killing ground," Jay said. "That's got to be close to a mile."

"Easily," Joab said. "If we're going to see them, this is where we're going to see them."

A rustling came from the bush to their right. A devil, in a down vest and ski pants, appeared on the shoulder. Nearly losing its balance before coming at them, it gave a gasping howl.

"Here we go," Wheeler said. Taking the machete strapped to his back, he brought it down into the center of the devil's skull and kicked it back to the edge of the road. "That's one."

"And here's two," Jay said, racing forward and bringing sharp metal into and through the bridge of the next devil's nose. Blood, like dirty oil, spilled down its face and chest before it dropped.

No one cringed at the splitting sound of cartilage, skull, and brain anymore. The grimy blackness that blood became in a devil and often launched like a tapped spout no longer gave shivers. The days of puking were gone. All the gruesomeness did was spin their eyes around for a possible third devil.

"Joab, you want to take a look at this?" Bird said, standing on the embankment. "That's not a big herd, but there's more than a few down there."

Coming next to the shorter man, Joab saw, through the trees, several devils working their way on a path next to a creek. "That's interesting."

"Three!" Jay announced and took down the third devil as it reached the pavement.

"Half a mile up is the turn-off for Cumberland," Duran said, looking at a map. "From The Garden, this creek stays on the far side, the east side, of 19. This means we have the buffer of an embankment to the highway and the creek's distance to the embankment. Some of the devils might stray, as these did, and reach our area. But the majority are going down the ravine and into the flatlands."

"That's huge," Bird said.

"Providence," Joab muttered.

"Great news to take home," Jay said.

"Maybe we should be sure they're coming from Sky Porch?" Wheeler suggested. "We're assuming these devils are from Sky Porch, but what if they're not? We could still be dealing with something big."

Joab rubbed his beard. He wanted to keep going north, but, by the reading of the map, they'd already put four miles between themselves and the Utility Road to The Garden. If they went beyond the turn-off to Cumberland, they could risk getting cut off.

"We know this creek passes through Big Sky," Wheeler said. "If we're wrong, and we haven't seen anything from Sky Porch yet, that could turn out bad for all of us."

"You think we should go into Cumberland?" Jay said.

"At least," Wheeler said. "Based where Big Sky sits above The Garden, west of 19, it helps us that these devils are siphoning from there. Which is great except when you consider Sky Porch and when and where those devils begin to move."

Jay breathed in through his teeth to mimic the pain of the long walk. "If we do that, we need to hotwire a car to bring us back."

"We'll need Sandoval for that," Bird kidded.

Joab knew Wheeler was right. "Guys, I'm going to Cumberland," he said. "You don't have to come with me."

Duran studied the map again. "The turn-off's up ahead, and that's two more miles to Cumberland. That means it will be nearly five miles to get back to this spot. And we've come close to four miles already."

"Sounds like fun, I'm in," Wheeler said. "Besides, we've got to know. The better information we come back with, the better everyone's going to sleep."

"We don't have a clue about what we're going to find in Cumberland," Joab said. "We haven't been anywhere near it since last November."

"I'm down," Jay said.

Bird laughed. "Big, tall, Joab's concerned."

"Bird?"

"Joab, we love you, but we're not doing this for you," the small man said. "We're doing it for The Garden."

His fear was they'd die instead of him.

Ping.

"Okay," he said. "We're going to be exhausted. If we go in and come out, we have to hope nothing comes down this highway and cuts us off. It's a risk."

"You're always preaching clarity; well, this is clarity," Duran said. "Whether they're from Sky Porch or not, the devils going down this path are bypassing us. And this is something else to consider. Nothing was bottled up in Big Sky like Sky Porch. We know there's been a steady drip from Big Sky since this whole thing started."

"True," Joab said, looking at the faces of his men and seeing no dissent. "We go to Cumberland, and if we see huge numbers passing by on the creek trail, then it's likely they're coming from Sky Porch."

"And we'll have caught a huge break," Wheeler said.

The men shrugged, smiled in agreement, and started north again. The sun beautified the day, and the mountains did their best to persuade them it was the world before The Tilt.

"Can you still see the creek, Bird?" Duran said.

"It's starting to curve away," Bird responded, "towards Cumberland."

Half a mile later, they reached Mountain Road 27 and the turn-off to the small village.

"What's in Cumberland?" Wheeler asked, stopping under the sign at the t-section of road and highway. "Old timers? Witches? Warlocks?"

"Retired grandchildren of hippies if memory serves," Joab said. "There should be an abundance of herbal tea available, but I don't think there'll be any baseball caps to take back."

"There could be some Cannabis Free America lids available,'" Jay said.

Clouds rolled over the top, momentarily shadowing them before sailing on.

"Hey man," Bird said to Wheeler, "maybe Roberta's up here?" He snorted a laugh.

"Bird, that's cold," Duran said. Then they all laughed except for Wheeler and Joab.

"What's with you guys and Roberta?" Joab said. "You're always cracking jokes about Roberta, and you never tell me. I live in Mandalay, too. Clue the old guy in."

"Let's save it for another time," Wheeler said.

Joab took a step toward Cumberland, but Bird held him up.

"Why don't I park it there?" he said, pointing to the car with its trunk open, across the road.

"What do you mean, park it?" Duran said, tucking his map into the backpack.

Bird trotted to the car with its trunk open, and the rest came. It was a silver Chevy Cavalier with its tires half deflated. Its windows were intact, and no bloodstains or bodies were inside. It looked like it had run out of gas and spent the winter parked in this spot.

"This will work," Bird said. "I'll leave my radio on, and I'll park it in here. I can keep track of anything coming down behind you."

"Are you out of your mind?" Jay said.

"I don't know, let me see," Bird said, yanking on the handle. "Nope, it works. Manual locks," he thumbed necks of the door locks twice over, "no, I'm not out of my mind."

Joab thought about it. Bird wasn't crazy, but he should have lived with more fear.

"So, you're saying you want to kick it in this car and keep an eye on the road for us?" Joab said.

"And I'll warn you when or if something dangerous shows up," he said. "Better to know there's trouble a few miles away than to come back into it. From here to there, the radios should work fine. You don't even know what's going to be in Cumberland. You may need to jet out of there. With me in the car, at least you have time to find an alternate route."

"It's a great idea, except for one thing," Duran said. "What are you going to do when a hundred, or even a thousand, devils come by?"

"What I do best," Bird smiled, "get real small."

NOEL
(5)

"Pato, pato, pato,….gonzo!"

When the hand slapped the top of Noel's head, she didn't know what to do. The kids in the circle were laughing.

"Run!" They screamed. "Run!"

"I thought we were playing Duck-Duck-Goose?" she said as Elias danced around the circle, waiting for her to chase him.

"It is Duck-Duck-Goose!"

"Oh!" She sprang and began the pursuit. Elias, who was supposed to sit when he came to her spot, kept running, which forced Noel to keep chasing. On his second time around, he plopped down, and now it fell to her.

The older kids and adults were clearing rocks. Todd, disappointed it was to be a tennis ball version of baseball, was counting distances between bases. Having gone so long without Little League, Noel knew he was itching to do something—anything— once familiar.

"Why did you change it on me?" she said.

"We didn't change it, Noel. We did it in Spanish," said Alison, The Garden's playground lawyer in residence. She continually explained how things were to be done. There was Alison's way, and then the wrong way.

"I don't speak Spanish," Noel said.

"You should!" Sandoval yelled from the parking lot. "You're from El Monte, homegirl!"

"Do you speak Spanish, Mr. Sandoval?" Noel called back.

"Three words!" He held three fingers high for everyone to see.

"What three?"

"Pato...pato...and gonzo!"

The group laughed, and she returned him a thumbs up.

"Noel! Come on!" The kids yelled. "It's your turn!"

Noel was happy. Cora and Alison were giggling and whispering. Elias and Teddy, wearing baseball hats turned around like Todd's, smiled at everything. Even though they'd lost so much, these kids had such a natural joy. Alison and Elias were orphans, Cora had an older sister, and Teddy only had his father.

"Duck..." she said.

She only had Larry, but he wasn't going to need her...

"...Duck..."

...But these kids will.

Noel felt it come against her heart. If it came to it, she'd die for them. She'd do anything to protect them.

"You good with that, Noel?"

She didn't argue with the voice because she was good with it.

When she still believed her mother was perfect and her father would be there to pick her up and carry her, Noel laughed and smiled like this. She daydreamed about them coming to her school plays and how they'd talk, tucking her in at night. This kind of joy was there when she could still smile and dream about tenderness. When it was a real hope that her mom would teach her how to bake or her father would put an arm around her as they watched TV together. She knew what it felt like to wait for something magical to happen, for something to reveal the enchanted part of life. Not even the enchanted, but merely the decent every kid wanted to see in their parents and home.

Every day she became willing to accept less and less. They didn't need to live at Disneyland, but could they go to Disneyland? Dad didn't need to be home every night, but could he be home one night? And the one night when dad was home, could he play with her? They didn't have to live in a big house, but could they live in an apartment and laugh and be happy like the families on TV? Could they look, just once, like those perfect families at church that arrived together and decorated their homes at Christmas time?

"…Duck…"

She couldn't make the devils go away or bring back the family they lost, but they were smiling now, and she could make sure those smiles never wilted or were lost to fear of the dead.

"…Duck…"

I'm good with it, God. I'm so good with all of this.

"Goose!" She tapped Loren on the head and ran.

The little girl bolted. When Noel made the turn, she pulled Elias's trick and ran around a second time. The cheering grew. Peeking out of the corner of her eye, she saw a smiling Loren, bandaged arm and all, closing in. Loren's hand touched her.

The circle applauded.

"Noel's in the mush pot!" Alison hollered.

"Mush!"
"Mush!"
"Mush!"

Noel rested back on her hands in the center of the circle, blew upward at the bangs on her forehead, and smiled as they razzed her. Beth and Karla stopped what they were doing to ask Liz what happened. She told them, and they clapped approval.

"Dogpile!" A voice yelled behind her.

Teddy jumped on her back, Alison followed, and the rest came.

As the weight mounted, Noel felt a knee push into her thigh. Her hair was getting tugged and pulled from its ponytail. Curling to protect herself, she hoped for Sandoval to drag them off.

The kids kept laughing.

Sandoval never came.

And they kept laughing and laughing.

***

"We're almost ready!" Wolfman said. "Just another minute or so."

The games, including the dogpile, were broken up, and they sat on the grass. More kids joined them, and some of the moms as well. Heather was there with Loren next to her.

"Where's your mommy?" Teddy said, sitting closer to Noel. She remembered when he and his father came to camp that first winter. Hurt and wounded in body and soul, it seemed like they'd never find joy again, but God had done it, and it was another great testimony to his power.

"My mommy's in heaven," she said.

"Did the devils kill her?"

The question was much more problematic than the answer. In a split second, Noel knew she'd be able to say her mother died before this all started. The question begged her to think about why Teddy was asking. What had he seen? What did he hear?

"No, she died a long time ago," Noel said, straightening his baseball cap. His features were Asian, but his and his father's accents and vocabulary were all apple pie. "But she's in heaven with the other mommies."

"How do you know that?"

Pastor Chip told me.

"What's heaven like?" Jenny, the eight-year-old on her left, questioned.

"It's beautiful," she said.

"You've never been there, how do you know?" said Ben, nine. He was Kelly and Alan's son.

Noel didn't have to think. They were sitting on the grass, enjoying the morning, watching the adults, and Todd, get the baseball diamond ready. Wolfman and Ken, Teddy's father, were filling any ankle-breaking holes they could find. The day wasn't perfect, but it was close.

"No, I haven't, but if God's preparing it, then it has to be beautiful," she said. "Look how beautiful this day is, there are trees, grass, and you can smell the pines. God made all of this in six days, and it's beautiful."

She pointed at Ben, then at Jenny, Alison, Loren, Teddy, and Trinity. "And God made all of you in nine months inside your mothers, and all of you are the most beautiful things I've ever seen."

A flash came of Alex and the clinic, and Noel swallowed to hold herself together.

They lie to you, they lie to you, they lie to you...

The adults were listening now. Sandoval stopped the small chat he was having with Beth behind her. Heather looked her way for the first time all morning. "When Jesus rose into heaven, he said he was going to prepare a place for us. And that was, what, like two thousand years ago? So if the earth is this beautiful after six days, and you are all amazingly beautiful after nine months inside your mommies, how beautiful is heaven after two thousand years of Jesus hammering nails?"

"Wow," Jenny said.

"Wow, is right," Noel said back.

"But I don't think Jesus would be hammering all the nails," Ben said. "Aren't the angels helping him?"

"Probably," she said. "The most important thing to remember is Jesus loves us. Do you guys know that?"

"You're supposed to say, 'do ya'll know that?'" Alison said.

"Okay," Noel said. "Do ya'll know that?"

The kids nodded.

"Someday, someone might try to tell you something different. Promise you'll never forget Jesus loves you."

"We promise."

Wolfman walked halfway over to where they were. "Hey! You people want to play some baseball or what?"

BRICKLANDER
(5)

Bricklander stood when the truck stopped. They were behind a pickup loaded with carpentry tools near the Kellog Interchange of the 10, 57, and 71 freeways. To the right was the Via Verde Hills. Off to the left, he could see Cal Poly Pomona's buildings.

Barnes pulled out and bypassed the line of cars to where a CHP officer was directing traffic. Squashed dead were all along the road. "Hold for a second," the officer said. "We're going to get you through this real fast. Brackett Field?"

"Yeah," Barnes said. "What's going on?"

"Breach last night on the highway. We got it cleaned up about a half-hour ago."

"Bad?"

"It wasn't good. They came up through the riverbed." The cop touched the radio clipped to his shoulder. "Alright, you're good. Happy hunting."

As they edged through the checkpoint, Bricklander got a better view of the campus. So many of the dead were milling about. He couldn't count them. Further south, where the landscape stretched to Diamond Bar and the hills beyond, was a wasteland.

"Before this is over," Jarvis said to Bricklander as he strained to see more of the deceased terrain. "We're all going to become Romans. You know what I mean?"

Bricklander shook his head.

"They're going to give us swords, shields, and reconstitute the legions. NORM's going to send us out in battle squares because there aren't enough bullets."

Barnes revved the engine and took the exit. The road to Brackett wasn't entirely secure but continuously patrolled. After three miles through the rolling hills, the airport was in view. At the end of the McKinley Avenue entrance was the main building. It was a one-stop shop modeled after the travel centers on the interstates. Beyond the building was the airfield.

With a high chain-link fence rounding the perimeter, lots of killing ground, and NORM-contracted security patrolling, Brackett Field was a safe place to be.

Sitting outside the shop, to the east, was an Apache helicopter. More than a dozen warehouses and offices were at the other end of the complex--businesses no longer viable due to the virus. A handful of parked Cessnas were producing rust.

The men hopped out, and Lieutenant Farmer circled the truck to join them.

"We're hanging all afternoon, right?" Gibson said.

"Yeah, we're good," Farmer said. "But let's get the gas pumped now. Jarvis, take care of it."

"Why me?"

"Because if I ask the black guy, he's going take offense."

"Why you always dragging me?"

Farmer ignored Doughty. "And if I turn it over to Gibby, Crowder, or Barnes, they'll blow the truck up."

"So I'm the only one you trust not to blow the truck up?" Jarvis said.

"Take it as a compliment. And be sure to bring the totals in. I've got to sign for it."

Farmer, requisition orders in hand, led the rest inside. Crowder talked about the old days when truck stops usually had a Taco Bell or Subway operating in the corner. "The one in Buttonwillow had a Popeye's in it," he said.

"I'm just glad they still run their showers," Doughty said.

"That's a good chunk of change," Gibson said. "You can shower in the barracks for free."

"They got more hot water here," Doughty countered. "And I don't have to worry about you guys checking me out."

"I ain't getting glowed up over you," Gibson said. "I've got other things I want to see."

"I wouldn't mind the privacy, but I'll shower at Braggs," Barnes said. "And load up on the beer."

"You drive the truck, Barnes," Farmer said. "You ain't loading up on anything."

"Go halves with me, Barnes. We'll down it back at the base," Doughty said, and Barnes agreed as the men separated inside.

A day away from standing a post and waiting for someone's six-month dead uncle to break out of a garage made coming to

Brackett a real—albeit pathetic—holiday. Bricklander felt the tension release in all of them.

"Hey Jose, where are the chicks?" Crowder said.

"Your Tio NORM made it illegal," Jose said from behind the counter. "But I've got some magazines under the counter for purchase."

"Any DVDs?"

Jose shook his head. "Been cleaned out for a while. Had to make some deals to get the magazines. We got plenty of family-friendly DVDs in the back. Some Benji, some Mary-Kate, some Disney, all the old school stuff."

The private magazine industry no longer existed. There wasn't a Cosmo, Playboy, Entertainment Weekly, or Sports Illustrated to be had. With the internet mostly disabled, there was a very active black market for old porn mags and exceptionally trashy homemade shorts on DVD.

Browsing the aisles there were some items of value. A few truck drivers were shopping, country music played, and an ancient situation comedy was on the flat screen above the counter. Written in red on on a dry erase board over Jose's soldier was an announcement that "The Burger Guy" would be at the truck stop in three days.

Farmer delivered his request sheet as Doughty bought a shower. Barnes, Gibson, and Crowder studied the cold brew options. Bricklander bypassed the marked-down DVDs for what remained of the reading material.

The first sergeant thumbed through "Our Times"—a newsprint tabloid co-produced by the Associated Press and NORM. It banged the drum about how things were improving. Beyond that, there was nothing new. There was a stack of old paperbacks, word searches, and crossword books.

Unsure if he wanted to spend money on the newspaper, he considered buying a 12-pack of beer and taking it back to lift Lancaster's spirits. His eyes then spotted a small note taped to the empty bottom shelf. **"1978 Edition of Playboy at the cash register! Like New!"**

Bricklander didn't want to consider what *like new* entailed.

"Look at that, Sarge," Barnes said, walking by, holding a case of beer and seeing the same thing. "We should pool our money and bring a copy back to Braggs. It'll be good for the guys."

"You realize the women in these mags, if they're still alive, are probably pushing 80, right? Keep drooling over Holsopple. It's free."

"Holsopple's happening," Barnes said and walked on and shouted. "Jose! Why isn't The Burger Guy here today?"

Bricklander kept browsing through the tabloid. Safe zones were being declared and expanded into New Jersey. The Texas National Guard, which had liberated much of Dallas, was preparing to hit Austin from three sides this summer. A pair of refugee movie producers announced plans for a major motion picture release next spring. That meant about ten heavily guarded theaters from California to Maine. Everyone else would only see it if they had access to streaming.

Major League Baseball and the National Football League maintained office structures in upstate New York but were years from resuming play. The idea of these leagues having an "office structure" was comical, but Bricklander understood. The mere mention of professional baseball, basketball, or football gave hope. It caught the eye and facilitated fantasies of everything becoming right again.

Returning the tabloid to the shelf, he went into the coffee shop area. The singular light source came from the west side's rectangular windows that showed part of the landing strip. There were plenty of tables and chairs, all empty. Starbucks had replaced their baristas with automated machines. Fishing for coins, he dropped in what was needed, and the motor inside began generating his request.

"Of all the gin joints and saloons in the world, Jeff Bricklander shows his ugly face in this one," said a voice from a shadowed corner.

He turned and saw two men sitting. The black man with the shaved head was his age and built similarly. His cargo shorts and light gray sweatshirt confirmed he was Brackett security. The white guy, who spoke, was the Apache pilot. He was a bit younger with all gray hair.

"Brick," the black man said, getting to his feet, "long time, no see."

Since he was so homesick, not much made Bricklander smile from his core. But happiness blushed through him at the sight of Cliff Smith and Terry Belton. The machine kicked out his latte, and he went to see his old friends.

"Smith, I haven't seen your butt since...."

"...Since you got it out of Afghanistan. I remember, I promised you ribs when I saw you next." They hugged tightly

"How are you here?" Bricklander said. "I thought you were doing contract work? What the hell?" They hugged again and sat down.

"What does it look like I'm doing?" Smith said. "I'm holding the fort."

"What's happening, Brick?" Belton reached and shook his hand.

"I guess I haven't been out of San Quintana for a while."

"Since at least January," Belton said. "I know because NORM's made Brackett my office."

"I got here in February," Smith put a big paw back on Bricklander's forearm. "It's really good to see somebody I know still alive."

"Cliff told me what you did for him," Belton said. "My estimation of you climbed a bit."

"Bacha Bazi," the sergeant sighed. "Sick."

The carnage the dead inflicted on the living didn't trouble his soul the way Bacha Bazi did. Bacha Bazi was an expression for an adult Afghani male keeping a young boy as his personal sex slave. Horrific to its victims, it ate at the life of those who knew about it but were told to stand down.

Under protest, they all ignored it except for Cliff Smith. He killed an Afghani colonel—shooting him twice in the kneecaps before putting the third round through his brain. The battalion command declared the Taliban to blame and quickly arranged for Smith's departure. Bricklander got Smith to Bagram to expedite the discharge and journey home.

"It's a sick part of the world," Smith said.

"And we danced with it," Bricklander said, rapidly replaying all of it in his mind. "Not all of the shame sticks, but that one does."

190

"You had Rosa and the girls to think about," Smith said. "They had you, they had all of us, by the shorts. I was the one with the least to lose—so screw Sandland."

"I had some Brits and Poles pull me out of the fire once," Belton said. "But, yeah, you can keep it."

"Another brother?" Doughty passed the coffee shop with an armful of potato chips and beef jerky. "I thought I was the only black dude at this stop?"

"Where's this boy from, Brick?" Smith said.

"Texas."

"Texas?" Smith laughed. "Sorry, kid, Texan trumps black."

"Why am I getting dragged?"

"Get's some hair on your chest, and I'll tell you," Smith said.

"I thought you bought a shower, Doughty?" Bricklander said.

"Just taking some goodies in with me," he said, heading down the aisle.

"Goodies?" Smith smirked. "Any dude that uses the word *goodies* is softer than his mama's love.

"He's a good kid," Bricklander said.

"Even when the dead are biting?"

"No complaints, he does his job. So, I lost track when you went into contracting. How did you end up here?"

Smith glanced out the window and back at Bricklander. "Soon as I got back, I went out on contract with the Kurds. Got a little hairy,

191

lost myself a bit, and when it ended, I came home. Back in Central LA, for the first time in twenty years, and listened to the preacher tell me any brothers serving were Tom-ing for Uncle Sam. So, I slugged him."

"You slugged a preacher?" Belton said.

"Right there in the church. He knew who I was and thought he could chump me. Actually, I didn't just slug him. I beat the crap out of him." He gave a quick laugh at the memory. "I ended up doing 90-days in County for that. By the time the world ended, I was doing security in San Diego. Eventually, I transferred here."

"Glad your close, brother," Bricklander said.

"Man, Brick, it is so good to see you."

A moment passed between all three of them. No one spoke, but Bricklander was sure they were all reflecting on the roads bringing them to Brackett Field. He appreciated the men he was leading now, but Lancaster was the only one who could have sat at this table with him, Belton, and Smith.

These were the men he could start a conversation with, take a decade-long pause, and pick right up where they left off. These were the brothers he never had to ask or order what to do when caught in a storm of hate because they already knew.

"So you're still in San Quintana taking day trips to the mountains," Belton said.

"You heard?"

"I got nothing better to do with my radio."

"In that case, you want to fly the three of us to Virginia?"

"If I could get the fuel," Belton sighed. "Do you know what my daily routine is?"

Bricklander shook his head.

"I sit right here until NORM calls. I don't patrol. I don't do rescue. I just sit here." Belton was a lifer who rotated into Afghanistan after Smith left. "I got all that hate mounted on that machine, and NORM can't find a good enough reason to use it."

"You ever get in the air?" Bricklander said.

"Once a week, I fire up the engine and take a little spin round LaVerne, but that's it," he said. "I can't even drink the beer because they tell me I'm permanently on call. So, I listen to your chatter on the radio. I picked up your trip yesterday. I was surprised to hear Minister Kevin had the nad to stay overnight with the freaks on the hill."

"What about when our people get in a tight spot somewhere?"

"Unless NORM says so," Belton pointed down at the table. "Believe me, I'm itching to push a few buttons. I got a kid riding shotgun with me who's all Stars and Stripes. We're dying for a fight."

"NORM's a bastard," Smith said.

Bricklander raised his coffee in agreement and took a swig. "Well, since you're both parked here, what's the word?"

"You want to know if things are getting better?" Smith said.

"Yeah."

"How big do you want the lie?"

"The only thing NORM's got control of is us," Belton said. "NORM's the Feds, the Feds are NORM, the same people who invented DMVs. We've got resources to burn down a place like Sky Porch and that whole mountain. But they're working off computer models projecting things that aren't even close to happening."

"Models?" Bricklander said with disgust.

"There's scuttlebutt about clearing out and consolidating behind the Rockies before making a return in force to the coast," Belton added.

"NORM's saying that?"

The pilot nodded.

"That's the chatter," Smith said. "I find it hard to believe, but you never know."

"We can't even take back LA, and they think we're going to be able to leave and come back and retake the west coast?" Bricklander did an intentional shifting of his eyes around the empty coffee shop. "This ship's going down, isn't it?"

"Hence the rumors about pulling back," Belton said quietly. "Especially if the IE falls."

"You two sticking around for that show?"

"Tell me about Sky Porch," Belton said.

Bricklander shook his head. "All I can say is, if it opens, you can kiss the baby."

Smith and Belton exchanged looks to confirm, seemingly, a point from a previous conversation.

"You two sticking around?" he asked again.

"It's easy for us, Brick," Belton said. "I'm divorced with no kids."

"I'm neither," Smith said. "I'm free to kill another officer if I want."

"So you do think about bailing?"

"Every day," Belton said. "But where to?"

The sound of voices rising came from the store side.

"You fellas might want to see this," A truck driver interrupted them. He wore a Dodger baseball cap and a leather biker vest with a sweat-stained gray tank-top beneath. A United States Marine's *Semper Fidelis* tattoo highlighted his right bicep.

"What's up, Gus?" Smith said.

"You're not gonna believe it."

"I believe you're the cop around here, Smith," Belton said. "But we'll follow for the entertainment." The three trailed the truck driver into the retail area. Bricklander saw, stitched on the back of Gus's leather vest, *Sons' of Trump*.

"Gus from Bellflower!" Jose called out. "Want to deal some oranges?"

"Turn it up, Jose! And there ain't no Bellflower anymore."

Crowder and Gibson lined up behind Bricklander with open cans of beer in hand.

"What's going on?" Barnes said, walking up with an ice cream sandwich.

"Where you guys been?" The first sergeant asked.

"Arcade."

A breaking news graphic lit the flatscreen. Jose's first attempt to turn up the sound didn't work. He slammed the remote to the counter and tried again. "There we go."

"What's happening?" Gibson asked.

"I don't know," Bricklander said. Others crowded in anticipation.

A female reporter appeared in front of the capitol building.

"Oooh! That's Claire Peete," Crowder said. "That chick's got it!"

"I'll take that over, Holsopple," Gibson said. "Break us off some of that, right, Sarge?"

"Shut up," Bricklander said.

"Word out of the White House is the President will sign the agreement between both houses...."

The screen split, and the news anchor reappeared. He didn't have Claire Peete's body, so no one knew his name.

"She's torture," Jose said. "Mama! I'm ready to crack one-off right now."

"They need to pull back a little," Crowder said. "A strong wind can blow that skirt...."

"Crowder, chill," Bricklander said.

"Claire, is there going to be any legal challenge to this? There certainly must have been opposition. And when is the Supreme

Court expected to weigh in?"

"That's it!" said Gus, the former Marine. "That's what I heard! Listen!"

She put a hand to her earpiece, nodded, and then spoke. **"In normal times, of course, but Howard, with so much happening, the belief is scaling back the national election is the best approach to keeping things on track. All of the spokespeople here on the hill are very careful to point out that the measure was bipartisan. Both parties want this. I'm also getting word this was floated unofficially by Chief Justice Richards."**

"They just canceled the election," Gus said.

"Sources are telling us, Howard, given the extraordinary situation we are in, that lawmakers feel they have done the background work. They are sure this is legal and will stand against all the lawsuits expected to follow."

The worst people in the country to Bricklander were the NORM-supported ministers. Second, by the slimmest of margins were the politicians. They were all crooks, but the people wanted the right to vote for the crook of their choice. Fraudulent as it all was, an unelected crook still remained an unacceptable crook.

"None of the lawmakers I've spoken to wanted this. They based the move on where we are in terms of recovery. While things are getting better, a shakeup right now could set the nation and, even, the world back. Many expressed the clear burden the United States shoulders in leadership through this crisis. And that they must act with global intentions and not merely with national interests."

"Thank you, Claire." The anchor focused back on the camera. **"We're expecting to hear from the President within the hour on this fast-breaking story. Again, breaking this afternoon out of Washington DC, November's national**

election, which includes the office for President of the United States, has been scaled back. It will include only those living in the secured area of the District of Columbia. Congressional and Senatorial elections are canceled indefinitely."

"Doesn't sound like a big deal to me," Jose said. "It makes sense. Why rock the boat just when things are starting to get back on track?"

Jose was alone in his sentiment.

Bricklander imagined how this was playing in San Quintana.

"I can hear my dad screaming in Idaho," Gibson said.

"They can't do that!" Gus said.

"They just did," Smith said. "NORM's got his shack in DC, and homeboy ain't about to give that up."

"They say one thing and then do something else!" Gus said, kicking over a rack of water bottles.

"Dude!" Jose said. "Take it easy. I got to clean this place!"

"Gus," Smith said. "We're all upset, but if you can't hold it together, then you'll need to take it outside."

"What are you guys going to do?" Gus said to the soldiers. "You going to let them do this to us?" He issued an expletive. "I'm breaking the seal on my truck. If you've got something good to trade and want some oranges, come see me. I'm done." He marched out.

"What's the big fricken deal?" Jose said.

While it may have been lost on Jose, Bricklander knew the military had held together because the Constitution held them together. It held the country together because it kept in thought that the nation's fundamental laws remained intact. They were fighting, following orders, giving of themselves because it mattered. The United States mattered, and in that framework, a future was possible. And hope that a life with their families could return.

Now, especially for everyone outside of DC, that trust was broken. Were they fighting for a shared future or for the elites in high places? Bricklander felt a ticking in his heart. How long would the soldiers hold their posts? Why would anyone continue if the very thing they were fighting for was taken away?

Why does an election have to be canceled if things are getting better?

Bricklander likened it to where his hope would be if Rosa told him she found another man and someone else to be the father of their children. Three thousand miles away, there'd be nothing for him to do but give up on everything. Now three thousand miles away, the very thing the country had been using as a compass to recovery, the Constitution, was being shredded.

"Dictatorship," Gibson said. "My father said they'd use the name, the sound of the Constitution to keep us in line and obedient, but DC would run things like a dictatorship...." His voice tapered off. "It's really happening. I can't believe it...I really thought...."

"What? That this is America?" Jarvis said. "For them, it is." He shook his head at the screen. "For the rest of us," he exhaled a four-letter expletive, "it's the broken end of the bottle."

"NORM's the antichrist," Barnes kidded, but no one responded. The road trip's good cheer vanished. With one breaking news story, Stars and Stripes was dead.

"I gotta get home," Gibson said.

"Hey, Brick," Belton said. "They want me in the air to do a perimeter check. It's good to see you, and I'll keep an ear out for you as well."

"Stay safe, brother."

LARRY
(7)

The sun, like an egg sunny side up, shined with white clouds fluffing around it. By the amount of heat it gave, the day felt like early spring instead of approaching summer. The late morning was pretty, but things weren't right.

There was the question of Sky Porch. There was Owen, and, worse, there was nothing in sermon form building in Larry's brain. Walking The Garden's perimeter, he and Mason could hear the baseball game's sounds through the trees and structures.

"Doesn't it seem perfect at times?" Mason said. "All of this with the kids having fun, it makes me feel like I'm dreaming."

Beginning behind the amphitheater, they circled the lower meadow to the dining hall, the cabins, and Utility Road. Pausing there, they watched some of the game before circling behind the cabins on The Garden's north side.

Noel, playing left field with a half dozen kids around her, saw them and threw a wave. They answered in kind.

The Garden's immune, Larry thought.

It was easy to believe nothing bad could happen here. As if God had lifted The Garden from the terrestrial to the celestial. Larry wanted to declare it invulnerable to attack, but would that be bold faith or vanity?

"I used to hear about people going to church camp, but I never got this kind of picture in my head," Mason said. "I always thought it was a bunch of RV's and campers with tents."

"I went to junior high camp once," Larry said. "It was fun but gross. I was in a cabin with a youth pastor who got into a competition to see who could go the longest without showering."

"Sounds demented," Mason said.

"In those cabins, there was no ventilation. Just wooden slats, you slid open during the day but couldn't at night because of the animals."

Radio chatter stirred beneath their conversation. Every thirty minutes, security around the perimeter checked in.

"I should have tried it," Mason said. "My family was AG. Do you know what AG is?"

"Assemblies of God?" Larry said.

"Yeah, that's it. They used to pray so loud. It freaked me out."

The radio squawked.

"At the half-hour, we're clear at 19 and the Utility Road," Anspach said. **"Crazy Chang wants to know who's bringing lunch or if he needs to come pick it up."**

Mason ignored them. "That's why I got away from church. That, and everyone telling me God had great plans for me."

"Nothing else?" Larry didn't have to be a minister for twenty years to know that there was always something else when people stopped going to church. Departure from a congregation came with a long grocery list of reasons.

Larry never stopped going to church; he just stopped paying attention. Everything was about the Rapture, the Second Coming, and no time in history ever being as bad. It made being at church a bummer. Why be there when you could be at the beach with your friends feeling the breeze and riding waves?

"So we're AG and all into the tongues stuff," Mason said. "There was this Sunday night when the entire church was at the altar. Everyone—everyone, like 40 people—is commanding sickness and infirmity to leave. They're ordering demons out in Jesus' name in that weird way of talking."

"Doesn't sound very Free Wesleyan," Larry said.

Mason let out a small laugh. "No, it wasn't."

"Checking in from beyond the amphitheater, this is Big Leon, and Brewer—we're clear."

"...So we're there, and all of this is going on. The ladies in the church gathered around this girl who came that night with her friends. And I know I'm not supposed to say, 'hot looking chick,' but she was a hot looking chick. I mean, she had it all. We didn't get very many visitors, but that night we had four. Three girls and a guy—I mean, at least I think he was a guy...You know?"

Larry, knowing he missed critical developments in the sexual revolution, smirked but didn't speak.

"I mean, I was only about 14, but, suddenly, church was interesting again. I was hoping she'd stick around for a while. If she sticks around, I might want to get right with God as well—a bunch of us would. So she left her friends sitting in the back and makes it down to the altar. The ladies were praying her straight through the pearly gates when she busts out with what we joke about now. All that '*UntieMyBowWhoStoleMyHonda*' stuff, right? And everyone's praising God. They're hugging her, hugging each other, they're even hugging me. Then the Pastor says..."

"This is Kuykendall, with Hutch and Gavin, in the bush north of The Garden. Clear and hungry."

"...The Pastor says, '*this is proof the Holy Spirit's here with us tonight.*' Everyone is saying, '*Amen, Amen.*' Then the girl raises her hand to testify. She looks down and looks up with a massive grin. We're all ready to hear her redemption story... '*Fooled you!*' she shouts and walks away, laughing. In the back of the church, her friends stand up, busting with laughter, and they all leave."

"Best spot in town, fellas," Drew's voice came over the radio. "On top of the dining hall with Bash, ready for lunch as well."

"Serious?"

"What messed me up the most was the Pastor saying the Holy Spirit was there," Mason said. "But if the Holy Spirit was there, how come it didn't reveal to him the girl was a fraud? So that was really it for me. I was still a good kid. Grew up, I got a job, got married, and tried to have this really cool deal where my wife and I could each have a sex-buddy."

"Sex-buddy?" Another layer of the revolution Larry didn't comprehend.

"We didn't say sex. We used the f-word. We allowed each other to have an f-buddy."

"While you were married?"

"Yeah, because we convinced ourselves it was only sex and didn't mean anything." Mason's expression conveyed a personal stupidity. "Of course, everything fell apart. We got divorced, and eventually, I realized my life was screwed up. Then the virus hit," he looked at Larry, "The Tilt happened."

The Tilt happened to all of us.

"The sucked part is," Mason continued. "I wanted to find my ex-wife and try to make things right. We loved each other in the beginning, but we listened to everybody else. I still love her, but I don't know if she's alive or dead."

"Did someone say we have wings?" Bash said.

"Jerk!" Anspach said.

"There are no wings," Drew clarified.

"I got movement," Kuykendall said.

"I was on the short end that day, Bash," Anspach said.

"Say that again, Big K.," Drew said.

Larry and Mason stopped their conversation.

"I got big movement..."

BRICKLANDER
(6)

"DC's safe because we're standing post and keeping the lights on," Jarvis said. "They ain't giving that up."

"Not unless we do something," Gibson said.

The heat was building inside the truck stop. Commerce came to a halt as people began weighing what the announcement meant for them and their future.

Bricklander's mind went to Virginia and what may be happening there. He stored the anger coming alive in him but saw it growing in his men. The thought of mutiny, no longer abstract, now had definable features.

"Nothing changes," Farmer said. "Our mission's the same. Our responsibilities are still here."

"Sarge," Barnes said in a begging tone. "What should we do?"

Bricklander looked at them. "We keep working because our brothers depend on us to keep their people safe—and we depend on them to do the same."

They'd been juggling hand grenades since the virus came. The people may have been scared, but they weren't stupid. Anyone could die at any time. A pause in focus the span of eye-blink could punch someone's ticket. The decision on the election was a loss of focus, leaving the country only a few small steps from collapse.

Stars and Stripes had cultivated hope and was an easy buy-in. No matter the crisis, sneak attack, or virus, America always won.

Almost divinely, the USA found the better angels of its nature through terrible times and gained victory.

Americans believed they'd always conquer and overcome. If not in the literal, it was in the figurative DNA of the citizenry. American exceptionalism, embarrassing to the politicians before the virus, became good business after its arrival. From the get-go, it was the foundation of all propaganda out of DC.

The cancelation of the election was a hard kick to the gut. Like a bad meal in the stomach, it just rang wrong, hurt bad, and thumped in a way that couldn't be ignored. To Bricklander, Uncle Sam had punched his own ticket.

"NORM controls everything," Gibson said. "They control it because they got us taking all the risk. If we all walk, they're done."

"Gibby, is your butt covered back home?" Bricklander said. "I know mine's not. I've got a family in Virginia, and I depend on guys like you to do their frickin jobs to keep them alive. You've got family in Idaho. Some of you have family up 395. Do you want those guys to walk?"

The double doors opened, and another driver came inside.

"What did you guys say to the dude hauling oranges?"

"What's he doing?" Farmer asked.

The truck driver, sickly looking and reeking body odor, tossed an orange into the air and caught it. "He's screaming and emptying the back of his truck."

They raced outside in time to see Gus, formerly of Bellflower, climb back inside his Peterbilt and gun the engine. Hundreds of oranges were littered across the pavement.

"You don't think he's stupid enough..." Farmer started and then stopped when the truck began to accelerate toward the closed gate.

Cliff Smith and three other security members opened fire as the truck rammed onto McKinnley Avenue. An alarm let everyone know there was a perimeter breach—and notified every ghoul in the vicinity of an opportunity.

Farmer looked at Bricklander. "Brick, plug that hole. I'll get the alarm turned off."

Without word, Jarvis, Barnes, Crowder, and Gibson sprinted with Bricklander for the truck and their weapons.

Gus's gas tank exploded. Fire consumed the rig as it ran up the side of a hill and rolled on its side.

The soldiers, taking their M4s, found a box of oranges in the bed.

"Well, that was cool of him," Barnes said.

"Dang," Crowder said. "There must 50 oranges in that box!"

"75," Jarvis said, pulling his lever and releasing it to chamber a round. "And we ain't sharing."

"Oh hell no!' Crowder ratified.

"Focus," Bricklander ordered. "Take direction from security. They're the home team."

Another truck, racing out of the yard, took care of the four dead that had entered.

Smith waved for Bricklander and his men to join him.

"What do you need, Cliff?"

"They can only come from one direction," Smith said. "I need your men to hold the road while my guys reset the gate."

"Bayonets!" Bricklander said.

The soldiers walked carefully onto McKinnley. The heat of the burning truck pressed around them, but the fire on the hillside didn't spread. The stink of the dead became acrid as they picked up the low cull of growling headed their way.

"Hold on!" The first sergeant yelled. "Wait for my word. Let them get a little closer. Hold on…

"How long?" Barnes said.

"Okay, light'em up!"

JOAB
(7)

Mountain Road 27 narrowed after it t-boned into Highway 19. Two slim lanes lined with pine trees on both sides stretched east. Its benefit was a comfortable canopy of daytime shadow and a relatively flat grade.

Bird, in the Chevy Cavalier, was playing lookout. It was a good idea, but since The Tilt—compounded by memories of the

Bradbury Church rafters—Joab always sided with movement. Going through the front door and then immediately locating the backdoor was instinct now.

"I guess when you're five-two, anything's possible," Duran said and then looked at Jay. "Sorry, didn't mean anything by it."

"I'm five-six, jackwagon," Jay said.

"I'm sorry about that too."

They kept moving.

"Talk, but keep your eyes wide," Joab said. "Don't get lulled to sleep."

He walked on the left, and ten yards behind him was Wheeler. Directly to Wheeler's right was Duran. Trailing was Jay, who spun periodically to make sure nothing was gaining. Because devils often shuffled and dragged a limb or spilled entrail, they weren't good coming up from behind. And in anticipation of a victim, they let out a growl or hiss. But if someone was distracted, the dead could, seemingly, materialize from nowhere. And when it happened, there was no Mulligan to take—no do-over to protest for.

Joab was beginning to notice the devils also had motivation beyond hunger or a need to feed. Their blatant hatred for the living put things in play the secular world didn't, couldn't, or wouldn't admit. Giving the dead intentions and spiritual components moved the deliberative needle from science to theology. And that was a no-go zone.

"Let's say a herd comes, and Bird warns us," Wheeler said. "Are we going to double back for him?"

"Bird's a big boy, figuratively," Joab said. "If a train of devils rolls down, we're re-routing, and so is he."

"I wouldn't worry about Bird," Jay said to Wheeler. "Guy's got ruby slippers. He clicks his heels, and he's there for lunch, or patrol, or twenty feet up in a tree."

"Ruby slippers?" Wheeler said.

"Really?" Jay said.

"I don't know what you're talking about."

"You never saw the Wizard of Oz?"

"You mean the remake?" Wheeler said. "No, I didn't see it."

As long as it stayed peaceful, devil-free, the walk was refreshing. The road was easy, and the shade got better by the step. Again the scent of pines hit them, and, again, Joab had to remind himself it was closer to the end of the world than the beginning…

Ping.

…And his life was reduced, rightfully, to mending the things he broke in ministry before The Tilt.

"To preach and teach justice is to preach and teach Jesus." He once wrote. *"Be like Jesus, love the unlovable, but don't get caught up in repeating the magic words of salvation. As if salvation, something already attained, could or should be purchased again. Or even something necessary to ask for. Action, action, action is*

our calling and mission."

Ping.

"So, Wheeler, tell me about Roberta," Joab said to distract his memories.

"I don't know if that's a good idea, Jefe," Jay said. "Wheeler's a little sensitive about the Roberta subject."

Joab could hear both Jay and Duran squashing down a laugh.

"We can leave it alone," Wheeler said.

For the moment, they walked in silence. The wind, either in their favor or remarkably clear, bore no odor of the dead. Here, outside of Cumberland, may have been Joab's most pleasant walk in the mountains since his high school camping days at Tara Pines.

"Duran, this is strange," he said. "Is that creek bed winding into Cumberland? Because I don't hear any water running, and I don't smell the devils. I thought we would've by now."

Duran reached for his map, and they stopped. It was never good to walk and read at the same time. Jay kept his back to them and his eyes in the direction of 19. Wheeler looked north and into the woods. Joab went a few more steps and faced the south side of the road into the forest.

"Just ahead, we're going to come to a bend," Duran said. "And according to the map, the creek runs around this hill at one o'clock." He pointed to the east and off to the right. "You can see the hill through the trees. On the other side, it converges with Cumberland. Plus, we've been through Cumberland before. We've seen the creek and the bridge."

"I know," Joab said, seeing the hill. "Maybe because the day's so nice, it just didn't seem right. I was worried there was another creek. It's throwing me off. Let's go. Maybe they got a coffee shop in C-Town."

"Cumberland's not C-Town, Chief," Jay said. "Covina is C-Town. Monrovia is M-Town. Alhambra is A-Town. Cumberland is only Cumberland."

"Alright then," Joab said, and they started to move. "Let's get to Cumberland and find some coffee."

"Ravioli," Jay said. "You keep your coffee. I need authentic Italian ravioli."

"Wouldn't that be a bummer?" Wheeler said.

"Why?" Jay asked.

"To find a functioning restaurant after all this time and have it be Italian?" Wheeler said. "That's just too depressing."

"You gotta be kidding me, Wheeler?" Joab said.

"I think it's time we talked about Roberta," Jay said.

"We don't need to talk about Roberta," Wheeler countered.

"Yeah, we need to talk about Roberta!" Jay and Duran repeated in chorus.

There was nothing fresh to debate. No sports sites to browse. No ESPN to watch. No baseball, no football, no big fight on the docket in Las Vegas. And Joab had put the kibosh on all talk about The Garden's single women's plusses and minuses.

Everyone—save for the married men, Joab, Drew, and Larry— talked about the women in private. Noel was the prize but was hands-off for two reasons. One, they held her in too high regard. Two, Joab watched over her like a hawk.

Without discussion Mountain Road 27 was becoming a lullaby and way too comfortable. The Roberta story had legs and, in Joab's thinking, became necessary to keep them sharp.

"I need to hear it, Wheeler," he said. "I give you my word. What happens in Cumberland stays in Cumberland."

"We've got about a quarter-mile," Duran said. "There's time."

The road began to bend, and the hill hidden behind the forest fell into view. A green road sign with white printing welcomed them to Cumberland: population 110.

A minute later, completing the curve, Joab saw it.

"I've got this," he said.

Twenty yards ahead, a devil was feeding on the carcass of a deer. A few seconds later, the odor hit. Subtle, faint, but enough to let them know the devil wasn't alone. Joab unsheathed his machete.

"You still want to hear about Roberta?" Jay said.

"Lay it on me."

The devil was oblivious to their approach.

"Wheeler was popular in school," Jay started. "He was Sammy Wheeler, starting wide receiver, and junior college-bound."

"That true, Wheeler?" Joab said as the devil's eyes turned from its recent kill. "You a football player?"

"It's true," Wheeler said, his tone happy to share. "Best hands in the Valle Vista League."

"According to Wolfman, Wheeler got elected Prom King," Jay said.

"Give me a second, guys." The devil came towards him, and it was evident hunger wasn't the motivation. Closing the distance in a jog, Joab swung the machete through the top of the skull and then kicked it backward.

"Okay," Joab said. "Wheeler's Prom King, go ahead." He wiped the machete off on the devil's dirty slacks. The remnant of a button-down shirt with a loosely fastened tie indicated it wasn't a Cumberland native. There were only two button-down-shirt-wearing communities in these mountains; Sky Porch and Big Sky.

"We good?" Duran asked as the rest of the men came closer.

"We're good. Finish the story."

"So Wheeler's elected Prom King," Jay went on. "And…" A smile creased his face.

"Yeah?" Joab said. "Go on…"

"That's it," Wheeler said. "I was elected Prom King. That's the story."

"Where does Roberta come in?"

"Roberta was elected Prom Queen," Jay said.

The forest thinned as they came into full view of Cumberland. Small shops, cabins, and zero stoplights. The two lanes narrowed into a single road. Slowly they continued. The options to Joab were to either sweep the town carefully, door to door, or speed through to the bridge stretching over the creek.

"Was she a dog?"

"Dog? Yes," Duran chimed. "She? No."

"I don't understand."

"Roberta," Jay jumped back into the lead of the conversation, "was actually a Robert, who became Roberta."

"That's it?" Joab said. "That's the story you've been sitting on?" Wheeler nodded. "Well, I might have sat on that one myself."

"They wanted us to share a dance," Wheeler said.

"Did you?"

"No."

"Did you get in trouble?"

"Yes."

"What did they do to you?"

"They wouldn't let me march at graduation unless I publicly apologized in front of the whole school. I wouldn't, so they sent my diploma in the mail. And when the junior college found out through the message boards, they wouldn't let me play unless I wrote an apology. I wouldn't, and that was that."

"Good for you," Joab said. "Of course, if I'd been your youth pastor, I'd have been all over you for being judgmental."

"Good thing you weren't," Wheeler said.

Joab looked thoughtfully at him. "I'm so sorry people like me put people like you in spots like that." He shook his head. "We were Woke in sheep's clothing."

"Did Roberta cry?" Jay said.

"Yeah, they tried to guilt me, and I wouldn't bend. I got unfriended by a bunch of people, but a few friends stuck by me. The newspaper did a blurb, and I got a lot of hate blown my way. So did my parents."

"Was it because of your faith?" Joab pressed.

"A little bit, but I just wasn't going to let anyone force me. No one was going to tell me what to think or how to believe."

"Wow," Joab said. "And it cost you, I am sorry." He knew Wheeler wasn't pinning this on him, but he felt responsible.

Ping.

Paused, at the entrance to Cumberland, they waited for movement and tried to pick up sounds beyond the breeze rushing through tree branches.

"Sweep or sprint?" Duran said.

"Okay, even if we can't see them, we can smell them," Joab said. "So I say sprint. We're gonna take this sucker right down the middle, get to the bridge, get a gander, and get out. Chatter ends here. Watch our flanks. Jay, protect our six."

"And what are we looking for again, exactly?" Jay said.

"We want to see if the devils are exiting down the mountain from Sky Porch via the creek bed or if they came to Cumberland from Big Sky," Duran said. "If there's a traffic jam of devils in the creek..."

"...Then we're in good shape at The Garden," Wheeler concluded. "It means the devils from Sky Porch are bypassing Highway 19."

"That's it," Joab said, pulling his machete back out. "Alright, blades before bullets. The only thing we're stopping for is the Italian restaurant."

They took the main street three-wide. Joab in the center, Wheeler to the left, Duran to the right, and Jay a few steps behind. The smell of death grew. Cumberland was alive with the dead, and Joab laughed inwardly at the paradox. "You guys feel that?"

"Feel what?" Jay said.

"Doom?" Duran said.

"Yeah," Joab said. "The closer we get to crowds of them, despair grows."

"That's what that is then," Wheeler said. "I feel it. I've always felt it."

"I don't," Jay said. "I just smell the stink."

A faded, decaying boardwalk connected shops on either side of the road. They were individual structures with similar front windows, doors, and porches. An emergent weed here and there rose to daylight in spaces beneath the boards.

An art shop, tea shop, head shop on the south side was matched on the north by a used book shop, another art shop, and coffee shop. A small general store, doubling as a post office with a tattered American flag hanging upside down, cornered a ten-yard intersection. Across from it, on the north side, was a cabin with a jutting sign reading, "Palm & Tea Leaf Blessings."

Further down, on both sides, were small cabins built in the same manner as the shops. Battered and weathered wood, battered and weathered picket fences protecting small yards of overgrown grass and weeds.

Joab raised a hand, and they stopped. He looked at Duran, who shook his head. Then to Jay, who shook his head. Then to Wheeler, who gave him a nod. Noise arrived in the small intersection as the devils came out of the tall weeds. Joab counted before acting. There were only eight.

"Take'em down or bypass them, Jefe?" Wheeler said.

"Let's go see the bridge," Joab answered.

Then a mob stepped out from between the buildings in front of them. The total now was more than two dozen.

"I got some bad guys back here as well," Jay said.

Duran didn't wait. Putting his machete to work, he lobotomized the first devil to get close.

"Cabin, right here!" Joab said. He went to the porch rail of the psychic reading business and dispatched the devil standing there. "On the awning of the porch, onto the roofs, and we'll hop out of here."

Jay sheathed his blade and went to work with three shotgun blasts.

Joab went up, then Duran. They reached and pulled Wheeler to the roof as Jay unloaded his Remington 870. When Wheeler was secure, Duran fired twice, and Jay quickly scrambled to the top.

The devils, now pushing forty, gathered around the base of the porch, hating and howling.

"These cabins are only a few feet apart," Joab said. "We'll hop across them to the bridge. It should give us some distance. Jay, take the lead!"

The smaller man went over the peak of the cabin and hopped across. Wheeler followed. Duran patted Joab on the back for him to go while he fired twice more into the mob to keep them seething.

When Duran reached the second cabin, Wheeler was crossing over to the third with Joab close behind. The smell of devils grew stronger even as the noise of the mob grew distant.

Jay cleared to the fourth cabin. "I can see the bridge!" He leaped for the fifth as Wheeler jumped to the fourth and went through the roof.

"Wheeler!" Duran yelled, hopped across, but Joab kept him from going in.

"Go to Jay!" Joab said, pointing to the edge of the cabin. Duran did and landed safely.

Wheeler screamed.

Joab looked down into the dark…

…*Ping*…

…And leaped in.

NOEL
(6)

When Noel saw Larry and Mason move out of view, she didn't think anything until Drew jumped from the dining hall. Shotgun slung, he didn't sprint across the field. Fast walking, he tried to give the impression he wasn't running to danger.

Teddy was at-bat. Ken, his father, was pitching. The kids were aware of only the game. Wolfman was still sitting on the picnic tables, and Sandoval was still in place by the vehicles. They weren't racing anywhere.

Drew came by Noel in left-center.

"Everything okay?"

He smiled and gave her a thumbs up. If Noel's day needed to get a little bit better, it had. She beat back the voice chirping in her head about being selfish. Selfish would have been chasing after Drew.

Teddy popped out to his dad.

"Dad!" he said.

"Ah, Ken," she crowed, proud of her choice to stay with the game. "Give him something to hit!"

"Yeah, Dad!" Beth said, sitting with the kids and a happy Tammy under the shade of trees. "You're supposed to drop those! Come on, don't be such a brute!"

"Hey, do you want to do it?" Ken said, hands apart to the crowd as Todd picked up a bat. "This isn't as easy as it looks."

"You're supposed to let your kid hit a home run, jerk!" Liz called from outside the dining hall. Liz's gift was a lack of filter. No one had to wait for Liz's opinion because she always gave it. A widowed mom of three—none at The Garden—Liz lived a hard life before The Tilt and only softened when talking about her moment of salvation.

"I never thought I'd long to live, Noel," Liz said to her.

"That's exactly, I mean exactly, how I felt," Noel answered.

"Yeah, Ted!" Wolfman called. "Don't suck!" He high-fived an approving Liz from a distance.

It feels like a real baseball game, Noel thought. *One ball, one bat, 100 experts.*

It was Todd's turn. He batted left-handed. In his first at-bat, he bounced the ball to first base. The second time he popped up. Noel didn't have to be standing next to him to know he was frustrated.

He'd waited all this time to play baseball, and when he finally got to play, he had to do it with a tennis ball. Gavin, his dad, was working security. Candida, his mom, sweet but sad, was most likely sleeping. Noel kicked herself for not foreseeing this--Todd needed his parents.

"Watch out for this guy, Ken!" she said, cupping her hands. "He thinks he's Reggie Jackson!"

"Who's Reggie Jackson?" A healthy Aaron asked from center-field.

"Mr. October?" she said, running around him to get into position in right. "Man, you kids don't know anything."

"You're like one year older than me," Aaron muttered. "Who's Reggie Jackson?"

Todd barely tipped a ball foul and hit the head of the bat to the ground.

"Last batter before lunch!" Karla called.

Noel positioned herself next to Darcy, who was busy talking to her boyfriend, Ryan. He was sitting in a beach chair down the first baseline. Getting closer by the day, they were, maybe, a week away from making out in public. Everyone was sure Ryan and Darcy were already making out in private. They were 15, and Noel prayed again that she didn't look as stupid or obvious when fawning over Drew.

"Come on, give him something to hit, Ken!" Liz yelled again. "Do we need to dust off home plate?"

"Take it easy," Ken said.

Noel's plan was—as Ken's next pitch was out of the strike zone—if Todd hit the ball high, she'd charge and let it go over her head. If he hit it at her, she'd play the part of a girl and duck. As long as he hit it, he was going to get on base.

Another pitch by Ken went wide.

"Let's go!" Karla barked again. "Lunch is getting cold!"

"Bring in a reliever!" Wolfman heckled.

"What are you talking about?" Ken said. "Lunch is always cold."

"Get with it, Ken!" Beth shouted. "You afraid of him? Give him something to hit, or you're not getting any lunch!"

Everyone laughed but Todd.

"Come on, kid," Noel whispered. "Come on..."

Another pitch was short. Todd swung and tipped it foul.

"I thought you said this kid was the next Reggie Johnson?" Aaron said.

"Jackson, Aaron! I said, 'Reggie Jackson!'"

"Whatever," he said. "You're weird."

If they only knew how weird Larry and I were.

Ken got the pitch over the plate, and Noel saw—as if in slow motion—Todd hold back, lock his eyes, and turn on the ball. It cleared second base, and before she could pretend to misjudge it, it cleared her and was by Darcy before she could ask what was going on.

Aaron chased after it as Todd scrambled around first base and then second. The Garden cheered.

"Oh Todd," Noel felt burden come off her. This was a great moment.

Your parents should have been here.

Rounding third, Todd headed for home. Those that had been sitting were now standing and applauding. They knew what it meant to Todd, what it meant for him to swing the bat.

Then he stopped halfway to home plate.

"Go, Todd! We love you!" Alison yelled, clapping her hands.

The cheering continued for a few seconds and then ended. No one knew what was going on. For a moment, Noel thought a devil had come into view.

"Run it out, slugger!" Bash called from the top of the dining hall. "You got it!"

Todd put his head down, and Noel ran to him. He was sobbing.

"What do you say, Todd?" Wolfman said, coming closer. "Step on that plate, brother!"

"Go to lunch! Just go to lunch!" Noel said, waving her hands on arrival.

The adults began corralling the kids and moving to the dining hall.

"Friend," she said, kneeling in front of him. "You just hit a home run. That was awesome!"

He wasn't in hysterics, but having the simple cry one might have at the end of a movie. The type of tears that came when something was over and all there was left to do was cry.

"Todd, what's wrong?" she said. "What do you need?" She put a hand to his shoulder. "Tell me."

He quivered and drew in a breath. Then he looked at Noel.

"It's never going to be the same, is it?"

"Oh Todd, I don't know," Noel said. "Maybe someday, maybe it'll be something better."

He looked home plate.

"I was happy," he said, "but I saw home plate, and I knew. I just knew."

"What did you just know, Todd?"

"I'm never going to see my sister again. I'm never going to play Little League again. It's a Frisbee for home plate. I hit a tennis ball, and I knew." The crying picked up. Noel hugged him but received zero response.

Todd pulled his head back with a loud sniffle. "Can I go to lunch now?"

"Sure," she said. "Or we can talk?"

He walked from her to the dining hall. The wind gusted, and the scent of pines came strongly. It was beautiful but still false. She didn't need to smell death to know evil was doing its thing because evil's best talent was stealing hope.

LARRY
(8)

"Everyone hold..." Drew said. **"Are you safe?"**

Larry and Mason ran for the hill on the north side of the cabins. When devils came near before, it was down the mountain's small, ancient paths.

"We're holding still..." Kuykendall's voice came through the static.

"I'm on my way," Drew said. **"No one else move!"**

Mason, pulling his machete, took the lead, and Larry realized he didn't have anything to fight with. Not much was needed beyond willingness when confronting a single devil, but confronting several was something else.

They crunched through the brush and fallen leaves until Mason raised the machete for him to stop. "Listen," he said.

"What's the count, Big K.?" Drew's voice came through the radio.

Mason lowered the blade and motioned for Larry to tiptoe with him. It wasn't his first time in the midst of things. He kept eyes on Mason and ears honed for a bad sound.

"They're...right...on...us..." Kuykendall whispered.

Heavy footfalls came behind them. Mason and Larry paused and spun their eyes in an arc. Raising his blade, Mason stepped in front of Larry. More steps, then, fifteen yards away, Drew emerged. All three shared a smile of relief.

Shotgun blasts broke the quiet above them.

They raced to the sound.

"Everyone hold!" Drew shouted into his radio for the others on watch.

The grade of the hill produced a clearing and a pack of devils with it. Larry counted eight.

Mason caught the first with a right-handed swipe of his machete. Drew fired his shotgun twice. Mason's blade got wedged inside the next devil, with two more closing in. Larry churned his legs and launched into the attackers.

Two devils landed with Larry in a bed of shrubs. A mouth clamped down on his right hand. The teeth cut, but they weren't razor-sharp. Flat, crumbling incisors gnawed to the bones on his knuckles. His back, pinning the second devil over a thick bush, had branches dig into his shoulders. Larry's feet were in the air, and the devil chewing on his hand was on top.

More shotguns spoke nearby and in the distance.

Larry swung with his left hand while trying to shake the right free. He punched and punched until his fist went through its softened skull. Looking upside down, he saw Drew bringing the butt of his shotgun down on the pinned devil as he rolled off.

Mason picked him up. His hand throbbed and bled.

"No!" Mason said, grabbing the hand. "Larry…I'm sorry!"

"I'm gonna be fine," he said with a wince. Being fine didn't mean without pain. It hurt.

Mason ripped off his gray tee shirt and wrapped the wound. "We can't lose you!"

"Mason," Larry put his left hand on the man's shoulder and met his eyes. "I'm gonna be fine."

Three more shots came, there was yelling, another blast, and then it got quiet.

Drew led them up the slope.

"Kuykendall?" he said into his radio.

"We're going to need some help." The voice was Gavin's.

Drew told Larry to go back, but he continued. They moved through an opening in the trees and bushes until it leveled. There was a path spilling to the left. The year before, they reasoned, this was the trail devils took to reach The Garden. It was the easiest way for them to come down the hill.

"You guys going to tell us what's going on?" Anspach called over the line.

"We're alive," Gavin said.

Thirty seconds later, they found them. Hutchinson was wrapping Kuykendall's leg. His left arm already had a blood-soaked bandage on it. Small trickles of blood were streaking down to his elbow.

"Can you believe this?" Kuykendall said with a grin.

"What happened?" Drew said.

Larry got closer to Kuykendall and kneeled alongside Hutchinson.

"He got bit in the leg," Hutchinson said, "and his arm is mangled above the elbow."

"Leg hurts worse than the arm," Kuykendall said.

"We saw a dozen moving--right where we expected them to be," Gavin said. "We hid in the brush. The plan was to let them pass and take them from behind and then..." He stopped and shook his head.

"...Another mob hit you?" Drew said.

Gavin nodded. "We were careful," he said, still trembling. "But it was close. I don't know where that other group came from."

"Praise God, you guys are okay," Larry said, feeling at his right hand.

"You bit?" Gavin asked.

"He didn't cut himself shaving," Mason said, walking past the two and further up the trail. "We got a problem, Drew."

"Besides this mess," Drew said, "what else is there?"

Finished with Kuykendall, Hutchinson joined Mason and Drew.

"You gonna be okay, Big K.?" Larry said.

"Do I get bonus pay for this?"

"Yeah, we'll hustle you up a plate of wings."

"Promise me a pizza, and I'll let them have another bite," he grimaced.

Larry smiled at the big man, who was still joyful. "What's at the other end of this stretch, guys?" He asked, feeling like he needed to let it go and focus on Gavin. The married man, still rattled ran a canteen over his head, and shook the water free from his beard.

"There's a trail further up covered by the brush," Mason said. "We knew about this one." He pointed to the one the men had been keeping an eye on. "But this other one didn't show, and the way they came around on you guys, it means there has to be another. And that's our problem. Devils don't work through the thickets unless they got fast-food in sight."

"Where did these devils come from?" Hutchinson said. "For our sake, it better be Big Sky."

"I'm guessing bleeders from Big Sky," Drew said. "It's too soon for Sky Porch."

"If they're from Sky Porch," Hutchinson sighed, "that's ball game."

"That was a mob that hit us," Gavin said. "It wasn't just bleeders."

There was a rush of nerves that hadn't been there when the devils were attacking. Larry put his trust in Joab and his men. They could handle it. Right now, they needed to get Kuykendall back to camp, and Gavin was going to need time to chill.

"I don't think Big K. can walk," Hutchinson said.

"Big man," Drew said. "I'm going to need you to hop part of the way down. I'll get Bash to meet us along the way in the golf cart. Larry, you and Gavin go into camp. I'll have Bash stay with Hutch, Mason, and me. We'll figure out a short fix."

"I'm thinking we come back down the grade to where the opening is," Mason said. "It's defendable, and they shouldn't be able to flank us so easily."

"Makes the most sense," Drew said. "We can talk about something permanent when Joab gets back."

"Flank us?" Gavin said. "You know what that sounds like?"

"Strategy," Drew said.

"Intelligence," Mason added, and they all shared a shiver.

"Have we heard from Joab?" Gavin asked.

Larry shook his head. "Not yet."

BRICKLANDER
(7)

The Battle of Brackett Field easily won, but the mood going home was joyless. The election announcement wrecked the pleasure of the get-away day from San Quintana.

Bricklander, reading the faces and body language, wouldn't have blamed them if they cut out.

"It was with a heavy heart that I read the proposal that came from congress."

Through a single earbud, he listened to the President address the nation while hearing the men talk. Doughty, beside him, freshly showered, was eating oranges and drinking beers with Jarvis and Crowder. Gibson only stared at the passing road.

"While I understand their motives were not political but practical, I also, selfishly, did not want this to be part of my legacy. No matter the circumstances, no matter the crisis, the American people deserve an honest and fair election. I seek to continue to be your President, but I wish it done the traditional way. The American way."

Crowder fired an empty beer can onto the freeway. Doughty tossed another.

"Be cool," Jarvis said. "And don't think about bailing."

"If Abraham Lincoln was able to conduct a fair and honest election during the Civil War, I knew it was what I wanted also. In doing so, Lincoln took extraordinary measures. Make no mistake; we will still be holding an election for the office of President. It will still be national in scope. The varied and

diverse population we have in the District of Columbia ensures representation of the entire country. Some will criticize, and that is their right. Still, my purpose for signing this extraordinary—bipartisan measure—is to preserve the United States of America for ourselves, our children, and our children's children."

"If I had someplace to go, I'd consider it," Crowder said, taking another orange. "I'm from here, Granada Hills, and what's left of my family is up the 395. Even if I could get away with desertion, I wouldn't want to live in one of those camps."

"And if you desert, they ain't going to let you," Doughty said. He took an orange and held it to his nose. "I'd go back to Texas, but how would I get there?"

No one offered an answer as the truck bounced on I-10.

"I think Gus, the truck driver, was more Stars and Stripes than any of us," Gibson said.

"Gus is extra-crispy right now," Jarvis clarified. "He acted like a fool and died like one."

"I don't know, and I don't care," Crowder said. "Because if we're talking like this, everyone else is, and it's all just a matter of time."

Gibson turned and looked past his friends to Bricklander, who pulled the earbud. "I'm leaving Sarge," he said. "I love all you guys…But first chance I get, I'm gone."

JOAB
(8)

Joab landed on a table, and its legs gave out, carrying him into a paneled wall that cracked when he rammed into it. Focusing through shadow and dust, he saw a devil biting into Wheeler's shoulder and another locked by its teeth onto a forearm.

Lunging, Joab grabbed for the one on the shoulder. His hands slid down, peeling strips of skin came before he could pry it loose. Smashing its head into the wall by the front door, black blood flowed. The second devil lost its grip and fell, and Wheeler used the heel of his shoe to crush its skull.

The front door pushed open. A devil entered, but Joab shoved it back to the porch. With more coming, he let go and closed the door. Putting his back against it, he felt for a lock and turned it as pounding came from the other side.

Wheeler, shotgun in hand, was disoriented and staggering.

"Wheeler!" Joab yelled. "Find a backdoor!" The pressure from outside pushed him forward. He tried to dig in, but his boots slid as the rotting shag carpet began to rip. "I can't hold it!"

Wheeler came towards him.

"No! Backdoor!"

Hands broke through the window to Joab's left and began to feel for him. They ran over his forehead and chin. His shotgun was on the floor next to the demolished table. More force came against the door. "I can't hold them!"

Wheeler stepped to the window and cut loose with his shotgun. After five rapid rounds, he backed away and kneeled to reload. The pressure, briefly, eased but mounted again.

Firing came from the outside.

With blood running out of him, Wheeler finished loading and chambering his shotgun, then raised the barrel upright, but not himself.

The door splintered and broke. Leaping to the other side of the living room, Joab picked up his shotgun as the devils rushed in. Wheeler fired three rounds before folding. Aiming high, Joab fired. The recoil jabbed against his shoulder and sent his second blast wild. Adjusting for the third, he sent a hail storm of buckshot through the devils.

Pulling his pistol, Joab aimed as a devil took another bite out of Wheeler. He fired, but they kept coming. Using his machete, he fired and slashed, fired, and slashed, fired, and slashed.

With multiple rounds going, he couldn't hear but felt the click of the pistol. Putting both hands on the blade's handle, he swung. Black blood sprayed his face and painted his clothes. Through the fog of the fight, Joab wasn't aware he was breathing. All that mattered was finishing them. There was no panic but essential focus as he worked the machete in an aimed frenzy. This was clarity.

He continued to slash, going through the door, more shotgun fire came. On the overgrown yard, a devil came face to face with him, not running--none of them ran. They never cowered; their evil was always heroic. His blade slipped from his hands as he stumbled into it. They crashed into a dilapidated picket fence and landed on the road.

Machete gone, he hammered away with his fists until its skull opened, and he was able to rip apart its mushy brain.

"Joab, I hope you learn sooner than later that you're not as smart as you think."

Shots passed through the air above, and the fog lifted. Joab moved off the devil's chest and stayed on his knees. Arching back, he raised his hands and knew what he wanted most; a touch from heaven—a taste of the one form of forgiveness that had never come.

Memory loss.

Ping.

"Joab?"

Breathing heavily, he saw Duran a few feet away from him.

"You good?"

He looked down, then back across the yard, to the house's porch, where Jay stood by the door. Bodies of devils were littered everywhere.

"Wheeler's had it," Jay said.

Ping.

"Joab, we've got to go," Duran said, "we've got to go now."

NOEL
(7)

"Thank goodness for peanut butter," Karla said.

Standing by the fireplace, Noel watched the consumption of peanut butter and jelly sandwiches and potato chips. The Garden's official beverage, thin lemonade, was the drink. Karla, with her bobbed black and gray hair, was next to her.

"If it wasn't for the peanut butter, these people wouldn't be getting any protein."

"All these people and nobody who knows how to kill and clean a deer," Noel said. "Not even Joab."

Karla stood closer so as not to be overheard. "The good news is, we've got enough food. Bad news is, enough is all we got. If anyone else comes..." She stopped and issued a serious expression.

"I understand."

"We're gonna have to try planting food again," she said, raising some lemonade to her mouth. "We don't have a farmer, a gardener, but if your computer breaks down, we got you covered."

Noel smiled. "The only farmers I knew grew pot."

"Ever smoke it?" Karla said.

"Sophomore year, friends and I went to the park across the street from school."

"And?"

"I puked my guts out before we finished. After that, I just stuck to guys."

"I had a good time for a long time," Karla said as they continued to look at everyone else. "But it made me fat. If it weren't for The Tilt, they'd be calling me Big Karla."

"I spoke to Kiln, Charles, I mean," Noel clarified, "and he thinks most of the land we're on doesn't go very deep before it hits solid rock. I think we should build planters behind the kitchen, but then we have to start talking about fertilizer."

"I know what it smells like, but I don't know how to make it."

"I don't know if I want to know." Noel saw Wolfman by the back corner window with a cute brunette from Owen's group. "What's Wolfman doing over there?"

"Sweetie," Karla laughed, "that's why he's called Wolfman."

Anytime Owen came into the dining hall, it was a small victory, but he didn't need to see Wolfman charming one of his girls. Noel needed to give him something to do.

"I'll bring up the food issue with Larry soon as I see him," she said. "Right now, they're all focused on Sky Porch."

"I get it," Karla said, "and I don't want to add anything else to your plate, but we're also running low on gas and propane. We're using a lot more water, and it takes a lot more than just solar to run the pump."

"So much for solar."

"Preach."

"Larry does the preaching." Noel started for Wolfman when Heather, walking through her line of sight with a pitcher of water, said, out of the side of her mouth, "Can you do something about that before Owen explodes?"

"On my way."

The epitome of an upside-down world was Noel, 19, getting ready to tell a 20-year-old guy to back off someone else. She could see the brunette was hardly suffering. Wolfman talked a great game, and the girl's smile showed it. For the first time in months, she was being chatted up by a charismatic dude.

"Hi!" she said, making eye contact.

"Hi, I'm Noel."

They shook hands.

"You're the one that prayed with my friends on the bus. Thank you," she said. "I'm Angie."

"I wasn't the only one, but you're welcome. We're very happy you're here. Do you mind if I borrow Wolf for a second?"

"Sure, no problem," she giggled. "Funny, she calls you Wolfman, too. I'll see you later." She walked away as Noel led him out the double doors.

Keeping watch from the parking lot, Sandoval, chewing on a sandwich, looked their way and gave a bend of the head.

"What's going on?" Wolfman said when they reached the three trees.

"Are you out of your mind?" Getting the sensation of being watched, Noel exaggerated her hand motions as she spoke. "Are you thinking?"

Wolfman glanced around and let out a small laugh. "About what?"

"You know exactly what I'm talking about," Noel said. "I'm not your mom, but you can't do this."

"I was just talking to her," he said, acknowledging he knew exactly why Noel was cutting into him. "I wasn't doing anything. Ask her. I didn't put a hand on her." Then he smiled. "At least not yet."

Everyone liked Wolfman. He'd proven he could handle all the stuff the security guys had to deal with, but he still maintained the charm of an adolescent.

"That's not funny. You know how her youth pastor feels about this place," she said. "You know he's looking for any excuse to leave. Don't give him one. And I'm moving my hands like this because he's watching us, and I want him to believe I'm chewing you out."

"I get it, but I wasn't doing anything, I swear." His eyes moved beyond Noel to the north. "It looks like they're back."

She turned and saw Kuykendall riding in the golf cart with Gavin driving and Larry sitting in the back. Plain as day was the red bandage on Kuykendall's arm. Sandoval directed Gavin to take the cart to the trees.

"Oh no," she said.

"Are we done?" Wolfman said.

"I know you're a good guy, and Owen's a jerk, but we need to keep the peace."

"Okay," he said. "I'll cancel tonight."

"What?"

"I'm kidding."

"Don't kid like that."

Noel could see Kuykendall trying to smile through the pain as they converged around the cart.

"Just the arm?" Sandoval said.

"I got it on the leg too."

"Anyone else?" Noel said, and Larry lifted his wrapped hand. "Goodness."

Drew was still out there, and no one was giving her the impression that whatever took place was over. Another soft, deceiving rush of wind came across The Garden. The leaves spoke back in rustles and aroma, both familiar and foul.

"What happened?" Wolfman asked. "Do I need to go?"

Larry shared about the attack. "Drew's working on a plan but wants to run it by Joab. Is he back?"

Sandoval shook his head.

"If you guys don't mind, I'm going to go see my wife," Gavin said.

"Hey Gavin," Noel said as he walked by. She wanted to tell him about Todd's breakdown but held off. "I know you have to share with Candida, but can you try not to tell her with other people around?"

He nodded. "For sure."

"You doing okay, Big K.? Can I get you something?" Sandoval said.

"I'd like two cheeseburgers, access to Netflix, any pain killers we got, and a ride back to Mandalay," he said. "And in any order, you want to give them."

Wolfman climbed into the back, and Sandoval got behind the wheel of the cart. Noel said she'd bring him food and have Debbie come clean his wounds, then they drove for Mandalay.

"What about you?" she said to Larry.

"I think I'll live," he said, peeling back the blood-stained shirt to expose the knuckle bone at the base of his middle finger. "I could probably use a little peroxide."

"And stitches, and gauze, and reconstructive surgery," she said. "That's nasty."

"Like we haven't seen worse?"

He sat in the shade at the picnic table and let her examine the hand. "Is the camp in trouble?"

"This happened a half-mile away, and no one else has reported anything," he said. "So maybe not. Joab will have it figured out by the time he gets back."

"I'm not worried," Noel said. "But we need to get you cleaned up and, oh, by the way, Karla said we're getting stretched with food and fuel."

"What's on the menu today?" Larry said.

"Braised PBJ with a hollandaise sauce. It's delicious," she said. "Get up, let's go. That hand needs to be washed and cleaned."

They walked wide and to the right of the dining hall's main doors. They didn't have another building or cabin to serve as a nurse's station, mainly because they didn't have a nurse. Like everything else, Joab filled the need for most of the first aid issues. He'd had EMT training in the past. For scrapes and cuts, the best remedies remained at the kitchen's back door. Debbie, Karla, Beth, Liz, the camp moms, always had some water, a harsh cleanser, and bandages at the ready.

"I guess I'm going to have to wait another week on this," she said as they passed the shed. He didn't answer.

Several pitchers of water were out, and Larry sat down. Noel began taking the shirt off the hand.

"How's Mr. Personality doing?"

"He's inside," Noel said, pouring water over the wound. "I had to pull Wolfman away from one of his girls."

Larry didn't look right, and it wasn't because of the bite. Trouble and danger were constant things, but this was something else.

"Do you want to talk about Denise Hemingway?"

He took a breath and pulled his hand away from the water. Grabbing a paper towel, he dabbed at it to soak up the moisture. The wound had coagulated. Noel poured peroxide and began applying gauze.

"I don't have a sermon tonight," he said.

"Because Denise is in your head?"

"Drew's not in yours?"

Noel fastened the gauze with tape and looked at him. "I don't have to preach. I only have to keep moving, and that keeps Drew away." She looked from his hand to his eyes and smiled. "Plus, I'm sorry to say, I've never had a moment with Drew like you did with Denise." She began wrapping the hand a second time in flesh-colored, flexible gauze.

"Yeah, some moment."

Drew did come into her thoughts, but she could put him on the back burner. He was in camp, unattached, and that was more than enough to occasionally inspire a hopeful daydream. For Larry, it was more challenging because Denise Hemingway was gone.

"I pray every day, I study my Bible, I'm doing what I should be doing, but I'm afraid about tonight because I can't get focused. You know what I almost did?"

"What?" she sat next to him on the bench.

"I almost told Mason the camp was safe."

"The camp is safe."

People were getting up from the tables and beginning to exit out the front of the dining hall. Some would go clean cabins, others to rest, and others to Bible Study. In another hour, Noel was supposed to be part of a women's study.

"I don't know that for sure," Larry said. "And my prayers don't seem to be getting through."

"You saying God's not listening to you?"

"No, he's probably just tired of me praying for the same old stuff. But I don't know how to ask for anything else."

"Larry, I love you, you're my brother." She stood, readjusted her ponytail, "but stop praying about Denise Hemingway. She's gone."

"Eighteen months ago, I saw her. I saved her."

"Yes, you did," Noel said. "You saved her, her children, and her husband."

BRICKLANDER
(8)

By the time they reached San Quintana, the impossibility of getting from California's Inland Empire to McCall, Idaho, was made clear to Gibson by everybody. And when he shook off their facts, the conversation turned blunt.

"Gibby," Crowder said as the truck pulled in and parked at Camp Braggs. "I'll kick your butt before I let you go AWOL."

"We all will," Doughty affirmed. "Like I said, if I thought there was a way back to Texas, I'd already be gone. No one's flying, no one's driving, and, believe it or not, I thought about bicycling." He laughed as they got out and slung their weapons. "Bicycling? How stupid is that?"

"Guys, if I'm going to die," Gibson said, "I want to die with my family."

Barnes joined them, and Farmer went to check-in.

"No one has to die. That's not written anywhere." Bricklander said. "But you will die if you go AWOL. The dead will get you, the cops will get you, or NORM will you get you. You need to let that bake between your ears for a while."

Two soldiers from Third Platoon, coming to unload the truck, caught the First Sergeant's stare and turned back.

"All of you, listen up. You know I've got family in Virginia, and I'm just as motivated as any of you to bail. I'm guessing there'll be desertions, but I'm staying put. We have to trust our brothers. We have to hold our end because they'll be trusting us."

"My parents aren't young, and my sister's dead," Gibson said.

"McCall, Idaho?" Bricklander said. He ran his eyes around the near-empty playground to be sure no one was listening in. The last thing he wanted was Minister Tim butting in.

"Yes."

"Then they most likely got National Guard, plus neighbors armed to the teeth. Your dad armed?"

"Like a Texan," Gibson said.

"That's why no one screws with us," Doughty slipped in.

Bricklander stepped close to Gibson and put a hand on his shoulder. "Trust your father, trust your neighbors, trust Idaho. All you're going to do is make them sick with worry when your rotation for a call comes around." Gibson bent his head, and Bricklander spoke to all of them. "We got screwed today, that's all. When you make a career out of the military, it's SOP—everyone gets screwed. Before, it was some general doing the deed, and now it's NORM. It's not pleasant, but don't let emotion take the best of you." The men, including Gibson, nodded. "If one of those ministers hears any talk about desertion, you know they're going straight to NORM. Swallow your squash, do your job, and we'll make this work. Now get some chow, and then get some sleep because we're back on the clock in a few hours. You guys get me?"

"We get you."

The men walked away. Trailing behind them, Bricklander took better notice of the lack of activity. The campus seemed to have lightened in their absence.

"Brick!" Lieutenant Farmer coming across the playground, called, and they met in the center. The lined space beneath their boots looked like it had been the pitcher's circle for an old kickball infield. "How are the guys?"

"You heard?"

"I heard them talking when we got back, and I saw you call them together. Any tea to spill?"

"Gibby wants to run," Bricklander said. "Hell, we all want to run, but no one's going to. I chilled them out and talked them down. But the last thing they need is for Minister Tim to get on the PA and announce the wonderful news from DC."

"He wanted to," Farmer said.

"No way? Seriously?"

"He did, but Torres pulled the plugs on the system." Farmer laughed. "The porker's skipping around here like it's Christmas. I don't get it."

Bricklander never measured his smarts against anyone else's. In the field, when bullets were calling out names of friends, he didn't trust anybody else to be the final answer. But in a place like this, he couldn't figure out how the college-educated officer could be so simple.

"You don't, LT?" The lieutenant shook his head. "The guys were talking about it at Brackett. Power's concentrated in DC, and the longer NORM has authority, the longer Minister Tim and his friends call the shots. I'll tell you this. We can clear the dead everywhere, reclaim all the cities, revive the economy, and bring back football on Sundays, but NORM's never retiring."

Farmer looked away and spit. "Did you hear about Second Platoon?"

"No." And now Bricklander knew why the campus was empty. "Shipped out?"

"Shipped out."

"All of them?"

"All of them."

LARRY
(9)

Larry entered the dining hall through the kitchen and reminded himself he was a preacher. That's what God brought him into the world to be. Still, thoughts kept swimming for a sermon. It was never this difficult before.

He was a big boy, with big boy responsibilities, and calling out sick wasn't an option. His brain kept feeding him a steady dialogue about how unprepared he was for everything. When his mind stretched this way, it always reverted to the slacker teen he'd been.

Loafing Larry was always trying to reassert control over the person God had remade.

Everyone scattered for their post-lunch happenings around camp. Charles Kiln and Ken Hong were settling in for a Bible study with some of the other men. Larry walked by them and stood looking through the windows of the double doors.

"You feeling good, Larry?" Kiln called from the table.

"I'm feeling good, Chuck," he said, smiling back to the older man.

"Then rock on, man. That's all I need to know. Lord's going to work through you again tonight."

Because of what he did at The Garden, they didn't ask him to join the study. They didn't press him to do much beyond preaching each weeknight and a little rah-rah on Sunday mornings. It would have been nice to sit down with them instead of preparing for the sermon.

But his calling didn't give him the luxury of choice. The calling was a thumb persistently pressed to his back, telling him not to worry but to get going and take action. Bugging out of hassles, whenever and wherever, was who he'd been. When he and Noel came through the closet door, the sensation of getting away with something changed to a dreadful fear of letting people down.

Inspiration didn't always have to be there, Joab said. He didn't have to have exploding passion with every sermon. He only had to believe every sermon he preached. That's what mattered when sharing.

"See, I didn't do that," Joab had said. *"I wanted to deconstruct people. I wanted to create doubt and empty them. And then come back and refill them with my beliefs, not necessarily the Lord's."*

"How could you do something like that?"

"I was so evil I didn't even see the evil I was pushing. I thought I was doing so much good, but I was warped. I wasn't a clean vessel."

When Larry stood in front of the people, they wanted hope. They wanted assurance of victory over this nightmare. So he gave it to them, but he only gave them what God wanted them to hear. Noel wasn't holding up cue cards, and Joab wasn't intercepting questions or providing in-depth insight about doctrine in the middle of a message. His was a total dependence on God, but right now, only silence was speaking to his heart.

Outside the dining hall, he crossed paths with Wolfman.

"I know, I know," he said, holding up his hands in surrender. "I didn't do anything. I never touched her."

"Don't stress," Larry said. "Just ease off and keep your radio handy. Drew might need some help." He had a sermon to work on, and lecturing Wolf was not a priority. "How's Big K.?"

Wolfman shrugged. "He's Big K. He says two bites means he deserves two sandwiches."

"Well, talk to your mom or Karla and make sure he gets them. I gotta prep."

Wolfman nodded. "I didn't touch her."

"I believe you," he responded as they parted.

Halfway to the trees, Legaspe caught him. Before he could say what he wanted, Larry cut him off.

"Have you heard from Joab?"

"No."

"I'm going to be in my cabin prepping. Let me know when he gets back."

"Do we want to alter chapel tonight?" Legaspe said. "Joab's group still isn't back, and we're down Kuykendall. Might be a good idea, you think?"

"That would make things a lot easier, but no. You guys and Drew can hold the fort until Joab gets back. Do whatever you have to, but we're staying with our regular chapel."

"Okay," Legaspe said. "I'll send Wolfman and Orlando up to relieve Hutch and Drew."

"I'm not worried," Larry said, but a part of him was wondering about Joab.

He passed the trees, and Owen's voice called out and approached him. Mr. Personality had found him.

"You had somebody bit today? Don't lie because I saw the big guy in the golf cart."

A devil growled and chomped its teeth when it came after you. It never gave the impression it was better than you, but Owen appeared to love the high road.

"Thanks for assuming I'd lie to you," he said. "And we call the big guy Kuykendall or Big K."

"I don't care," Owen said.

"Never thought you did."

"And I heard the shotgun blasts. Those things are close to the camp."

"It happened a half-mile away," Larry said. "And if you want to leave, leave." He gestured with his hand to the parking lot and saw Owen's eyes travel to the bandage. "You're starting to tick me off."

"You got bit too," Owen said.

Larry couldn't be sure but thought he saw a gleam in Owen's eyes. "Are you happy about this?"

"You've been bit," Owen answered. "It wasn't on the butt, but it had to hurt, and now you know how much danger we're all in if we stay."

"Are you saying we're ignorant to the danger because The Garden's been safe?"

Noel, the night before, took her swing when it came to Owen. He knew he needed to do the same.

Noel should be in charge of everything.

"I've lived in Sky Porch, I know…"

"…No, you don't," Larry interrupted. "You may understand the danger, but we know the cure. I was bit. You want to feel my forehead for a fever? You want to see if there are any veins in my arm turning black with infection? I'm immune."

"That's not the point."

"It is the point. How are you going to fare when your time comes?"

Larry hit the nerve. The youth pastor's face turned red.

There was a sermon to prepare, mental notes to make, and consideration about Kuykendall being bit and what it meant. He was going to have to answer questions about where Joab was. There was zero mental energy to deal with this ridiculous man.

"You've got nothing to say, do you?" Larry said. "Everything you were taught and believed is coming up short. You have no relationship with Jesus and, therefore, no way of defeating this enemy."

"You believe you're so smart!"

Larry shook his head. "No, I'm just saved! I've been bit down to the knuckle, and I'm immune!"

Owen took a step closer, and Sandoval's voice came from nowhere.

"Whoa, take it easy! What are you guys doing? I can hear you yelling from the parking lot."

Owen pointed at Larry. "You keep that Wolf kid away from Angie!"

"If her survival hinges on you or Wolfman, she has a better chance with Wolf."

Owen relented and stomped off. The anger felt good to Larry, but it didn't last. He needed to get on his knees to pray because the day was unraveling.

"Do you need me to throw him out of The Garden?" Sandoval said. "Or pour a few buckets of cold water on you?"

"I'm sorry," Larry said. "Dude caught me at a bad time."

"It's cool, but you've got a sermon to preach. Go to your cabin. I won't let anyone else get close."

Larry thanked Sandoval and went on.

"Mr. Garrison, Mr. Garrison!" It was Teddy and a group of friends stopping him at the door.

Mr. Garrison?

"Hey guys," he said, pulling back hard on his frustration.

"Are we going to sing *Pharaoh Pharaoh* tonight?" Teddy led the begging.

"We always sing *Pharaoh Pharaoh*."

"Well, we want to do the motions tonight," Teddy and his group argued. "Alison and her friends are always hogging up the motions when we do them."

"Good point," he said. They were good kids and draining off his aggravation rather than increasing it. "Why don't you find Noel and ask her who's leading worship tonight. That way, we'll be sure to get you guys your shot."

"Cool!" They bolted to find Noel.

Larry went inside and fell to his knees. "God, thank you for Big K."

The mob of devils coming off the trail could have made things so much worse. "Thank you for your protection, Lord..."

When he learned how to pray, it was refreshing. As a kid, he knew the *stealing heaven* prayer, which was the quick prayer before going to bed at night—just in case something happened while sleeping. He knew all of the forms and derivatives of, *Good food, good meat, good God, let's eat.* But as experience educated him on the power of prayer, falling to his knees in his little cabin was like being in a room with flowing fresh air. It was clean, promising, and brought belief anything could be done.

"...And Lord, please let Joab and his group get back safely. We need you, Lord. We need Joab."

The air thickened, the smell of dust and old wood rose. It was as stale as a dark abandoned basement. There was enough breath for life, but not a victorious life. There was no fresh air. There was no gentle breeze.

JOAB
(9)

Shadows had stretched, covering places that had been in direct sunlight. The sun wasn't stopping, the earth kept spinning, and feelings kept hitting.

Wheeler's death brought no effort to rationalize or eulogize. Instead, the focus was getting home. Their friend was dead, and they'd have to mourn later. And, since the creek running through Cumberland wasn't packed with devils, there was no clear answer if those leaving Sky Porch were bypassing The Garden or not.

Stripping Wheeler of his personals, including remaining shells, machete, radio, and pistol, Jay and Duran placed him inside a Sundowner pickup near the post office. They put a blanket over him. There was no time for anything better.

"We've got to go," Duran said.

Joab put a praying hand to the truck's window. The fight kept replaying in his mind. There was the comfort that Wheeler was dead in the way people were supposed to be dead, but sickness at the thought of explaining his loss.

"It's not your fault," Duran said. "It could have been any of us, or even you. Joab, you are not providence. Wheeler's number came up, and God called him home."

Pulling his attention away from the truck, he looked at Duran but had no words.

"You're not, and we've got to get back. Are you with us?"

"I'm with you," he said, straightening up and wiping at his face. "Let's roll."

"We're going to have to hoof it to get there before dark," Jay said.

Duran gave the map a once over, checked out where the sun was in the sky, and put it away. "We'll make it if we go now."

Fastening the straps of their backpacks and drawing their machetes, they got ready to run.

"One of us stops, we all stop," Jay said. "Stay aware. We're not running a 5K, don't groove into a mental zone where we block each other out."

"I agree," Joab said, his thoughts starting to loosen. "Listen, I'm the old man here. I may not be as fast as either of you, but I'm smarter. If I want your help, I'll call for it, but don't help me until I ask."

"We ain't showing up at The Garden without you, Joab," Duran said. "I'm not answering those questions."

"I'm not saying I ain't making it back to The Garden. I only mean I might have to find a different way because I'm not quick enough. Get me?"

They gave the nods he wanted.

"I don't want to die," he said, feeling like it was a lie. "Our priority is still The Garden. And it's for me to break the news about Wheeler."

They exited Cumberland the same way they came. At the edge of town, four devils met them on the road. They didn't break stride.

Each lifted his blade as if to return a tennis serve, and craniums opened in a near synchronized fashion.

Joab, bringing his blade back to the right from the left, caught the fourth devil and disposed of it. There were snarls behind them, gnashing of teeth, but Jay and Duran's footfalls stayed with him.

They reached the bend, and the road was clear. Joab could feel his pace remaining steady. Jay was behind to the right, Duran behind to the left. The volume on their radios was turned high to hear any calls from either the camp or Bird.

A devil stumbled towards them through the woods, but they rushed by it.

Two more appeared on the road, and Jay sped up. Cutting one apart, the other he shoved to the ground. Joab hurdled it, Duran went around, and Jay fell back into formation.

It wasn't a sprint. Joab knew he couldn't handle a sprint, but the easy jog they blended into kept him from burning out. A lather of sweat began to swell around his neck.

"We got devils!" Duran said.

"Keep going!" Jay said. "They can't catch us."

Wheeler...Those kids...Elias...

Ping.

Like a light bulb being iconic of a new idea, the ping for Joab revived terrible thoughts. He could make his theological case for forgiveness, but he couldn't reach inside and turn off the memories. And the Lord didn't seem inclined to take them away.

With perspiration drenching the inside of his shirt, Joab felt no constriction in his lungs or pain in his side. If anything, he had to fight the idea of running faster. They continued, but Wheeler's ghost kept pace.

"Dear White People..." he remembered starting a message to great applause at a college chapel. *"...I speak to all of us. You and I have been the problem for far too long."*

The *Dear White People* sermon was first in his regular rotation of messages. He shared it at churches and campuses when fundraising for awareness of Social Justice in all its forms. If he needed to disguise it, he would couch it in terms like Social Holiness, but it was always the same old garbage. It aggravated the mature, inspired the young, and activated the soft-headed into action. He didn't author the line, but he loved saying, *Dear White People*, and following it with boatloads of shame and accusations of white fragility.

Joab could die now and make it go away or live as long as he could, fight, and try to correct as much as possible. But he'd never be able to right all his wrongs. For that to be possible, Wheeler would have to be resurrected.

Ping.

Static, then, a garbled, indistinguishable voice came over the radios. They didn't stop to fine-tune.

In front of them on Mountain Road 27 were three, then five, and before he stopped counting, Joab saw 11 devils glaring hate and emoting despair with their rotting faces.

Rage hit him. Red anger closed off his peripheral vision, and all he saw he wanted to kill. He'd do it for Wheeler. He'd take them all on, and when strength and bullets were exhausted, he'd willingly die. Adrenaline persuaded it wouldn't be a bad way to go. He deserved to go. He needed to go. His trot was about to turn into a sprint when Duran's voice rose.

"How we doing this?"

"Shotguns!" Jay said. "Two blasts and run around the rest to the left!"

Joab unslung his shotgun and saw Duran and Jay come even with him. The mob had come onto the road from the north, fully activated, with outstretched hands. Their fire-yellow eyes reminding that the spirits empowering them were from another place. Jaws rehearsed, up and down, their intentions. They weren't hungry; they were evil and fed because they hated.

The men put the breaks to their jog, lodged the butts of the Remingtons to their shoulders, and squeezed off a 12-gauge volley that decimated their attackers.

"Again!" Jay screamed, and another barrage opened enough road for them to keep moving as more devils closed in from behind. "Run!"

Creating distance between themselves and the devils, they kept shotguns in hand. The sky looked good, there was plenty of light, but the conditions on the ground worsened as another platoon of devils rose ahead of them.

NOEL
(8)

The afternoon grew late, and stress rose about Joab and his group's return. Orlando and Wolfman rotated onto the trail. Big Geoff then replaced Wolfman, who was going to lead worship. Hutchinson and Drew were back. Karla and her staff were working on dinner.

Candida had not let go of Gavin since his return. It was what Noel expected sitting with the two of them outside their cabin. As shared by her husband, Candida never recovered from the loss of their daughter, which highlighted The Garden's strangest oddity. There should have been more people mourning like Candida, but there weren't.

The death of a loved one didn't incapacitate or affect everyone the same. Joab taught them this lesson at the beginning. Everyone handled death differently, and there could be no certainty in anyone's response. The shock was so many were able to keep moving forward.

"I'm only sharing for you to be aware of what happened with Todd earlier," Noel said. Todd was currently running around with Teddy and Elias.

Gavin and Candida were on metal folding chairs while an ancient tree stump served Noel.

"I haven't talked to him," Candida said. "What happened?"

Noel shared what took place as Todd rounded third.

"We'll deal with it," Gavin said.

"I know you will. I only wanted to make you aware," Noel said. "He's a great kid."

"They're all great kids," Candida said.

A tiny spark wanted to ask—knowing how important it was to Todd—how they could miss the baseball game. There was no requirement to walk patrol, and Candida had zero responsibilities, but Noel held back.

"Yes, they are," she said, standing to leave. They were a married couple in their early thirties with a young son and a dead older daughter. There was very little she was in position to press them about. "I'll see you at chapel."

"Hey, Noel," Gavin said. "You and Larry are great people."

The expectancy of another sentence hung like a guillotine, ferociously, over her. Something else was coming.

"But…"

The blade fell.

"…We think it's time for us to move on. This is just too much after today, and things are more secure in the flatlands."

Would this cause a groundswell of folks wanting to pull out? Their leaving, along with Owen brushing elbows with others, could lead to it. It would solve Karla's food dilemma, but the ramifications, spiritually and to morale, would be considerable.

"I think it would be a mistake, but no one's going to force you to stay."

"We know that," Candida said. "But if things are getting better in the city, we'd be more secure than we are here. And with Sky Porch open, there could be real trouble."

"I feel we've done all we can," Gavin said.

"The Lord's seen us through everything," Noel said, smiling with open hands that slapped down to her hips.

"He'll see us through down there," Gavin said. "Are you going to tell Larry?"

"If I see him, but you can tell him if you want. I'm not your boss, and you're free. I wish, with all my heart, you'd stay. I worry for your son, but it's your decision."

"We know what's best for him," Candida said.

"Of course, you do," Noel said, careful she didn't let the sarcasm she was feeling enter her voice. "I'll see you at chapel. Afterward, we can talk to Karla about getting a backpack of food put together for you."

"Thank you," Gavin said.

Walking away, a thought struck her, not in mind but in heart. One of those moments where she knew she had to say something—something unpleasant. Noel kicked herself for not seeing this coming, but then again, how was she going to see it? It was her first end of the world experience. Perhaps she'd be wiser at her next end of the world party.

She turned around. Gavin and Candida were entering their cabin.

"Things might be normal down the hill--that's for you to judge," she said. "But you have to know if you get bit in the flatlands or, God forbid, Todd gets bit, they aren't going to wait for signs of fever. They'll shoot you, just like they were ready to shoot those kids on the bus yesterday. They'd shoot Big K. right now, and he has no fever. So think about it. Please think about it."

Without giving them a chance to respond, she left.

There was so much churning through Noel's soul. Sky Porch, attacks near the camp, Owen, Joab, and Larry not feeling right all seemed like bad spiritual omens. How much of it was true, how much of it was Satan hitting with doubts? She didn't know. The Lord was in control, but, like Joab said the night before, it did feel like something was coming.

"Noel!"

Sandoval and Drew were talking at the picnic tables to her right. To her left, folks were working in the dining hall. In front of her, coming from the amphitheater, were three of Owen's students; Aaron, Jessica, and Angie. "Noel!"

They weren't in a panic but definitely wanted her time.

"What's up?" she said.

Aaron stood between the girls. All fresher and looking like they should for their ages.

"Jessica, you and I still have some business to take care of."

"I know," Jessica said, gliding a finger through her brown hair and tucking a strand behind an ear. "That's why..." she paused and looked at her friends.

The Lord healed Jessica, but it was a healing only. To Noel's knowledge, she'd yet to accept Christ. The urgency for that melted other concerns.

"That's what we want to talk to you about," Aaron said. "We want to stay here."

"You know your youth pastor's looking to leave, right?"

"That's who we've been talking to in the amphitheater," Angie said. "A lot of us are over eighteen now, the three of us are, and we feel like this is where we want to be. And our families would want us to be safe."

"Where are you at in your faith, Angie?" Noel said.

"I'm not going to lie," Angie said. "I could use a refresher." Noel gave her an odd look, and the girl clarified. "I was told at junior high camp, about seven years ago, that I was saved, but it doesn't seem right. I didn't make any decision. The speaker just said we all were."

"It happens a lot these days. We're told we're saved," Noel said, "but what we need to understand is that, yes, while forgiveness is there, we have to acknowledge our need for forgiveness and accept it. It requires an action of the heart."

"I know they're not just magic words," Angie said. "I mean, don't I have to feel them in my heart?"

"Yeah, you do," Noel said. "When do you want to talk?"

"Tonight or tomorrow morning?" Angie said. "We've got some friends we want to connect with right now. We want to convince them to stay."

"I'm glad you all want to stay," Noel said. "The only thing is—and I know I sound like a grandma on this—but because you're adults making an adult decision, you're going to have adult expectations here."

"We know," Aaron said. "I want to help with security and move into Mandalay."

"Security could use the help, but I don't know if I'd have the courage to move into Mandalay," Noel joked. "Now, what's your hang-up, Jessica? What more do you need to know before accepting Christ's forgiveness?"

Jessica's eyes locked on hers. "I want you to be the one that prays with me."

"Why me?"

"I trust you."

"Girls, Jessica, Angie," Noel smiled, feeling a rush of God's provision. "What are we waiting for?"

BRICKLANDER
(9)

The effect of Second Platoon's departure was greater emotionally than visually. Through the PNN, it became clear Carlson's platoon shipped due to fallout on the election announcement. The troops remaining weren't scared. They were too experienced to be scared but anxious to see what the next few days would bring.

In the cafeteria, Bricklander filled his coffee mug and surveyed the room. It was mostly vacant, with just a few personnel scattered about the long tables and green commercial tile. He could sit alone, sit with his men, or sit with Lieutenant Gayle Holsopple, who was filling in figures on a clipboard.

Being middle-aged—Bricklander guessed late-forties and prematurely grey—Holsopple was easy to notice. Not that she rationed any provocative comments or flirtatious expressions. But because she was straightforward, did her job, and was the epitome of Stars and Stripes. For the first sergeant, her attractiveness wasn't a consideration as he went toward her.

"I heard you put in some work at Brackett," she said without looking at him. "Glad you made it back in one piece."

"Glad somebody cares."

"We're short enough around here. I'd hate to see us lose anyone else."

Technically, she was an officer, and he had to respect that, but since they were deployed and off duty, he took the seat across from her.

"You realize you should only sit down with an officer when asked," she said, still not acknowledging him with her eyes. "My suggestion, with Second Platoon gone, would be to rack out. Sleep's going to be hard to come by this week."

"Why?"

"Call it a feeling."

Bricklander pressed. "What's going on?"

"They took a platoon away from us today."

"Yeah, but why did they take it?"

She looked at him and exhaled. He noticed while her hair was platinum, the brows above her blue eyes were dark. "Does it matter? They're gone, we're shorthanded, and sitting in the shadow of a mountain about to pop."

"That's why I'm curious, what trumps San Quintana right now? Normally, I'd think they'd have been sent to the Arroyo Seco."

"And normally, you'd be right." She resumed her scribbling.

"I think they got called to a different chore."

"Like what?" she said, putting down her pen and returning his gaze.

Bricklander knew she was with him but only wanted to hear him say it. "That Brackett Field business, today, started because someone lost faith after hearing the news from Washington. There was a healthy discussion among my men on the way back about going AWOL. And now something's more important than San Quintana?"

Holsopple's eyes shifted around the cafeteria. She sipped some coffee and leaned forward on her arms. "When news got to Hawaii, a military base revolted. The Marines holding it down are from Pendleton, and they want to come home. There was a problem at the docks in Long Beach, and NORM shipped Second Platoon to San Bernardino because a squad of soldiers hijacked a convoy of trucks and had to be gunned down."

"What about the rest of the country?"

"Similar things have happened up the coast, but no one on the other side of the Mississippi is sharing."

"Virginia?"

The TOC officer shook her head. "NORM's gagging everything."

Bricklander hoped she wasn't reading his mind because his thoughts were processing, and he knew what the answer was going to be.

"Have we heard anything from Minister Kevin?" he asked.

Holsopple shook her head, uninterested in the fate of the minister. "Let me ask you a question. Those roads up to Sky Porch were pretty clear, right?" He nodded. "How long do you think it would take to walk from there to here?"

"A day or two—have you heard something?"

"No, just a feeling. You know when your tires are ready to blow, they don't care about the condition of your engine. They just blow, and all the bad stuff happens at once."

Bricklander's brain spit out the answer.

"Well, Gayle," he said, holding on to a form of cool and rubbing the growth on his chin, "my family's on the other side of the country. What do you think I should do?"

"Well, Jeff," she said, a sardonic grin ebbing to her lips, "I'd be thinking about getting my butt out of here the best way I can. If my husband were still alive, we'd have made a rendezvous point soon as this thing started."

"No kids?"

"Miscarriage, second year, was the closest we got."

"I can't even dream of a con good enough to get me to the east coast," Bricklander said. "Can you?"

"I can't. We're stuck here, just like everyone is stuck every place else. So we have to hope there's still some life in this Stars and Stripes thing."

"Stars and Stripes," he echoed in an exhausted manner. When he said it this time, it felt like he was standing over a casket about to go into the earth.

LARRY
(10)

Prayer time hadn't been so much about seeking God but more about being lectured by the big guy. Since arriving in this world, obedience had been a straightforward, easy, super-highway to follow. Now it was a haunted, scary path Larry wanted to avoid.

What was supposed to be right didn't feel right. Instead, it felt like the sound of an inexperienced driver grinding a clutch in search of an elusive gear.

"Can't find them grind them," Joab said. *"If you can't recognize anything transcendent in your message, don't worry about it. Grind on what you know and believe: Jesus, Jesus crucified, and that empty tomb. The truths of God will always see you through, and you'll find the correct gear for that particular night. Trust*

me."

For the last 18 months, Larry went into his cabin, closed the door, prayed, wrestled with doubt, prayed some more, and ground out a message. Some days, the sermons came easy. Some days, they came hard, but they always came.

Now it was time, and there was a truth he needed to share with The Garden. He knew the scripture, the connecting stories, and illustrations but desperately wanted to find another gear. He didn't want to preach this sermon.

And the first rule of preaching was to believe in what you preached.

Edging open his door brought no fresh air. It remained stale and depressive. Kuykendall, sitting on the picnic table, talking to Frank, caught sight of him.

"Boss! How's it going?"

Larry returned a tilt of the head, sucked in a breath, and headed to the trees. Big K. looked pretty good and sounded even better despite nearly becoming fast-food.

"I was telling Frank we ought to have a big hunting party for deer. And then have a major cookout, what do you think?" Kuykendall gave an enthusiastic thumbs up. These two, chronologically pushing thirty, were fun people to be around.

"I'm all for it, guys, but the problem's the other stuff you run into out there," he said. "And no one around here knows how to clean a deer."

"Frank's got a plan," Kuykendall said.

"Is Joab back yet?" Larry asked.

271

"No, but listen to this," Frank said, unconcerned about Joab because everyone knew you didn't have to worry about Joab. "Big K. and I figure if we drove to another part of the mountain range…"

Larry's concern for Joab was growing. "…Huh, uh."

"…We start a fire…"

"A fire?"

"Yeah, listen," Frank went on. "We start a fire and let it flush the deer towards us. We shoot them and load them in a truck and bring them back. Then…"

"Then it's all trial and error," Kuykendall jumped in. "We make our mistakes carving the first few, but if we have a lot, then we'll learn what we're doing wrong and eventually get it right."

"What do you think?" Frank said.

"What about the fire?"

"It'll burn itself out," Kuykendall said, exchanging a concurring nod with Frank.

"Guys, I gotta preach." Larry smiled and began moving away. "We probably need to think this out a little more."

They continued to talk.

"I told you not to mention the fire," Kuykendall said.

"Well, how else are we supposed to get the deer?"

"You save the controversial stuff for the last," Kuykendall said. "Get them to commit, and they won't have a choice."

Saving the controversial stuff for the end sounded like good advice as he passed the shed and trudged the sloping gravel to the amphitheater. The music was kicking in with the sun dangling in the lowest part of the sky.

Hiram, shotgun slung over his shoulder, met him on the trail. Wolfman's voice came with the guitar.

"What do you think we should sing tonight?"

Larry couldn't see the faces but knew the kids were demanding, *Pharaoh, Pharaoh.*

"You're not staying for chapel?" Larry asked Hiram, who was good-natured but stubborn.

In his late twenties, Hiram was a throwback-biker with a balding hairline and matching goatee. His sleeveless shirt revealed a run of non-decipherable tats down the length of both arms.

"Picking up Frank by the trees and heading out to the road. Drew thought it best if we pushed out a little bit tonight. Sorry, I didn't get the shed torn down. Before the week's over, I promise."

"I'm not complaining," Larry said. "Keep a low profile out there, and don't try to bag a deer by starting a fire."

"Agghhh, those guys," he sighed. "I told them that was a stupid idea."

"Be safe," Larry said, and Hiram walked on.

It hit Larry that he didn't tell Hiram The Garden needed him. This was because all The Garden really needed was Joab.

And that was the problem.

JOAB
(10)

Because they were men and not boys, there was a lot Joab could ask of his men. Even the youngest—Wolfman, Orlando, Chapman —were unlike their peers. They had more than the courage to speak but also the courage to be selfless and place themselves into any breach.

Another 20 to 25 bodies should have been among The Garden's defenders, but the courage required was hard to find. The group of men unwilling to commit to stand a watch or even wield a gun were victims of Joab's generation. A generation that encouraged those they led to put off their masculinity and--aided and abetted by the church--to be ashamed of it.

When Joab led Jay and Duran off the road and into the woods to avoid the herd at the highway, he knew the danger. There were shadows, rocks, and dead tree limbs to navigate over and around. In an instant, a rolled ankle, fractured foot, or popped knee could turn someone into fast-food.

But he could put them through this because there was no aura of fear about them. Even if death got hold of them, they'd never be victims. They'd never be devils.

The growls and footsteps behind them grew distant through the woods, brush, and low branches. Joab's awareness, though, couldn't have been more heightened by a pound of caffeine. Boiling in sweat, still covered in blood, he emerged on Highway 19 with Jay and Duran. Panting for air, they reached for water after being sure no devil was insight.

"I don't know if it saved us time," Duran said between drinks and gasps. "But this is a good place to be with the sun going down. We're not too far away now."

"There they are," Joab pointed north and took a breath. "Try Bird on the radio."

Duran thumbed the yellow box on his waist. Joab looked at the devils coming in their standard limp and then tried to get a glimpse of the creek but couldn't see it.

"We're going to make it," Jay said, sliding fresh shells into the gut of his Remington.

"He's not answering," Duran said. "Or it's turned down because he's pinned."

"Bird handles his business as well as anyone," Jay said. "Let's get home."

They agreed with Jay and started south on 19.

Passing familiar territory, they came in contact with more devils. Some they pushed over, others they slashed at from behind. But there were no mobs, only individuals.

From the bridge at Sky Porch, it was, maybe, a day's stagger for the dead. They all thought the devils should have been passing in droves, but they weren't. It was becoming more evident to Joab they were scattering. Many devils found the going easier through the creek beds and places like Cumberland. Some took the highway, while others likely discovered the trails outside of Big Sky above The Garden.

A mile from camp, radios picked up the voices of the men setting up security. Kuykendall's voice went out to Hiram and Frank. Orlando and Hutchinson were going back and forth. Bash was asking Drew if Gavin was available.

Static... **"Has anyone heard from Joab?"** ...Static.

It was Anspach.

When they reached the Utility Road, they happily phased to walking. The cool-down period intensified the sweat. Joab knew their energy level-- plateaued--would eventually crash them into deep exhaustion.

"This is Joab. We're back..." He said into the radio.

"About time, Jefe..." Big Geoff said.

"Where you at?" Drew asked.

"Utility Road, I'll meet you at the trees."

"We got stuff," Drew's voice was severe.

"So do we..." Joab said. **"Hiram, Frank...Is it you two on the highway?"**

"Affirmative." Frank radioed back.

"Stay sharp. The highway's hot, lot of singles, but most of the devils seem to be bypassing."

Joab expected to hear a few amens because everyone on security had radios plugged into their ears. The silence made him believe critical things had happened.

In the distance, they could hear Wolfman and the kids singing.

"Do you think we got hit?" Jay said.

"I don't know," he answered. "They're still doing chapel. If there was a catastrophe, I think things would be different. How you feeling?"

"Sad, good, wired."

"You feeling good enough to do security tonight?"

"Absolutely. If I go to Mandalay," Jay said, "I'm only going to think about Wheeler."

Jay and Duran had been out and engaged all day. There was real fatigue, but they were still sharp to every sound, every snap of a twig or odd-sounding step.

"I appreciate it."

"I can help out too," Duran said as they came to the entrance and saw the large frame of Kuykendall sitting on the picnic table. "Where do you want me?"

"Let's find out what's up, and then both of you, get something to eat, catch your breath, and be ready."

Drew met them at the tables with Mason and Bash.

The sky was deep purple toward the amphitheater. East and out to the highway, where Hiram and Frank were, it was dark. It was a gorgeous time of day, except when there was no power for lights and devils were storming in the vicinity.

"We got devils in the woods, above camp," Drew said.

Kuykendall raised his hand.

"You got bit?" Duran said.

"Twice."

NOEL
(9)

If Larry was having a bad night, nobody—except Noel—knew because he'd learned to preach.

Standing next to Joab at the top of the amphitheater, Noel was aware of Larry's struggles. His tugs on the heart, attacks of doubt, but over the past 18 months, he'd turned pro. In her opinion, he was better than Reverend Joe Hyde, who preached the message landing them at The Garden.

"Our God is a great God, but he's not looking for loopholes to keep you out of Heaven. Instead, he's going and has gone the distance to make clear how much he loves you! How much he loves me! How much he loves this world and desires for it to be in right relationship with him."

"He's a good preacher," Joab said to her. His voice sounded flat and exhausted. The comfort for Joab, Noel was sure, came not with the stiff mattress he used for a bed or the lousy sandwich he'd eat for dinner, but with the words the Holy Spirit was giving Larry.

"You have to give this some thought, folks. You have to decide how far you want to go with God. You've seen a glimpse, you've experienced part, but none of us have seen or experienced all he wants to show and do for us. We tend only to go so far and then rest in that revelation instead of depending on him, Jesus, for more."

Unaware of Wheeler and Bird, Larry pressed on. But Noel knew when something was off. Tempo, timing, tone, she couldn't finger it, but her brother in the Lord hadn't worked out what he needed to work out.

"You have something in front of you tonight that, even though it's dark, you can clearly see. You see it clearer now than when it was behind stained glass or while sitting in comfortable pews and dining in warm houses with massive selections of food and drink. You couldn't see it then, but you can see it now in this place where God is speaking and saying 'Come further with me!'"

When Noel heard Joab's report, relief came that many devils were taking the creek path to the flatlands. Wheeler's death hung heavy even as she held out hope for Bird. The camp would remain safe in their absence but never the same.

And Elias...who was going to tell Elias—Wheeler was gone? It hurt to even think it.

"I look, and I see all Christians here, I see all believers here, I see 180 people..."

It was a good sermon, and it felt good to hear what Larry was saying. The message was hopeful. If words painted, then they were painting life as sky blue and limitless in the Lord. They were good words, but something nagged to be heard.

"Why do people have to die, Joab?" she whispered.

"Because it's an imperfect, fallen world," he said. "How's that for a pathetic answer?"

"I don't know how the kids are going to take it. I keep seeing Elias' face when he finds out about Wheeler." She leaned into Joab, and he put an arm around her.

"I know," Joab said as Larry continued to preach. "We incur a big debt to people who are in our lives only for a very short time. And the gift they give can either haunt or inspire us forever. I think Elias will be sad but eventually inspired by Wheeler."

Noel heard Joab sniffle and straightened up. Larry was about to open the altar. She sensed a lot of people were ready to pray. "You gonna be okay?"

"Yeah," he said, touching at his eyes.

"...And maybe tonight is not your night," Larry said. "Maybe tonight, you know God is talking to you, and maybe you're a little scared about stepping forward. That's okay. It has to be your decision and not peer pressure or persuasion."

What are you saying?

"Did you hear that?" Noel said. Fingernails down, a chalkboard couldn't have pained her more.

"...I don't want to pressure you...I want you right with God, but I don't want you to feel forced. Maybe tomorrow will work better for you. Maybe tomorrow's your day."

Just like the snap of a finger, the dead were dead, and Wheeler didn't matter anymore. The present had trouble enough of its own.

Noel felt a fury come over her. The message Larry had been preaching hit the clunker her heart had been anticipating.

Noel had never heard Larry say he didn't want to pressure anyone before. Never heard him say, '...tonight may not be your night.'

Joab wrapped a hand around her bicep and turned her. "We're in trouble here and not because there are devils in the woods." He didn't yell. His voice was low.

"What do we do?"

"We got to keep things safe tonight," he said. "I think tomorrow's going to be the day."

Larry kept speaking, and a few minutes later, he opened the altar.

For the first time in 18 months, no one came.

BRICKLANDER
(10)

"Not happening," Tom Lancaster said, lying on his bunk with a beer in one hand, skin magazine in another, and orange peels on his stomach. "No one's running because no one's got any place to go."

"If you had a place to go, would you?" Bricklander said, stripping out of his fatigues and into a sleeveless muscle shirt and blue athletic shorts.

The commercial tile was cold, but having his boots off brought relief. Outside the window of the classroom, he shared with Lancaster, the playground was quiet. Spring in Southern California was enter music for summer. The days were always ugly, the nights were almost always beautiful, and at dawn, it turned cold.

"I got a couple of brothers in Michigan," Lancaster said, putting down his beer. "But I have no one to worry about. Which is a pretty good deal because I'd hate to have a grandkid sit on my lap and ask about the worst things I've ever done."

Bricklander flipped off the lights and got into his bunk. The conversation felt like it was hanging open. "So you're cool?"

"Cool?"

"Kristen Block," Bricklander pressed. "Are you cool?"

"Would you be?"

"No, but better I ask you than Minister Tim."

"You know I've never gotten anything but drunk," Lancaster said. He got out of bed, slipped on his shirt and sandals. "I've never done drugs, never been high. But if someone offered me something to forget about Kristen Block—for just a little while—I'd take it."

"I'm sorry I brought it up."

"Don't be," he said, walking to the window and searching for something to see. "She's the last one. I mean it, Brick. I'm done." He paused, and an exhausted laugh escaped him. "You know who I was thinking about today?"

Bricklander didn't speak.

"I was thinking about God today. In Sandland, he was in my thoughts all the time, but we got home—and all this happened—I didn't think about God at all. But I've been thinking about him a lot lately."

Bricklander sat up but didn't go to his friend. Lancaster wasn't looking for reaction or affection but an ear to pour into. For someone to catch the sickness weighing him down. He knew what it was to want someone who understood what it felt like to have bullets fly by and live for months in perpetual anticipation and anxiety.

Would today be the day? Would tomorrow be the day? If not mine, then whose day would it be? Who's turn?

Just flirting with those thoughts and remembering that place sped Bricklander's heart. It made him long all the more for Rosa and the girls.

There'd be a moment to go to his brother, but it wasn't now. For now, Lancaster needed to purge.

"I'm going to Hell," Lancaster said, standing in the silver nightshade lancing through the window's blinds. Bricklander saw his chin quiver. "That girl, that girl, that girl...Kristen Block...was looking at me. She's still looking at me...I should have ate that bullet." He rubbed his forehead and walked to the door. "I should have ate that bullet."

Bricklander heard him go into the bathroom and then water running through the pipes. Everyone had one that was one too many. The last person he capped was an old man begging to die. For Lancaster, it was a young girl begging to live.

Laying in the dark, he disconnected. He couldn't shoulder Lancaster's pains anymore than his friend could shoulder his. Brothers in battle, brothers in life, but there were limits to what they could do for each other. It was a pernicious loneliness only remedied by the touch of family.

After Lancaster, silently, went back to his bunk, Bricklander sank into sleep.

When winter broke in Virginia and the air warmed, the jasmine began to break out in the evenings. He supposed it did in other places, but other places weren't like the Shenandoah. They didn't have large porches and expansive lawns that were more joy than chore to mow.

It was home, sunlight, and the bright green lawn he cared for under the tires and blades of his John Deere. It sloped down the long drive until it reached a buffer of cypress trees that kept the highway unseen. Rosa, smiling, wearing a yellow print dress, held Margie in a glider on the porch. From the steps, Bricklander watched Shelby and Marcia playing with their American Girl dolls on the grass.

He didn't doubt he was asleep. The question was, how long could he stay asleep? How long could he stay knowing this place wasn't real but a medication his mind and soul were providing after a stressful day.

Remaining on the porch, he let the smiles float his way with the laughter. If he demanded too much, if he reached out for Rosa, if he took a step toward the girls, the vision would shatter and hurl him back to the place of desert and dead—California.

…A bell sounded. Rosa looked at him, and Lancaster's voice came from her mouth.

"Brick, we've got a breach!"

LARRY
(11)

If the preparation for the sermon was off, the end proved to be more out of whack. Yet, Larry knew and did nothing about it. Like sticking a hand into a running fan, knowing he'd get cut, and not stopping himself.

It wasn't the fumbling of words. Larry had words. The decision to hold back the truth caused the perpetual strength—always present when he spoke— to evaporate. The altar call died. No one came to pray. By holding back the truth, Larry took away the urgency. The Garden's citizens left the amphitheater the same way they came in and, very soon, would face a world different from the one they were living in.

The sense of failure didn't dissipate as the amphitheater emptied. It was going to be a long night, probably sleepless. He'd get to his cabin, repent, get some rest, and at breakfast, he'd tell the truth and leave the reactions to the Lord. Which was the very same thing he could have done tonight but, out of fear, held back.

Larry reached the top, but Noel and Joab weren't going to let him pass.

"What was that?" Noel's question carried no sisterly compassion.

"What?" Pride. And again, he saw clearly what needed to be done. He needed to tell Noel and Joab what he did wrong, get to his cabin, and pray for forgiveness. "What are you talking about?"

"Are you out of your mind?" she said. "Telling them that maybe tonight isn't their night and that maybe tomorrow is? What the heck is that?"

"I was preaching."

"You weren't preaching," Joab said. "You were hiding something."

Larry raised a hand as if to argue but dropped it. He wasn't ready for a review of his spiritual condition. "I gotta get to my cabin."

"Larry," Noel grabbed his arm. "Wheeler's dead, and Bird's missing. We got devils in the woods all around. We have to talk about what we're going to do because Owen, Gavin, and others are pulling out tomorrow. These people needed something more than what you closed with tonight."

Before the last two nights, Noel never gave the impression she'd willingly get into someone's face. He'd never underestimate her again, or her look that could cut stone.

"All the more reason for me to pray," he said. Tears welled, one spilled. Others could cry at The Garden, but not him. "We'll talk in the morning. I need to go."

"Larry, this is us," Joab said. "I'm not feeling good either, but we've got to talk about what's going on and what you're not telling us."

"Make the camp secure tonight," he said. "Make it safe."

"Do you just want to talk to Noel?" Joab said. "I'll back off, at least talk to Noel."

Larry noticed Noel's eyes widened as if to say, '*yes, that would be a good move.*'

He walked away and then turned. "Listen," he said. The distance made it easier for him to speak. "I did fail tonight." The weakness in his body mingled with newly arrived honesty, but it didn't improve his mood. "I was supposed to share something with the group. I'm going to pray, and in the morning, I'm going to confess everything."

"Were you supposed to share about where we came from?" Noel said.

"No, it's not that."

"Are we leaving The Garden?" she pressed.

"No, but some of us are. Some of us have to go."

Leaving his best friends, Larry fast-walked for his cabin. People were getting themselves settled for the night. Voices, sounding like whispers, came across the grounds and harassed his conscience as he went inside. On other evenings it had been like sweet music, hearing people talk while brushing their teeth, making mention of the chapel service, talking about plans and dreams.

The vocabulary wasn't much different tonight. Except, now, sensations of failure were whisking between Larry's lobes. They were still brushing their teeth, still talking, but, he knew, they were in danger. And they were his responsibility.

Like a computer, scripture was fundamentally new to him. A computer answered when you asked a question. When he asked about Denise Hemingway in Pastor Chip's office the day they arrived, it gave him an answer. And like a computer, scripture gave answers to the thoughts he had.

"A man who strays from the path of understanding comes to rest in the company of the dead."

Where was the address of that scripture? Psalms? Proverbs? Surely the Old Testament.

It made no difference because now he felt like he was in the company of the dead.

JOAB
(11)

Karla wasn't too protective of her turf in the dining hall, but she was a bit protective of her cache of candles. Any lighting source was a premium, and she didn't part with her wax and wicks as freely as she did PB-&-J.

Joab took four from the drawer in the kitchen. He placed them around a 16 by 20-inch map Legaspe, with some art experience, had sketched the year before.

"We got Hiram and Frank just south of the Utility Road," Drew said. "They're actually at the turn-out where we met the bus yesterday. Hopefully, sunk a little deeper into the brush."

"Why are they south of the Utility Road exit?" Joab asked. "Shouldn't they be north to see what's coming?"

"It was Frank's idea, believe it or not," Drew said. "If we really believe they smell us, he suggested it made more sense to be south of the Utility Road. So there'd be no chance, if chased, of leading them into The Garden."

"That's a lot of thinking for Frank," Noel said.

"It is," Drew said.

It was out of context, but Joab caught the look in Drew's eyes when he spoke to Noel. It wasn't long enough to label but sufficient to confirm he had feelings for her.

Drew put a finger back to the map. "I got two, two-man teams out here." He touched the space directly north of camp.

"That's out a little far, isn't it?" Joab said.

"It is," Drew said, "but there's a trail up there, and that wasn't just one or two that hit those guys today. I don't know where they're coming from, but if they get through that section, they'll be knocking on Larry and Noel's backdoor."

"Who are the four out there?" Joab said.

"I have Crazy Chang and Anspach over to the left, just north of the amphitheater." Drew slid his finger to the right. "Kuykendall and Gavin were hit, here. I know it's a little high to have them up the hill, but this is where that mob came off the trail. I put Hernandez and Pena there since they're our best rested. Hutch knows the ground well, so he's set back about 20 yards to make sure nothing comes in behind them."

In all, 18 men were guarding the perimeter. If he could have ordered another group out there, Joab would have. But Wheeler and Bird were gone, and Kuykendall was injured. And the married men were done and leaving in the morning.

"Utility Road?"

"Bash and Legaspe."

"That works," Joab said. "I don't want anyone bothering Larry tonight. If he comes out of his cabin, fine, but unless things get crazy, no one bothers him."

"I'll be up all night," Noel said.

"We got Wolfman and Brewer on the roof," Drew continued. "They aren't going to see much, but you can hear a lot in the dark with the way the sound carries. Mason and Chapman are at the three trees. What do you want to do with Big K.? I can park him at the table and have him work the radio."

"No, he talks too much," Joab answered. "God bless him, but he needs to be back in Mandalay. Where do you have Vegas and Duran?"

"Walking the inside perimeter with me," Drew said. "But I told Duran to take a couple hours before coming out. Scott and Jay are behind the amphitheater. It's a quiet spot and a good place to put Jay. He won't admit it, but I know he's tired."

"Okay," Joab said. "Now, all we have to do is get to sunrise."

NOEL
(10)

Noel felt strong.

Things often left to Larry, and Joab now required her voice. And more was at stake at The Garden tonight than any time before. Joab was tired and grieving. Larry was, hopefully, prayerfully, righting himself. She was sure they'd be okay, but it didn't change the reality. Tonight, she was leading The Garden.

It wasn't without compassion, but compassion weighed less when factoring the camp. So if Owen, Gavin, and the others wanted to leave, they could leave. She wasn't going to beg anybody to stay.

At her bedside, she prayed while Joab and his men made things secure. She prayed for no awful sounds, blasts of shotguns or screams, nor the anthem of the age, the gnashing, and gasping through rotting teeth.

Noel prayed for the morning to come, the transition to end, and the kids to be safe. She prayed for Joab, not knowing what to ask because every time she prayed explicitly for him, her thoughts stopped. She prayed for Larry to get his head on straight.

It hurt to confront him...

...*Drew*...

Drew pushed into thought, and she pushed back.

When she said amen and wiped the tears away, she rose off her knees. It felt like two hours had passed, but it was only a few minutes. Through her window, she saw the black silhouettes next to the benches under the oaks. She recognized the rounder silhouette as Kuykendall, who decided he didn't want to be in Mandalay.

Drawing back her hair and tightening the scrunchy, she wiped her face and grabbed a flashlight off the nightstand. She considered a darker coat than the gray sweatshirt she was wearing but figured it didn't matter. Too much was going on to feel the cold.

Outside the cabin, Noel expected to hear Big K. chattering away about where he used to buy the best pastrami in East Los Angeles. But with Joab and Mason standing around him, Big K. was quiet.

Everything was quiet.

"So far, so good?" she said, reaching the trees.

"So far, so good," Joab said. "We're pushing midnight. Sun comes up at 6:35."

"You read my mind," she said. "I was just thinking about sunrise."

291

Of course, Joab could read minds. He can do everything but hunt deer.

"Nothing else matters tonight," he said and then turned away and spoke into his radio. **"You looking good, Hiram?..."**

Static... **"Good."**

Three shadows came through the area in front of the cabins near the parked cars. Noel recognized Drew's walk immediately. His shotgun slung, a baseball bat in hand.

"Kismet or Yahtzee?" Noel muttered, trying to figure what keyed her attraction.

"I always preferred Yahtzee," Kuykendall said.

"You heard that?"

"I heard you mumble." Big K. smiled. "It wasn't my ear that got bit today."

BRICKLANDER
(11)

The jeep's headlights reached the center playground, a truck came behind it, and Lieutenant Farmer jumped out.

"Brick, I need Squad A on the truck," he said. "Montview and San Antonio are under siege."

"Edge of town, north side," Bricklander said.

Captain Torres met them. "Secure the area, and get me an update. I don't think this is the show, but it's likely a preview. We're going to secure here and wait for word."

Holsopple was outside the TOC, M4 in hand, scrambling Third Platoon's soldiers to their stations.

"You know the routine! Everybody up! Everybody hot!" Bricklander said, taking the wheel of the jeep. Farmer took shotgun with Barnes in the backseat. Tired but experienced, the men complied. They rolled out of Braggs and headed for the intersection.

APCs (Armored Personnel Carriers) were used at different entries to San Quintana as checkpoints. The intersection of Montview and San Antonio was the last stop before Highway 19 resumed its trek to Sky Porch.

"Any idea how many?" Bricklander said.

"About two dozen," Farmer answered.

"Two dozen?" Bricklander said, and sick thoughts of Sky Porch came.

"One man dead, another bit," Farmer said. "They crawled inside the APC and called for help. Apparently, it happened very fast."

"Sounds like no one was paying attention," Barnes said.

"Someone was jacking around," Bricklander said.

They made quick time. Driving by several ghouls, Bricklander stopped the jeep and ordered the soldiers out of the truck. More of the dead were popping up less than half a block from the intersection.

"We're in a friendly neighborhood," he said. "Fix bayonets and only shoot if necessary. Work your way to the intersection."

The men went to work with thrusts to the head and kick's to the body. The distant sound of sirens came closer, and the Civilian Patrol set a blockade on the street behind them.

Bricklander took the left, Farmer the center of the road, and Barnes the right. They moved carefully. Barnes' gun cracked, and he looked at his superiors.

"What do you want me to do?" he said.

"I don't want you putting a bullet through someone's window. Use the fricking blade!" Farmer barked.

The street lamps were slowly glowing to life, along with the lights inside the homes. When an area became compromised, the power grid turned back on. It served as a warning to the citizens.

"Right in front of you, LT!" Barnes said before launching a bullet through the monster.

"What did he just tell you?" Bricklander said.

"I'm not going to get close to them if I don't have to," Barnes argued. "We're not trying to save the country anymore. We're trying to stay alive."

Within the platoon, Barnes was the easiest going, but tonight his fuse was short. Rage or fatigue, Bricklander wasn't sure. The dynamics were changing fast, and Barnes's actions reflected how close to the edge they all were.

They reached the edge of the homes. Directly beyond the APC, Montview rolled on to become Highway 19 with an open field on either side. San Antonio Road ran east and west—where a series of orchards began. At one time, the property was in development;

different fences and stretches of barbed wire made it difficult, but not impossible, for anyone alive or dead to pass through.

The street lamps had taken effect when the sound of suffocated gunfire hit their ears. The hatch to the APC opened. A soldier pulled himself out with a hand wrapped around his ankle. He fell backward and hung upside down, screaming.

Farmer raced to the far side and fired twice. Barnes leaped onto the vehicle and put a bullet through the head that popped out. Bricklander caught the soldier that fell and set him down.

"Oh, god! Oh, god!" The soldier, panicking, rolled on the ground and stood. He began feeling all around his chest and shoulder. "I don't know if they bit me, I don't know!"

"Barnes, can you see inside?" Bricklander said.

"It's a buffet in there." Barnes' thumbed the grenade on his belt, and Bricklander nodded. He pulled the pin, held it over the opening, "Fire in the hole!" Dropping it inside, he jumped to the ground. The vehicle shook, and smoke belched out.

"NORM's going to be hacked about the APC," Farmer said.

"You, you, and you!" Bricklander ordered the rest of the squad as it arrived. "Secure the area. Get the jeep and the truck up here and put their lights towards the mountains. I want to see what's out there." Then he stood with Farmer and Barnes facing the soldier who had come out of the APC.

"Are you bit?" Farmer said.

"I can't hear...my ears..."

"Are you bit!"

With his jacket shed and shirt ripped, he knew what they were asking. "Look! Look!" he said, spinning around and holding his hands high. "Look!"

"Drop your pants!" Bricklander ordered, and the man complied by letting his cammies fall to his ankles. Nude from the bottom down, he short-shuffled around in a circle. "Pull 'em up."

"What's your name?" Farmer said.

The soldier shook his head.

Bricklander knew who he was. The kid from Fresno, Melker. He didn't need to be trapped in an APC to be nervous. Melker got the frights from a flushing toilet.

"Melker, Lee Melker."

"What happened?" Farmer said. Melker didn't respond. "What happened?"

"It just happened! They just came. Grabbed Wilkins...I don't know how...I don't know."

"Is that him they were chewing on the other side of the APC?"

"Before we knew it, we were surrounded. They bit Silva in the neck, so we dragged him inside the APC, but he died and turned on us."

"Four United States soldiers on post, in a hot zone, get caught off guard by a couple of monsters?" Farmer said. "What the hell were you doing?"

"That's not exactly Stars and Stripes, Melker," Barnes said. "Dude, do your job."

"It wasn't just a couple," Melker said.

"Barnes," Bricklander said. "Check the highway."

With bodies of dead lying around them and up the street, the count of two dozen was correct. Melker and his friends may have been far too relaxed, no question, but they weren't hit by one or two. More gunfire came further back on Montview. Civilian Patrol was ending the remains of the assault.

Things aren't getting better.

In Sandland, Bricklander lost a friend to a sniper. The double indignity of it was having a portion of his buddy's skull, and brain matter sprayed on him. He cried, got mad, but soon boxed and crated it and returned to the game. Bricklander never got sick. With all the gore, vulgarities, and consequences the virus brought, his stomach never turned, never convulsed over something being rejected by his system or soul.

Until now.

The lights lit the blackness beyond the checkpoint. There was nothing to see, but it didn't make any difference. The point was they were a herd, a pack, and there weren't supposed to be any herds or packs in this area.

Bricklander stepped away.

Things aren't getting better.

Circumstances were forcing his decision sooner rather than later. Three thousand miles. There were three thousand miles to navigate to do what he knew was right.

The first sergeant walked to the edge of the field and heaved until his insides went dry.

LARRY
(12)

"Lord, is this you or me? I have to know."

The panels of the wood floor, under his knees, had no give to them. Larry's hands were on the back of his head, pressing his face further into the thin mattress. The extra push hopefully blocking out selfish thoughts and achieving clarity from the Lord.

"Clarity, amigo."

The great lesson—learned through experience—was about being uncomfortable. Larry wasn't comfortable preaching, teaching, leading, or speaking out on complicated matters, but when he followed through, they brought comfort in unexpected ways.

What were the arguments for working out? No pain, no gain? The cliched thoughts did nothing to encourage, but they resonated. Same old stuff; nothing worthwhile is ever easy. It was as if he was still running cross-country.

Until The Garden, Loafing Larry had no experience with hard things. Get to school on time, make Dad happy by getting the trashcans to the curb, make Mom happy by going to church. These had all been overwhelming then. Now, his mind boggled in recollection of old complaints of unfairness.

Someone didn't stop breathing because he failed to take out the trash or because he didn't go to church. But if he failed now, someone could stop breathing. They could stop breathing and come back and make someone else stop breathing. They could spend eternity apart from God.

Larry had to be right; he had to be on. He had to be uncomfortable every single moment of every single day to feel comfortable at the end of the day. That meant there was no time for pity and no room to dwell on Denise Hemingway. Not her smile, not her body, not the hour he spent with her that October morning.

Prayer wasn't always comfortable. Shutting out distractions, he accepted the discomfort of praying on his knees. It would have been much easier to do it in bed, but the distractions were greater in bed.

Discomfort brings comfort.

"I really don't want to be in this position."

"So much easier to go the easiest way. That's what you always did before, right?"

"It's easier to go the way that makes sense." Larry didn't know if he was praying anymore or talking to himself.

"Limit what I can do by attempting to make sense of what you can do? That's why we're here, isn't it, Larry? To try and make sense of what you can do?"

"I've made tough decisions. I've done everything asked of me."

"Joab?"

"You gave me, Joab."

"And now I'm taking him away."

There was a distant boom of a gun. The sound wave curled under Larry's ear lobe, and he lifted it off the bed in anticipation of more.

Dread came, and a moment later, two more blasts thundered. It would have been nice to think of the blasts as the proverbial atmospheric discharge, but he knew the sound a Remington 870 made. Not a crack, not a pop, but a boom, and the worst of the night arrived with it because it wasn't target practice.

He waited for a knock at the door and another boom. The Garden needed him. He stood.

"Where you going?"

"What would you have me do?"

There was still no voice speaking directly in his ear, but his heart tolled it out. The gunfire felt like parole from a difficult prayer time. He was needed; he could get back to this later.

Boom!

"Where are you going?"

"They need me."

"They need you here."

"Is this is you, Lord? Or is this me?"

Back on his knees, head back into the mattress, Larry prayed for something new. A new revelation, perhaps a softer one, but it didn't come. Nothing came but the reminder that he already had his answer.

Could he depend on God? He had no choice. Could he confidently share with the people of The Garden? He had to because Joab wouldn't be around any longer to depend on.

Feet ran outside, and Larry heard voices conversing. No one knocked. He got up and went to his window and saw the darkened shapes of Joab's men and Noel standing by the trees.

"Don't underestimate her."

"She's strong."

"She'll be with you."

Larry put his eyes down, and in shame, moved back to his knees. Joab had to leave, but not Noel. The two of them would become stronger in the Lord. She was a decision-maker and a leader.

"Lord forgive me..." he said. "...Again."

Boom!

"Larry, you are not among those who shrink back and are destroyed but of those who believe and are saved."

He heard that. He didn't know if he heard it audibly, but somehow he heard the scripture and knew its address from Hebrews 10:39.

"God, just tell me it's you and not me thinking or talking to myself."

"My love for Joab is great, but so is my love for you and these people. I have different plans for Joab and those that go with him."

He prayed, not for Joab but the moments after Joab's departure. And as he did, it became clear Joab and his men--with their guns and blades--didn't keep The Garden safe.

"It's you, Lord."

"It's me."

"You keep The Garden safe."

"I do."

JOAB
(12)

"Are we going?" Mason said.

"No," Joab said.

"Drew...?" They heard Hiram's voice through their earpieces.

"...Copy..." Drew said.

"...We've got problems..."

Gunfire came through the line.

"Make that big problems..." Frank chimed in.

"You want us to help?" Bash's voice came into the conversation. **"We can get there. We're on the Utility Road."**

"Nobody moves!" Joab made clear.

The shotgun booms came separate from their earpieces. Joab stepped away from the trees and stared in that direction. Hiram and Frank weren't just good men in the sense that they were good guys, but they were also good fighters.

"...Hiram...Hiram, talk to us..." Drew said. He shrugged in frustration at Joab. "...Hiram, can you fall back?..."

It was quiet. Static came on the line.

"...Hiram...Do...you...copy?"

"We're cut off...About a hundred, maybe more, I don't know, came out of the dark on the highway. There were too many, we didn't engage, but one got a hand on Frank. I fired, and it brought them down on us..."

"Can you get back to the Utility Road...?"

"...No..."

Joab went back to the table. "Move over Big K., Chapman, open the map."

The younger man unscrolled the camp map. Flashlights pointed to it.

"Drew, come here," Joab said. "They started where we met Owen and his bus yesterday, right?"

"Yes," Drew said.

Boom!

"But the two of them were further down the road, and then they took the back trail to return to camp. Ask if they can take that trail."

Two louder booms came back-to-back north of camp. The men at the three trees shifted their attention.

"That's close," Mason said.

"Pena, Hernandez...?" Drew called.

"We're cool." It was Pena's voice. **"We just had four come at us. Hernandez fired twice. We took the rest out with blades...That's it...There's no more."**

"Stay sharp..."

Boom!

"Amphitheater?" Kuykendall said.

No shots followed.

"What's going on?" Wolfman's voice came on the line.

"Get off the line, Wolf!" Drew said.

Things were spinning faster than Joab expected. As the new gunfire came, his thoughts remained on Hiram and Frank. If the herd was significant, they might fly by the trail and be unable to get back.

"Drew, follow up on Hiram and Frank, make sure they don't forget about the trail. I'm going to check the Utility Road with Chapman and Mason."

"What do you want me to do?" Noel asked.

"Besides, pray? Stay here with Big K. and be available. Do you have a weapon?"

Noel shook her head.

"Here," Kuykendall said, sliding his sheathed blade across the table. "If they get in this far, we're not going to be worrying about the noise my shotgun makes."

Joab ordered everyone to stay off the line unless it was an emergency. His heart grew sick at the thought of Hiram and Frank being lost. Running to the Utility Road, he saw a cabin door crack open, and Charles Kiln stick his head out.

"Shut the door!" He shouted, and the older man complied.

He paused at the edge of the Utility Road and dropped to a knee.

"We're going to go up to Legaspe and Bash. I'm going to leave one of you there to make sure these guys aren't surprised if the devils come off the road. Only fire as a last resort."

"Isn't it a little late for that," Chapman said. "Hiram and Frank are already firing."

"No," Joab made clear. "With the herd on the road, we want them chasing Hiram and Frank. Their firing leads the devils away."

Mason and Chapman moved with him. The steady trot of their feet hitting the gravel told the men in front of them they were friends, not foes. Devils didn't run.

"...Hiram, talk to me...Tell me where you're at..." Drew's voice carried into Joab's earpiece.

Static answered.

They kept on the Utility Road.

"Jefe?" Legaspe's voice came out of the dark.

"Yeah," Joab said and then made out the spot where Legaspe and Bash had settled. They were in the bushes to the right, the mid-point between the camp and the highway.

"Where are the other shots coming from?" Bash said.

"North," Joab said. "Listen, if it starts getting hairy out here, I'm gonna pull you back. If we have to make a stand, we'll make it at The Garden."

"We're good," Bash said. "It's quiet. We don't even smell anything."

"We can't have any firing," Joab said. "This herd needs to keep chasing Hiram and Frank."

"Sucks for them," Bash said.

"Yes, it does."

Drew's voice came back. **"...You've had enough time Hiram...Talk to me...Did you reach the trail?"**

As the men crouched, Joab went onto the Utility Road. He thought he heard the far away movement of feet going down the highway but wasn't sure. There was no sound of anything coming their way.

Boom!

It came farther south.

"We're outta here," Joab said. "Chapman, you stay. I want the three of you in a triangle. Eyes everywhere; stay sharp!" He tapped Mason on the arm and motioned it was time to go.

"Nothing's getting by us," Bash said.

"...Hiram?...Frank? This is Drew..."

Static... **"Hiram's bit..."**

NOEL
(11)

"Hiram got bit," Drew said. "I don't know how bad."

Noel wasn't concerned about one bite but instinctively rubbed the scarred area beneath her sweatshirt.

"Come on, Frank, talk to me..." Drew said.

Duran and Vegas stepped from the space between her and Larry's cabins. They paused as if waiting for another sound to come. Vegas squatted to get a better look at something.

"It be nice if they tipped the rest of us on why they're doing that," Kuykendall said in a calm voice. The night's tension had quelled his barking style of speech and big laughter, but not the peace running through him.

"It would be," she said, following them with her eyes. "Can you run, Big K.?"

"Nope," he said. "I'd like to say it's my last stand, but it's more like my last sit." He squashed a laugh into a grunt. Kuykendall was always the best fan of his humor.

"Then, my friend, what are you doing out here?"

"I don't know," he shrugged and grinned, "It's my home, my family. Mi barrio, ese."

"Troy turned an ankle yesterday and hasn't left his bunk since. He's got Karla bringing him his food. You got bit twice today, you should be in Mandalay."

"I'm not Troy," Kuykendall said. "And if I were in Mandalay, I'd be all by myself going crazy."

"Karla didn't bring you any of the hot pastrami we had, did she?" Noel sat beside him.

"No, she didn't, but if you close your eyes when eating peanut butter and jelly..."

"...Does it taste like pastrami?"

"Nah, it tastes like peanut butter and jelly."

Noel smiled. "You're a good soul, dude."

"I try to be." He elbowed her and whispered, "I'm rooting for you two," then bent his head toward Drew.

She let a moment pass, not knowing if he could see her blushing in the dark. "You can go into my cabin and still be close to the action."

"I like it out here," Kuykendall said. "And I ain't waiting for something to happen to me. Before these devils feast, they'll eat all six of what Betsy has to offer." He lifted the shotgun.

"Betsy? Like Davey Crockett?"

"Fifth-grade teacher," he said. "Mrs. Betsy was meaner than sin."

"That's funny."

Vegas and Duran gave up and came to the trees.

"Sorry to freak you," Vegas said. "Thought we heard something behind the cabins."

"Don't be," she said. Ever since moving into her glorified closet, there were countless times Noel heard uncommon noises in the middle of the night. Bumps and scratches at the wood that didn't rhyme with the everyday sounds she'd grown accustomed to. "There's always something crawling around out there."

"Everyone check-in," Drew said.

"Can I listen?" she asked Kuykendall, and he pulled his earpiece and gave it to her.

"Perimeter check-in...Crazy Chang-Anspach?..."

"We're good..."

"Hernandez-Pena?..."

"All quiet here..."

"Orlando-Big Leon?..."

"**Did you say Orlando?...**" Orlando's voice came back. "**Yeah, yeah, yeah...we're good.**"

Static sparked up...

Noel caught sight of Joab and Mason coming back to the trees.

"**...We're not going to make it back...**" It was Hiram's voice.

"**Go again, Hiram...**" Drew spoke. "**Did you miss the trail?...**"

The line opened up, and they could hear the heavy breathing of Hiram; "**I got it...**" Frank said...The static stopped, and the line opened again.

"**I got bit on the shoulder...**" Hiram said. "**Frank took some pellets in his leg when I fired at a devil grabbing up at us...**" Hiram was panting... "**Tell them how you shot me...**" Frank's voice came... "**We bypassed the trail. They're too close to us. We wouldn't be able to shake them. They'd follow us back to The Garden.**"

Boom! Boom!

"**We're going down the hill...lead them away...we'll try for the old church. Maybe you can pick us up in the morning...or...**"

The line went still.

Drew spoke into the radio. "**Nobody even think about it... Check-in; Legaspe-Bash?**"

Noel knew others would want to save Hiram and Frank, so Drew cut them off before they could offer. They couldn't help, and with both of them bleeding, they were likely to be tracked and devoured on the highway. A shudder went through her.

They had gone so long without losing anybody. Now four were as good as dead in less than 24 hours. When the sun came up, the only thing preventing Owen and an exodus would be the traffic of devils on the highway.

"We're good..." Bash reported.

"Big Geoff-Matts?..."

"Still here like a couple of fools..." Big Geoff said.

"Sandoval?..."

"Still in business..." The old Marine responded.

Noel never knew a Hiram growing up, never knew a "Bird," a "Big K," or a "Crazy Chang." They were 30-Mighty Men with names, nicknames, and skin colors as different as fingerprints. Young men who needed a world upside down—like she and Larry needed a closet door to come through—to discover their worth. But if granted gray hair, old age, and grandchildren, she'd always talk about them and make people remember who they were and what they did.

"Wolfman-Brewer?..."

Joab and Mason reached the trees. She felt sadness trying to drown her and forced herself to stay present. There'd be a time to cry later and let it all go.

"We left Chapman on the utility road," Mason said.

"Good on the roof," Brewer's voice spoke back to Drew.

"You heard about Hiram and Frank?" Noel said before remembering they were all listening to the same channel.

Joab nodded. "Anything going on here?"

"We, I, thought I heard something behind cabins..." Vegas said.

"Jay-Scott?..."

"Nothing?" Joab said.

Duran and Vegas shook their heads.

"We haven't heard a shot north of us since you went to the utility road," Drew said. "Maybe we're catching an expensive break with the devils chasing Hiram and Frank."

"If they're both bleeding, there's no way they'll lose them," Joab said. "They've done something amazing for us. We have to trust the Lord will take care of them."

Noel gazed at the stars building in the black sky and quickly prayed.

"Jay-Scott?..."

Sorrow continued to punch at her. These men couldn't die.

"Jay-Scott? Check-in, let's go." Rare agitation was in Drew's voice.

Please, God, please don't let anyone else die.

"Jay, come on!" Drew shouted.

"They should be answering," Joab said.

BRICKLANDER
(12)

Sipping water helped.

When Bricklander finished puking, Jarvis checked on him. The medic explained an aggravated stomach should be expected after running around all day and night while inhaling his chow in between.

"People your age, Sarge, don't even ride rollercoasters anymore," Jarvis said. "You shouldn't push it."

"And the horse you rode in on, Jarvis," Bricklander said.

"Thanks, but no. I'm saving myself for marriage."

No one needed to know what his mind and body were working through. It was okay to vomit. It was okay to be vomiting because of too much Jack Daniels, the flu, or even fatigue. But in the first sergeant's line of thinking, there was no way he'd let anyone know the real reason. Especially when Minister Tim showed up, with his lying smile, to take notes and account for all the bullets spent dealing with the breach.

An hour had passed since the last shot, and the power grid was going to be shut down. Things would darken, but Bricklander liked it better when the street lamps were off and the light was natural.

Without his jacket, he was cold. There wouldn't be frost on the vehicles at daybreak, but the cool air attacked his bones. The type of bones belonging to people who didn't ride rollercoasters anymore.

"You think NORM's sending us out there when the sun comes up?" Lancaster asked, sidling beside him. Their backs were leaning against the deceased APC, looking north. Steam venting from their mouths.

"I gotta feeling we're going to beat feet to that church."

"You cold?"

"Just a little."

"PNN's reporting Holsopple would warm you up if you showed some interest," Lancaster said.

"It's the end of the world, and thousands of dead are ready to fall all over us, and your biggest priority is Holsopple?"

"She is," he said in a sullen voice. "To tell you the truth, she's the happiest thought I can come up with."

Bricklander tasted some excess bile and swallowed some water. "I owe you a lot."

Lancaster never took a bullet for Bricklander, dove on a live grenade, or patched him up after being wounded. What he did was his job. He was clockwork, the very eyes you wanted to be looking out for you, which multiplied into thousands of moments to be thankful for.

"That's for sure."

"Okay, here's some payback. When the sun comes up, we're going to get royally screwed. NORM's going to send us down the road to be his eyes and a buffer if Sky Porch is open. Reinforcements will be brought to San Quintana. But we'll be left to die out there."

"Wow, scoop city, Brick," Lancaster joked. "I never would've figured that out on my own."

"But I'm not going to die out there," Bricklander turned to face his friend. "I'm not kidding. I'm going to whack anybody in the way of me getting back to Virginia."

"You're gonna bounce?" Lancaster said. "How is that paying me back?"

"I need a wingman, you've got no place to go, and the Old Dominion beckons. So start believing you're not going to die. No matter how bad NORM sticks it to us, keep believing you're not going to die and that Gayle Holsopple won't be the last woman you long to nail."

"So it's really happening? It's all getting ready to collapse?"

"It's already started. Mutinies in Hawaii, Long Beach, up and down the coast," Bricklander said, "You've got nothing, and I've got a little bit to offer. Some isolation, a roof, and eyes to watch your six."

He stared deep into Lancaster's eyes until his friend turned away in awkwardness. Their attention went back to Highway 19, and a few cloudy breaths later, Lancaster spoke. "Do you have a plan?"

"It starts with us not dying and ends with NORM believing we did. We survived the Arroyo Seco—we're not dying here."

"Stars and Stripes," Lancaster said. "We going to bail on our boys?"

"No, we fight with them until the church falls. But let's be honest, they're probably all going to die."

"But we're not?"

Bricklander answered with a shake of the head.

"How can you be so certain?"

"I've made a decision. It's not happening."

Lancaster grinned. "What about Minister Tim?"

"If he CAB chases with us out to the church, then he's dying today."

LARRY
(13)

A burning bush would have been fantastic. The Red Sea parting, a fiery chariot, or club level seating at the resurrection would have cleared things up real nice.

Larry's sign? Best he could figure--Sky Porch. On that point, Owen was right about something.

That sign, reinforced by sounds of gunfire, running feet, and gatherings around the three trees, testified The Garden would be a different place when the sun rose.

He wanted to turn on his radio, wanted to hear what was happening, but tonight it wasn't his fight. His fight was in the cabin with fears, thoughts, and the search to find functionality to his faith before it eroded.

"How long until you trust me?"

Voice of God or the purer part of his soul? He couldn't confirm the source of the counseling. Not because it was harsh, but because it was true. Its authority required deep, personal effacement. To disobey would be akin to never being obedient any day of his life.

"How have I not trusted?" He raised his hands—scrunchy in the right—upward, wanting to shout an expletive to drive it home. "I open a door, and, suddenly, I'm at the end of the world. You've taken everything, every dream, every plan, everything I wanted. I trusted people I didn't know. I trusted because you wanted me to trust, and now this?"

How could God ask for more? He was just a doobie roller with nothing left to give, except for that small piece of comfort, making it easier for him to put his head down at night.

"Everything, Larry? Be honest."

"I've given you Joab."

"Now give me someone else."

"I won't say it. You want me to say it, but I won't say it." Larry paced to the door of the cabin. Pressing his face against it, he smelled the distressed wood. "This isn't cool. I don't talk to her, I don't see her, and you made sure she was married. So because I think about her, it means I'm not living the life you want me to live?"

"Free yourself. Give me Denise Hemingway."

"God, I love her," he said, sliding to his knees. "I love her. You give me one moment with her, and then you take me away. I'll always love her."

"Trust me."

"I know I'm never going to see her again. I'm never going to touch her, never going to kiss her, she's never going to love me, and now I can't even think about her?"

"She's a millstone around your neck."

Poets dramatized emotions to the point of ludicrous. Larry hated those assignments, couldn't stand them, couldn't stand whining and groaning about lost love. It was easy to mock those who said they gave their heart to another. Yet it was here, at this moment, he understood the ferocious pain of God asking him to put away thoughts and dreams of Denise Hemingway.

"She's *not evil, she's not wicked, I love her, but she's not what I have for you."*

"What could you possibly have for me?" He knew he didn't need to qualify it by mentioning forgiveness, salvation, and eternal life, which he clearly understood. On this earth, though, what was there to make him feel the way Denise made him feel? When he dreamed of her when he thought of her? "What's going to comfort me, Lord?"

"I know the plans I have for you. Plans to prosper you and not to harm you, plans to give you hope and a future."

He teared up and smirked, "There are times you make me hate scripture."

"Truth hurts. When they fell, it hurt, it hurt bad, but it didn't change what was true."

Going back to his bed, tears turned into a heaving cry he masked by pulling the sleeping bag over his face. It hurt physically. It was doom being poured all over him, finality. There was no choice to make, no decision—not really--only the opening of a previously well-guarded corner of his heart to the Lord.

He did it. On the strength of his faith, he pushed it open, and the Spirit flooded in.

Denise dug in her claws, which were images of her beauty and the distant but familiar sounds of her voice. She relented, and a new wave of tears came as she left his thoughts. His true love—he was certain Denise had been his true love—Larry set adrift.

"I don't feel any better."

"Let go of the scrunchy."

Without smelling it a last time, Larry hurled it across the room.

"I still don't feel any better."

"You will."

Exhausted and flat, the Lord began to reset Larry's heart and priorities. It became clear to him that much of his goodness and obedience he'd considered a point system—a way of earning Denise.

"She'll come back. Don't let her in. You can't stop the first thought…"

"…But I can stop the second," Larry said. "Yeah, I know."

A worse terror than devils marching on The Garden? It was, but as emotion abated, he did feel the release. By surrender, he'd put all the pressure back on God. God was going to have to show him, prove to him, that he had something better.

JOAB
(13)

"I'm going to the amphitheater," Joab said. "Mason?"

"Yes."

"Everyone! No more firing tonight unless it's a last resort," Joab said into the radio. **"Something gets through the perimeter use blades, bats, or the butt of your guns. We do not want the herd on the highway changing direction."**

How he learned tactics, Joab didn't know. Like a blind man with heightened hearing, he felt it must have been a dormant ability until other gifts were shut down. Like a well-prepared and often used sermon, directions came out of him with little to zero debate between the ears.

Moving away from the trees, he studied the bend of ground leading to the amphitheater. Nothing could surprise them unless it came from the one place that wasn't reporting.

Joab looked at Drew. "If you think we need help, come running."

"You think devils are inside?" Drew said.

"I don't know, but we're about to find out. Mason, let's go."

"Be careful, boss," Kuykendall said. "It's stormy out there."

They took off. Joab stopped at the shed and shined his flashlight inside. "Better safe than sorry."

"I'd have checked it if you didn't," Mason said.

The pitch from the center of camp went downhill to the amphitheater. From the trees, it was the only blind spot at The Garden. To the left was the meadow, but it was on slightly elevated ground. The grade beyond the meadow, pushing to the south and west, was so steep, it was impossible for the living, let alone the dead, to climb without a rope.

Beyond the amphitheater, there were no structures, and the forest was thick. But there was a slight slope that might have allowed intruders, so they guarded it.

When they reached the trail, Joab stopped.

"You see something?" Mason whispered.

He held a finger to his mouth for them to listen and then spoke. "Stay a few yards back. Keep me in view."

Joab went onto the foot trail. Low weeds, dead grass, nothing impaired his line of sight. A feeling of being ambushed came over him. He didn't see anything, wasn't even sure if he heard anything, but his blade was out as he reached the top row of benches.

He came to the second step, checking to the right and left. Counting the rows, he passed the third and fourth row. Pausing, Joab turned to see Mason at the top protecting his six as gamers Kuykendall and Frank taught them to say.

Fifth row, sixth row, steam ebbed off his lips. At the seventh row, he saw it.

A dark figure, overweight, foul-smelling, was sitting on the aisle seat in the next to last row at the theater's base. Joab, with machete in his right hand, rose to the tips of his feet to minimize any sound.

Thoughts raced. Jay and Scott were gone, or, worse, someone inside the camp had turned.

Ping.

Knowing Joab was getting closer, the devil didn't budge. He hated its stillness, but that stillness was action, a brain function. They were more purposeful than anyone wanted to believe. And there was a growing, albeit rudimentary, coordination to them. Evil's best disguise was convincing the good, the holy, that it didn't exist, have purpose, or strategy. But the longer the Sin Virus was with them, Joab began to subscribe to the devils owning intelligence.

They're learning.

Feet raced from behind. Turning, Joab saw Mason running and diving with his blade in front of him. A hand touched his shoulder and let go as Mason's body drove it back into the benches.

There was the crash of broken wood and a quick glimpse of Mason's blade coming down before rolling to the bottom. The devil in the seat came for Joab. Growling, it nearly caught him off guard. Backing a step to improve the angle, Joab chopped the machete into its skull. Bone shattered, and brain separated.

"Mason!" Joab moved to the floor of the amphitheater.

Mason, feverishly, was hacking the devil apart. Through the dark, Joab could see rage taking him.

"Mason," he said, keeping it from a shout.

"It scratched me," he said. "It scratched me!"

"Mason," Joab held out a hand. "It's okay, it's okay."

Mason lowered the machete, took a breath, and acknowledged Joab.

"Cool down," Joab said. "You saved my life, brother."

"I hate them!" He seethed, sucking air back through his system. "I hate them."

They heard snarling and gnashing of teeth. Both thumbed their flashlights to the far side of the amphitheater.

NOEL
(12)

"Drew!" Duran said. "Amphitheater!"

Noel spun and saw lights coming from the lower end of the camp. The rule was to never aim a flashlight skyward, and if so, never for any length of time to avoid attention.

"Vegas, stay with Big K., Duran, come with me," Drew ordered. Both broke into a sprint, and Noel didn't hesitate. Fear was secondary because this was The Garden, and as Kuykendall said, The Garden was home. It's what she'd say to Joab when he got after her for not staying by the trees.

Passing the shed and reaching the bend, she heard a struggle.

"Coming in! Coming in!" Drew shouted to make sure Joab and Mason didn't shoot. From the top row of benches, she saw the roll of flashlights on the ground. Drew and Duran took the center aisle.

Joab picked up one flashlight as he swung his machete at three different devils. Mason, finishing off another, could be seen in the shine of a second flashlight resting on the steps. It illuminated the corpses of three devils splayed out across the ground.

Drew swung his bat through the head of the devil Joab was tangling with. Freed, Joab hacked off the extended arms of another and kicked it back. Mason, flashlight back in hand, lit the final one for Drew to turn his Louisville Slugger on. Two swings from a left-handed batting stance ended the devil's run.

Joab circled left of the armless devil as it howled at him in a loud voice. Drew moved to the right. The sound of it told Noel it was a recent transition. It was short, and when Duran put light on it, she knew why it had been quicker, stronger, and louder than the rest.

"Iccchhhabosh!" The devil verbalized. "Iccchhhabosh!"

Noel came to the bottom step. The situation wasn't what she thought it would be. It was worse.

Duran shined his light over the benches before aiming it to the back of the amphitheater to make sure nothing else was coming in around them.

"How can this be?" Drew said.

It bore its white teeth in a seething growl. Firey yellow eyes issued hate to all of them. Red blood, not black, poured from its wounds. A red stain on the side of its neck fell to the chest of a dark sweatshirt.

"It's speaking," Duran said.

"Oh god," Mason said.

"Take him out," Noel said. "Take him out, Drew!"

Drew approached Jay, now back by virus.

"Iccchhhabosh!"

His eyes, burning yellow, fixed on her, and Noel felt pity instead of fear. The hatred, the sin, the demonic in the tent of Jay's body could do nothing to her. What had been his mindset for him to miss all the grace Christ had to offer?

He bolted at her.

Noel didn't have to react. Drew took care of it with a thud and sickening splat. Jay, their guy, one of Joab's Mighty Men, was down and dead at their feet.

Quiet came. The kind of quiet a whisper could explode. The one who spoke first needed tremendous courage because it was the most terror they'd faced since coming to The Garden.

Duran went behind the amphitheater and shined his light.

Noel's adrenaline boiled. She could cry, or she could think. Because The Garden needed her to be right, she fought the temptation of despair and chose to think.

Drew kneeled alongside Jay. "Noel, how can this be?" Examining him, she saw the lost look on his face before Joab thumbed off his flashlight.

"I counted eight," Mason said, turning off his light. Their eyes began to readjust to the night. "There were eight."

If Joab had been in the disposition to speak, she would have stayed quiet, but he wasn't. He made no sounds or movements. It was odd for him not to have a response and direction to give. But Noel had the answer come.

Duran came back. "There's nothing else back there."

"Does this mean we're not immune anymore?" Mason said.

"It can't," Drew said. "Noel's been bit. Kuykendall was bit today, so was Larry."

Noel knew. Not only was there a gap in the perimeter, but worse, somebody had lived with them for 18 months and acquired no faith.

"Jay wasn't a believer," she said. "This can't happen to a believer. The virus does not affect those with a believing loyalty. We know this," she said with conviction, "nothing's changed."

"What do you mean he wasn't a believer?" Duran said. "He was with all this time. He was at the chapels..."

"What do you think that is, Derek!" Mason exploded. "Looks like a devil to me."

Where are you, Joab?

"Noel, that's the truth, isn't it?" Mason said. "Jay wasn't a believer. Because if he was, I'm doing myself right now." He pulled a snub-nosed .38 from the back of his waistband and put it to his temple.

"What are you doing?" Drew said. "Put the gun down!"

Mason turned his shoulder for them to see the blood running out of his upper bicep. In the dark, there was enough star shine for Noel to see the separate streams spilling down. "I've got to know because it's not happening to me."

"Jay wasn't a believer," Noel said, stepping to Mason. "Big K.'s our proof, and so is Larry. Mason, are you a believer? Have you accepted Christ?"

"Yes."

"Then put the gun the down, brother," she said, coming closer. "You're going to be fine."

"Something new in the virus?" Duran asked. "A mutation?"

"Only if Kuykendall and Larry suddenly start developing a fever," Noel said. "Hear me, we are immune."

But The Garden was now vulnerable. What hit Noel the hardest was that they had become too dependent on...

..*Joab and his men.*

Now she knew why Larry was struggling. The one who needed to leave was the one they depended on more than God—Joab.

"Scott, are you out there?...Over." Drew called into the radio.

Joab, sitting on a bench, ran both hands through his hair hanging free on his shoulders. "I was certain of him."

"This has to be something new," Duran said.

"Go easy on the something new talk," Drew said. "All that's new is that not everybody in The Garden is what we believed they were."

"I'd appreciate that," Mason said. "I'd appreciate it a lot more if somebody stuck a thermometer in Big K.'s mouth."

"Nothing's changed," Noel spoke, but it didn't sound like her to her ears. Strange confidence, more robust and less amiable, came upon her. "Nothing's changed in the virus. Only our assumptions."

Staring at the mutilated body of someone they thought part of their family, Noel, compelled by obedience, began to share.

"Believers, don't turn," she said. "We can still manage ourselves a bit with the sword, but our reliance has to be on the blood. Don't ask me how I know. I just know. Jay was a good guy, but he believed in his shotgun and his strength. Now he's dead. The devils getting in tonight are the least of our problems. We have to consider how many in camp are just going through the motions but have not decided for Christ."

"You think there are others?" Joab said, shaken.

"Owen," Duran said. "That's one."

"Jay fooled us," Noel said to Joab. "We have food, shelter, pretty good security…Who wouldn't repeat the right words just to be here?"

"Mason, you alright?" Joab asked, standing back up, sheathing his blade.

The younger man put his head down, exhaled, and looked up. "Do you trust me, Joab?"

"And that's a bingo," Noel said. "That's our problem." She looked directly at Mason. "Believers cannot turn, but you're the only one that can answer the question about being a believer."

"Scott's not answering," Drew said. He looked at Joab standing next to Mason. **"Vegas, you copy?"**

"…Yes…"

"Put a hand to Kuykendall's forehead and see if he has a fever."

"…Copy…"

"We need Scott's body found," Noel said. "We have to find it or what's left of it to confirm he didn't turn."

Drew and Duran began turning bodies over as Noel examined Mason's wound. It wasn't a bite but three deep scratches.

"…I have no fever…" Kuykendall clicked in.

"... He's good..." Vegas voice came.

"We'll set up a new line at the top of the amphitheater for tonight," Noel said. "Drew, Duran, it's yours. Let's get Vegas to help you out." Words came so fast she didn't even look to Joab for approval.

"...Vegas come on down...," Drew said.

"Mason, we'll get you cleaned up at the trees. And Joab, you're tired," she said to him as they came up the steps. "You need to get some sleep. I've got this."

"She's right," Drew added. "You've been going all day. We'll get you in a few hours."

"Okay," Joab said.

Vegas, going the other way, passed them at the shed. "How bad is it?"

"Bad," Noel said. "Drew and Duran will clue you in."

They kept walking, and Joab veered to the dining hall without saying anything more. Noel saw his tears.

"Am I going to live?" Mason asked.

"I don't know how long you're going to live any more than I know how long I'm going to live. But, these scratches aren't going to do you in."

Mason stopped and began to sob. "I'm sorry. I'm not afraid of dying, but..."

"You've seen my scar," she said, "I've had my moments. This night's terrible, but this night is also confirming who you are in the Lord, right?"

Mason wiped at his eyes. "I feel weak."

"You shouldn't. You're as normal as the rest of us. You're his temple." She jabbed two fingers against his heart. Strength returned to Mason's expression. "I'm not kidding you. He dwells in you. So come on, let's get you patched and ready to rumble because the night's not over."

When they reached the trees, Noel told Kuykendall to pass the word about Jay. Joab's men had a right to know.

"Jay?" Kuykendall said.

Mason took a seat alongside him and confirmed with a nod.

Noel ripped open the plastic containing gauze. "It looks good," she said, going to work on his wounds. "I don't think it's going to bother you much. You seem like you're a bleeder, though."

"Always," he said. "The tiniest nick, and I gush."

She taped over the gauze and pulled the shirt down on the shoulder. "Might not be a bad idea for you to get some sleep in Mandalay as well."

"We probably need…" Mason began, but his attention went to something behind her. "Excuse me." He casually walked from the picnic bench to the spot between her and Larry's cabin, pulled his machete, and took out the devil.

BRICKLANDER
(13)

Sunrise was a mesh of dawn and dusk. The perfect niche where it didn't matter if the sun was coming up or going down. It was beautiful, and California beautiful meant no humidity, temperatures in the low sixties, mild breezes coming from the south…And a strong chance of flesh-eating monsters striking randomly from the foothills.

First Platoon remained deployed along the intersection, facing the mountains. They leaned against posts, found spots against rocks, and continually kept their eyes out to the open stretches investors once dreamed of developing.

Bricklander passed the night with his back against the APC, thankful his gut had quieted. When he heaved, he heaved. Rosa said she never saw anyone vomit the way he vomited. *"It's like you're puking out every meal you've had since high school."*

The jag was over. Only an improving raspiness lingered at the back of his throat.

Currently, under a purple sky, the field was clear. Assured nothing was moving their way, the men began breaking out rations. Bricklander nibbled at a nutrition bar.

"Sarge?" Barnes said. "LT wants to see you."

"Where is he?"

"Other side of the APC."

"Are you embracing the suck, Barnes?"

"I'm cool."

"Then, I don't want to see what I saw last night," Bricklander said. "It has nothing to do with Stars and Stripes but thinking. You stop thinking, and you die. You get me?"

"I get you."

Coming around the APC, he could see neighborhood people coming out of their homes ready to start the day. A sanitation truck, two blocks away, was picking up trash and corpses.

"It's black," Doughty said, handing him a paper cup with coffee. "I was told you didn't like candy-boy creamer."

"That's right," he said. "Do you?"

Doughty shook his head.

"I'm starting to love Texas more and more," Bricklander said, gulping the brew and wondering how something could taste so lousy and good at the same time.

Sitting on the APC, helmet off, smoke hanging from his lip, Farmer looked worse than any ten miles outside Kabul. Something other than fatigue was wearing on him. He stared towards San Quintana, mouthing an expletive.

"Is it all that bad, LT?" Bricklander said. "You need some bad coffee for perspective?"

The lieutenant looked at him with no expression. "We're to push out on Highway 19 and set up a forward position near the foot of the mountain."

"Just us?"

"Just us."

Bricklander, glad to finally hear it, wasn't shocked.

"Torres and Holsopple will remain in San Quintana. We'll set up in the church and play lookout," Farmer nodded to convince himself. "Then NORM will decide what he wants to do."

"We knew it was coming," Bricklander said. "Just a question of when and where."

"Well, now we know when, and where we'll be hung out to dry," Farmer said.

"Scrounge up some air support and burn Sky Porch down. There's a fully locked and loaded Apache at Brackett. It could put so much hate on the mountain we'd never have to worry about it again."

"NORM's got other things on his plate." Farmer spat the cigarette out of his mouth and slid off the vehicle. Putting his hands to his face, he ran them over his shaved head. The sun's rays were filtering out the purple.

"What else is going on?" Bricklander said.

"Just have everyone loaded and ready to go by 7:15."

The total count, two squads, including Farmer, was 24. This left 52 behind to defend San Quintana.

"Are they going to order the people to fight?" Bricklander said.

"Not our problem," Farmer said.

As depressing as the situation was, Bricklander knew something else was hanging over them.

A jeep reached the intersection. Minister Tim, collared and all, was in the passenger seat. A black book was in his hand, no doubt to take a census on the number of shots fired the previous night and determine if they were necessary.

"Talk to me, LT," Bricklander said.

"You really want to know?" Farmer said. "I'm supposed to keep it under wraps, but what the hell? We're probably all going to die today, anyways, right?"

"Go ahead," Bricklander said, reminding himself he had no intention of dying.

Farmer exhaled and faced him. "At six o'clock this morning, Eastern Time, China attacked Taiwan." He rubbed his eyes. "It's not official yet, but we're at war with China. So short of going to nukes, they'll likely, in a few hours, have an unobstructed path all the way to Hawaii."

A laugh shot out of Bricklander. Instead of being surprised, Farmer began to grin.

"With the fleet scattered and everyone bogged down, how could it not happen?" Bricklander said, working to tamp down further laughter. "Perfect timing. Sorry." He kept laughing. It was too funny not to laugh. There was relief in knowing that no matter how the day turned out, he'd be making his way to Virginia because this party was over.

"And I don't have all the details," Farmer continued, "but there was a mutiny in Hawaii, and everyone's trying to get out. I've got family there."

Bricklander sobered. "I heard something about the mutiny. I didn't know about family, I'm sorry."

"No worries, but now you know why I look like I'm hanging by a thread."

LARRY
(14)

Devastating.

Before Noel told him about Jay and the others, he knew the night had been The Garden's worst. Adding to it, a devil slipped through the perimeter at dawn and took a chunk of Sandoval's left forearm. Two hours elapsed before Sandoval passed the acid test Jay hadn't.

A little after eight, most of the adults gathered by the three trees. Larry stood on the picnic table. Joab, behind him, leaned against an oak while Noel stood with those facing him. After passing tea and Tang, Karla, Beth, and Debbie were feeding the children in the dining hall, where Wolfman sat on the porch next to Tammy.

Again, Larry didn't know what he was going to say, yet he knew. When things were right between him and the Spirit, the words always came. Yesterday every word felt like he was bench pressing three hundred pounds of Kuykendall. Today, the truth was the truth, grace was grace, and though the burden was there, the burden was lighter.

Did the people want to hear the truth Larry was about to share? He didn't think so. They wanted comfort. They wanted a promise of safety, and, after he shared what he needed to share, they'd, likely, want to put a rope around his neck.

"A lot of you know it was a bad night," he said. "It's been a bad twenty-four hours. We've lost Wheeler, Bird, Hiram, and Frank as well as Scott and Jay." As he spoke, there was a rippling gasp working across the crowd. "Kuykendall, myself, and Sandoval have been bit, Mason deeply scratched, and Gavin had a very close call. The devils are working down from Sky Porch."

If he didn't have their attention before, he had it at the linking of the deaths and Sky Porch.

"The report from Joab says they're going down in a stream bed on the other side of Highway 19 toward the flatlands. But many have found their way to the road by smell or scavenging. Thanks to

Hiram and Frank, dozens, maybe hundreds have blown by us since last night."

No murmur. No talk. Still no disapproving shake of the head. Not even Owen, tired and looking like he'd spent the last few hours beating himself up, offered any attitude.

"We're assuming Scott's gone. We never found his body," Larry said. "But Jay, we know about for sure. So stick with me because I have a lot to say, and it doesn't get better." He paused, cleared his throat, then continued. "Jay turned last night."

"What?" Several voices came out of the crowd.

"That's impossible." Several different voices said and repeated. "Impossible."

"During the night, Scott and Jay were overwhelmed on the west side of camp. They never got off a radio call. Joab and Mason found Jay and seven other devils in the amphitheater."

It was quiet. They processed the loss, they processed shock, and then they processed the scariest part.

"So, our faith doesn't shield us anymore?" Ken Hong said.

"It does," Larry said. "Mr. Sandoval?"

The old Marine raised his bandaged left arm.

"He was bit early this morning and shows no sign of infection. Kuykendall was bit yesterday and has no infection." Larry held up his wrapped hand. "I was bit yesterday. I have no fever."

"So, some of us get it but not others?" Charles Kiln said. "I don't understand."

Larry hesitated.

"Tell us, Larry," Liz called out in her unfiltered style. "Tell us the truth. We believe you."

Liz didn't know how much her statement blessed him. It didn't make what he had to say easier, but it felt good to hear.

"What it means is, up to this point, we've never questioned anyone's faith," Larry said. "When anyone said they accepted Christ, we took it that they had accepted Christ. For the most part, fruits of living the life bear those things out. Some of you might think this is judgment on Jay and inappropriate. But out of fear of being labeled judgmental, the church has conditioned you not to assess or discern the actions of those among you. Truth has become something we're too frightened to share. And the truth in this situation is, Jay was not a Christian."

"That's not true," said Kiln. "I knew Jay and saw him work hard to protect this camp. He was a good man."

"I was with him on patrol yesterday, I agree," Joab said. "But a few hours ago, I saw him in the amphitheater, eyes yellow, trying to kill me. This virus is a spiritual truth serum. You cannot have a form of godliness; you've got to have the real thing. I know this by the way I lived before The Tilt. I know this because Wheeler died right in front of me, and he didn't turn."

The group reflected, and murmuring spread.

"Then how are we going to know if people truly believe?" Gavin said.

"We're going to have to ask," Larry said. "We're going to have to do a better job of teaching. Jay's proof you can fake it—at least for a while."

Owen's hand went up. "I have to ask then," he said without sarcasm. "How do you defend this place now?"

It was time for part two. Larry looked at Noel, and she flexed a smile of approval.

"I've been leading this camp as if it was the last bastion on earth. As if we were supposed to stay here and stand," Larry said. "Friends, you might not want to hear this, but we are not supposed to stay here. We're supposed to train here. To train others to depend and trust solely on God. To a degree, I've failed."

"What do you mean?" Kelly said, standing with her husband, Alan.

"The Garden was provided by the Lord to make us ready to go out, in dependence upon him, and preach the gospel," he said. "And I mean the gospel, not good works, not service projects, or soul-soothing social work as Joab describes it."

Owen's face gave a wince.

"We've both failed," Noel said unexpectedly. She came and stood below him. "We've been faithful in sharing the gospel, but we haven't been putting our faith in the Lord about protecting The Garden."

"We've been putting too much faith in Joab," Larry said. It was a heavy blow. Eyes became pallid, and jaws hung. "Joab's a Christian man," he turned to his mentor and then back to the crowd. "But in this world, he's a warrior. His calling is not to defend this camp."

"Are you crazy?" Kiln said. "Without Joab, we'd all be dead!" Loudly, others agreed.

"Our problem's not the devils," Larry said, gaining strength as the words left his mouth. "Those souls are lost, and they're in the way of those we have to reach. Listen to me; we will never reach them if we depend on something other than God. We'll always be too small, too weak, and the enemy will always be too many."

"There will never be enough bullets," Joab said.

As if on cue, stepping from between the north cabins, a devil entered the camp. Its lone snarl carrying malevolent intent to where they stood.

Without hesitation, Drew sprang with his bat triggered. Some became alarmed and shrank back. A devil inside the perimeter was something the ordinary citizens of The Garden hadn't seen in over a year. Covering the distance, Drew unloaded. The thud and squash made them shake.

"Joab needs to leave!" Larry said in a voice that rose above them all. "The defense of The Garden belongs to the Lord, not Joab. You've all acknowledged Noel and me as leaders, you've done this because you believed the Lord was working through us, but we surrendered too much of that mandate to Joab."

"This is crazy," Kiln said. "Without Joab and his men, we'll get overrun. This is your ego talking."

"Larry has no ego," Joab said. "Listen to him."

"I am listening, and he sounds like somebody who feels threatened."

A smile emerged on Joab's face as he looked at both of them. "I envy you guys," he whispered.

"Why?" Noel asked.

"I'll tell you someday."

Drew came back, the barrel of his bat darkened by blood. He stood at the rear of the crowd. "People listen to me," he said. "We can't defend this place. Especially with thousands coming down from Sky Porch. God's going to have to defend this place."

"Drew's right, and so are Larry and Noel," Joab said. "The Garden's a starting point, not a final destination. This is the right thing. The Lord's been speaking to me as well. For me, this door is being closed. I'm leaving within the hour. If any of my men wish to go with me, they can."

"You can't expect people to stay after you take away their protection!" Owen said. "My group is leaving. I have a forty-passenger bus, and there are other vehicles here. We can drive almost everyone to San Quintana."

"Where the devils are headed?" Liz said. "You're out of your mind."

"Where there will be soldiers to defend us," Owen countered.

"Where they will shoot your daughter on sight," Liz snapped back.

"I'm going with you," Kiln said. "I'm not sticking around to be part of this slaughterhouse. It's time for us all to leave."

"I won't make you stay. I've never made any of you stay!" Larry said, grabbing back their attention. "Something's changed, but the Lord hasn't! He will protect this place."

A few continued debating, some broke into groups to make plans. Noel raised her hands, clapped them together, waved them, and snagged their attention.

"Do you hear yourselves? God has done miracles here; you've seen them. Owen, you saw it with Aaron and Jessica. You still deny God's at work?"

"God is at work, Noel," Owen hollered back. "He's saying it's time for all of us to leave this place."

"We've been here for 18 months! A year and a half of safety, provision, miracles! And now you're talking about leaving down a dangerous road to a heartless city. And not one of you has suggested going to the Lord in prayer."

"We'll pray when we're on the road," Gavin said. "Everyone meet by the vehicles, but bring only what you need. San Quintana is less than an hour away."

"Don't do this," Joab said to Gavin. "You've been out there. The mountain's storming with devils. They're on that road, and their numbers are growing. You won't make it to the flatlands."

"As if we'll make it here?" Gavin said. "Joab, I love you, but no."

"What about the orphans?" Liz yelled.

"The orphans stay here!" Larry shouted. "If they have no parent, no family, they stay here!"

No challenge came, and they dispersed.

"Everyone, get packed!" Gavin yelled.

There was nervousness. People were pinballing between those leaving and choosing to stay. Noel intervened where emotions ran high and tried to calm them down. Larry jumped off the picnic table and was about to join her when Joab grabbed him.

"For the record, kid," Joab said, putting an arm around Larry. He never called him 'Kid' before. "This is a good call, but the next time you fire an associate, give him a heads up. I could have been gone before this meeting and saved you a lot of trouble."

"Old man," he said, not remembering a time before when he had called Joab, 'Old Man.' "Thank you..." When the next thought came, he translated it to action instead of speech and hugged him. "...I don't know what God has for you. I don't even know if we'll ever see each other again. Be careful."

"I needed to give my men the option of staying or coming with me," Joab said. "Most of them are unattached."

"You do," Larry said, seeing Owen approaching from the corner of his eye. "Because I can't have someone staying and thinking they have to fill your shoes."

Joab put a hand up to Owen for him to stop and extend his moment with Larry. Stepping close, he spoke softly into his ear.

"It seems everything attracts them," Joab said. "We know they can hear, I believe they can see in the dark, and they smell us. And don't underestimate their ability to coordinate."

"What can I do about that?"

"Noel's idea. Take the food off the table for a while," he said, but Larry didn't understand. Joab pulled him close and looked into his eyes. "Go inside for about three days. Pray, fast, whatever, but stay out of the breeze, and they may stick to the road."

"Cabins or dining hall?" Larry said.

"Go into the dining hall. Whoever stays is going to need to hear you preach," Joab said. "And they're going to need to see Noel's beauty." He paused. "Take care of Noel; I owe her a debt I'll never be able to repay."

The two men shook hands, and Joab said he'd connect with him before leaving. Owen approached.

"Owen, sorry," he said to head off debate. "For 18 months, this place was safe. I can't say that it is now, but God has a plan."

The youth pastor looked spent. His eyes were geriatric.

"I know you think this is my fault," he said. "But, I had to get my people out of Sky Porch."

"Let it go," Larry said. "It's nobody's fault."

"They'll overrun this camp. You all need to come with us."

"You're not going to get a better shake in the flatlands. Don't let anyone get bit. Don't let them see your daughter's wound. I beg you."

"Have you considered God is using me to speak sense to you?" Owen said.

"Stay, and we'll spend the next three days talking about it."

"Goodbye."

JOAB
(14)

Joab, keeping from debates, focused only on his departure. Fifteen were joining him, including Drew and Mason. Three decided to go with the caravan down the hill; the married men, Gavin, Alan, and Troy. Derek Duran was staying along with Wolfman, Big Leon, and Sandoval. Kuykendall didn't have a choice—he had to stay.

Karla and Beth were filling backpacks with food and water bottles for the men going with him. They'd have rations for two days.

"Beth, what are you crying for?" Joab said as she handed him a backpack. "This is a God thing, and if it's a God thing, then it's going to be a good thing."

"I love all of you," she said, "you've been so good for my son." Working for composure, she drew in a breath, smiled, and lightly slapped his face. "You be safe."

"I promise, Beth," he said. "The Lord's going to take care of all of us."

They hugged. Karla followed with a hug and zero words then both ladies left. No tears came from Joab. These were great ladies, he cared for them, but this was feeling like a ministry departure. Sweet thoughts, hugs, and gifts expressing he'd never be forgotten.

He'd been all over as a pastor and activist from San Dimas to Auburn, to Arroyo Grande, to Oregon, briefly Alturas, to La Canada, and then Pasadena. Most of those places ended with a hug, sometimes two, a few tears, and declarations about staying in touch.

Being professional clergy meant being a professional at saying goodbye. And, of course, like all ministers, with time, he became a fuzzy memory.

Joab felt no ping over that outcome.

"Everyone gets what this is?" he said, coming to his men outside the back of the kitchen. "Everybody understands, we're going out there to fight. I'm not promising you anything, except that The Garden's no longer our concern. I'm not coming back."

No disagreements.

"I be in," Crazy Chang said.

"One more thing, if you're traveling with me, you better not have a faith issue. Larry's going to keep preaching here, so if you have a faith issue or questions, my advice is to stay."

No push back.

"Any questions?" he said.

"We're not going down the highway with the vehicles, are we?" Anspach said. "If that's what we're going to do, I might have to reconsider. Those folks are fixing to be fast-food."

"I have no intention of affirming what they're doing," Joab said. "That's not my job. They should be staying here. I'm leaving, and I opened it up to you because, like me, you're unattached."

Vegas put his hand up, "I'm ready to roll. And if it comes to it, where I'm cornered or about to cash in--do me."

"I think that goes for all of us," Chang said. "It's not my nature to give up a place to sleep and regular meals, but I'm glad we're going. I need a change. I'm ready to brawl with some bad guys."

"Me too," Vegas added.

"We going to San Quintana?" Legaspe asked.

"I don't know," Joab said. "I want to get off the mountain first."

"You think Hiram and Frank made it to the church?" Chapman said.

Joab wanted to say yes, but he only smiled and gave a shrug.

"Hitting the church would be a good thing. We can decide what to do after," Bash said.

"How we getting to the flatlands, which way?" Hutchinson said.

"Right back here," Joab pointed into the brush. "There's a trail that goes down, just to the left of where the meadow drops off. It's steep, but about a mile down, it leads to another fire road. Going east will take us back to 19, which I don't want to do. If we go west, that will take us to Mountain Road 37 and Wintercrest, population; small. It might be a good place for us to catch our breath and some sleep."

"Okay," Big Geoff said. "When do we leave?"

"Grab your gear, and we'll blow," Joab said. "I don't want any prolonged goodbyes or sad moments with those kids. Stay out of all arguments. Meet back here in ten minutes." He clapped his hands. "Go!"

The men scrambled. Some ran. Some moved slower, knowing this was the last time they'd see The Garden and its people who had become family.

Back through the kitchen, the dining hall was empty. Between the tables, Joab took a knee and begged God, again, for the forgiveness he knew he'd already attained. The brain told him repentance brought forgiveness. His heart, however, was more hard-nosed on the issue of peace.

How could he be forgiven for wasting so much of his life? For dealing so much evil council, for teaching so much bad theology, for leading so many astray?

Ping.

"God forgive me," he uttered, thinking of Jay, not Wheeler. "Please forgive me."

"Joab," Alison said from out of nowhere with her blonde bangs and sunshine smile. She put a hand on his shoulder. "God always forgives us, and I would always forgive you."

He began to cry.

NOEL
(13)

At daybreak, when Larry started to tell Noel about Joab, she stopped him. She already knew.

"How did you know?"

"You do remember we came here together?" she said.

"I do."

After a short absence, Larry was back.

Practical, smart spiritually, but toll taking on the heart was parting with Joab. She knew everyone wasn't going to get it, but enough of them would. To God's glory, Joab understood, and his humbleness made the message all the more powerful.

Drew's leaving with Joab.

"You should come with us," Darcy said. Chronologically she was 15, but her blue eyes were still childlike. "I'm scared for you, Noel."

"I'm going to be fine, Darcy," she said. "I wish you, and your mom would stay."

Darcy shook her head and went to the bus. Ryan ran alongside her, and they boarded together.

Noel drifted near the parking lot. People were bringing blankets, clothes, and pillows. They put them inside trunks of cars and put bags in the seats of the bus.

"People!" Gavin yelled. "We're less than an hour from the city. You're not going to need any of this. We have to get going!"

Ken, leading Teddy away from the group, saw her.

"This is hard to see," he said. "We were all together for so long."

"Why don't you go into the dining hall," she said. "I'm sure Larry's going to want to talk to us."

"Are we going to see our friends again?" Teddy said. "Is Todd going to come back?"

Noel lowered herself to look him in the eye. "I don't know, Teddy," she said, readjusting the baseball cap on his head. "But we'll pray for them, won't we? Why don't you go with your dad and see if Karla's made the lemonade?"

Straightening up, she met eyes with Ken. He'd lost a wife and a daughter but always had a smile. A programmer just out of college, he was brought over from Taiwan years before. When the century turned, everyone thought something was going to happen to the computers. It didn't happen, but Ken and his wife stayed and had a family.

"You and Larry just stay true to God's word," Ken said. "We're going to be alright."

She smiled because to speak would have brought tears. Ken took his son to the dining hall.

A hand tapped her shoulder. It was Kelly, Alan's wife; she was 31 and mother of Ben and Trinity. They'd been blessed to this point as the family was still intact.

"You need to come with us, Noel," she said with Trinity in her arms and Ben beside her. "Please change your mind. You're too young..."

"Kelly!" Alan called from the cars. "Baby, we gotta go!"

"My place is here," Noel said. "I wish I could get you to change your mind. The Garden's not finished."

"It's not safe anymore," Kelly said. "And this is the best move for our family."

Alan, a shotgun in hand, came. Noel didn't know him as well as she did Kelly. He always came across as serious, reserved, and never commented on spiritual matters. His faith? Salvation? He professed it, but was he living and growing in the Lord?

She thought of Jay.

"Kelly, we got to get on that bus," he said. "Noel, you've been good to my family, thank you."

"I'm not trying to guilt you," she said, feeling a sick pull in her stomach. "But I wish you'd reconsider. This isn't about being loyal but safe. This place is going to be safe."

"I'm sorry," he said. "I just don't see it that way."

Kelly hugged her again. "Love you, Noel."

"Love you too."

Watching people load up, she began counting. Initially, it seemed like everyone was going, but it became clear everybody wasn't. The seats in the back of the bus were empty.

Many were heading for the dining hall with sleeping bags and pillows. Duran, with his gear, was with them.

"Derek!" she called. "What did I miss?"

"Larry wants everyone staying to move into the cafeteria for the next three days," he said, passing by. "Something about taking the food off the table."

"Noel," She spun and saw Heather and Loren approach her. "We wanted to say goodbye."

"I didn't want this to happen," Noel said. They embraced.

Heather's eyes were red. "I lost the argument with Owen when you said you were sending Joab away."

"Noel, where do we go?" Aaron said.

"You and the girls really aren't coming?" Heather said.

"I'm staying," he said. "I know what's out there, and I know what I almost became. Goodbye."

"Dining hall," Noel said, and he took off. It struck her odd that Aaron and Heather didn't hug after so much time together in Sky Porch. There was no tearful separation.

A scream came, followed by a gunshot.

"This place is like the Titanic, Noel," Heather said. "It's sinking. You need to come with us."

Noel shook her head, hugged Loren, and they went.

"We can't wait!" Gavin came to the hood of the jeep with his shotgun. Alan and Charles Kiln joined him. They spread the map. "Troy's got eyes on the highway. He says we need to hurry. Where's Owen? Owen!"

"We take the Utility Road out and let the bus lead the way," Alan said. "The highway's open, but not if we wait much longer."

"Then, stay!" Noel shouted at them. A compulsion overrode any sense of dignity or respect and forced her to shout again. "We're gonna be safe here! Where are you going to go if the road gets blocked or a vehicle breaks down? And you're going to have kids with you! Think about this! You've seen and experienced the miracles of God here!"

"Noel, that's a promise you and Larry can't keep!" Gavin answered. "You heard the gunshots, and you know what happened last night. It's happening right now!"

She was afraid for them but not mad at them. So what came out of her mouth next wasn't meant for spite or to crown a disagreement. It just came because it had to come from her lips.

"No one staying here is going to die!"

BRICKLANDER
(14)

"So much for that next Chinese Revolution," Farmer said from the passenger seat, his boots on the dash. Barnes was driving, Bricklander sat in back next to Minister Tim.

"I wouldn't know," Bricklander said.

The two vehicles, the truck following, were moving less than fifty miles an hour. A decent pace and slow enough not to miss a ghoul on the highway. To this point, they'd seen a few in the fields but none on the road.

"My brother's in Hawaii," Farmer said, looking into the distance. "His wife, kids, and our sister is a student at Chaminade."

"Military?" Bricklander said.

"No," Farmer said. "Academics, they teach. My sister-in-law's from there and very big into the keeping the islands rural movement. She probably knows a lot of places to hunker down."

"Why would China hit Taiwan now? They've got to be taxed just as bad as everybody else by the virus," Barnes asked.

"The PNN had them fighting a civil war," Farmer said.

"The PNN's hit and miss," Barnes said. "And when it misses, it misses big."

If China's move had come during a game of Risk, it would have been brilliant. At present, Bricklander couldn't think of it as anything but beyond evil. With every nation at or near collapse and militaries weakened from the fighting the dead. It didn't add up.

"I think it best we didn't discuss it until NORM has provided better clarity on the situation," Minister Tim said. "It could discourage the men."

A tumbled weed, blowing west, cut across the path of the jeep. An abandoned car with a dead body on the ground was by it. For Bricklander, who saw it before, it was a marker letting him know they were halfway to the church.

"All leaves have been officially canceled," Farmer said, leaning back.

Barnes shook his head. "Shocker."

"Again, I think it best if we stay focused on what's in front of us," Minister Tim said with his grin of superiority. "Stars and Stripes, as you gentlemen might say."

"Why are you here?" Farmer said, then held up a hand. "And before you answer, don't."

"CAB chaser," Barnes muttered.

For so long, they'd shown deference to the ministers. They were the designated—NORM appointed—encouragers bringing calm to horrific events. As secular as American society had become, professional clergy in a white-collar still carried nearly universal respect. And NORM knew it.

"I'm here to make sure you do your job," Minister Tim said. "Your job is to kill the enemy. My job is to make sure we are all being efficient in our work."

"That's why Minister Kevin was with me the other day," Bricklander said. "To make sure I double-tapped the young people on that bus."

"Controlling this infection is the priority," Minister Tim said. "And, yes, despite your marvelous record Sergeant Bricklander, there is some doubt about you."

"But it's not like you can fire us or replace us, is it?" Farmer said. "Right now, you need every bad dude you can get."

"You have..." Minister Tim started, but Barnes cut him off.

"Lieutenant," Barnes said with eyes never leaving the road. "Do you know what the good luck sign in Hawaiian is?"

"No," Farmer said.

Bricklander knew what was coming.

"Mind if I show you?"

"Go for it," Farmer said.

Barnes took his right hand, formed a middle-finger, and aimed it back to Minister Tim.

"Is that supposed to be funny?" Minister Tim said.

"Stars and Stripes, candy boy," Barnes said.

"Maybe you'd like to experience life as a civilian?" Minister Tim said. "It's within my power to make it so."

"Only if he gets to eat like you," Farmer said. "All of us have been trying to figure out how you stay so fat."

Minister Tim ignored them, and Bricklander thought about how quick, again, the world had changed. Yesterday, a private wouldn't have dared insult a minister. Now, it was open season and full mutiny felt only a few hours away.

Barnes snapped the pause. "Question, if that was a herd from Sky Porch, why aren't we seeing more than these stragglers?"

Bricklander had run the same question through his head. "There are two ways of looking at it, and I just thought of a third. One, they could all start walking down the highway. The road is clear, and it's downhill. Two, while they could still work down the highway, they're stupid enough to stray off the road. Maybe, walk-off cliffs, get trapped in canyons and ravines, and scatter themselves throughout the entire mountain range."

"So what you're saying is they could be anywhere," Barnes said.

"Yes, just like like always; they could be anywhere."

"Thanks, Sarge," Barnes said. "I'll sleep easy tonight."

"Or three, Sky Porch is still sealed, and the dead we dealt with last night and see walking now are from someplace else."

"When we get to the church," Farmer said to Bricklander, "let us out. Then take Barnes and scout up the highway. I'll get command set up and have the men rack out. They're all dogged."

The long road revealed the church in the distance on the left. Initially, it looked like a fortress, a castle keep. A little closer, and it looked like a fort on the frontier. On arrival, they recognized what it was; an old broken church abandoned long before the apocalypse.

The remains of the parking lot consisted of knee-high weeds and shrubs. Broken bits of asphalt and faded white lines marked where parishioners parked their long-forgotten cars. The buildings, a dingy yellow stucco, had every window gone or broken out.

The pastor's office, church office (as indicated by a jutting sign), and the nursery made up the building parallel to the highway. North was the sanctuary, a short gap, and a single building—marked Fellowship Hall—completed the horseshoe on the west side.

They parked, and Bricklander stood in the back of the jeep. The men got out of the truck. "Secure the perimeter, eliminate anything lurking, and wait for orders."

Gunfire came.

The soldiers moved their M-4s into the ready position and fanned into the square. Bricklander moved across the cement slab, stepped on a mound of debris, and looked in through the broken window. Shattered glass, overturned benches, trash, dirt, and two men, covered in grime, were firing out the other side of the sanctuary.

LARRY
(15)

"Toss your things in the center," Larry said. "We're going to push tables against the windows. Then stack the rest on them, on their side, against the glass."

"Should we drop the sun blinds first?" Beth said, rolling Tammy's wheelchair in front of the kitchen.

"Yes," he said. "Good thinking."

Everybody wasn't leaving in a panic, which was the initial concern. By Larry's count, Joab's group was at 16, and another 50 were going to San Quintana, leaving 115 at The Garden. He didn't have time to count how many of the 115 were kids.

The next 72 hours should have had all of them in nervous anticipation, but instead, it was bringing everyone to life. New energy kicked in as people went to work preparing the dining hall, and sermon ideas began popping.

Larry was curious about how they'd be holding up tomorrow. Three days inside the dining hall wasn't exactly the belly of a fish, but potentially testy. They had food and plenty of water. To manage the bathroom situation, a long blue tarp would be stretched from the back of the kitchen to a single compost toilet—previously unused due to proximity.

"Meals?" Karla asked. "Do you want us to cook?"

"No, dry foods, dry cereal, dry whatever for the next three days. I'm fasting and asking others to join me."

"Let's go!" he encouraged. "Get these benches moved." Sandoval and Wolfman were dragging tables. Beth, working ahead of them, was dropping the rolled plastic blinds.

Joab appeared in the doorway and motioned for him to come outside.

"Duran," Larry stopped Derek Duran as he came through the doors. "I want you to get some help and secure that tarp for the compost toilet. Use the spikes and find rocks to cover the spikes with."

Outside, he looked and saw the people loading and getting ready to roll.

"Larry, I need to give you something," Joab said as he walked him away from the entrance toward the decaying tool shed. "At first, I was going to take it with me, but if something happens, I don't want it laying around in the woods for the next twenty years. You know what this is?"

Joab unveiled a silver rectangle.

"A computer."

"Technically, it's called a laptop. I know you're not too familiar with it, but you're a bright guy. You'll figure it out. Ask Duran or Ken if you need some help." He handed him the computer and a small folded black item with a wire coming out of it. "This is the solar pad I use to charge it, but it's charged now."

"Aren't you going to need this?"

Joab shook his head. "Not out there. Listen, I told you I had some pretty good connections. In ministry, you always hear stories and accounts of things that sound ridiculous. But when everything started to happen, I was able to download some reports."

"I don't understand," Larry said.

"I've added notes. But inside are accounts about when this has come close to happening before."

"You mean the virus?"

"Yes."

Larry was shocked. Joab had never shared any of this. "Is there an answer?"

"Just Jesus," Joab said. "But there might be a time you and Noel will want to read some history on the subject. Maybe for some encouragement. Some of it will be very close to home for you. I also left a personal note for Noel."

"Close to home?"

"Coincidence, or the Lord? You decide," Joab said. "It was when I read these reports the Holy Spirit confirmed, again, the conviction in my life and my ministry. I respect you, Larry, and I know you were conflicted last night, but you can't let the circumstances pollute what you know to be true. Keep preaching, and don't ever be afraid."

Over Joab's shoulder, he could see, coming with purpose, the leaders of the group leaving The Garden.

"I'm listening to God right now," Larry said. "And he's saying you better split, or you'll never get out of here." He looked again at the older man he had depended on for so long. "Go!"

"Take care of Noel," Joab said and was gone.

The men arrived and appeared ready to trade punches.

"Larry, tell us the truth!" Gavin yelled.

"What are you so burned about? You got your vehicles, you got your guns, and you've made a plan. God bless and Godspeed."

"Do you know what Noel just said to us?" Kiln said with a rage he'd never seen in the old man.

Larry didn't like thinking he'd been suspicious of his number one cheerleader, but he supposed, at this moment, he'd always been. Kiln, openly supportive since the beginning, had jumped ship.

"I don't know what she said," Larry shrugged. "Probably told you to stay and that you'd be safer here."

Gavin spoke. "She said in front of everybody that no one staying here is going to die. What does that mean? Are we cursed if we leave? She can't say that. She can't use God to create fear in the people going down the hill."

"Do you hear yourselves?" Larry said. "You decided to end this fellowship. You're making this move because you believe you're in the right. So what do you care? Go in peace."

"She was out of line," Kiln said.

"Brother, you're out of line. You all are. When has Noel ever lied to you? When has Noel said something crazy or irrational?"

"You can't curse us like that. We've got children going with us!" Kiln shouted.

"Curse? What is she a witch, now? God has told us to stay, and we'll be under his protection. Leave, and you'll be on your own. That's not a curse." Larry didn't know if it was a thumb at his back or an invisible arm pulling him, but he stepped closer to the men. The provocative move caused them to retreat. "I wouldn't doubt the words a living God puts in the mouth of a woman like Noel. I'd heed them."

It was a crusher. The men, looking weakened, drifted back to the vehicles.

Another of the mountain's sweet-smelling breezes came across the camp, lying about the kind of day it was. Larry was hesitant to think of it as a revolt. No one was threatening him, and they weren't fighting for control of anything but the narrative of which group was in the right. And that need to be in the right was enough to drive passions.

Gavin remained. "Will you pray for us?"

"Gavin, we've been together since almost the beginning," Larry said. "Of course, I'll pray for you. But you have to think about this. You know better. I know you know better."

"I have thought about it, Larry," Gavin said. His tone was different than before. "I can't help but think it's time, and I can't let the actions of a group dictate what I know is best for my family. We've got to go." Then, again, his frustration broke through. "You're only 19! How could you possibly know what God would want! Why you?"

361

He'd played the youth card, and another flame of anger flickered for Larry to snuff out or nurture.

"Brother," he said, snuffing it out. "Those are your doubts, or you wouldn't have been so concerned about what Noel said."

"You don't have any doubts?"

"None."

JOAB
(15)

Joab cupped water from his canteen, splashed his face and waited behind the kitchen.

The men began gathering. Chapman, Vegas, Orlando, Anspach, Legaspe, and Hutchinson were there. Drew, Mason, and Bash then rounded the corner, checking their gear.

Joab remembered all he wanted as a kid was to be out of church. Sunday morning service ended at the stroke of noon but, Corrine, his older sister, dragged him to the evening service and all the youth activities.

He came to recognize the morning sermon as seeker-friendly and sanded down to avoid any offense. Evening messages, however, were like a chainsaw unleashed in a horror movie. In the A.M., God loved them all. In the P.M.—with few to zero visitors—you were going to fry if you didn't accept that love.

Hiding from people who said they were praying for him, getting back to the car, and getting home, was his weekly mission. Now he was leaving this home, the only place he'd ever done any good in ministry, and it didn't feel like he'd find another.

"Everyone else on the way?" he said, turning to Mason.

"I think a few of them are hitting the bathroom before we split. I know I did."

"Big Leon ain't coming, huh?" Vegas said.

"No, he says he likes it here," Chapman said.

"What about Wolf?" Brewer questioned.

"You think Wolfman's going to leave a place with so many available females?" Hutchinson said before letting a savage leer overtake his face. "Come to think of it, staying might not be a bad idea."

"You're a little old for some of those females, Hutch," Vegas said. "We all are."

"Don't sell the kid short," Bash said. "There's no way Wolf was going to leave his mom and Tammy. He's better than that."

"Then what are we?" Brewer said. "Are we bad for leaving?"

"No," Vegas said. "We're the unattached."

"The back pew people," Hutchinson said.

"The get out before they knew we were there crowd," Bash said. "That was me."

Pena, Hernandez, Brewer, Crazy Chang came through the kitchen. Big Geoff and Matts turned the corner. Behind them was Noel, and Joab knew why.

"Guys, we got to hit it," Joab said. "Bash, take the lead. Drew, hold on a second."

Bash led the rest of them into the brush. Duran and Wolfman came out of the back of the kitchen carrying the giant blue tarp. They said something to Noel, and she busied herself with them.

Joab pulled Drew aside.

"Jefe?"

"Drew," he half-smiled. "Stay."

"Why?" He followed Joab's eyes to where Noel was standing. "No."

"You sure?" Joab said carefully. "Don't kid me, and don't kid yourself. This thing doesn't go one way."

"She's attractive, I like her, but," Drew shook his head, "no."

"You're not being honest."

"What am I going to do, Joab?" His voice was low but firm. "Take her out on a date? Go to the movies? Get married, build a home? I appreciate everyone wanting to play matchmaker, but God's kept me alive for a purpose, and I don't think it's to set up house with Noel."

"Drew, if you haven't figured it out," Joab said, "I'll tell you. All we're doing is going out there to die. We'll do some good work for a while, we'll get into a scrape or two, some of us will die, and some of us will break up and go in different directions. We don't have anything profound waiting in our future. But you've got something right here."

"I know that's what it looks like," Drew said. "But God will lead us to something. I believe that with all my heart."

"So going out there to die is preferable to trying to build something here with this woman?"

Noel finished helping Duran and Wolfman and started their way. A flashlight in her hand.

"I'll be on the trail."

Joab gave Noel the warmest smile he knew how to give and hugged her. "I left a note for you on the computer I gave Larry. I don't have time to get into it now but ask him when you get a chance. I love you, Noel," he hugged her a second time. "I love you and Larry."

"I don't know what to say because there's so much I want to say." She cleared her throat, and a small smile emerged. "But for the sake of it, tell me why you envy Larry and me?"

"You're both right where God wants you to be, and people are mad about it..., And it doesn't matter to either of you. I was there once, briefly, and then everyone started agreeing with me, and I started agreeing with them. Where you two are in the Lord is beautiful. Make sure you stay there."

Noel gushed tears.

"And stop shedding tears for me," he said. Noel wiped her eyes. "Be happy. You're serving the Lord." He wanted to say more, he wanted to tell her about her mom, but it was time to go. "God bless."

NOEL
(14)

"Drew, can we talk?"

Noel was relieved she hadn't missed him. Glad when he indicated he had a moment--and worried when she considered the condition of her hair and the dirt under her nails.

"I wanted to say goodbye," Noel said. His body language became like someone forced to listen to an Amway pitch. It was an unusual waste of movement she'd never seen before.

"You're going to be good," Drew said. "God's going to take care of this place."

"I thought maybe you could use this," she gave him the flashlight. "It's an extra one." She turned her eyes down and away from his and fought to bring them back up. "Joab picked it up for me last fall. It's been on the shelf, but I put fresh batteries in."

The warming morning was turning a hundred shades of beautiful with the surrounding canopy of trees. To Noel's thinking, the word amid the scents of pine and death was; paradox. The Garden was as much a paradox as optimism and romance were at the end of the world.

"I like you, Noel," Drew said, handing her back the flashlight. If he stopped there, she might have been satisfied. Like was better than dislike and only a little below love, but he didn't. "And I know you have feelings for me, and I've tried not to lead you on because I don't want to hurt you."

"How can anything…" She began.

"…I know," Drew said, cutting her off.

"But…"

"…I know," he said calmly. "And it's okay. I'm flattered, but it won't work. You have to understand that."

She hated the false modesty associated with someone being flattered. It was merely another slow-death weapon used to break the loser's heart. Someone wasn't going to get the one they loved, and they were supposed to be mollified by the word, flattered?

The old Noel would have inserted a choice expletive at this point. Instead, she reached into her reserves, controlled her emotions, and continued the fight. Eyes could become wet, a few tears could spill, but leaders didn't break down. 'Stoic' was another word she was coming to understand.

There had been days with long thoughts spent on the idea of kissing him and dreaming how a first kiss might be. About the kind of father he'd make, how his eyes would never change even as they grew older. His eyes always being gentle poetry, cooling her terrors, and warming her heart. Promising she'd never be alone or vulnerable again, reminding that her past only served as the voucher for forgiven sin. And there would be the home with children. Children who knew—with no doubts— the magical feeling of Mom and Dad loving them and each other.

"I don't know what feeling I'm supposed to have, but I love you," Noel said, her heart racing. She took comfort, knowing she could be bold in things not involving Owen. "I want you to stay. You held my hand once…That night, by the fire…" She paused to combat the lump in her throat. "…I want you to give us a chance."

"Noel," he said, not touching or taking her hand. "I remember that night, and I wasn't thinking." Now he stopped and re-started. "Truth is, all I'll end up doing is hurting you. My heart's not here. God has something out there for me to do, but not here."

"Take a chance," she said. "Give us a chance, Drew. I know I'm not wrong." He turned away. "I know you feel something for me."

"I gotta go," he said without looking back. "The Garden's going to be fine." He left with nothing more—not even the over-done side hug Joab had taught them all to master.

Noel held still long enough that some might think she was praying. If more time passed, people would think she was only crying about The Garden and those leaving. She heaved tears and sadness. But fear of being discovered broken-hearted ended when a scream came from the far side of camp.

It was the kind of scream only a devil straying into the perimeter could produce. She ran around the corner of the dining hall. Her wet eyes swept the grounds and located Alan crushing the butt of his shotgun into a devil's head.

The van, two pick-up trucks, and bus were running. Owen called for Alan to get on board. The bus took the lead. In the backseat, she could see Todd wearing his baseball hat. In the front sitting behind her father was Loren. Heather had an arm around her. No eyes looked her way. No one turned to take a last look at The Garden.

Everyone staying carried pillows and blankets to the dining hall. Duran and Sandoval were hurrying the last of them inside as everything else at The Garden fell to a haunting quiet. The tool shed to her left, the benches by the trees, the cabins, Mandalay, were all abandoned. The camp, save for the dining hall, was a ghost town.

The day before, they all loved each other, laughed, prayed, and played games. Family one day and strangers the next. All the confessed love for each other, all the declarations of bonds never being broken, were all gone.

And so was Drew.

BRICKLANDER
(15)

The attacking dead were less than a dozen. Lancaster took a squad around the front of the church to chop them down. Bricklander went inside the sanctuary and saw what they were after.

On the floor, below the windows, the two men, with backs against the wall, didn't respond to Bricklander's appearance. Before asking any questions, the first sergeant pulled their shotguns away. They were too exhausted to protest. If not covered in dirt and some blood, they could've passed as being hungover. One of them had been bit on the shoulder. The other had a bloodstain coming through the calf of his jeans and crusted blood on his Nikes.

"I'm Sergeant Jeff Bricklander, United States Army. You boys need to identify yourselves."

The one who had been bit, with shortly cropped balding blonde hair, barely turned his eyes upward. He grunted out a smile, too tired to speak. The dark-haired one licked his lips and began to build the strength to talk.

Minister Tim and Lieutenant Farmer came into the sanctuary and stood next to Bricklander.

"Find out who they are?" Farmer said.

Bricklander shook his head. "Where you two from? You're not in trouble, not yet anyway, so talk to us."

"You from the city?" Minister Tim said. "Out here to do some hunting?"

It was an informed thought by the Minister. It wasn't uncommon for young men to load up a vehicle and go monster hunting. But with no car parked outside, he knew it was something else.

"I think they're from the mountain," Bricklander said. "Did you make it down from Sky Porch?"

The darker one licked his lips again and pushed a crazy smile to his face. "We claim this planet in the name of Mars. Isn't that lovely?"

The balding one gave a weak laugh.

"Funny," Bricklander said. "I guess you can laugh when you know you've got nothing to lose. But your friend's been bit, and I'm the guy with the gun that can end it mercifully or watch him rot."

The balding blond man readjusted himself against the wall and stared at Bricklander. "Then I guess we'll be together for a long, long time."

"Dead!" Private Flores said, sticking his head inside the sanctuary doors. "We got another wave coming in, Lieutenant."

Bricklander and Farmer moved to the window. The dead were coming across the field and not by the highway.

"That's more than a dozen," Farmer said. "Let's get everyone ready to go. Minister Tim, you babysit our boys here. I want to talk to them after."

"Sarge…" Doughty called by radio from the steeple of the church. **"I've got about a hundred bearing down."**

"Are the groves to the west clear? Anything flanking us?"

"That's a negative…"

Letting the herd approach, the men took careful aim, waiting for Farmer to give the order. It was an uneasy feeling to let the dead move close. NORM issued monthly memos encouraging troops to employ the tactic of waiting until they were in the optimum range to save bullets.

When firing broke out, the dead melted in the first hail of 5.56-millimeter rippers. Walking behind the men shooting out the windows, Bricklander exited and passed to the space between the fellowship hall and the church. Barnes calmly delivered rounds, often getting two for the price of one.

"You!" He grabbed Private Decker, who stepped through the opening behind him. "They're focused on the church." Then pointing to orchards. "You stay in this gap, here, and guard Barnes' flank. Don't let anything sneak up on him—understand?"

"Yes, Sergeant."

Back inside the church, Bricklander half expected Minister Tim to be someplace else. But he was still standing over the two strangers.

"We're going to have to slow down our fire," Farmer said, meeting Bricklander in the center of the sanctuary. "We don't know what we're going to be facing or how long until resupply."

"They're concentrating on the sound of the gunfire," Bricklander said. "Let me take some men and swing around on the highway itself. We'll fix bayonets and get a twist on them."

Farmer agreed, then put a hand on his arm. "I'm going to call for a cease-fire, but give me a ten-second pause. I don't want anyone getting hit with a stray bullet."

He grabbed Gibson, Crowder, Rickman, Belst, and Zavala. They went backstage through what had been the Pastor's office, then to the church office, and nursery before going out and down the short steps to the deceased lawn.

Bricklander pulled out his blade and held it up for his men to see. They fastened bayonets and were ready to go.

"Stars and Stripes," Bricklander said because old habits were hard to break.

"Stars and Stripes," they responded.

The firing stopped. Bricklander held them back with a raised hand and counted to ten.

"Go!"

The soldiers wheeled out from the direction of the highway. The initial danger was stepping over the dead bodies before attacking. A trip and fall could turn things serious in an instant.

Because he fought in some of the worst places on earth, it helped Bricklander that the dead were so mangled and decomposed. Their monstrous appearance produced less consideration of their original dispensation. It gave better focus on dealing with what they were now. He wasn't killing people. He was killing monsters.

Even after turning, the hair on the dead continued to grow. Wild and pasted up with dirt and jams of mud until eventually bending over on itself. The hair hung in hardened but harmless layers. Fingernails, which also continued to grow, weren't harmless. They were sharp and as deadly as a bite.

Using textbook thrusts, the six men dropped them by the dozens. They used the butts of their rifles with perfection. Pivoting north, they cleared the field. A hundred yards from the church, the assault was ended.

Nothing else appeared on the horizon. Looking back to the south, Bricklander saw a church as tired and sick as the world. The structure was ready to fall with the next quake. If he intended to get back to Virginia, then this was the long way home.

"Sergeant Bricklander?"

"What do you want, Crowder?" he said, not looking at his man.

"Sergeant?"

"What is it, kid?" he turned to see the private holding a bloody hand.

LARRY
(16)

"You okay?"

"You and me, Jefe," Noel said, standing by him and the double doors as they studied the empty grounds. "By the way, who sang *I learned the truth at 17?*"

"Janis Ian," Larry said.

"Well, she was a couple years early."

Noel's eyes were wet. While he shared everything there was to share about Denise Hemingway, she never spoke in great detail about Drew. It always seemed Noel and Drew were a short countdown away from becoming an official item. They had to be. They were an excellent match—but apparently not.

"You gonna be okay?"

"Is everybody in?" Noel said with a quivering in her voice.

"Noel?" he pressed.

"I'm sorry for not being understanding about Denise," she said and broke down. Larry held her. "Joab told me to be happy, but I'm so sad. I'm so, so sad, and I know I can't be...Not now."

"Be sad," he said as she soaked his shirt with tears. "But get yourself together and go forward. That's what you've been telling me, and you were right. We can't stop sadness, but we can go forward."

Noel pulled back, sniffled, and wiped at her nose. "Okay," she drew in a breath, "I be in. How do I look?"

Larry let out a laugh.

"What's so funny?"

"That we actually thought we knew what we were praying for that Sunday night."

"The pool's a lot deeper than we thought." She giggled and dried her eyes. "Well, I'm thankful we're not attracted to each other."

"That would be gross." They embraced again and released. "You gonna be okay?"

She bent her head.

"Come on, then, let's get inside," he said.

They went in, closed the double doors, slid the lock, dropped the blinds, and let Wolfman and Big Leon move the tables to secure it. The heavy wooden tables gave finality to everything about the day. The sun was still young, it wasn't even noon, but the outside portion of the day was over.

"I'm gonna give a pep talk. Can you get Joab's guys that stayed to meet me in the kitchen afterward?"

She went to the kitchen, and he walked to the front of the dining hall. The fireplace they never used was made of stone. It had a stone porch stretching two feet outwards to keep embers from hitting the floor. Larry stood on it.

"It feels like I should say thank you for staying," he began, "but I don't want this to sound like a victory speech. We stayed, they left, we'll show them, and we'll win. It can't be that way. We're here because the Lord wants us to be here. We've chosen this, and he's going to keep us safe. I believe that. I don't know how many devils are going to pass through, but we'll be safe."

Larry spoke to the camp but engaged in another conversation with himself. The Gospel would have to be preached and shared like it was in the beginning. He'd go over the nuts and bolts to make sure these people were not only calling Jesus, Savior but Lord as well.

"I'm going to ask you to be patient, and I'm going to ask you to pray and read your Bible a lot. These next three days will pass quickly, but I'm sure this first day will feel awkward as we settle in."

Hopefully, like the creatures in the ark, like the lions with Daniel, these 72 hours inside the dining hall would pass in relative peace.

"We're also going to pray for our friends who left. We might disagree with them, but we're going to pray for their safety."

No dissenting voices or expressions came, and he went into prayer.

When the amen came, he stepped down, and there were small eruptions of laughter and smiles. It didn't make sense, but trying to make sense of the Lord's work was a waste of time. The appropriate action was to let the Holy Spirit do its thing and stay out of the way.

Coming into the kitchen, it was critical to let the faces looking back at him know they were no longer Joab's men. They weren't even his men but part of The Garden. They'd still need their weapons, The Garden would need their strength, but they weren't going to be walking patrols and going out to engage devils.

"We are not going to get caught up with anything that happens outside of this dining hall for the next three days," Larry said. "And after that, I'm not sending you out or putting you on the Utility Road or having you secure the perimeter. Those days are done. We'll do what we need to do for food, but the perimeter's the Lord's."

"And if a devil comes into the campground?" Big Leon said.

"Kill it. If this dining hall comes under attack or if one gets in here, kill it," he answered. "God kept you here for a reason, I didn't ask any of you, but I'm glad you've decided to stay. There's nothing wrong with what Joab or any of you were doing. But we got side-tracked thinking it was the muscle and not the Lord keeping this place safe."

"Make a circle, spread out, push everything back…" Noel's voice came from the dining hall. People started shuffling around. "…

let's make some teams."

"That looks like a game of dodge ball she's trying to get going," Duran said.

They saw the game starting to form. The kids were excited. Larry felt release because the Lord was speaking, but not through Joab, a burning bush, or writing in the sky. Instead, he used the cooperation that went into setting up a game of dodgeball. It affirmed what they were doing.

"If I weren't so ugly and bald, I'd ask that woman to marry me," Big Leon said. "All you fellas know black men are allowed to marry white women, right?"

"Get in line with the half-breed Mexican," Kuykendall said.

"I don't think you Room 222 kids have any idea how long that line is," Sandoval said.

Larry got the reference, but the rest of them missed it.

"Essentially, what we're all saying is, is that Drew's the dumbest person on the planet?" Duran said, raising a hand. "Can we all agree on that?"

"Absolutely," everyone raised a hand in testimony.

"What a moron," Kuykendall said.

"Drew's the proof Owen wasn't the only jackwagon at The Garden," Big Leon said.

"That's a bit harsh," Sandoval said.

"But is it true?" Big Leon asked back, and Sandoval gave no argument. "Who walks away from a woman like Noel?"

"On a day like this," Wolfman said, straining for a better view of the hall, "who else could talk everyone into playing a game of dodgeball?"

"So the Drew-Noel thing was obvious to everyone?" Larry said.

The men burst into laughter.

"Wow, okay, then," he said. "I didn't know. I thought it was under wraps."

"You've had other things on your mind," Sandoval said.

Noel's eyes, no longer looking wet, met Larry's. She smiled and gave him a head gesture to finish his business in the kitchen. "I got this," she said before Teddy fired a ball into her hip. "Teddy!"

Larry started again. "Our weakest spot is going to be this bathroom thing."

"The tarp stretched perfectly," Duran said. "We got it spiked, but we could only staple it to the back wall here. I don't know if it will hold in a good wind."

"We can't barricade this door," Larry said. "So we're going to need to guard it. At least two of us should be in here at all times. This window above the sink is high enough, but the door's pretty flimsy."

"I was on the roof last night with Brewer; maybe we can put a spotter up there to see if anybody's in the neighborhood when we send people to the bathroom?" Wolfman said.

"There's no access to the roof from inside," Kuykendall said. "Which makes me think about air. I don't think we'll suffocate, but it could get pretty stuffy."

"These doors aren't sealed. You can feel the air coming beneath them," Sandoval explained. "You have heat vents in the ceiling, and we will be opening this back door off and on. It might get stuffy, but we'll be okay."

Cheers came as the first round of dodge ball concluded.

"Winner!" Noel shouted while holding up Elias's right hand in victory. The kid was happy.

"Does Elias know about Wheeler?" Wolfman asked. "Has anyone spoken to him?"

"I don't think so," Larry said.

JOAB
(16)

The men continued on.

Carrying sleeping bags, backpacks, and any lid for protection from the sun. Most of them, like Joab, wore baseball caps. Pena wore a fisherman's hat, Crazy Chang wore a Panama, and Big Geoff used an ancient fedora to cover his bald scalp.

Some wore hiking boots, but most wore basketball shoes or some form of sneaker. Joab and Drew wore jeans. The rest wore baggy shorts, cargo pants, whatever they had available to make hiking bearable.

They were an hour south of The Garden when the trail emptied onto a firebreak, and options presented themselves. They could go west or east. North went back to camp, and south put them in thickets, brush, woods, with no discernible path to follow.

"I thought we'd have seen some by now," Mason said.

"This isn't an easy place to get to," Bash said. "The devils would have to leave 19 to come this way. The highway's easier."

The men sat to catch their breath and sip water. It was a nice day, but clouds were building.

Leaning back on a rock, Joab sensed Mason's eagerness for a fight growing. Rage was a valid option when there was no place to run or family was in danger. But when rage took over in an open area, in situations where clear thinking was the best option, things got dangerous.

"I know it's a long way," Drew said, reading a map. "But if we swung back around, above The Garden, we could open up and deflect any devils from coming into the camp."

"Draw them down Highway 19?" Mason said. "Why not? Let's get to it."

"We are out here to drop devils, right?" Drew said.

"The Garden's no longer our priority," Joab said before drinking from his canteen. "And we need to stop spoiling for a fight."

"Then what do we do?" Chapman said. "Where do we go, where will it count most?"

"Our job's to kill bad guys, but we're not going to be able to if we don't find a place to rest," Joab said. "I'm not the only one dragging."

"That's for sure," Orlando agreed.

"We can pause at Wintercrest," Joab said. "I'm sure much of it's been looted, but if we can steal some winks and scrounge a few edibles—then jackpot."

Two miles west, on Mountain Road 37, was Wintercrest. Joab remembered the citizens as spiritual types, much like those in Cumberland. Hospitality wasn't a Wintercrest virtue. Tourists were welcome to shop but never invited to stay. Just pass through, spend some money, drink tea, visit the head shop, and split.

"If we push through Wintercrest, we could get to that old church by nightfall," Drew said.

"We could, but if we don't make it, we could be in a world of hurt. You're all tough guys, but most of us have been up for the better part of 24 hours," Joab said. "We've got to get some rest."

"I'm for where the devils are," Mason said.

"That's what I'm worried about," Joab responded. "The devils are everywhere, there's no shortage of devils on the planet, but if we run into a bunch while exhausted, we're gonna have problems. At The Garden, I had some say, but not out here, so I'll leave it to you. Do you want to look for a place to crash in Wintercrest, or do you want to push the flatlands?"

"I'm for Wintercrest, if it's safe," Bash said. "If it's trouble, we keep moving."

"I think it's worth a shot," Legaspe said. "I'd like to grab some sleep with something over my head."

"My dogs, Jefe," Crazy Chang said. "They're getting angry."

"And that means?" Big Geoff questioned.

"It means his feet hurt," Anspach said. "And so do mine."

"Let's do it then. We're looking at about two more miles after we intersect with 37," Joab said. "You good with that, Drew?"

"Wintercrest it is," Drew said. "We have to pass through it anyway."

They moved along the fire road.

"Remember," Bash said. "If you find any mushrooms in Wintercrest, don't eat them."

"Why?" Legaspe asked.

"You'll be as high as a kite and listening to the fiddlers," Hutchinson said.

"How would you know, Hutch?" Brewer asked.

"Hutch knows," Bash said. "It's his field."

NOEL
(15)

"We're going to worship," Larry said from the fireplace. "Then we're going to share the Gospel. We're going to be absolutely sure everyone in this place knows about Jesus crucified and resurrected."

Applause followed.

Noel was exhausted. The night before, the efforts to convince people to stay, spilling her heart to Drew this morning, left her frail between the ears. She felt good, she had peace, but wanted a pause in remedying the logistics around her. She wanted the pillow, sleeping bag, and backpack she'd forgotten in her cabin.

Duran went to the front with his guitar. The people clapped. Noel knew he was exhausted as well, but instead of yawning, he smiled at them.

"We love you, Derek!" A voice called out.

"I love you too," he said. "How about this?" He began strumming a familiar song. All stood and started clapping. The new place of worship was small, but the noise was big. "Let's have church!"

The Garden cheered.

"What can take away my sin? Nothing but the blood of Jesus."

It was a different camp. They all suffered losses. They loved Wheeler, Hiram, Frank, Bird, Scott, and Jay, but this group was worshiping, not mourning.

"Maybe it's time, Larry," she said into his ear. They were standing by the doors.

"What?"

"How precious is the flow that makes me white as snow."

Noel touched his shoulder for him to face her. "Maybe it's time to tell them who we are?"

"I thought we weren't going to talk about that?" Larry said. "Joab was right when he told us not to share it."

"Things have changed," she said. "And, by the way, who's Joab?"

She knew she surprised him by saying that.

"Do you trust me, Larry?"

"I trust you," he said.

"It's time."

Larry panned his eyes over The Garden as it worshiped. Duran was giving as much as he could with his guitar while the adults and kids passionately sang. "Now?"

"No other fount I know."

"Let's do it," Noel said as worship became louder.

"Nothing but the blood of Jesus."

While some Christian expressions caused her to pause and bite a lip, being 'born again' wasn't one of them. These people hadn't stopped believing, they were nowhere near giving up their faith, but it was as if they'd been born again. They were being made new. No hesitation came as Duran led them.

"What can make me whole again?"

The subtractions brought power to the Garden.

"Let them come," Noel whispered, thinking of the devils outside the dining hall. "Let them come."

"Nothing but the blood of Jesus."

She thought of Alison and wondered where in the dining hall she was. Impossible to see who was upfront, she went to her tiptoes.

"This is all my hope and peace."

Alison, standing on a bench in the back of the dining hall, arms raised, sang to her fullest. In the context of the recent days, through this hurricane of worship, even Alison was rejuvenated.

"Nothing but the blood of Jesus."

The song ended, the people applauded. From her spot, a narrow walkway led across the dining hall to the kitchen entrance. Noel saw Tammy sitting in her wheelchair with her hands, previously incapable of coordination, clapping.

Thunder broke out above them in three loud and distinctive booms. They looked up, waiting for more. Pelts of rain began hitting the roof.

"You hear that?" Duran said before leading the next song. "God's talking."

BRICKLANDER
(16)

The strangers introduced themselves as Frank and Hiram.

"Should we cap this one now?" Barnes said. He kicked at Hiram's boot.

"Is this how you guys make friends?" Hiram said. "No wonder everyone wants to stay with us."

Lieutenant Farmer squatted to make eye contact. "I'm easy going, but when I come in contact with people bleeding, I get suspicious. You can understand."

The two men looked at each other and laughed.

"That's funny?" Farmer said.

"We ain't infected, Eisenhower," Frank said, "I got buckshot from his gun in my calf, and he was bit about ten hours ago."

Barnes put the muzzle of his M-4 against Hiram's head.

"Before you pull the trigger, take his temperature, take a good look at the wound. He's not infected," Frank said. He gestured to Crowder near the double doors. "On the other hand, your boy doesn't look so good. He's got a fever and is throwing up. How long ago was he bitten?"

"Everyone bitten gets infected," Farmer said.

"Unless you're us," Hiram said. "So either get me a pillow or pull the trigger. I've got to get some sleep."

Bricklander stepped into the conversation and pushed Barnes back. "Where you guys from?"

They didn't answer.

"You with the group that says it has a cure?" Bricklander turned to Farmer. "I think they're part of the group I left Minister Kevin with two days ago."

"Have you seen Minister Kevin?" Minister Tim said, jumping in. "If you know where he is, you better tell us."

"I don't know anything about a priest, man," Hiram said.

"But you are from that group?" Bricklander said. "I met a man named Joab, and he's supposed to be one of your leaders. He talked about a cure."

"We do know the cure, but you have a more immediate problem," Frank said.

"What's that?" Minister Tim said.

"Sky Porch is wide open," Hiram said. "We intercepted the bus you people were supposed to meet because they had infected. They weren't near Sky Porch. They were in Sky Porch. To get out, they opened the passage across the bridge."

"I gave a radio to Minister Kevin," Bricklander said. "He would've warned us."

"I never met this priest you're talking about," Hiram said, "but I have a feeling The Garden, our camp, was overrun. And you don't have to guess where those devils are going next."

"Devils?" Minister Tim said.

"The dead," Frank made clear.

They backed away from Hiram and Frank.

"We thought Sky Porch might be open," Bricklander said. "And they just confirmed it."

"Barnes put a call into command," Farmer said. "Explain our situation, and see what comes back."

"They'll also tell you to put these two, and Private Crowder, out of their misery," Minister Tim said. "We should do it quickly."

"LT, he's getting worse," Jarvis said to Farmer. The medic made the gesture of a pistol with his thumb and index finger.

"You're going to take care of him, right?" Doughty said. He was pacing the sanctuary and nervously bouncing to and from Crowder's spot on the floor. His tears were obvious.

"Not yet," Farmer said and went back to Frank and Hiram. "Tell me about this cure. What's the abracadabra?"

Hiram pulled the bandage off his bicep and shoulder. "You know what a bite looks like. You can see your man's hand from over here. I was bit last night. It hurts, it's ugly, but you can see that it's already starting to heal. There's no discoloration, no root system of blackened veins. I have no fever, and I'm not puking."

"Then what is it? What heals you but not him?" Farmer asked.

"Christ."

"Oh, garbage," Minister Tim said. "Don't waste your time, Lieutenant. These are the regressive types always fighting against us."

"Then how come he's fine, and Crowder's dying?" Farmer said. "I'd like that answer before I put two in his head."

"The call's mine, not yours," Minister Tim said.

"Someone make the call!" Doughty shouted.

Crowder screamed again. His pain and struggle caused anyone who didn't have to be in the sanctuary to leave. Any detail would suffice. Climb the steeple, dig a latrine, go to the east side of 19 for a smoke—anything, to avoid their brother's agony.

"Fix him," Farmer said. "If you've got the cure, fix Crowder."

"They can't," Bricklander said. He knew how the routine went. "Crowder has to do it. He has to accept Christ. That's how it works, right?"

"That's pretty good for a NORM employee," Frank said.

"We're soldiers," Farmer corrected.

"We can share who Jesus is," Hiram said, "but Crowder has to choose. He can be saved, and we could play a part in that, but it doesn't mean he'll experience healing from the virus."

"What the hell does that mean?" Farmer said. "He's dying over there. You say you got the cure, but you can't heal him?"

"He's talking about his soul, LT," Bricklander said.

"Shouldn't you be doing this?" Hiram said to Minister Tim.

"I'm talking about his flesh and bone!" Farmer fired back. He squatted back down and twisted Hiram's arm just below the bite. "I'm talking about healing like this."

With his left hand—rather boldly Bricklander thought—Hiram reached out and grabbed Farmer by the collar and pulled him close. "I can share what he needs to save his soul, but I do not have the power to lay hands on him and guarantee his healing. The Sin Virus has its consequences."

Farmer slapped the hand away. "Sin Virus?"

"He's going to die, Lieutenant. We can't stop that," Frank said. "But we can pray with him, and if he accepts, we know where he'll spend eternity."

Another wail came.

"One of you white boys better do something," Doughty said. "Or I will."

"Doughty get your butt back in the tower," Farmer said. "Now!" The private didn't until he made eye contact with Bricklander, who nodded at him.

"He won't come back," Hiram said.

"Everyone comes back," Minister Tim said.

"No," Frank said. "Not everyone."

"Who can heal? Who can put their hands on him and physically heal him?" Bricklander said.

"The only two we've seen heal by the laying on of hands are at The Garden," Hiram said. "Larry and Noel, and by now, there are a few thousand devils between them and us."

"Stop using that word 'devils,'" Minister Tim said. "And stop talking in spiritual terms. This is a virus, not a Sin Virus. It takes over the body; it has nothing to do with a man's spiritual condition. This is my business, and I know my business. It's unfortunate, but all three of these men need to be terminated to contain the infection. Lieutenant, I'm ordering you to eliminate these infected men, or I'll be forced to take action."

Bricklander pulled Farmer toward the platform. Minister Tim tried to join them. "Back the hell up!" The authority of his voice stopped the Minister's approach.

Crowder's agony fell into a persistent moan as he balled into a fetal position.

"LT, listen, Crowder's going out—nothing's going to stop that. We know what a bite looks like. That biker dude on the floor was clearly bit, but he doesn't have a fever. We've got nothing to lose, so let's have them pray with Crowder." Farmer's shoulders turned away. He wasn't having any of what the older soldier was offering. Bricklander moved in closer to make his point. "Nothing's going to happen, but our men are sick of killing civilians. Ask them to end this for Crowder, and they'll likely go along because he's burning up. But to ask them to shoot those two, who have no symptoms and only one of them is bit, means we're asking for trouble. So unless we're prepared to kill Minister Tim and bug out of here, we have to let this play out. We're close to a mutiny right now."

"What about Crowder?" Farmer said. "Minister Tim's right. He deserves that bullet."

"Either way, it will be over, and he'll get that bullet," Bricklander said. "It's terrible, but let's say; he's taking one for the team. Or maybe, just maybe, those two really have something to offer."

Bricklander felt compassion, but his words to Farmer weren't entirely true. Morale wasn't his motivation. He was desperate and wanted to know if Hiram and Frank could change the equation. This was about taking some hope back to Virginia with him.

Despondent approval came to Farmer's face. "Jarvis," he ordered. "Get those two over to Crowder. They're going to pray with him."

The civilians heard and didn't hesitate. They slid up against the wall. Hiram held Frank, who nearly lost his balance as they began to shuffle across the room.

"I feel like I just played five hours of hockey," Frank complained about his body. "You want to join hands, Lieutenant? Always room for one more."

"No, no, no, no, no, I cannot allow this," Minister Tim said. "Lieutenant Farmer, Private Crowder deserves the mercy of a bullet. You cannot put him through this. It's inhuman."

"Ah, come on, we'll show you how it's done," Frank said.

"This does not happen," the Minister said. "This is a violation of the regulations that are mine to enforce."

"We'll make a note of it," Farmer said. "You two, get busy."

"I won't allow it!"

Bricklander stepped in front of the Minister. "When the President decided to cancel the election, he not only took away the lie that things were getting better. He took away Stars and Stripes. And it was Stars and Stripes keeping your fat butt safe."

"And that means?"

"It means we've killed children on orders from people like you," Bricklander said. "The hate we have for you is greater than the hate we have for anything else. I swear to God if you try to give another order around me, you'll be dead before Crowder."

"I'll second that motion," Frank said.

They knew they were close to death, but Bricklander was starting to appreciate Frank and Hiram's wit. They were living these last hours unconcerned about being eaten or bullets going through their brains.

Barnes stepped in behind them. "Sir," he said to Farmer. "I got a message from Captain Torres. NORM wants us to hold our ground. They're building defenses in San Quintana."

"They sending us any more men?" Farmer said.

"Food, water, and ammo," Barnes said. "But no boots."

"Air support?" Bricklander said.

Barnes shook his head.

"Yeah, I didn't think so."

A lesser officer would have begun his tale of woe, but the lieutenant immediately set about dealing with it. He went outside the sanctuary to the front of the church and called for Lancaster.

"I need to use the radio," Minister Tim said to Barnes, who walked away from him. "I said, I need to use the radio!"

"I'm not allowed just to let anyone…" Barnes said, heading to the courtyard.

"Jarvis," Bricklander said. "Give these two their space with Crowder, and come get me when they're done."

LARRY
(17)

Derek Duran aggressively led worship. It was the Duran they knew, but it was a Duran who glowed. He played the guitar and paved the road for them to come to the throne. As he transitioned to the moment for Larry to speak, the hearts and minds of The Garden transitioned with him.

Larry came to the fireplace and stood. The rain had passed, but occasional thunder still sounded.

They were ready for a sermon and unprepared for what he was about to share. Everyone sat, some on the floor, some on benches against the walls. Kuykendall, and Sandoval, looked on from the kitchen.

"Noel, I need you up here," he said.

"Noel's going to interrupt me if I make a mistake." Larry smiled, amazed this moment had come. "Only Joab knew our story. I'm sure a lot of you thought something was off about Noel and me. A little out of step. We don't know about cell phones, the internet, or Starbucks and lattes. And it's because…" he stopped and looked at Noel for a final affirmation.

"Just say it, Larry," she said.

"We aren't from here."

The response was a loud quiet.

"What I mean to say," Larry started again, hoping for feedback.

"Clarity, amigo," Joab's ghost whispered.

"Well, we aren't from another planet." He laughed nervously. "We're from another time."

The explosion of laughter didn't come, no eyes rolled, and the dining hall continued in silence.

"I…" he put his head down.

"Talk to us!" Liz called out.

"We were both born in 1962," Noel said. "And on October 1st, 1979, God brought us forty plus years into the future."

"You're saying you traveled through time to be with us?" Ken Hong said.

"Yes, but it was God who moved us," Larry said, feeling relief the conversation had begun. "God brought us from our time to yours. You can say it sounds crazy, you can say it sounds like a lie, but it's true. You've seen how God has worked through us by the laying on of hands. That's not our gift--that's God."

"Incredible," Wolfman said.

"We know," Noel said. "We know it sounds crazy, but is it crazy to believe God can do the extraordinary?"

The crowd began doing calculations and putting pieces together in their heads. Larry supposed if the whole Garden were here, he might be fielding protest questions, but instead, there was awe to all of it. The right people were here to hear it.

"It's a miracle," Duran said. "I didn't know, but I feel like I knew —somehow."

Though still shining clearly with love for them, the eyes in the cafeteria began to reflect as if they were looking at something otherworldly. Larry picked up on it right away. "We're not special! Don't think of us as any more loved by God than you! You've been with us, you know we don't glow in the dark!"

"You know we went to high school together," Noel said. "We both came to the Lord during a Sunday night service on September 30th. That night we surrendered our lives to God. The next day we were in business class—October 1st, 1979—and got sent out to get supplies from a storage closet. We opened the door, there was a flash, and before we knew it, we were here."

"Amazing," Debbie said. "Crazy, but amazing. I have no words."

"I believe it," Karla affirmed. "It's just...I've got goosebumps."

"Dead people walking sounds crazy," Big Leon called out the obvious. "No cure for the virus, except Jesus. No healing except for what God has done through you. All kinds of crazy is happening," he shrugged and let out a short laugh. "This makes perfect sense to me."

Half the crowd issued an "Amen" at Big Leon's statement.

"It makes sense," Beth said. "You were both too ignorant about so many things."

"That Sunday night," Larry said. "The Lord broke us at the altar. There were a lot of people happy and crying for us. As if God had answered their prayers."

"When we got up, Pastor Hyde asked if anyone wanted to give a testimony," Noel said. An unmistakable shiver ran through her body—tears, now unrelenting. "I got up, in front of the Arcadia

FWA Church, and declared that the rest of my life belonged to the Lord. I knew God, but I never acknowledged him. I fought with my mother and partied a lot. I...I had an abortion." Her head went down. Larry took her hand. "And that Sunday night, Jesus set me free."

Now, "amens" came in abundance.

"For the first time in my life, I longed to live!" Noel shouted and then convulsed into another jag of tears. "Just like we talked about Liz, remember? For the first time in my life, I was free. And I wanted to live."

Larry put his arms around Noel and wept with her. Sniffling could be heard throughout the dining hall. A few more isolated "amens" and "hallelujahs" came. Liz came close and put her arms around the both of them.

Thunder boomed.

"The reason it makes sense," Tammy said from her wheelchair, "is because our God is perfect!"

Every head swiveled her direction. Those standing by her backed away. Larry, Noel, and Liz let go of each other. He could feel his legs buckle a bit from her voice.

"The Lord knew he'd need two pure ministers for The Garden. Two ministers unpolluted by false teaching."

Beth and Wolfman kneeled by the wheelchair and put their hands on her.

"Tammy?" Beth wept. "Tammy...?"

"I love you, Mom," Tammy said. "I have to go, but I'll be back." She looked around at everyone else. "The Lord lives! The Garden is his, and you are in the center of his will." The appearance of her face returned to what it had been before. Her head slumped, her lips pursed, and a small, thin line of drool began to spill again.

Duran came back to the fireplace and held a hand for Larry and Noel to go down. Without giving any reference, he began to play.

"What can take away my sin? Nothing but the blood of Jesus."

The Garden sang like a choir of a thousand.

"What can make me whole again? Nothing but the blood of Jesus. How precious is the flow, that makes me white as snow? No other fount I know, nothing but the blood of Jesus."

There was no preaching, no teaching, Duran played, and they spontaneously prayed. The occasional thunder continued as the rain came off and on, and the afternoon turned late. By the spirit they embraced, they engaged, and amid a world slowly dying within a nightmare—they rejoiced.

JOAB
(17)

In the lead, Joab and Drew walked alongside each other, blade and bat, respectively, in hands. Hearing thunder, Joab knew they'd have to pick up the pace. Without shelter from the rain and wind, a lonely mountain road could birth terrible misery.

Mountain Road 37, well-paved, was easy terrain. The weeds, growing off the shoulders, were in desperate need of a DUI work crew. But there was nothing in the way of human, or formerly human, activity to be seen.

Thunder cannoned, and Joab smelled the coming rain. He hoped it would only be a ten-minute blow, which wasn't uncommon in the mountains, and blue skies often followed.

"Ever been caught in the rain up here?" Joab said. He turned his head to make sure the men were keeping pace. "Last year, with Big Leon and Bird, we got caught over by Big Sky."

"I remember you talking about it," Bash said.

"It came down so hard it knocked over the devils chasing us," he said.

"So, it's a good thing?" Drew said.

"Not if you're out in the open."

Joab didn't want Drew out here. An unspoken, emotionally notarized responsibility attached him to the young man. Joab knew he needed to get him back to Noel. "So, you're telling me this is better than being at The Garden?"

"I'm not interested." Drew took his eyes off the road and put them on Joab. "I don't want to talk about it anymore."

"Put your eyes back on the road," Joab said. "I'm too old to let things go."

"Positively ancient."

"I'm trying to figure how you're so smart about everything else and so stupid when it comes to Noel," Joab said. The road was easier on his knees than the trail. "A shot at happiness...I don't know what you're thinking."

"Yeah, it's none of my business," Crazy Chang offered from behind. "But if Noel looked at me, the way she looks at you, I would've said; 'happy trails, guys.'"

"You ever have a woman in your life, Joab?" Drew said. "A serious woman?"

Something came in the air. The men raised their noses upward and smelled the scent of rain and death.

"When I was your age, I was so marvelous. I never stayed with anyone longer than a couple of weeks."

"Couldn't make up your mind?"

"No, Mr. Marvelous couldn't stop talking about Mr. Marvelous." The smell became potent, Joab tightened the grip on his blade. "I was all that and a bag of chips as the saying went, and everyone needed to know."

"So you never settled down," Drew said.

"I'd move on. I always figured something better would come my way."

"Well, I'm moving on too."

"It's not the 90's; it's the end of the world," Joab said. A drop of rain hit his forehead. "There aren't a lot of options. And you're not going to find another Noel."

Coming over a slight grade, they arrived outside Wintercrest. To Joab, calling it a town was a stretch. He guessed it to be half the size of Cumberland. A single stop sign, peace flags in various places, "Impeach 45" bumper stickers in dirty windows of closed businesses decorated the village. A small general store indicated it accepted the mail, sold necessities, and, likely, answered directions for people who got lost on their drive to Sky Porch.

"Got one," Drew pointed. "To the right, by the side of the road."

"Got it!" Mason began to race, and Joab stuck out a foot that sent him sprawling to the road. "Joab? What the hell!"

"Drew, take care of it," he said.

The tall, gangly thing was gray and with black veins running down its neck. It limped out of the high grass, smelling like it had turned early. It moved by its right foot, dragging the broken left behind. Its exposed teeth chomped at the sight of them.

Drew cocked his bat and blasted straight through the devil.

"You okay?" Joab said, squatting down and offering Mason a hand. "Sorry, but I'm worried about you."

"Why did you do that?" Mason took his hand and stood.

"You're going to get yourself killed and somebody else along with you. You need to get your head together."

Mason didn't respond.

"Do you understand? I'm saying I like having you around."

"It's hard."

"I know, but be cool," Joab said. "You're gonna get your shot to explode, but do it when it matters."

More devils appeared in the distance, and the rest of the men passed to take them down. They did it carefully, almost--if it could be said-- professionally, with their blades and bats. It was good to see, but Joab doubted they were thinking of a backdoor.

Until last night, he didn't believe the devils strategized anything. They weren't supposed to talk either, but Jay spoke before going down. It took Joab his whole career to grasp, but intelligent evil was now something they'd all need to factor into their decisions.

They entered the abandoned village and gathered in Wintercrest's lone intersection. Mountain Road 37 continued west after the stop sign—and that would be their backdoor. A decomposed gravel road went 30-yards north before stopping at the forest, and it went the same distance south before stopping at a guard rail.

"Be careful," Joab said. "Don't lose control. Remember, we're here for the goodies and a place to crash. Coordinate with each other when you start going into these shops. If you see a place that looks secure enough for the night, come get me."

Another drop of rain fell on him. The loaded sky rumbled with thunder, and Joab was getting a bad vibe. The clouds were ready to unleash, but the woods, he could smell, were already storming with bad guys.

"You picking up on this, Jefe?" Legaspe said.

"Yeah, we won't be crashing here tonight."

"This motel is booked," Crazy Chang quipped. "Time to get back on the road."

The men scrambled for supplies. Two devils stumbled out between wooden storage units near the end of the road on the south side. He kept an eye on them and saw a third, its lower half missing, crawl into view.

They hit a mini-jackpot, scoring three boxes of candy bars, some bottled water, and dragged it out to the intersection. Hutchinson put down a package of beef jerky. Mason dropped two boxes of granola cereal.

"I don't know how all of this could still be here," Hutchinson said.

"No barricades, no bones in the street," Joab said. "The residents must have bailed first chance they got."

Devils came—three, four, then a half dozen from the woods to the north. Mason again went into attack mode.

"Mason! God bless it!" Joab yelled in frustration. "Brewer, Matts, Anspach, go with him and just hold the line. Do not pursue into the woods!"

A shotgun fired in one of the shops from where they came in. Hernandez came out, holding his forearm, blood flowing between the fingers. He and Pena got to the intersection and threw down two small boxes of animal crackers.

"He's alright," Pena said.

"Bandage him up," Joab said. Devils began to flood the streets at the east end as the rain started to fall. He counted a dozen. They couldn't be tactical...

They couldn't be tactical!

…but it felt like they'd been lured in.

Intelligent evil.

Still not resorting to their guns, Mason and his group dropped devils as fast as they arrived. Firing only one shot to get out of Wintercrest would have been like winning the World Cup.

"Drew," Joab said, pointing west. "Secure the back door."

As the rain came harder, a shotgun blast came from behind him. It was Legaspe.

"Load up!" Drew said. He fired his shotgun as a devil got close. "Everybody! We are leaving!"

The men began packing up. Pena, kneeling, worked a fistful of napkins and duct tape around Hernandez's forearm.

"That hurts, man!" Hernandez said.

"Next time, listen to me!" Pena said.

"Go!" Joab said, and the men took off, but Drew came back.

"You go!" Drew said. "I'll get Mason and the rest."

Joab shook his head.

"I got faster feet. Go!"

Joab joined the rest of the men, but he lingered at the edge of the village. Mason and his group were standing and fighting. "Mason!"

Finally, they began to fall back. The men retreated, another surge came, and Matts tripped. He was gone before anyone could help. Instead of running, they fought as more devils arrived.

Legaspe and Hutchinson held the south side. Drew pumped and fired three times into a mob of devils from the east. "Get out of here!" He yelled, and Legaspe and Hutchinson pulled out.

"Fall back! Fall back!" Drew shouted, and Anspach and Brewer did, but Mason did not.

"Mason!" Drew fired in his general direction, "Go!" he said to Anspach and Brewer."

From where he stood, Joab saw the two men running his way, but Mason, in full rage, stayed. He fired his shotgun, and when it emptied, he went back to his machete.

"Drew!" Joab began drifting back to the intersection. "No! Don't!"

Mason was pushed back as Drew went forward, continuing to fire. Devils engulfed them. Blood flew into the air, Joab could see the top of a machete waving. More of the dead came from the east and south. The sound of a handgun came, and then all he heard was the gnashing and growling of devils to complement the rain.

He couldn't compute how fast it happened. It was as if a sniper had suddenly picked off one of his men, but it wasn't one. It was three. The devils in the intersection were dining on three of his men, and Drew was one of them. Mason, who he had just warned, was one of them.

Sick inside, he defended himself to his thoughts. He tried to get Drew to go back. He tried to get him to stay at The Garden.

Nothing he said to Drew was unjust or any perversion of truth, but the kid hadn't listened.

Blood rolled on the ground under the feet of the devils. A new fountain shot upward. Joab fired twice...Then it came and nearly took him off his feet.

Ping.

Nothing in his life became him like the leaving it.

Joab was ready to leave. His gun dropped, and he was about to sink to his knees when hands tugged him backward and out of Wintercrest.

NOEL
(16)

The radios were quiet. Not a burp, squelch or squeal of static all day.

Probably best, Noel thought, sitting in the corner. Pressing her head back to the wall, she could see, between the window and the tables barricading it, the trees, the shed, and slope of ground towards the amphitheater.

Twilight was passing, and the rain was merely a drizzle. She liked the rain when it came this way. It fell softly enough to walk in or stand under the branches of the trees without being drenched. It brought freshness, hope and squashed the scent of devils.

The conversations around the room created the soft din of a restaurant. People were relaxing as the day—at first troubling—fused into a peaceful evening. Some were fasting, some were snacking, some were sleeping. Aaron was helping Wolfman put together groups to take to the toilet. And some were still buzzing over Tammy's awakening.

Noel bit her lower lip, looked to the twilight, back to the room, then down to Elias—asleep and resting against her. When she told him about Wheeler, the kid capped it before she could.

"He's with Jesus?"

"Yes."

"That's better than here." Then he wept himself to sleep.

Her eyelids were heavy, and she adjusted against the corner and the cold floor. The virus was going to end because there was no other outcome to be had. God wouldn't have brought them here or this far if victory wasn't possible. There was struggle, of course, but there would be a turnaround and, ultimately, triumph.

If not, what was there to say to Elias?

When things were over, she'd move to New Hampshire or somewhere far away and live a long life--Drew, her, and their children. It was the daydream she tinkered with on hard days. Sometimes it was a beach house, sometimes it was a farm. Of late, it was a house with a wrap-around porch in New England. A place where they'd spend time together, and their children would never have to reduce their dreams.

"New Hampshire," she whispered, and her breath fogged the glass. No one heard her, and she thought of it this time. *New Hampshire.*

A blanket landed on her and Elias.

"I always thought Drew was kind of slow," Karla said with a wink. "If you need anything else, let me know."

"Thank you, Karla."

"I've known your pain," the older woman said. "But don't let it eat you. It's just a memory, and memories can't feed you, clothe you, or stop you from breathing. Like Paul says, 'Press on.'"

BRICKLANDER
(17)

Distant thunder and lightning boomed and blinked on the horizon, but it was a dark night. And Bricklander knew from experience in the Arroyo Seco that the ghouls—devils—only had one gear, and it was always forward. Middle of the day, middle of the night, it made no difference. They were always going forward.

"We don't have anything to block the highway, Brick," Lancaster said. "There's no way we can keep them from getting to San Quintana."

The smell of rain came on the wind, and they felt the chill. Standing twenty yards from the front of the church, they were looking to the mountains.

"They'll come at our gunfire," he said. "It'll draw them to us. Unless…"

"Unless, what?"

"I don't know." Bricklander was hesitant to mention what popped into his thoughts. "Either way, our mission is about buying time."

"Question," Lancaster lowered his voice, "when do we go Elvis?"

"Have you told anybody?"

Lancaster shook his head.

"We're going to fight, and when the time comes, we'll bail. We won't leave our guys hanging."

"Hell no, I wouldn't do that," Lancaster said. "But I'd like to stick around long enough to see Minister Tim get chewed twice."

"I think we'll know when to hit the road," he said. "In the meantime, let's strengthen the barricade at the gap between the fellowship hall and sanctuary."

"What about the orchards?"

"If they spill out behind us or attack from the orchards, it'll be over faster than we think."

The orchards were vast. Bricklander's first assignment on arrival was to rescue a family inside a ranch house surrounded by apricot, orange, and peach trees. They got the family out but had to fight to get to the trucks.

"Should we put an ambush team out there in the morning?" Lancaster suggested.

"Sounds good, but the problem with being inside those groves is you can't see anything. Those trees aren't tall, and the branches hang low. I think we should torch them."

"Do we need NORM's approval?"

"Are you kidding me?"

Lancaster's lips pulled into a smile. "Old habits."

"Go rack out," Bricklander said. "Tomorrow will answer everything, and at the end of the day, we'll be on the road to Virginia."

They bumped fists, and Lancaster headed for the church.

Bricklander took off his helmet. The cold air landed on his head. He had to remind himself this wasn't desertion. As long as the fight continued, he wasn't leaving. But when could he bail without putting someone else in danger? A point was coming where getting back to Rosa and the girls needed priority.

On the surface, they were doomed because NORM wasn't going to reinforce them with more men. The best thing they had going—and what NORM and the politicians couldn't reconcile—was what was inside an American soldier.

Over and above the cosmetics of Stars and Stripes, platonic soul ties connected soldiers living in the proverbial meat-grinder. They'd fought, bled, and survived together, but only in the shadow of certain death would they speak or act on their devotion to each other. In Bricklander's mind, those things were purchased and sealed in blood.

NORM was a conglomeration of politicians, academics, desk jockeys, and bean counters who had never been in a foxhole. They never concerned themselves with anything beyond themselves, so they were incapable of understanding the depth of a combat soldier.

Rosa, the girls, Virginia.

Bricklander cursed to the sky and began his walk back to the church. Coming to the barricade at the gap. "The Gap," he said, officially christening it. The busted tables, chairs, pews, and wood planks linking the sanctuary steps to the fellowship hall wouldn't hold when a good push came.

"Another smoke?" Bricklander said, finding Farmer on the steps with a lit butt.

"Well," Farmer took a long drag. "It can't do much to me now. How we looking?"

"We ain't going to keep anything from going down the road, but as we fire, they'll close in on us. And, eventually, we'll run out of bullets."

The lieutenant gestured with a nod to the surroundings. "When that happens, and they press in, this church is going to collapse right on us."

"LT?"

"What is it, Flores?" Farmer said.

"Jarvis sent me to get you—Crowder's dead."

"We're on our way," Bricklander said.

"That was quick," Farmer said, dropping the cigarette and stamping it with his boot. "And I didn't hear anything."

"Neither did I," Bricklander said, surprised. "What do you want me to do with the other two?" He wasn't going to kill them. Taking their weapons and sending them on their way made the most sense.

"Let them go, or convince them to stay. It doesn't really matter."

"Believe it or not, we've got a case of 12-gauge shells," Bricklander said as they went up the steps. "They could do some work for us in The Gap."

Three battery-powered lamps parked in different corners lit the room. Hiram, sleeping, and Frank, half-awake, were back against the north wall. Crowder was on the floor, legs stretched out, arms folded across his chest.

"Couldn't save him, could you?" Farmer said. "All your talk, and you couldn't do jack."

"Says you," Frank answered.

Bricklander came closer to Crowder but couldn't find the head wound. "Did you do something to him? Is he dead?" he asked Jarvis.

"Almost 30 minutes," Jarvis said.

"Why didn't you get us?"

"I wanted to see what would happen," Jarvis said. "I'm twisting in the wind, same as you."

"So he died and already came back?" Bricklander said.

"He didn't come back," Jarvis said with rising excitement. "Sarge, he didn't come back!"

Bricklander thought he could see a tear of joy building in the medic's eye.

"They always come back," Farmer said.

"Dude, look at him!" Jarvis said with no consideration of rank. "Look at that man against the wall. He was bit before Crowder; he still has no fever. I didn't put a bullet in Crowder, and I didn't have to split his head open because he didn't come back. Beavis and Butthead, over there, are telling the truth."

"It doesn't make sense," Farmer said, going to Hiram and Frank.

"It makes perfect sense," Jarvis said as a big laugh came out of him. "They just changed everything!"

"What did you give Crowder?" Farmer said to Hiram and slapped him awake. "What did you take?"

"Dude, be cool," Hiram said and turned to his friend. "I'm asleep, and you couldn't help me out?"

Frank shook his head. "You shouldn't be sleeping; we've got a lot going on here."

"Why didn't Crowder come back?" Farmer said.

The two men volleyed smiles in return. Bricklander expected to see smugness in them, airs of arrogance--instead, it was exhaustion and zero fear.

"Dude," Hiram said. "Just put a 9-millimeter right here," he tapped a finger between his eyes, "I gotta get some sleep. You people are killing me."

"That's funny," Frank said.

"Where's Minister Tim?" Bricklander said.

"How did you do this?' Farmer asked again.

"They prayed with him," Jarvis said.

"Jarvis, where's Minister Tim?"

"He's in the courtyard. He's been on the radio."

Bricklander kneeled by Crowder and moved his lifeless head from side to side. There were no marks on him. None of the virus's effects of blackened blood outlining maps of veins and arteries were present.

"Sarge," Jarvis said. "I've been watching people die and turn since this all began. These guys get a few minutes with Crowder, and he dies but doesn't turn. I watched. All they did was pray, speak, and hold his hand until he cashed out."

An adrenaline rush came through Bricklander. If he was to believe what he was seeing, then there was something else at play. He didn't want to smile, he didn't want it to register on his face, but the same optimism working in Jarvis began working on him.

"Is this true!" he half-heartedly raised his gun to Hiram and Frank and lowered it. "Is this true?"

The two men, who did nothing but joke, and insult Minister Tim, looked at Bricklander with stone seriousness.

"It's Jesus," Hiram said. "Look at me, look at Crowder. It's Jesus and his truth."

Rosa, the girls, Virginia.

"I spy with my sleepy eyes," Frank said, "a sergeant with a smile on his face."

Speechless, Bricklander wiped his expression.

"Everyone from the top down has been telling us these people were lunatics, but it was a lie," Jarvis said. "We just caught the biggest break in history. And hear me on this, I'm not taking orders from anyone if it means capping these two. You shoot them; you're going to shoot me first."

"There's no distress on his face," Farmer said, coming back to the body. "He passed peacefully. I don't know what to say."

"Okay, I believe you healed him," Bricklander said to Hiram and Frank. "But how come he still died?"

"We remedied his soul," Hiram said. "Don't ask me to explain it all because I can't. But we hallowed his physical body so no spirit could take possession of it. This is because of Christ dying for us. We can share that--any believer can. We can remedy our souls, I've been bit, but I'm not turning because Christ was already dwelling in me. Frank could be bit, but he's not turning, and that's half the battle."

"You should meet Larry and Noel," Frank said. "They can lay hands and heal," he snapped his fingers, "just like that."

"Why have you people been hiding?" Farmer questioned.

"Maybe you should ask that guy," Frank said, pointing at Minister Tim, who arrived back in the sanctuary. "He's your biggest problem. And, I might add, a real douchebag."

"You two are in my custody," Minister Tim said. "You'll be returning to the city with me in the morning."

"Yeah, KMA on that," Jarvis said.

Minister Tim shot an angry look.

"How do you think you're going to get them back to the city?" Farmer said. "I'm not letting you take them."

"You're giving me three men and the truck," Minister Tim said. "And the three men will bring back the supplies."

"The supplies are already on the way," Bricklander said. "By helicopter."

"Not until I drop off our two friends. It's NORM approved." The minister smiled. "NORM needs to be sure you men are holding your ground and doing your job. And then the supplies will be sent via truck."

"So you can safely slide out of here," Bricklander said, trying to rationalize what was happening and what was needed. A savior, prayer, faith, a cure? All crazy, all impossible, except when you matched it against the dead returning to life and feeding on the living. "You're not taking these two."

"You're not taking the truck," Farmer said. "You can walk or run, but you're not going to ride."

"I'm in authority," Minister Tim said. "NORM has reemphasized I'm in complete charge. You will do as I say."

"We've got to get this information out to everybody," Jarvis said.

"You have no evidence," Minister Tim said. "If you send a report back, it won't mean anything. NORM knows there's no cure."

"Then what just happened with Crowder?" Farmer said.

Two days before, Bricklander, while studying tire tracks, listened as Minister Kevin and Joab discuss the complicated issues of the Cross and Resurrection. Minister Kevin had said something about the church interfering with a secular problem. The other man, Joab, argued it was a spiritual problem spilling into the physical world.

"There's no cure," Minister Tim said. "No antibiotic can fix this. Prayer doesn't fix this."

"Well, the world's going to hear about this, and we don't need NORM," Jarvis said. "We can take pictures of Crowder and send them out."

Minister Tim found a heavy leg to a broken chair and pulled on it until it separated.

"You threatening us?" Farmer said in disbelief.

"Never, Lieutenant," he said, walking to Crowder's body. He raised the leg and swung into the dead man's head until it cracked open. Blood released like an open dam and spread from the soldier's body. Tossing the leg aside, he glared.

"That cross and resurrection stuff does get complicated."

"Now, take your picture," Minister Tim said.

"Are you...?" Jarvis started.

"I am in charge!" Minister Tim said and then to everyone in the room. "There's no cure! And if there was one, what happens when we come out and say the only cure for this virus is the blood of Jesus Christ? Will there be some wonderful coming together and great healing? Do you think that will save the world? It won't. It will only divide us more, and more blood will be spilled. So there is no cure!"

"Did you know?" Farmer said. "You knew!"

Bricklander understood. Of course, NORM knew, but when everything was equal—religions, cultures, choices—how could the government now come out and say the only hope was Christianity? Why would they give Christianity that status? When enforcing the equality of everything cloaked the government in virtue and delivered ultimate power.

Jarvis unholstered his pistol.

"Put it down!" Bricklander shouted.

"Good advice," Minister Tim said, "and I'll add to it. Start thinking about your families. Lieutenant, where's yours from? Hawaii? Sergeant Bricklander, Virginia, correct? Medic, your family's up 395, right? Remember, even at the end of the world, phone calls

417

aren't hard to make. Soldiers who mutiny are executed, and their families are thrown off base. You still have young daughters, don't you, Sergeant Bricklander? It would be a shame to have them see Rosa taken off base. But I wouldn't worry. NORM will take real good care of Shelby, Marcia, and Margie."

"Wow," Frank said from his spot on the floor. "I'm glad I don't work for this guy."

"I'm taking those two back with me in the morning," Minister Tim said. "NORM's sending supplies after I arrive back in San Quintana. If I don't get back, NORM, at my recommendation, will declare a mutiny, and you can kiss your resupply goodbye. And I've just explained what that means for your families."

LARRY
(18)

Larry woke to whispering and soft snoring. Candles burned in the middle of the dining hall and kitchen. He didn't know how long he'd been out, but the sleep helped. All appeared calm.

Denise Hemingway cartwheeled into thought, but he stood and stretched before settling back into a dream about her.

Farrah hair, great dimples, tons of teeth.

Stepping around slumbering bodies, she cartwheeled back to the past when he entered the kitchen.

"Chief," Big Leon said, sitting on the counter by the sink. "Need some water?" He held up a water bottle, and Larry took it. It tasted good as it slicked his dry mouth.

Kuykendall sat in the serving chair to the right. Sandoval, on the tile, rested against the backdoor.

"What time is it?" Larry said, drinking more water.

"It's after three," Kuykendall said. "Welcome to the graveyard shift."

"Duran and Wolfman?"

"Sleeping," Big Leon said with a grin. "And I believe the Wolfman's in love."

"Boy's got it bad," Kuykendall said.

"Angie?" Larry said.

"They might be the first wedding you do," Kuykendall said. "Of course, I don't know where they're going to honeymoon."

"Put'em in the shed," Big Leon said.

"I'm sure Noel will approve of that," Sandoval said. They didn't laugh, but small smiles came as they considered Noel's endless efforts to have the shed taken down.

Larry peered into the dining hall. There were still voices, but thankfully no sound of lips smacking. "Any noise outside?"

"Just the wind," Big Leon said. "The tarp's holding up. Duran did a good job spiking it down."

Another yawn came.

"You should go back to bed, Jefe," Kuykendall said. "Otherwise, I might have to bore you with Battlestar Galactica trivia."

"I'm cool," Larry said. Going back to his corner, where Denise was waiting and inviting him to dream dreams, would have been too easy. "I used to watch Battlestar Galactica, but it only lasted one season."

"You're talking old school," Kuykendall said. "I'm talking about the reboot."

"Like a remake?"

"A reboot," Kuykendall clarified. "They updated it."

"Why do they call it a reboot instead of a remake?"

"A reboot is when you turn something off and turn it on again. And the reboot of Battlestar Galactica was awesome. Even non-nerds like me loved it."

"You're not a nerd, Big K.?" Big Leon questioned.

"Half a nerd."

"You like Legos?" Big Leon challenged. "You like building Star Wars stuff with Legos?"

"Sure," Kuykendall answered.

"I rest my case. In my neck of the hood, you're a nerd."

"Where's your neck of the hood, Big Leon?" Larry asked, feeling like he should have already known.

"Duarte," the bald man said. "I was the brother in the neighborhood who stayed inside to watch Battlestar Galactica while everyone was else shooting each other."

"Ahh," Kuykendall said in a gentleness that was opposite his loud personality. "You did watch it."

"What more could a kid ask for?"

"Your hair not falling out," Sandoval spoke up from the door.

A chuckle worked around the kitchen at Big Leon's expense.

Sandoval was the old man, but he was in great shape. His gray hair was kept short. He always dressed the same: cargo shorts, sleeveless muscle shirt, and an occasional hoodie.

"You know," Larry said. "We've never talked. I mean, we've talked but never like this."

"You're a busy man," Sandoval said. "You don't need to talk to me. I'm good."

"No," Larry said. He looked over his shoulder and closed the kitchen door behind him. "It's not good. I'm sorry. What's your story?" Then Larry remembered you didn't just ask people their story. The background of every individual at The Garden was tragic. "I'm sorry, I shouldn't have asked like that."

"His story?" Kuykendall said. "Jefe, you are looking at the Vato Loco. He was the craziest dude around."

"Hey, Big K.," Sandoval said. "Don't try sounding like you're from the barrio, ese."

"Big K., you put the white in the coconut," Big Leon declared.

"What? East Los Angeles ain't the barrio?" Kuykendall said.

"Alhambra ain't East LA," Sandoval said. "It's Alhambra."

While Larry was preaching or preparing to preach, these men had spent time together in Mandalay, standing watch and fighting devils. They knew each other's pasts and interests. They knew how to push each other's buttons. They knew the backstories and the heartbreaks.

Sandoval enlightened with his history. How he got popped as a teenager lighting a cigarette in the back of the church. He and his brothers--bored during a Sunday evening service--taking a stroll on the sanctuary roof. Repeated instances of sneaking into theaters and ripping off candy counters confirmed Sandoval's specialization in accepting all challenges and every dare.

"Is all that true?" Larry said. "You don't look like a troublemaker. And you were FWA?"

Flashing his signature chipped tooth via a grin, he answered, "Free Wesleyan Alliance, New Lexington Church."

"I went to the FWA church in Arcadia. What did you do after high school?"

"God had some surprises for me." Sandoval made a fist with his right hand and turned his shoulder to show the Semper Fidelis tattoo on his flexing bicep.

A bulb lit in Larry's head. "Did you know a Pastor named Joe Hyde?"

"I heard of him."

Larry pressed, "Did you know a Pastor named Sheldon May?"

"Sheldon May saved my life," Sandoval said. His eyes, moving to a vacant section of the kitchen, reflected a library of shelved memories. "It feels like a dream now, but it was real." Looking back to Larry. "Maybe, I should have said something, but I've seen this before."

JOAB
(18)

The thick branches of a pine provided partial shelter, and the men got a small fire going. The fire was risky but, in this case, necessary to get through the night. They needed warmth and rest.

It was cold, but the stars were shining as if optimistic about their bad fortune. The rain had stopped, there were no sounds, no smell of death, and the shadows were empty. Joab jabbed at the flames with a stick as the dark worked its way to dawn. For these hours, they were safe. The men slept close together and as close to the fire as they could.

The storm was short, but with options out of Wintercrest limited, they were drenched racing west on Mountain Road 37. Bash, taking the lead, turned them east down a secondary road.

Anspach noticed the barbed wire on the right and called for them to stop. Shining flashlights over an empty horse corral, they went inside the fence, found the tall pine in the center, and set up camp. A tour of the perimeter showed the fencing and wire intact.

"Are you going to get any sleep, Joab?" Legaspe said, budging out of his bag. "I've been out almost four hours, and you're in the same spot I left you."

"I'm hanging in," Joab said, grateful no one wanted to talk about Drew, Mason, or Matts. Then again, these weren't the regular citizens of The Garden. These were the guys who battled devils and were consistently refreshed with new visions of gore. "I'm trying to think of our next step."

"We're with you, but I think we'd feel better if you got some sleep."

"Yeah," he mumbled. What was the point of sleep when he wasn't going to die? Everyone in his office died, but he escaped. He and Wheeler went through the roof, but he survived. Mason saved him in the amphitheater, Mason died. He told Drew to take off but Drew told him to go, and now Drew was dead. The reflexive pings were playing like *Carol of The Bells*.

So many years wasted taking people down the wrong paths and never to God. Burning candles, burning incense, writing your pains on an index card, prayer stations, prayer mazes, and services of experience instead of stuffing people like an ox with scripture.

Who needed to get saved if the work was done?

"Oh, God," he whispered and put his head down.

"Joab," Legaspe said. "You need to sleep."

"When the sun comes up, we've got to find what road this is. If we head east, there should be another fire road that will take us further down."

"Listen to Legaspe," Hernandez said, pushing himself up. "You've got to get some sleep, Jefe."

Joab pulled his revolver and held it in front of Hernandez's face. "Any fever?"

"What?" Hernandez said. "Joab, I'm cool!"

"Put the gun down!" Legaspe said. "It's Hernandez, he's fine. He's got no fever."

By firelight, he saw it in Hernandez's eyes and holstered the gun. "I had to be sure," he said to no one in particular. "I'm sorry. I'm so sorry I got Drew and everyone killed." He began to pray that he'd never see Noel again. What would he say to her? "I'm so sorry," he whispered.

The other men woke. Legaspe sat next to him. "You're exhausted, and you need to stop thinking. None of this is your fault, and you're not bringing anybody back. Come on, man, give your brain a rest."

"Jefe, sleep for an hour, and you'll feel better," Hernandez said. "Get two hours of sleep, get refreshed, and I'll go with you to the gates of hell."

"We all will," Big Geoff said.

"It's four-thirty," Legaspe said. "Sun's coming up in less than two hours. Sleep, and we'll get you up, give you some really crappy cold coffee, and then we'll get back in the game."

"Into the flatlands?" Joab said.

"Down the hill and into the flatlands," Legaspe said.

"We'll hit the church."

Legaspe nodded.

"Hernandez, I'm sorry," Joab said.

"You're not the first to act that way after seeing my face in the morning," Hernandez said, rolling over. "Get over yourself."

Joab laid down and closed his eyes. Sleep approached faster than he thought.

"Don't worry about him," Legaspe's voice came as he drifted into a doze.

"I'm not," Big Geoff said. "Fool's messed up, though. He needs to rest."

"How you feeling?" Bash asked Legaspe.

"Strong."

"First light, you and Pena scout down the road. If we can find out exactly where we are, we'll get off this mountain early."

NOEL
(17)

The sun was out, and its warmth strummed over Noel's body. People were passing her on the sidewalk. Some, she thought she knew, but they were the vaguest of memories. Like the people you saw at the mall but didn't recognize at the supermarket because they were in a different context.

On 6th Avenue was the Arcadia Church. She didn't know what day of the week it was, but Pastor Chip was standing on the steps. He appeared as old as she remembered him--a bald head with gray around the sides, but in decent shape for a man pushing 60.

"Noel!" He waved her over.

She looked both ways and crossed the street. There were no devils and no smell of them. She knew Pastor Chip was dead, but it didn't matter. It was good to see him. He'd been kind to her and Larry. Even if he didn't understand all they had to share, he welcomed them.

"How are you, Chip?" she said. "It's so good to see you."

He looked at her and shifted his head side to side. "We've got problems, and we need to talk some things out."

Opening the foyer doors, they went inside. It seated 150 people, but she noticed in an instant something was off. It was more crazy than scary. All the pews were turned away from the front of the church and facing the back.

"We need you to share," Pastor Chip said. There was a pulpit underneath the balcony. The pews were full of people she thought she knew but wasn't sure. They were waiting to hear her preach. "It's okay, Noel, speak from your heart."

There were adults and teenagers, but a group was missing. "Where are the kids?"

"They're in Children's Church. Teddy, Elias, Loren, Alison, Todd, Cora, they're all there," Pastor Chip said and then gestured to the lectern. "Please...."

A Bible was on the pulpit, and Noel dribbled its pages under her thumb. She had nothing planned. Larry was the preacher. She was only walking down the street on a pleasant day.

"I want to share how Jesus changed my life in this church," she started, and the crowd burst into laughter. She looked at Pastor Chip, who shook his head as if he didn't know what to say.

"Maybe I should share about what Jesus wants to do in your life?" They roared all the more. "He has plans for us and wants to show us things we never thought possible, but we must be obedient."

The congregation started talking to itself. People leaned back and spoke to others sitting behind them. A few crossed the aisle to start a conversation, and an older woman began knitting. Pastor Chip's head fell in shame.

"People, you have to listen to me," she yelled at them. "Trouble's coming. There's trouble in this world, and if you're not ready to talk about Jesus and the power of his blood...."

They laughed and carried on all the more. Noel tuned in and heard them talking about their projects and the good deeds they were planning for the community. They'd casually glance at her, laugh, and go back to their discussions.

All her old transgressions, the things she'd done and been so ashamed of, rose in her soul to meet the moment. Her pregnancy, her abortion, the boys she'd slept with, the rebellion that owned her heart for so long all felt like they were appearing as signs on her body. She expected the people to call them out to use them to shut her up.

"You have to hear me...." She yelled again. Still facing the floor, Pastor Chip wasn't doing anything to shut them up or make them listen. "Please! Nothing you're doing matters if Christ isn't the center of it!"

She knew they were going to mock her, call her a hypocrite. But she fought her inadequacy, and instead of shame, anger rose.

"Jesus is the remedy for sin! Jesus is the one you need to be serving! Not your egos!"

They continued to chatter and ignore her.

As Noel stepped away from the pulpit, banging came against the church doors. The people stopped talking. Fear filled the sanctuary.

"Where are the kids? Bring me the kids!" Noel called out.

The congregation fixed its attention on her. "Help us!"

The banging on the door continued. Wood cracked, and stained glass shattered.

"Help us!"

"It's too late! You didn't listen!" Noel said. "Where are the children?"

"Help us!"

The smell of the dead shot out of the furnace vents.

"Where are the kids?" she cried. "Pastor Chip, where are the kids?"

Pastor Chip's head was still bent down.

"Help us! They're inside!" The people scattered. Some came and grabbed her arms. "Help us!"

"Chip! We've got to get the kids!" She wrestled free. "The kids!"

"I'll get your kids, Noel," Pastor Chip said in a baritone voice. Raising his face, he flashed his fire eyes. "I'll go get your kids, Noel! Believe me, I'll get them all!"

The flesh on the hands pulling at her rotted away, and the dead were with her.

BRICKLANDER
(18)

It was seven, and Bricklander rotated his eyes from the front of the church to the mountains. Marine layer was the condition of the sky, but the sun was working its way in. Rain, always a threat in the high desert, seemed possible by the looks of things but far from certain.

His focus went to the field in front of him. If it had ever been tilled and farmed, it was a long time ago. Decaying brown prairie grass and weeds covered stretches before deteriorating into the bend of the mountain and Highway 19.

The night had been a busy one. Three separate attacks, all repelled, and resources diminished. No mass of ghouls came, only small gatherings. The last gunshot was at 4:30. Now, heaped with the shrubs and lifeless landscape were the carcasses of hundreds of dead. Their black ooze, one-time blood, irrigating the dust and collecting in puddles.

Back in the steeple after helping place Crowder inside a body bag, Doughty was eyeballing for movement. They all could see the dust cloud rising from the mountain and the indication of an army coming their way with bad intentions.

"That dust cloud is getting bigger," Doughty called out.

"Watch the orchards," Bricklander yelled back. "I don't want to get flanked."

The Texan returned a thumbs-up. Like Farmer, Doughty had grown so much over the months. His awareness was constant and didn't require a kick in the can to get started. He also displayed maturity in the wake of his friend's death.

Bricklander thought of Crowder and his suffering. But that suffering didn't end like everyone else's did. The world had changed, again, and it made clear that there was a shot of getting out of this nightmare—all because he didn't put a bullet into Crowder's brain.

"You do not appreciate our situation here," Farmer spoke into his radio as he paced in front of the church. He motioned for Bricklander to put on his headset and join the conversation. Ordinarily, the Sergeant wouldn't have felt right about this, but death was imminent, there was a cure, and Captain Reggie Torres was a good man.

That was in one corner. In the other corner was NORM, and NORM was a bastard.

"...This is what I'm telling you," Torres's voice came into his ear. **"I have nothing to send you. The people are trying to get out of San Quintana, and Holsopple and I are trying to get them to fortify. We've got chaos in San Bernardino and Riverside. NORM says he's sending reinforcements here, but we don't know when they're going to arrive."**

"Reggie, this is Brick." He cut in, and Farmer issued a nod that it was okay to speak. **"We're not saying we're not going to hold our ground. What we're saying is we need that re-supply now. We can't afford to send anyone back."**

"What about the two terrorists off the mountain?"

"Terrorists?" Farmer shouted. **"Those two have given us an answer. Crowder was bit. He died but didn't turn. Minister Tim is lying. Send us that Blackhawk! Tell NORM the conditions on the ground have changed. Tell him to look at the**

map again. If we fall, the whole IE falls with us."

"Reggie, we know what we're facing. We're ready. Just send us the stuff to fight with." Bricklander said. **"Better still, send us the Apache."**

"Hold on!"

Bricklander and Farmer both knew Torres was being pinched. But the Captain needed to see they had NORM in a bind. The higher-ups, no doubt, knew the map and knew they couldn't afford to lose San Quintana. There was no spinning the loss of the town and fall of the IE into a positive.

After the election announcement, NORM needed a win.

"If we're not re-supplied, we're dead," Farmer said. **"These jokers off the mountain won't make a lick of difference either way. But the men needed to transport them back will."**

"Hold on!"

As desperate as it all felt on the outside, Crowder's failure to turn kept panic from seeping in. Bricklander took off his helmet and considered the moment. What remained of his platoon was far from discouraged.

Farmer's voice went low and personal with Torres. **"Reggie, I'm gonna say this one more time; Crowder did not turn. Whatever Minister Tim is saying to NORM is a lie. Those people on the mountain have something...I know it doesn't change our mission, but you've got to let people know. Tell everybody, blast it all over San Quintana. This is our first break...Yes, sir..."** His voice became louder. **"Yes, sir... Out..."**

"Sarge!" Doughty shouted from the tower and pointed to the groves.

Bricklander saw a monster. Mangled, like its teammates, a coat stretched down over its arms, shuffling more than it walked. His best guess, from 50-yards, was it had been a man. He didn't know why he registered them as men or women anymore. A bite from either did equal damage. They both could kill, and both had better than expected strength.

Instead of raising his M-4, he walked to it. A recent transition, it came his way. The body wasn't falling apart. It snarled, growled, and its mouth chomped up and down.

Less than 25-yards away, its hands raised. Now closer, Bricklander saw dangling from its neck something white. It was someone he knew and spent time with, and now that person was a monster.

A cross was needed to stop a vampire. The purity of silver was required to finish a werewolf. Countless sequels, heroines, and providence were necessary to kill the unstoppable slashers in the films he saw as a kid. And it was always an evil motivating the slashers--some unknown force.

Evil spirit?

Monster was no longer sufficient to describe the dead that came back...but devil was.

Intelligent evil.

Torn skin was flapping down its right cheek, revealing bone. Its black tongue protruded out. Bricklander brought the butt of his rifle up through the jaw, straight through the head. The skull cracked, but it didn't go down until he gave it a second hammering.

He pulled the white item on the neck, and with the toe of his boot, he opened the coat's lapel. The handheld radio he'd given Minister Kevin was in the pocket.

"Brick!" Farmer called.

He stopped at the edge of the grove, squatted down to his knees, but saw nothing.

"Brick! We got the resupply!" Farmer came racing behind him. "What are you doing? Don't you walk out on me!"

He ignored the assertion. "It's odd, isn't it, that the guys telling us there's nothing spiritual to see are the ones in the collars?" He held up the collar for Farmer. "Funny how one day can change everything you used to believe about God."

"What did you believe about God?"

"Nothing. I went to church as a kid, none of it stuck, and I never went back as an adult. I figured I did my best work in Sandland, but my best work may have been not capping Crowder."

There was still a load on Bricklander's shoulders, there was still Rosa and the girls to worry about, but serious weight had come off. He'd be going home with Christmas presents in hand—real hope.

"I had good to talk with the Almighty last night," Farmer said.

"What did he say?"

"Well, I said the usual, you know, "if you get my butt out of here, I'll never ask for anything again."'

Bricklander, familiar with the 'Save My Butt Prayer,' laughed.

The lieutenant gave a slow shake of the head. "He didn't talk, but I felt him. It was like a whole bunch of stuff shoved into me as a kid spilled out. God didn't talk, but he did. I know that sounds weird."

"Everything's weird in this world," Bricklander said. "But I do believe God spoke through those nerds, and we need them to talk to the rest of the men."

"Don't we all get faith in a foxhole?" Farmer said.

"We do, but we need something a little bit more," Bricklander said. "Something that lasts after a chunk's taken out of a forearm. Something more than bullets because we don't have enough of them."

Farmer drew in a breath and looked around. "Real faith?"

"That Hiram guy doesn't die, Crowder dies but doesn't come back, and now you say we're getting resupplied." He shook his head. "Something's happening."

"And NORM seems to have cut Minister Tim off at the knees," Farmer added.

"You think those yahoos would be willing to preach to our platoon?"

***

Inside the sanctuary Minister Tim stopped Farmer at the doors.

"I want to talk to you."

"Yeah, later," Farmer said.

"Now!"

Bricklander walked over to Hiram and Frank, who were looking better. He put their shotguns in front of them.

"You boys healthy enough for these?" he asked.

"Oh yeah," Frank said. "Feeling good."

"Can you get around on that leg of yours?"

"Your man Jarvis cleaned and wrapped it yesterday," Frank said, "...when we led him to the Lord."

"We'll get to that," Bricklander said. "Right now, I got a case of 12-gauge ammo but no shotguns of my own to shoot them with. You know what's coming our way. You want to work those Remingtons for us?"

"Is the arctic cold?" Frank said.

"Is that supposed to be like 'is the Pope Catholic?'" Bricklander asked Hiram.

"I told you to stop using that stupid line," Hiram said and then looked at Bricklander. "Dude, took his first date to AM-PM for dinner."

"Not surprised," Bricklander said. "Get loaded up. Meet us outside these windows." Then he turned to everyone else. "Out front! Now!"

The soldiers came from their different stations and went through The Gap to the field. Doughty remained in the tower. As everyone prepared to hear from Farmer, the ignored Minister Tim went back to the courtyard.

"Bring it in!" Farmer said. "Eyes on me!"

Bricklander eyed the men, including Hiram and Frank, and got from them a weird optimism. It was tempered by Crowder's death, but like him, they were sensing a big change had occurred.

"This is real simple, and your only requirement is to hear me out," Farmer said. Behind him was Highway 19 and a weak breeze carrying the smell of dust and desert. "Any of you want to run, go ahead and run."

From the courtyard, everyone heard the jeep trying to turnover.

"I don't want to die any more than you do, but I'm staying. You want to leave, leave because there ain't no more Stars and Stripes. So I'll understand if you want to go and take your chances. You can take your weapon, but only the ammo already loaded. I won't have you shot for desertion, but I will have you shot if you take any ammo."

No one budged.

"We are buying time for San Quintana. There's no glory in this, and no one back there's going to buy you a beer to thank you for your service."

The jeep's engine kept cranking but wouldn't ignite.

"I'm going to ask you to hold your positions. Stay aware of the south side — it's our blind spot." Farmer stopped as the sound of the jeep became sicklier. The battery was waning. The men cracked smiles.

"Bummer," said Lancaster. "I always hate it when someone jacks with my ride."

Now the men were laughing, and Bricklander let the emotion show on his face. The sabotaging of Minister Tim was proof of unity beyond Stars and Stripes. They were going to stay and fight for each other.

"Rage is going to take you, it will probably take all of us, and it might not be all bad considering our position, but hold on as long as you can. We can kill more of them if we keep thinking. We'll last longer if we do our jobs and keep our cool."

"You think we're going to die today?" Doughty said from above.

"I ain't making any promises. Take a look at that mountain," Farmer said, turning upward and then back to the field. "But NORM's sending us a supply chopper. And he wants us to empty everything we have into what's kicking up all that dirt."

"I ain't dying today," Doughty called down.

"Then don't!" Bricklander said. "We don't have to die."

A locker room rah-rah seized what remained of First Platoon. Farmer nodded at Bricklander, and he nodded back. They didn't speak, but the telepathy viable in veterans gave them a connection.

Farmer raised his hands; "I'm going to tell you something else. Something Fat Minister Tim doesn't want you to know about. Crowder died last night, but what some of you may not know is that Crowder didn't turn."

The reactions on their faces confirmed most knew.

"I just want to be clear," Farmer said, then gestured to Hiram and Frank, who stood in the middle of them with shotguns resting on their hips. "These two said Crowder accepted Christ as his savior. Now that might sound bizarre to most of us, but before you dump on it, remember Crowder didn't come back."

Minister Tim came to them with far less confidence than he had the night before. "The jeep won't start, and I need to get to San Quintana."

Another round of laughter came.

"This isn't funny," the Minister said. "I need someone to look at the jeep."

"We're fresh out of mechanics," Bricklander said. "Start walking."

438

"Have you forgotten what I said last night, Sergeant?"

"We heard you, and now you're fresh out of ammo. That resupply is on its way. So you can just go."

Farmer continued.

"It will be a while before they get here. Doughty, keep an eye on the orchards," Farmer said. "If they're going to swing around behind us, they'll do it from there."

"That sounds like intent, LT?" Lancaster said.

"Call it a feeling," Farmer responded.

"Who gave those men back their shotguns?" Minister Tim shouted.

With the timing of professional comedians, Hiram and Frank pumped and chambered their weapons.

"My advice to you, Fat Minister Tim, is start walking," Farmer said and then to the men. "Fortify The Gap, but make sure we have a way in and out. We're going to want to lay some hate on the devils before they come against the church. And we want them coming to us, not passing us on the highway."

"Don't call them devils!" Minister Tim said in a tone desperate to hang on to control.

"Every directive given by Fat Minister Tim is to be ignored," Farmer said. "The only one who can shoot him is me, so don't get any ideas. Let's get the ammo, food, and water we have spread out. But we're coming back here to give you the how and why on what kept Crowder from turning."

"Scram!" Bricklander said. As the men went to work, he went to Hiram and Frank. "We need you to run a chapel service before the devils get here."

"I've never preached before," Hiram said.

Farmer joined them.

"Neither one of us have ever preached," Frank said.

"Well, you better figure something out," Farmer said. "Because we need what you know. We need it more than we need you working those guns."

"Think of it this way," Bricklander said. "You've got 23 of us in a foxhole, and we're ready to believe anything you say. Hell, we may even pass the hat and take an offering."

"Do you guys have cheeseburgers in San Quintana?" Frank asked.

"Plant-based."

"Well, if that's your best offer, I guess we'll do it."

LARRY
(19)

Joab's computer was small but intimidating. The computers Larry knew of but never dreamed of operating came big and wide with black screens and green type. What he held now looked like a flattened typewriter connected to a television screen. With the people sleeping off the rollercoaster that had been the day before, he guessed this the best time to see what the laptop had for him.

"You need help?" Duran said.

"Joab said he left some files for me to read, but..."

"Yeah, he mentioned you might need some direction." Duran took a spot next to him on the floor. In the upper right corner, he pushed a button, and the screen lit.

"Sometimes you have to give these things a few seconds," he said and then described how to use the 'mouse.' "This laptop's a few years old. It looks like Joab might have dropped in a new hard drive."

Larry didn't detour into questions about what a hard drive was.

"The files are on Word. The documents are here...there it is, see? He's got both your names on one and another just for Noel."

A little icon of a folder read: **Larry-Noel/This!**

"Double-tap the mouse—that's your finger on this pad—and it will open up. Then scroll down like I showed you. If you get lost trying to back out, just close it up, and it'll go into sleep mode. Got it?"

"No," he said, "but thanks, Derek."

Duran left him, and Larry moved the arrow over the icon with his name and double-clicked.

"These are reports I downloaded from connections at the Free Wesleyan Alliance Headquarters in Memphis. They are from the private files of the General Superintendents. These are critical pieces of five reports submitted over thirty years by two ordained elders in the church. There were more but, because of time, I went with names and locations that would be familiar to you. Reverend Sheldon May and Reverend Jerry Knight, with input from Reverend Grant McGee. I probably broke a law or five acquiring this information, but someone needed to get to them before they were lost."

Larry's eyes read further as an escaping yawn indicated he needed more rest.

Marcia Blaine: 1969
Marcia Blaine, Wisconsin, USA
The Account of Sheldon May, Ordained Elder Free Wesleyan Alliance Church

New Lexington Church: 1974
El Monte, California, USA
The Account of Sheldon May, Ordained Elder Free Wesleyan Alliance Church
The Account of Jerry Knight, Ordained Elder Free Wesleyan Alliance Church

Joab knew El Monte was Larry's hometown and that he attended the Arcadia Church. Sandoval went to New Lexington and knew both Knight and May. Resisting the temptation to click, he continued to scroll.

Pembrook: 1998
Pembrook (Lassen Mountain Range), California, USA
The Account of Grant McGee, Ordained Elder Free Wesleyan Alliance Church
The Account of Sherry Starne

Dane Power: 1998
Dane Power, California, USA
The Account of Jerry Knight, Ordained Elder Free Wesleyan Alliance Church
The Account of Quinn Rigby, Ordained Elder Free Wesleyan Alliance Church

Cambria: 2011
Cambria, California, USA
The Account of Grant McGee, Ordained Elder Free Wesleyan Alliance Church

Larry's eyes only scanned; his motor was shutting down. Still, he clicked the Marcia Blaine file for a glimpse.

"The episode in Marcia Blaine...I had no intention of sharing, but key members of the FWA's Marcia Blaine Church Board felt compelled to put together a report. To confirm their account, I agreed to share mine."—Sheldon May.

He read on.

"...Thunder came again, the windows shattered, and light came in shards from the outside. The smell was dreadful, like a rotting corpse. Through the thin light, I saw the four board members sitting at the table. Then I saw something else. Behind each of the men were hooded figures. Skeletal hands were resting on their shoulders. I could make out fiery yellow eyes under the hoods...."

His waning energy perked up. *Firey yellow eyes* were something he was very familiar with. He skipped further down to the date, 1969, and decided not to read anymore. Fear grabbed him as he closed the computer.

"They knew," he said under his breath. "...and did nothing."

The world tilted, and the Sin Virus came.

As he leaned back, Larry understood why the church had been silent. The product of the silence was the condition of the present-day church. Seeds had been planted decades before. The incident in Marcia Blaine, and other places, didn't fit the denominational narrative. Anything supernatural had to be ignored or stripped of everything exceeding the societal boundaries of accepted time and space. Miracles were symbolic, and Jesus was one of many with a Christ consciousness.

"Clarity, amigo," he heard Joab say.

JOAB
(19)

Joab didn't expect to see the orchards coming off the mountain but another utility or fire road. Instead, they arrived at the back end of an abandoned ranch with a long stretch of orange trees set to the west. Directly in front was an open field and, in the distance, the ancient church.

The house's remains indicated it was impressive in its day, with two fireplaces and a concrete foundation among its charred posts. Its perch on the foothill could have converted into a great camp with time.

But there wasn't any time.

Above, the trails were active, and what was unseen was easily smelled. In their march, the dead were exhausting dust like a steam locomotive coming down the track. Joab knew they were amid legions of devils but, for now, protected by the various canyons and ravines.

"We've fallen right into the middle of a perfect storm, Jefe," Vegas said. He and Chapman had scouted east. "None of it's good."

"Well, we weren't expecting taco trucks," Crazy Chang said, and the men laughed. "Frick, let's get to it. I'm sick of running. They want us, I can feel it. Let's give it to them."

For Joab, the few hours of forced sleep had cleared his head. Fatigue and sorrow were still there, but his brain felt functional. It also reinforced the vibe that his men were ready for a brawl. It was both healthy and hazardous. Great that the men wanted to fight, but treacherous because it was so easy for rage to set in and lose control.

One or a few devils didn't overwhelm emotionally the way hundreds could in a confrontation. Chang and the others were reacting to what was being foisted upon them spiritually. A growing mass of the dead didn't only bring physical danger but spiritual despair.

"What did you see?" Joab asked Vegas.

"It's a traffic jam of devils coming down Highway 19. Above us, everything is crawling. You can see the bushes and trees moving and the dirt kicking up. And in front of us…" Vegas smiled and pointed across the field. "…The United States Army is barracked at the church we're heading for."

"Why there instead of San Quintana?" Hutchinson said.

"My guess is they know our buddy Owen took the lid off Sky Porch," Bash said. "They're either fortifying or evacuating it, and those chumps are the buffer."

"How many?" Joab asked.

"Twenty? Maybe a few more." Chapman answered. "From what I could see, they're getting ready to fight."

"Last stand," Big Geoff offered. "I can dig that."

They'd left The Garden looking for a fight, and, now, one was right in front of them, prepped and ready to go. With what was coming into the flatlands and headed for San Quintana, Joab knew victory would be measured by saving souls, not lives. A lot of people were going to die today.

"You know, I always wanted to die flying in the shuttle," Anspach said. "I mean, that be a great way to go, right? Just boom and a long freefall down."

"A bit random, Anspach?" Crazy Chang said.

"Aren't we all thinking it?" Anspach said. "I got a feeling today's the day, and I'm okay with it. I just want to make it count."

"It boils down to how we want to look at it," Joab said. "We either stepped off the hill at the worst time or the right time. Thoughts?"

"I go with you, Jefe," Vegas said.

"We owe each other nothing," Joab said. "We're not at The Garden anymore. I'm not…"

"Save it," Pena cut him off. "The best thing that happened to us was hooking up with you…" He then turned emotional. "…Because you've led us to the right place at just the right time. If this is where I cash it in, then this is where I cash it in. This is clarity, amigo."

"The church," Bash said. "The church and those soldiers. Clarity."

"I'm not an amen boy," Brewer said, "but, amen."

"You sound like Kiln," Chang said.

"We got devils on our butts, a place to fight, and something to fight for," Legaspe said. "It's providence directing us someplace to share the Gospel and our guns. I love it."

"That's the US Army down there," Joab said. "They may not be thrilled to see us."

"Pardon the French," Hutchinson said with a smirk. "But I think they're going to be as happy as hell to see us."

"I wanted the shuttle," Anspach said. "But I'll take this."

"Thirteen of us going to make a difference?" Orlando asked.

"We were spoiling for a fight, and here it is," Joab said. "Yeah, I think we can make a difference. But you," he pointed to Orlando and then Chapman, "you and Chapman should probably head west and get out of here."

"You guys are young," Pena said. "Go, ride on."

"I don't owe you guys anything," Orlando said. "I make my own choices, and if we're going down there, then I'm going down there. I know how to pray, too. So don't despise my youth. I could have stayed at The Garden. But the Lord sent me here with all of you."

"I got no place else to go, guys," Chapman said. "Matts, Mason, and Drew went out like studs. I ain't running. I'm fighting with Joab's Mighty Men."

"Then let's dance," Vegas said. "Besides, who knows how to fight like Joab's Mighty Men?"

"Who's able to make war like us?" Big Geoff added. "Let's go empty our guns and make our machetes bloody." He looked at Joab. "I need this fight. Otherwise, I'm going to keep thinking about our friends and start to cry."

And then Big Geoff began to cry.

The men pressed around him and began to pray. It wasn't a prayer of survival, and it wasn't a prayer of victory or safety, but of gratitude. They thanked the Lord for one another and his bringing them together.

When they finished, there was no more discussion.

"Everyone good?" Joab said, and affirming glances worked around the group. "Any questions?" Heads shook side to side. "Okay...' And he set his face toward Jerusalem.'"

They stepped into the open field and began a steady trot toward the church.

BRICKLANDER
(19)

"I'm being honest," Hiram said. "I've never done this before."

"That's okay," Bricklander said. "After Crowder, I don't think we're going to need much convincing."

Bricklander and Farmer knew asking Hiram to share the God stuff would give the men purpose and keep hope present. And if they survived, new roads home could present themselves.

"You can't do this!" Minister Tim said. "This goes against every protocol!"

"Why are you still here?" Farmer said.

"Barnes, get Doughty down here," Bricklander said. "I want everybody to hear this."

"What do you need from us?" Farmer said to Hiram and Frank.

"He doesn't need anything because he will not be saying anything," Minister Tim interrupted. "I'm going to leave here, and when I leave, I'll be contacting NORM, and all your families will suffer unless…."

Farmer pulled his sidearm. "I'm sorry, can you repeat that business about our families?"

Minister Tim stopped.

"I apologize for the interruption," Farmer said, still aiming the pistol at the Minister. "What did you need?"

"Nothing, we're good," Hiram said. "I found a Bible inside, and…" he paused.

"…And what?"

Hiram laughed. "I'm nervous."

"Thousands of dead are on the way, and you're nervous about this?" Farmer smiled. "You guys are weird. Would it be easier for you if I capped Minister Tim right now?"

"Sarge!" Doughty called.

"Doughty! Come down!" Bricklander shouted back.

"Sarge!" Doughty was pointing north.

The men felt for their guns and pivoted, but it wasn't what they expected to see.

"Who are they?" Farmer asked, holstering his weapon and banking alongside the first sergeant.

"I don't know."

Hiram stepped forward, "No way."

"Unbelievable!" Frank yelled. "Yes!"

"What is it?" Farmer asked as thirteen ragged, baseball cap, Panama hat-wearing, long-haired men jogged toward them. "Who are those guys?"

"That!" Hiram exclaimed, "is prayer answered!"

"Are they on our team?" Lancaster said.

"Joab!" Frank called. He stepped in front of the soldiers, slung his shotgun, and began limping in their direction. "Joab!"

The formation of men eyeballed Frank, let out a cheer, and broke ranks. Hiram joined the sprint, and they met on the field away from the soldiers.

"Why am I feeling good about this?" Farmer said.

"Besides being given us thirteen more guns?" Bricklander said. "Call it a hunch, but I think we've been given thirteen more men who are immune to the virus. Better still, they know why they're immune to the virus."

The beating sound of a helicopter hit their ears. Beyond the church, they saw a Black Hawk coming their way. Bricklander would have preferred seeing Belton heading north to burn down the mountain in his Apache, but getting resupplied wasn't bad either. Farmer dispatched Jarvis, Barnes, and Flores to secure it.

"Torres came through," Farmer said.

"I'm leaving on this," Minister Tim said to them. "And I'm reporting this unit for insubordination and mutiny."

"Yeah, you do that," Farmer said.

Minister Tim raced through the opening in The Gap.

When the alumni celebration ended, Hiram and Frank escorted their friends to the church. Bricklander recognized Joab right away. In a few days, Joab had turned from scoundrel to saint in his eyes.

"Lieutenant Farmer, Sergeant Bricklander," Hiram spoke through the noise of the chopper, "this is Joab and the security team from The Garden."

"I assume you're here to lend a hand?" Bricklander said, not sure when or if he needed to give an apology for his previous opinion.

"We're here to drop bad guys," Joab said. "Do I have to tell you what's behind us?"

Farmer shook his head. "Only two things matter right now. First, we're being resupplied but not reinforced. What you see is what you get. Second, I don't want any of my men to turn."

The whooping of the Black Hawk's blades grew as it landed behind the church. Sand and small pieces of roofing tile came their way over the top of the building.

"So, you understand us now?" Joab said through the distraction.

"We do," Bricklander said, extending a hand that took Joab's. "And, I'm sorry."

"Not as sorry as me," Joab said.

"This is huge," Hiram said. "What I've been nervous about doing, Joab's been doing all his life."

"We're clueless about this business," Farmer said. "Yesterday, your men prayed for one of mine after he was bit. He died but didn't turn," Farmer said. "None of us have seen anything like that. So we know you have a cure, and we know it involves God."

"It does," Joab said. "Specifically, Jesus Christ. Any problem with the name?"

"None," Farmer said. "And before you ask me what the rest of my men think, it doesn't matter. There are no atheists in crumbling churches."

A rush of emotion kicked through Bricklander. Scarred physically and emotionally by war, distrust was his natural condition. At this moment, though past its prime, his heart was pumping. Something beyond his strength was putting Virginia within reach.

Thank you, he said inwardly because he didn't know what else to say or how to say it. A need came across his soul to weep at this unexpected grace. *Thank you, thank you...*

The Black Hawk continued to kick dirt and debris high into the air as it was being unloaded.

"We've got work to do," Joab said. "So, we'll do it right here." He pointed to the shade extending from the church, and the men moved. The soldiers introduced themselves to the recently arrived. "Does anyone have a Bible?"

"I found one," Hiram handed it to him.

Joab took it and looked inside. A grin came to his face. "You're kidding me. Awesome."

The Black Hawk lifted off. The men unloading the chopper returned. Lurking at The Gap, Bricklander saw a flustered Minister Tim. NORM had stranded him.

JOAB
(20)

All the men stood in the shade of the church intently focused.

How long had it been since Joab preached?

It was easy to say the last 18 months, but there was a difference between speaking and preaching. Before The Tilt, Joab spoke at college chapels, youth conventions, and other gatherings. He was good at informing and illuminating whatever plan he was advocating. It was easy, a couple of jokes about White Privilege and a few shots at "Karen," followed by timely calls for justice and restoration.

They always bit.

Preaching, on the other hand, required belief in something beyond his control. It needed passion to reach people. Unlike a talk that expected nothing beyond applause and donations, preaching couldn't measure the unseen changes in the heart.

Giving a talk was easy and self-edifying, but after preaching, the condition of his ego was a coin flip. And that's why dialing down on the miracles, and supernatural came so instinctively. The only expectation, the only thing to extend and grasp for--in the end--was the earthly. The attainable, the reachable, the black and white, all the things that didn't hinge on a resurrected savior.

Uneasiness washed over him about being out of practice and unworthy. It wasn't a condemnation from above but from within. As he surveyed the men, it felt like he'd never preached before. When he opened the cracked leather of the NIV Study Bible Hiram found, a surge of calm came.

To Russ Moyer on his Birthday. We love you, son!"

The year indicated was 1989. Beneath Moyer's name, in red ink, was the signature: ***Keon Mitchell.***

Joab had known Russ Moyer. Russ became a successful pastor in the FWA. They weren't friends, but through social media, he knew Russ as a respected Biblically conservative thinker with stops in St. George, Utah, and Arroyo Grande, California.

"Someday, Joab, you're going to look back and realize you're not as smart as you think," Wendy Sedaka told him.

This was redemption.

"Something happened to the world," he said as the words sprang, limber, with strength. "It got knocked off its spiritual axis, and things spilled into our realm that never should have. Evil spirits, spirits the Bible tells us to have nothing to do with, began claiming deceased bodies and moving them to action."

Part of him wanted to hurry, but they had time. Devils, in their stumbling march, moved like a marathon runner seized by cramps head to toe. He had time to make sure they were locked and loaded. Time to see the yellows of their eyes, time to contemplate running or throwing another piece of broken wood on the barricade they called, The Gap. And they had time to consider things of eternity.

"Part of the reason for this is because the church stopped preaching the need for a Savior. Salvation was found in helping the poor, attaining justice for the immigrant, and even protecting the environment. Salvation was your truth, the truth you cultivated, not God's. We eliminated all discussion about sin, and with that, we eliminated the need for Jesus to take away our sins. These devils carry the Sin Virus, and when they attack, it activates what is already inside us. Unless…."

"Unless we've been previously vaccinated by the blood," Bricklander said with complete understanding.

454

"The blood of Jesus, that's right. And we've had this remedy the whole time, but the church failed to share it."

"Why?" Another soldier, Joab judged, by his insignia to be a sergeant, asked.

"Because it was too awkward, troublesome, singular," he began rattling off reasons. As each one left his mouth, it seemed to turn and slap him in the face. "Isolating, lonely, you name it. We were God's church, but God wasn't enough. We needed affirmation from the culture."

"Clarity, amigo."

"When we live in Christ, the physical attacks of the enemy have no viral effect on us," Joab said. "When we're apart from Christ, we have unforgiven sin, and if exposed to a bite or wound--it activates virally--and we become susceptible to these spirits that hate us. Have you noticed that while they kill and eat, their priority is to keep killing?"

"Yes," an African American soldier said. "They seem to hate us more for being alive than for food." Other soldiers concurred.

"Have you noticed when they come in big numbers, a depression comes over us?" Joab said, and the men bent their heads in agreement.

"Doom," another soldier said.

"Right now, we know they're coming, and unless you've made a decision for Christ and receive what his blood provides, it's only a matter of time before the Sin Virus takes you."

"Tell us what to do," Farmer said.

"You need to acknowledge that you're sinners," Joab said. "You need to ask for forgiveness and accept Jesus Christ as your savior."

"Clarity."

"I was taught we were saved when Jesus did his work on the cross," the African-American soldier said.

Joab pointed at him politely, and the soldier understood.

"Doughty," he said. "Ben Doughty."

"I'm sure you were, Ben," Joab said. "I taught the same. Jesus did do the work on the cross, but it's like an unopened present. It means nothing unless you believe in it and accept it. And the key aspect of that is repentance--the turning away from sin. Not the expanding of your mind and the grand search for ultimate truths. It's you, us, turning away from our sins and coming to God."

"It's hard," another soldier said. "I don't even know what sin is. Is it what I did, or is it what someone else is telling me what I did?"

"A few years ago, answering that question took a little time. Today," Joab raised his hand and pointed across the field. The first ranks of devils were now in view, and their stench was moving ahead of them. "Do any of you identify with that?"

The soldier shook his head.

"You've all been given the gift of seeing your friend bitten but not turn. Of seeing our man, Hiram, bitten but not infected. That's because the blood of Jesus is the remedy for all of that. We will all die physically, one day, or even today. But in him, we will not be overtaken by sin. In him, we live forever."

"I understand," the soldier said.

"What's your name?"

"Adrian Gibson."

"Adrian, happy thoughts don't save us. Good deeds don't save us. Guns can't save us, machetes can't save us, NORM won't save us. We need a savior, a savior's blood, and that savior is Jesus Christ...risen from the dead."

Eyes were turning moist and beginning to glisten. Maybe yesterday they wouldn't have been ready, maybe tomorrow would have been too late, but today, at this time, when Joab and his men came off the mountain, they were ready.

"Some of you have had to do horrible things," Joab said, knowing what moved in him wasn't unfamiliar. The Holy Spirit began shaking free, and he heard its voice. It was the one giving him words.

All of the soldiers were crying. The sergeant who asked, "Why?" went to a knee and put his head down. Anspach and Big Geoff put hands on the sergeant.

"Things you believe there's no forgiveness for. I know that feeling, that feeling has been with me since this started. I can only bear it by the grace the Lord has shown me through his son Jesus Christ."

More soldiers took a knee, and more of Joab's men surrounded them to pray. Bricklander tried to remain stoic, but tears overran his battered face. He openly sobbed and went to a knee.

They were so ready, he thought. *It's like preaching at junior high camp.*

"Whether you think you deserve it or not, forgiveness is for the asking. Jesus's blood is the agent, the mechanism, for this. Though it's hard, you were doing what you thought was right. God knows that, and his Spirit is here to free you from that pain. You need only ask because he is our Lord, and he loves us with a love the world can't deliver through any of its supposed wisdom. And his love sits squarely between grace and truth. We need a savior who grants us peace that no one or nothing else can give--salvation no one or nothing else can provide."

The feeling was almost out of body, his mouth, his voice, but not his words. It had been so long, he desired to go to a knee with them.

"Jesus' resurrection isn't just a story with good values," he said. "Jesus died on the cross and physically rose from the dead. There's no work for you to do to gain or maintain salvation other than to live in a believing loyalty of its truth. And if that remains, everything else will come."

He led them through the *Sinner's Prayer*. When he was younger, Joab considered these words and phrases as fake as saying abracadabra. Just memorization to gain a daydreamer's entry into eternity. It insulted his intellect and made discovering God as easy as walking through the doors of a mall. He openly declared it a fraud.

"We have to discover God by our own journey and our own path," he once told a chapel crowd at Whidbey. *"This is not a one size fits all experience. We are all different; we all come from different backgrounds. Some of us need to grieve for what our parents, culture, even race have done. Others need to grieve for what's been done to them. And this is the purity that frees us--not a whimsical divine hope, but honesty and justice. Not the charade of American Christianity where money, mantras, and denominational oppression dictates. Our mission is to break down those corroding systems, to deconstruct those myths. And allow us to be reconstructed to live in the context of this present world's beauty, love, and opportunity instead of the next."*

Memory looped of the auditorium bursting into applause and the enthusiastic agreement of FWA-International Director of Youth, Barry DeJohn. There was great satisfaction in knowing he was helping to break the false notions and beliefs these young people had been coerced into accepting.

Now it brought him to the brink of nausea. He focused forward.

When he concluded prayer with a loud "Amen," the soldiers stood. "Remember this; they hate us because we bear the image of the creator of the heavens and the earth. We are the living testimony of their ultimate doom."

The men took their time. Wiping their eyes, they spoke to each other and embraced. For today it was good enough. He knew they'd need discipling, baptizing, they'd need teaching, and to stay close to each other. And on what could be the last day of his life, Joab knew something else—he'd been restored.

In the distance, they saw the devils approaching. They were coming via Highway 19, they were coming off Mountain Road 37, and Joab wasn't sure, but he thought he saw, in the distance, rustling in the unpruned and low-hanging branches of the orchards.

"This is bizarre," Bricklander's said, coming next to him. His eyes were red and spent with tears. "But now that I'm in the club, I can ask God for anything, right?"

"Well," Joab said. "You can ask for anything your heart desires. I don't know what the answer is going to be, but you can ask."

"How different would things be if I had this experience a few days ago?"

"I don't think you were ready," Joab said. "But a couple of miracles, here and there, the strong possibility of imminent death —just add water—and, pow, we all have hearts tender enough to receive salvation."

"Joab, I want to live," Bricklander said. "I have to get back to my family."

"Where's your family?"

"Virginia."

Joab grunted a laugh. "I do love a good road trip."

The breeze picked up, and the desert smells gave way to the aroma of rot.

"We should probably go over the game plan," Bricklander said. "By the way, what did you do to Minister Kevin?"

"I killed him," Joab said matter-of-factly, void of guilt or haunting ping.

"I thought so," Bricklander said. "He's laying, over there, by the edge of the orchard."

NOEL
(18)

"The doors! The doors!" Voices were in panic.

The dream was terrible. Hands were pulling and shaking her.

"Oh, no!"

Noel heard the shouting as she climbed to consciousness, but it was a haul. Like running the opposite way on an escalator, she couldn't remember the last time she fell so far into the depths of a sleep that wouldn't let go.

"I got it!"

"No, no!"

Glass breaking.

Doors?

Glass shattering.

"Noel, wake up!" Elias screamed at her. "Please, Noel! Please!"

Her eyes opened to people pressing against the barricade of tables. Before giving a guess, she knew devils were bringing pressure against the dining hall.

The table above fell. She shoved Elias away before it landed on her. Sandoval rushed to lift it back into place. They began setting it against the window but were stopped by a devil. With seemingly impossible strength for something so sickly, it resisted them. A thread-bare dress hanging from bony shoulders indicated it had been a woman.

Forcing its head inside, its ripped face snarled and snapped as it leveraged itself further into the dining hall. The table slipped from their hands, and the devil took hold of Noel. Behind it, more were coming.

Her gut tightening, Noel grabbed instead of pushed. Yanking the monster all the way through and off the table. Without hesitation, she stomped its skull with the heel of her shoe.

Orienting her attention, she saw the kids being moved back and every free hand coming against the tables. The wood was being pounded on, and there was a continuous sound of glass being broken.

"Move!" Sandoval said, wrapping an arm around her waist and pulling her aside. He fired his pistol out the window.

461

LARRY
(20)

Kuykendall limped through the crowd and pumped his shotgun. Sandoval and Noel dove out of the way, and the big man let go of three rounds through the opening. The table was put back against the shattered frame with no resistance.

The pressure was increasing. Every thump coming against the dining hall banged as if despair was trying to devour their spirits before the devils could their flesh. Big Leon came to Larry. "Let us go out the backdoor and fire a barrage at them from the corner. It'll take the pressure off the windows."

Larry agreed. "Take Sandoval and Duran! Unload your guns and come right back!"

The three men headed for the exit in the kitchen.

"Keep the pressure against the tables!" Larry encouraged from the center of the dining hall. "We're gonna hold!" In the hurricane, he marveled at the words coming out of him and how they were obeyed. If his parents could see their son now—the one who argued about the unfairness of having to bring trash cans in from the curb—what would they say?

"What happened to Loafing Larry?"

Kuykendall pressed his frame against the doors.

Karla, Debbie, and Liz replaced Noel at the far end as she went to Kuykendall.

"Big K., give me the shotgun!" He tossed it to her.

"It's loaded. Remember, red is dead."

"I know," she said and looked at Larry. "I'm going with them!"

"No!" he said. "Backdoor! Secure it!"

"They ain't getting in," Kuykendall said, angling his body against the table in front of the double doors. "Not ever!"

There was pushing, wood splintered, but no breach.

Outside, the shotguns volleyed five separate times, and the pressure eased. Small relief came over all of them. Larry turned his eyes back to the kitchen and saw Sandoval come back inside with Big Leon and Duran.

"It's not over!" Sandoval said. "There's more coming!"

"Let's go get them!" Wolfman hollered. "Let's take them!"

The young man's rage was checked by the point of his mother's finger. "You be cool!"

"Hold strong!" Larry shouted.

Pounding resumed, and the fight continued.

BRICKLANDER
(20)

The question, tactically, was where to place Joab and his men. They had pistols, but they didn't shoulder any rifles, only shotguns. The army would have to do the brunt of the work until the dead closed quarters on the church.

"We've filled The Gap with as much junk as we could find," Bricklander said.

Farmer, Joab, and two of his lieutenants, Bash and Legaspe, stood with them. They were in the sanctuary by the stage. A crudely sketched map was spread out on what had been a communion table.

Minister Tim, parked at the back of the platform, wasn't talking. Bricklander guessed he was beginning to experience the soldiers' feelings of abandonment and expendability.

"I suggest we leave The Gap to your crew," he said. "We'll focus everything we've got from the front of the sanctuary and to the highway. If you can hold that spot, the horseshoe will stay intact."

"We can do that," Joab said. "But I'm worried about them coming from the west."

"Doughty will stay in the tower," Farmer said. "And keep his eyes on the orchards."

"They're in there," Joab said. "It's just when and where they spill out."

"Let's burn it," Bash said. "We can torch it right now."

"What do you think, Brick?" Farmer said. "Once it gets started, there's no way of knowing which way it will go."

"It's going to burn out of control, but we've got to protect our flank," Bricklander said.

"Anspach! Crazy Chang!" Joab called out. "These guys love to break and burn."

"Okay, we torch the trees," Farmer said, "what else?"

"We have to get it in our heads that these things—the devils—have a bit more wit about them than we think," Joab said. "We'll need to keep a good number of guns pointed east and shooting out to the highway. I have a fear of them rounding the corner on us."

"I agree," Bricklander said. "We'll need to keep the shooting hot. We do not want them getting behind us."

Anspach and Crazy Chang arrived, got their instructions, and set off for the orchards.

They went over the remainder of the plan. Two men, Pena and Hernandez, would secure the fellowship hall and keep eyes looking west. The rest of Joab's men would guard The Gap and the steps into the sanctuary. Two men could shoot comfortably and pick their targets from each of the sanctuary's four windows facing north. On the east side, parallel to Highway 19, two soldiers were placed in each of the three windows of what had been the Pastor's Study, the church office, and nursery.

"What about the SAWs?" Farmer asked Bricklander. The Squad Automatic Weapon, also known as a SAW--was phased out by the military. The MK-46 fired 5.56, the same as the M4 rifle. As things became more desperate, NORM brought the weapon out of retirement. "We've got two of them in the re-supply. Four belts each."

"I'm thinking we don't want to let these things get too close," Bricklander said. "Enough of them pressing against the walls can topple this place. We should use those guns to do damage away from the church."

"Engage them in the field and thin them out?" Farmer spoke his thought.

"Yeah, as much as we can," Bricklander said. "Shoot and fall back. It should buy us a little more time."

"Why don't we all go out, mow 'em down, and race back to the church?" Bash suggested.

"It's a good idea," Bricklander said, "but I think we'd run the risk of rage taking us and losing focus. In the long run, we'll do a better job from the church."

"We lost three friends yesterday because of that very same thing," Joab said. "They got caught up in the fighting and were enveloped. The rage thing is real, and they use it to their advantage. Even if we send your men out to work those guns, they could still lose their focus. You've got to replace the belts and even the barrel if it gets too hot, right?"

"Right," Bricklander confirmed.

"So let's send out your men with an escort," Joab said. "My guys won't have anything to do until the devils get close. We could go out there and keep your men from getting too caught up and the pressure from building on their flanks."

"That works," Bricklander said. "At about 100-hundred yards, Lancaster and I will go to work. Sound good to you?" He offered to Farmer.

"Sounds good," Farmer said and called Barnes. "Tell Lancaster to get activated and meet us on the steps with the SAWs."

Static came, and Doughty's voice followed.

"Orchards are burning."

"Okay," Bricklander said to Joab. "I want three men each for Lancaster and myself. One on either side, the third on our tails."

Joab turned to Bash and Legaspe. "Myself, you two, Hutch, Brewer, and Vegas. Explain what we're doing and get them ready. Don't let Crazy Chang in on this. He's gonna want to worm in — too risky."

"Does Chang run hot?" Bricklander asked.

"Like a furnace when devils are storming," Joab said.

"I love your lingo," he said as they walked through the front doors and into The Gap. "It makes me feel like you've been doing this for a while."

Bricklander saw the army of devils closing in. After all the anticipation, the big dance was only a few football fields away. Lancaster met him on the steps.

"How many does that look like to you?" Joab asked.

"Couple thousand? Maybe three."

How do I pray, God? He asked silently. *How do I ask you for help? Let us live? Let me live? Oh God, my girls. Keep my girls safe.*

Lancaster handed him the SAW and four 200 round belts in canvas pouches.

"Give the extra barrels to Joab's men."

Kneeling, the veteran soldiers pressed, slapped, and chambered their weapons.

"I love the feel of this thing," Lancaster said, coming to his feet.

"I do too," Bricklander said, "but it's more dangerous than the first chick you meet coming out of Boot. Don't give in to it. Use your brain, and consider your wingman. That's what Joab and his boys are for. So listen to them."

Lancaster, spit and said, "I'm good."

"Are you?" He asked, wanting to see it in his friend's eyes. Wanting to know if he would remain professional and not try to make up for Kristen Block.

"I'm good," Lancaster assured him humbly.

Bricklander looked at Joab. "You about ready?"

"Yeah," Joab said.

They went to the front of the church.

"Listen to me," he said to Joab's men. "Joab picked you, so you must be good. But that's a long line of devils, as you call them, so don't lose your cool, or we're all going to die."

"I've got no intention of becoming fast-food," Vegas said.

Lancaster laughed. "Fast-food—That's funny."

"Stick with us," Hutchinson said. "We'll get you ready for the Mandalay experience."

"Mandalay?"

"That's too cruel," Legaspe smiled and shook his head. "We just met the guy, and you want to stick him in Mandalay with Big K.?"

Bricklander faced the church and The Gap. The faces looking back were determined but not crushed by the number of dead coming their way. Lieutenant Farmer came to them.

"When you two go black, get your butts back here," Farmer said and then to Joab. "Take care of my guys!"

The leaders shook hands, and Farmer went down the line bumping fists with Bash, Legaspe, Vegas, Brewer, and Hutchinson.

"Smoke them!" Doughty shouted from the steeple, and the voices of others rose behind them. Bricklander thought he heard words sounding like scripture, but he didn't know for sure.

"Get some!" Came from the sanctuary. "Get some!"

Frank's voice sang out.

"Hark the herald angels sing, glory to the newborn king...."

"Is he kidding me?" Bricklander said to Joab.

"I'm sure you've gotten to know Frank by now."

Everyone turned to look at Frank standing in front of The Gap. "What?" he yelled with tears pouring. "This is what we're here for! He's our king! And those things are going down! Those things destroy the ones we love. Those things deceive. Those things are evil...Those things..."

"...Peace on earth and mercy mild, God and sinners reconciled...."

Joab didn't know why Frank picked the Christmas song to inspire them until he realized they all knew the words. As the line went toward the devils, all the men were singing.

"...Joyful all ye nations rise, join the triumph of the skies. With angelic host proclaim, Christ is born in Bethlehem...."

"Is this what walking through the valley of the shadow of death means?" Lancaster asked.

"Oh yeah," Hutchinson said. "Except, I prefer sprinting through the valley of the shadow of death because, you know, you get out of the valley faster that way."

"That's funny," Lancaster said.

"Old joke," Hutchinson said.

"...Hark the herald angels sing, glory to the newborn king...."

JOAB
(21)

"Ichabod!" Was the chorus of the dead as they came closer. It drowned the singing of Frank and the others from Joab's ears.

Ichabod wasn't the Washington Irving character being tormented in Sleepy Hollow. Joab understood what others didn't. Ichabod was Hebrew for, 'the glory having departed.' It was the word Jay was trying to utter after his turn. It was the perfect concept of attack against those still clinging to the one true God. Make them believe they've been abandoned.

"Ichabod!" Repeated outward from the waves of thousands.

Joab felt his hate grow. The devils in front of them were the tangible evil of all the earth. Every provocateur, of every sin, ever to destroy a family, marriage, or life was represented in them. Spirits, part and parcel of the delusion that overtook him as a younger man, came in expectation of them all knuckling under in subservient terror.

The devils' arrogance fueled his fire. They stole from him, and this was a microcosmic opportunity for payback. His debt was so great, and he fought to tamp down the rage attempting to consume him. Wisdom reminded he couldn't correct the past, not even with a victory on this battlefield.

Veiled in flesh the Godhead see. Hail the incarnate Deity...Keep cool, keep cool...

But he desperately wanted to run into them and attack.

Mild He lays His glory by. Born that man no more may die. Born to raise the sons of earth. Born to give them second birth.

Bricklander's team, with Joab trailing, was set on the east next to the highway. Brewer took the right and Hutchinson the left of the first sergeant. For Lancaster, 20-yards to the west, was Legaspe, Bash as the trailer, and Vegas on the extreme left.

The dead emoted temptations of surrender and feelings of hopelessness. Shame struck Joab for being so familiar with these things and heeding them for so long. And, now, the devils were soliciting them all like a dealer with something sweet in a syringe.

"Ichabod!"

Brewer was trembling.

"You feel it?" he yelled, and the young man nodded. "They lie! Keep focused! Sing!

"Mild he lays his glory by...Born that man no more may die... Born to raise the sons of earth...Born to give them second birth."

"Surrender." Fired at his thoughts from the devils.

...Never again. He pushed back.

"Ichabod!" They chanted. "Ichabod!"

"It's hopeless."

...Not anymore

"They're speaking!" Hutchinson said. "Do you hear it?"

"Unforgiven."

...Not anymore.

"They lie!" Joab shouted for his benefit as well as the others. "Keep focus!"

"Ichabod," the devils seethed at and upon them like hot diseased breath.

"Glory to the newborn King!"

Joab knew if they didn't attack soon, it would overtake them.

"Do it!" he screamed. "Fire!"

Lancaster and Bricklander agreed on a spot. There was a silent count to three, and then they unleashed the SAWs. Bullets burst and ripped through the air and into the lifeless bodies. Devils collapsed, folded, and were torn apart as every shot did damage deep into the dead's ranks.

"Get some! Get some! Get some!" Bricklander shouted as he shot in bursts.

Joab heard Lancaster doing the same and knew it was a technique to conserve stress on the barrels.

Smoke from the burning orchard blew their way. Dust began to hover like fog, and vision became cloudier. And the dead kept marching. They didn't duck or veer, they kept coming. Yellow eyes locked on all of them through the field's integrated muck.

"Ichabod!"

"Get some! Get some! Get some!"

"Bash!" Joab screamed, and his man looked at him. Joab indicated Lancaster needed to back up. He tapped Bricklander on the shoulder, and the first sergeant hesitated, kept firing, then heeded the warning.

The devils closed in on the flanks requiring Lancaster and Bricklander to wave their guns, but this allowed the center to push closer. The desire to join the attack was powerful. It would bring satisfaction, but Joab knew it could lead to them being overwhelmed. Instead, he guided the eight men to forfeit ground.

Brewer fired his weapon, as did Legaspe. Bricklander dropped his first belt and loaded a second as the devils used the break to get within reach.

"Back up!" Joab shouted. "They're flanking!"

Bricklander locked, loaded, unleashed fire, and devils melted.

Lancaster struggled to reload, and Bash guided him backward. "Vegas! Legaspe! Fall back! Fall back!"

To compensate, Bricklander unleashed so many rounds his barrel began to glow. When it emptied, he stepped away.

"Brewer! Come on!" Joab said. "Tighten up!"

Brewer, holding his ground, fired shell after shell.

"Brewer!"

Joab and Hutchinson fired around the younger man until they went empty. When Brewer's weapon clicked dry, Hutchinson—machete pulled—reached for him. A devil clamped on his arm and ripped down the length of it. Joab stepped forward, broke Hutchingson free, but it was too late for Brewer. He was inside the mob. Blood exploded.

"Clear!" Bricklander shouted. He let go of another burst of bullets to finish off anything remaining of Brewer and kept firing until empty.

Devils began turning off the highway and coming straight for them. Some fire came from the church. Smoke and dust put them into coughing fits.

"Ichabod!"

"We've been flanked!" Joab shouted. "Get to The Gap!" Hutchinson went, his left arm painted red, and Bricklander followed.

He could still hear his men and the soldiers singing. **"Veiled in flesh the Godhead see; hail the incarnate deity!"**

Lancaster's group went into full retreat. Bricklander, holding the SAW, pulled his pistol, continued to fire, and slid back to the opening.

The devils kept coming.

When Joab and the others reached The Gap, the men opened up with their shotguns. Bricklander and Lancaster went down to their knees and quickly reloaded. He sent Hutchinson stumbling through. Doing an assessment, he knew Brewer was dead, but he was missing another. Bash and Vegas were firing to his left.

"Legaspe!" He yelled as the name came to him. "Where's Legaspe?"

Bash slashed a thumb across the throat.

"God!" He howled and emptied his Remington into the wall of devils.

The firing from the sanctuary caused ranks of the dead to fall, but they were quickly filled. Corpses were beginning to stack. Smoke from the orchards cut off sight of the rest of the legion. All the men could see were the devils closing in.

There aren't enough bullets.

NOEL
(19)

The blue tarp ripped away, and hands broke through above the kitchen sink. Stepping back from the door, Noel fired into the opening. Then, feeling the ease of the Remington's pump-action, she stepped closer and continued to fire until the gun was empty.

Wolfman shoved his way into the kitchen, fired twice more, and placed his back against the door.

"I got it!" He said and motioned her back to the dining hall.

Working through the crowd, Noel gave Kuykendall back his shotgun. The big man began to reload.

"You okay?" Larry asked.

"We're going to hold!" she said. Fearlessness had already worked through her, and recklessness began to mount. Noel felt she couldn't be killed or denied anything.

"Yes!" he said back to her and pointed to his head.

She knew what he meant. Rage was a narcotic so easy to slip into. There was pure pleasure in hurting the devils, in stopping them and making them pay. But before quelling the sensation, a push, to the left of the doors, knocked a table back. It began to slide away from the window.

Noel raced to it, but it fell. Hands grabbed her. Sandoval came fired once, but his gun clicked. A surge allowed the devils to latch and pull her. Noel fought, but she began to be dragged through the opening.

"Noel!" Elias screamed in a pitch that rose above all others.

Noel saw Larry spin and Sandoval reach, but her legs lifted and crashed through the wreckage of the window frame. Landing on the dampened, decomposed gravel. A devil bit through her jeans and into her thigh as firing cleared the space above her. She punched and kicked before rolling away and gaining her feet.

"Noel!" Voices called desperately for her from the dining hall.

And then she saw something worse.

Todd, running from the Utility Road, was lathered in dirt and mud. Behind him was Loren. Trinity, bleeding, was in the arms of Kiln as they ran and fell. They got up, then fell again.

She'd found her children.

Twenty devils were pounding at the dining hall, more were inside the camp, and a half-dozen were closing in on the kids and Kiln. She went after them.

Todd reached the grass, and a devil grabbed him. Noel tackled it. Hate, rage, had never been so strong in her. She fired a fist into and through the monster's decomposing forehead. Standing, she looked for more because these were the spirits that denied her a home, a father, mother, and family. Rage possessed her.

"Noel!" Todd screamed, bouncing on his feet. "Noel! Noel! They killed us! They killed us!"

She didn't hug or embrace him and fought off the urge to go after another. Taking Loren by the arms, Noel flung her into Todd and went for the others. Charging, she pushed a devil off its feet and pulled up Kiln and Trinity. They started to run, but a devil got hold of the older man. It took him down and bit into his hamstring.

Trinity came out of his arms and sprawled onto the dirt.

"Run!" Kiln screamed at her. "Run!" Blood sprayed upward as the devil took more bites out of the back of his thighs.

"Noel! Noel! Noel!" Todd continued to shout, with Loren shaking next to him.

Trinity got to her knees, blood rolling from her left shoulder. She wobbled, trying to stand, and then stumbled in Todd's direction.

A shirtless devil, skin a dark sewer-grey, locked arms with Noel. They went to the ground. Knowing she and the kids were dead if she didn't get up, Noel arched her back with all her strength and rolled onto the devil. Its teeth cut along her wrist and forearm, and blood poured into its mouth. A blackened tongue ran itself over the open wound. She slapped it away and stood.

Another devil descended on Kiln. Now two were eating on his legs. Noel kicked one into a second death and ripped at the other by the hairs until it released him. The older man dragged himself forward, only to stop again in pain.

"Come on, come on," she said out of breath. "Get up, Charles!" The children had found each other. Clinging together by the picnic tables, they weren't moving, only staring and screaming.

"Noel! Noel! Noel!"

"Run!" she yelled at them and pulled at Kiln's sweater. "Come on!"

Kiln, howling in agony, rolled over. He looked at her and shook his head.

"Go," he pushed through a mouth clenched in pain.

She left him. "Run!" she hollered to the children, but they only stood in terror.

More devils were at the dining hall, and several were closing in on the kids. She didn't want to see what was behind her. Reaching the trees simultaneously as a devil, she punched it. The skin on the back of her hand split as she hit it a second time to send it to the ground. Trinity jumped into her, wrapping arms and legs around her body. The other two took her hands.

"Come on, come on," she said. To her right, devils were coming between the spaces of her's and Larry's cabins. She kept moving and considered going around to the kitchen, but the siege had increased.

Noel veered towards the shed. The tiny latch was still on; no devils would be inside. Running, she tangled feet with Todd and hit the ground. He turned and looked at her, his eyes big.

"The shed!" she said, giving him Trinity as a devil landed and drove its teeth into the left side of her back—tearing downward. Feeling the blood coming out of her, Noel whipped an elbow around to dislodge it. It reached again, and she kicked a foot through its face.

Todd opened the shed, the children got inside, and his expression was horror waiting for her to come.

Because there was no time for it, the pain vanished. If she lived, she'd moan about it later. Pushing herself up, Noel went inside the rickety shack she'd wanted torn down. The rickety shack that was ready to blow over in every storm had now become a rickety lifeboat.

Pulling the door shut, a skeletal set of fingers raked across her left forearm. A shove of her hand to its face pushed it away, but it cut into her palm. Pulling the door closed, she felt for a latch. Half the planks on the roof were gone, and the kids' faces were lit and shadowed by the morning sun.

There were three aluminum bats, but there was no way to latch the door from the inside. She held the handle, leaned back, and watched the ancient wood vibrate as the devils slammed against it.

LARRY
(21)

"She's out there!" Sandoval said after pushing the flat side of the table back against the open window. "We gotta get her!"

If Larry lingered in his thoughts about Noel, fear would drown them all. He couldn't think of a way to get to her without putting everyone in danger. At this moment, there were no ramifications to her being dead because this moment wasn't over. He could cry later, but not now.

Window frames were cracking. Kuykendall dug his heels into the cement to hold a table against the doors. Big Leon joined Wolfman as the assault increased against the kitchen. Any hope of a back door escape was gone.

"Did you see how many are out there?" Karla said.

It was the first of the thousand questions he'd be fielding. Was this the moment they were going to die? Was God abandoning them? The panic and the crying were about to overwhelm. But Larry didn't wait for the questions or the feelings to arrive.

Pushing Noel aside, the answers came.

"We're gonna hold," he said to Karla and then to everyone. "We're gonna hold!"

Larry's mind scavenged for some point to panic on, but it wasn't there. The dining hall was going to hold. He didn't know what it meant for Noel, so again, he pushed her away. He needed to get rid of the pressure coming against the doors and windows.

"Sandoval!" he said. "You and Duran, lower the table and empty your guns into the window frame. And work your way down the line. Do you understand? Work your way down the line!" They moved without question. Aaron joined them along with Liz and Karla.

"I'm ready to shoot!" Kuykendall said.

Debbie, Jessica, and Angie replaced Kuykendall at the doors.

A table came down, and Big K's 12-gauge spoke five consecutive times. Aaron and Liz raised the table back up. Duran and Ken Hong lowered the next, and Sandoval went to work with his gun. They rotated down the line with Kuykendall and Sandoval alternately firing and reloading.

"You ladies, good!" Larry said.

The group by the doors held thumbs up.

Larry backed toward the kitchen. Wolfman was firing.

"Big Leon?"

"We're good!" He then fired twice through the window.

A hand clamped Larry's left wrist, and he flinched. Clenching his bandaged right hand to take a swing, he saw Tammy looking at him from her wheelchair.

"No one's going to die," she said with no slur to her words and a shine on her face he couldn't rationalize. No drool fell from her smiling lips, and there was no cloudiness in her eyes. At that moment, she looked like every other woman her age. Coherent, with the spark of understanding, and a little bit more of something only God could account for. "Larry, trust Lord. Trust the Lord with Noel. Give him the glory!"

He trembled, his spine numbed. Another blast came from Big Leon's shotgun. Another volley came from the barricade.

"God will take care of Noel," Tammy said again. "Trust God."

"Is she dead?" he said as quietly as he could. Tears pushed at the back of his eyes. The rest of the dining hall, The Garden, everything but Tammy turned to fog.

"You are badly mistaken," Tammy said with a joy he'd never seen on another human's face. She glowed as peace passed from her onto him. "He is not the God of the dead, but the living!"

The pressure eased. There was still banging, the sound of cracking glass, but the tables were holding. Aaron placed himself between the ladies at the door. Duran waved for others to join them. Young and old came to press against the tables.

"They're not coming through," Duran said. "They won't get in."

Kuykendall fired five times, and Sandoval, with Liz's help, put another table back in place.

Hand clapping began.

Tammy drew everyone's attention. She clapped harder, and her hands sounded amplified. **"I got to the Red Sea, and what did I see? I saw Pharaoh's chariots coming after me,"** her voice boomed. "**I took my staff and placed it in the sand, and all of God's people crossed on dry land. Pharaoh, Pharaoh, oh baby, let my people go! Pharaoh, Pharaoh! Oh baby, let my people go....**"

Beth kneeled by her daughter.

Alison came through the crowd, stood next to Tammy, and began to sing. Then Teddy. "**I crossed the Red Sea, and what did I see?**" Elias and Cora were with them now. "**I saw Pharaoh's chariots coming after me...I raised my staff, and I cleared my throat, and all Pharaoh's army did the dead man's float...**"

Cold and stale air evaporated as the dining hall became electrified. Power worked its way around them and filled the empty spaces. The hands outside ceased banging. Force began pushing outward.

Wolfman, seeing his sister sing, came and wept next to his mother.

"**Pharaoh, Pharaoh...**"Adults joined in. "**Oh, baby, let my people go!**"

BRICKLANDER
(21)

When he first heard the *thunk* of the M203 grenades launching into the devils, Bricklander thought of fireworks. A bullet cracked, but these were dull sounds followed by successive explosions.

The devils continued as the guns cut into them. Bricklander and Lancaster pressed Hate on their SAWs and sprayed rounds east and west to the extent of the march to prevent flanking. Devils literally broke apart in the wave of bullets.

Devils? He thought. They weren't monsters, they were devils. Which also meant they could think, and his concerns rose. *Flanking? They're flanking us!*

Lancaster cursed. "Jammed!"

"Pop it!" He said and thumbed for Lancaster to get behind the barricade. When his friend was gone, he duck-walked to the opening and resumed firing.

The smoke from the grove, blowing thickly, made it difficult to breathe. The unintended consequence of securing the west flank was costing them. If the wind didn't shift, they'd be overwhelmed at best or asphyxiated at worst. The only other option was to run.

"Fire!" Joab yelled, and his men let go of barrages of buckshot.

"Highway!" Doughty's voice burst through the radio. **"They're rounding us! Coming into the courtyard!"**

Bricklander went through The Gap. "Close it down!" And the men from The Garden closed the opening with piles of debris.

Lancaster was still working on his SAW.

"Highway! They're flanking us!"

Lancaster left the SAW and took his M4, and headed to the classrooms.

Bricklander removed his helmet and visor and coughed out smoke. He went to a knee and replaced his spent belt with Lancaster's. Pena and Hernandez, Joab's men, ran past him, firing at a group of devils that had turned the corner from the highway.

"Coming down! Coming down!" Doughty's voice came through the radio.

Another volley of shotguns came. Bricklander didn't have to see it, but the dead were pressing hard against The Gap. Chambering the

SAW, he knew there weren't enough bullets, and the fighting would soon be hand to hand. Getting to his feet, he came behind Pena and Hernandez as a platoon of devils arrived in the courtyard. "Move!"

Joab's men peeled to either side, and Bricklander chewed away. Knowing it was his last belt, he leaned into the weapon, unconcerned about the barrel, and took them all down. For the moment, the back of the church was clear.

"Pena, right?" he asked.

"Yeah!"

"Trees?"

"Burning!" Pena said. "Nothing's coming out of them."

"You got ammo?

Pena nodded.

"You've got to hold this spot; I'll get men to you, but you can't let anything get through, or we've had it!"

Bricklander turned and saw the struggle at The Gap. Several of Joab's men leaned against the barricade; others were firing over the top, but they were sliding back. He took the side entrance into the sanctuary.

Passing Doughty, who was coughing out a lung on the platform, Bricklander went to the closest window. Devils were pressing against the sanctuary. Tapping Barnes and Gibson, he pulled them away.

"Courtyard!" he said. "I got two of Joab's men out there. They're sweeping behind us!"

Barnes and Gibson raced outside, and Doughty followed.

Farmer came from the double doors. What remained of the sanctuary's furniture was piled against it. "They pushed back The Gap. The doors are exposed."

"I got Lancaster in the classrooms, and Joab's still holding."

"West?" Farmer said.

"Clear!"

The fight was gaining ferocity, and the passion—rage?—of the men growing. They screamed and cursed out the windows. Spent shells were piling on the floor, and ammunition was evaporating.

"Where do we want to make the last stand?" The lieutenant asked, confirming the inevitable.

"Here," Bricklander said. "We give up The Gap, secure the doors to the sanctuary and classrooms...and...."

"And wait for them to topple the building."

"That's about it," he said. "We're beating the hell out of them, but they're just too many."

Bricklander considered the truck. It was still available. Instead of holding to the last, they could get in and drive off. But San Quintana needed them to fight and take out as many devils as possible. Thoughts of Virginia countered through him. If he and Lancaster were going to go, he couldn't go back to the city. The time was now.

"Hold the doors," Farmer said. "I'll get Joab's men inside."

"We still have the truck. Do you want to bail?" he said, feeling ashamed the moment it came out of his mouth.

The church shook, and dust fell from the force coming against the structure. Pressure was coming against all of them. The best answer was to fight and not give in to defeat or hopelessness. He knew this, but running could...might...

"Do you want to bail?" Farmer asked back.

The lieutenant was giving him the call, and his brain paused. Rosa and the girls needed him, he needed to get to them. He shook his head. "No!"

"Stars and Stripes, then," Farmer said and went out the side door.

"Stars and Stripes."

Bricklander, with no alternative, encouraged the men in the sanctuary. "Keep it hot, keep firing!" Dust and smoke now filtered through the building. His eyes looked for anything to add to the doors—but nothing was left.

Hiram and Frank came in, and he sent them to the classrooms. A third, Chang, entered, and Bricklander pointed for him to follow the other two.

A surge came. The doors buckled but held. Flores put his back against the pile as he dropped a clip from his M4 and slapped in another. There was a cool to Flores he didn't have the other day on the mountain.

"You feeling good?" Bricklander asked.

Flores grinned, nodded, and then pitched forward as the sanctuary doors cracked and bowed. Faces of devils appeared in busted panels. Bricklander and Flores opened with their M4s.

JOAB
(22)

The barricade was disintegrating. The steps to the sanctuary were exposed, and devils were beating against its doors.

Wood splintered, a chair fractured, and a crease opened in The Gap. Orlando was taken by multiple arms.

"Grab him!" Joab hollered, but the kid was gone. He pumped two rounds into the opening to close Orlando's pleading eyes.

A shove by Anspach and Big Geoff came from the right to pinch the crease. Chapman guarded their backs and fired up at the devils on the church steps.

Vegas fired twice and leaned into the barricade. His eyes locked with Joab's, and they were in agreement they didn't have long.

Joab unleashed all five rounds of his .44 and unsheathed his machete. He jabbed it into the faces of the dead, trying to breakthrough.

Born that men no more may die....

They kept sliding, and the barricade continued to crumble. From his spot, he saw Pena and Hernandez combating devils at the entrance to the courtyard. One of the soldiers with them rolled pair of grenades into the crowd. The blasts launched body parts and blackened blood into the air and down on everyone.

Even if elaborately constructed, no nightmare could capture the horror Joab saw. His time in the Bradbury rafters was the sound of muffled chewing, heat, and mostly darkness. This blood and death came in high definition color. He could see eyes and faces under a bright sun—struggling to remain in the land of the living—being trampled by the stress of a battle that would never unhinge itself from their souls.

"It's giving way!" Bash said. There was a crack, and a pew broke apart. "Back off! Back off!"

The men stepped away and let go with their Remingtons. Big Geoff dropped his empty shotgun and went forward. Instantly surrounded, he began clearing space with his 9-millimeter and blade. He shook his head at Joab to abort any rescue. "Go!"

A hand took Joab by the collar and yanked him back. His men were firing the last of their rounds as they retreated.

"Sanctuary!" Farmer shouted at them. "Get to the sanctuary!"

Hernandez and Pena, with the other soldiers, ran up the short steps to the side door.

"Go, go, go!" Farmer stepped around him and unloaded his M4 at full automatic.

Big Geoff, blood running down his arms and shoulders, was now on the wide cement rails of the church steps, still working his machete.

The firing around Joab and Farmer faded as the rest of the men were forced to retreat or risk being cut off. A blur came from his periphery, and without thinking, he reacted. Swinging the machete, he decapitated a devil. Spinning all the way around, he saw two devils take Farmer to the ground.

"Joab!" Anspach yelled from the side door and then fired his pistol at an approaching devil.

Joab took out another devil as Farmer wrestled. When a third got to the lieutenant, he didn't scream. Like a scene from a movie, Farmer grinned at the pouncing of a fourth and fifth. He raised a grenade to indicate his intent.

"Joab!" Anspach shouted again.

He made for the door as the grenade exploded. Shrapnel displaced the dead, and their flesh and bones caught him in the back. Before Anspach dragged him off the ground and through the doorway, the last thing he saw was Big Geoff jumping into a crowd and out of sight.

Things went blurry, his head was spinning, and the sounds of the battle faded. He was dipping into unconsciousness when Anspach slapped his face.

"Jefe!" Anspach slapped him again. "Stay with us! Stay awake!"

Joab held on and began to focus. Water was poured on his face, and hearing started to return. His eyes reset, but his head was still in a spin.

"You good?"

Giving Anspach a nod, he sat up and looked around before falling to his side. Soldiers were firing out the windows. Another was working a radio.

Vegas straightened him up. "You're gonna be okay!"

"It won't stop!" Jarvis said, wrapping Hutchinson's arm, but blood kept pouring through. "Bash, keep his arm folded, or we're going to lose him!"

The fight continued at the sanctuary doors with guns and bayonets. The barricade there was little more than sticks and trash to step over.

Hark the herald angels sing...Hark...Hark...

"You with the program?" Bricklander said to Joab. "You with us?" He shook him by the front of his shirt. "Joab!"

He nodded again and tried to stand, but his legs wobbled.

"You're okay," Anspach said. "He's okay," he then said to Bricklander. "Grenade outside concussed him. The lieutenant...." He shook his head, and the sergeant understood.

"We've got the offices and the sanctuary," Bricklander said. "But the foundation's giving!" He pointed to the ceiling. Joab looked and saw the wooden roof rocking, pieces of it were falling.

He couldn't talk, so he grunted the words out. First, they were a slur, and finally, a swell of energy came. "I'm good!" He reached for his canteen and pounded large gulps of water. He had to be good. To be bad meant to be left for dead.

"Offices!" Bricklander leaned directly into his face. "Joab, support Lancaster. You," he pointed at Anspach, "come with me!"

Swigging more water and taking deep puffs of smokey air aided his balance. Joab nodded at Chapman and Vegas to get moving. Before following his men into the chaos of the Pastor's Study, he saw Minister Tim in the corner. He was hiding behind the Christian Flag's shredded remains.

No one noticed what Joab did because he did it quickly with a sudden and surprising strength. He didn't know if he'd be alive at the end of the day, but dealing with Minister Tim confirmed he was back in the game.

In the first room, two soldiers were shooting out the window facing the highway. Crazy Chang, leaning too far through the opening, was firing with them.

"Chang!"

His man turned wild-eyed. "They took my hat!"

Hiram and Frank came racing into the second room. "Get down, get down!" They yelled

Stepping around them, Joab saw Lancaster and another soldier race through the door from the nursery. "Fire in the hole!"

Grenades exploded, more debris mingled together to heighten the madness.

"Secure the door!" Lancaster said, but the door was missing. In the middle room, there was no furniture, and then they saw the devils materialize. Chapman and Vegas went to work. Joab, surprised to find his pistol in its holster, began to reload.

"Belst, wrap it up," Lancaster said, sliding down the wall next to the doorway. With a crooked smile, he held out a bloody left hand minus its pinky and ring fingers. "We're still immune, right? If not, give me another grenade, and I'll dive back in!"

"I thought there were no atheists in crumbling churches?" Joab said, spinning the .44's cylinder.

"No ministers either," Lancaster said, grimacing. "Tie it off, Belst. Let's rock!"

"Done!" Belst said, helping him to his feet.

Chapman and Vegas' shotguns clicked.

"Blades!" Joab shouted as a new batch of dead appeared at the door. He went to work with his pistol. Corpses accumulated, but sensing a trapped prey, they moved beyond their methodical pace. They weren't fast, but they were ferocious. Cracks, then holes emerged in the wall connecting the nursery to the church office.

When his pistol was empty, Joab beat its handle into the skull of a devil. The door jam broke, the wall crumbled further. As the opening between the rooms grew, the men backed to the Study.

Joab pushed Lancaster and Vegas through, but Belst got pinned to his left. As the devils bit into him, Chapman moved to help but was swarmed. His wail rose as he began to be devoured in a cluster of dead. Blood began painting the floor.

With nothing left to end Chapman's misery, Joab slipped inside the Study, and the thin plywood door, hanging by a single hinge, was closed. Vegas and Lancaster put their shoulders against it. Hiram was crouching and reloading his shotgun.

There should have been mourning for Chapman like there should have been mourning for Orlando and Big Geoff, but the only time they had, was time to fight.

The church trembled, and the powerful sound of air displacing came from above. Joab saw Frank reaching, screaming, at something through the window out to the highway.

"It's coming down!" Lancaster said.

NOEL
(20)

The shed rocked, planks separated, and more light rushed in. The kids, clasping at Noel, were crying. She had an answer. Grab a bat, open the door, and go to work until they got her down. That was the response she wanted to embrace because she hated them.

But it would have killed the children.

So she held the door and searched for an escape. Growls came with the smashing of wood. The devils grew more animated, more hateful, reaching hands inside and fingering her shoulders.

Noel reached for a bat. Her hand ached as it wrapped around the handle. With no place for the kids to hide, no backdoor, no cellar, she had them crouch below stretching hands.

Plywood gave way at another spot in the wall to her left. Faces of devils pressed inward, their jaws chomping. The shed shook harder, nails were bending, breaking, and screws were popping. Crying rose, the door broke, and she took the bat.

LARRY
(22)

In the center of the dining hall, Derek Duran began playing his guitar. As the atmosphere built and the energy grew, everyone was worshiping. Larry saw the tables against the window vibrate.

"There's not a friend like the lowly Jesus."

To the right of the doors, a table pushed outside. Devils collapsed.

"No, not one!...No, not one!..."

As they sang, Larry couldn't remember when he felt something so powerful except for the Sunday night at the Arcadia Church. First, it seemed to caress around them, like the embrace of a parent bringing comfort, and then it rose in power before bursting with a roar outward.

"None else could heal our souls' diseases."

The tables shot through all the windows and into the center of camp. A rush blew out the damaged window frames in the kitchen. The double doors ripped from their hinges and flew out and up into the sky. Light flooded the room, and shadow vanished.

"...No, not one! ...No, not one!..."

Reason tried to interfere with what his eyes were seeing as the concentration on worship bore upward. Larry looked at Alison, standing next to Tammy, her hair lifting, being blown by a great wind. And Tammy standing with raised hands, proving again what couldn't be, what shouldn't have been—was.

"Jesus knows all about our struggles; He will guide 'til the day is done...."

BRICKLANDER
(22)

A crack came above shouts and bullets. Large amounts of dust fell from the ceiling—a section of the roof shook over the sanctuary doors. Bricklander saw blue sky come through the timbers. A part of the wall nearest the doors collapsed to expose the marching devils.

Unable to reach trapped men, the rest—near and on the platform—fired into the opening.

"Sarge!" Barnes said.

Devils began to enter through the wreckage. They found no footing, but their faces hissed, and their hands reached for those that were left.

"Sarge!" Barnes shouted again. "NORM's here!"

Air, smoke, and dust pushed north as Bricklander heard the roar of helicopter blades.

"Belton says to get small!" Barnes said.

"Down!" Bricklander yelled and re-attached his earpiece. "Get down!" The men that could still move--dove.

"Get'em low...." Belton said.

"This is unauthorized...you will report...."

495

The Apache fired. Its guns, sounding like drums with no end, laid hate. The walls crumbled as the bullets swept over the soldiers and then to the north. The tune changed when the hellfires detonated. Tiles from what remained of the church's roof blew away. Bricklander determined Belton had settled near the highway and was cutting loose on the devils coming against the church.

It became clear the Apache was saving nothing. Its rockets unleashed.

Bullets ripped through the walls and passed above them. There was another crack, and another portion of the church fell outward to the field. Bricklander got a view of the chopper rolling up and over the remaining devils coming off the highway.

The firing of the bullets sounded like they'd echo forever. Terrifying but wonderful all at once. And then it began to fade as the machinery throttled back.

Bricklander stood and went to the opening to see the miracle. Belton was clearing the field all the way to the mountain. As he thought, 70,000 residents from the mountain hadn't come down. But by what he saw and assumed had already passed on the highway, maybe, 10,000 had. The hurricane was still storming, but for now, his old friend had placed them in the eye.

Barnes dispatched a pair of devils coming through the rubble and climbed on what remained of the north wall next to Bricklander. The ground was moving beyond them. Not all of the dead were dead, but they were cut down and had ceased advancing.

"Any of my guys still around?" It was Anspach.

"The offices are still standing," he said, "but I don't know."

Belton, going south, passed overhead. Bricklander heard the Apache as it hovered beyond the church for a bit. It was a tactic, employed with success in the Arroyo Seco, to draw the devils' attention. In essence, he was leading them to San Quintana.

"I told you I'd keep an ear out, Brick," Belton's voice came.

"Thank you!" He said, thumbing his mike.

"Stars and Stripes, baby! Now excuse me, I've got someone waiting at Brackett to court-martial me...Cliff sends his best."

"Stars and Stripes."

The fire in the groves spread in both directions. Patches of the desert, interspersed between the pile-up of bodies, were burning, but the smoke had shifted west. More of his men emerged and went to work. They pushed bayonets through foreheads, clipped off single shots.

Steps crunched behind him, and Bricklander turned to see Doughty.

"Did we just survive this?" the Texan asked. He was cut, bit, but very much alive.

"I think we did," Bricklander said. "Gibby?"

Doughty shook his head.

"Secure the perimeter. I'm going to see what we've got left."

Bricklander stopped when he got to the back corner of the platform. Minister Tim was pinned to the wall by a machete. With bullet holes through his chest and abdomen, he was gasping and snarling. The sight brought relief as he passed into the first room.

Hiram sat on the floor, elbows on his knees, mouth to his fists. Frank was face down with the back of his head obliterated. Bricklander knew he'd caught a round from the Apache.

"I'm so sorry," he said, and he was. Belton played a part, but Hiram and Frank were the reason he was still alive and the reason he'd see his family again.

"Friendly fire," Hiram said with a shrug. "What are you gonna do?"

There was noise and grunting as Bricklander went into the second room. Lancaster was sitting on the floor drinking from his canteen.

Bricklander surveyed the mess. "Where's Joab?

JOAB
(23)

Anything sitting above three feet in the Pastor's Study was sawed in half by the helicopter's guns. When the door broke apart, rage clicked inside Joab, and he pursued the devils. Finding Chapman's machete, he went to work on all he could see.

When there were no more devils, the blur surrounding his thoughts and actions lifted. He was outside and could see the chopper leading the dead away from the church.

Blood dripped inside his left pant leg. Above his knee, a mouth had clamped down and broke the skin. A piece of wood had broken off from the force of the wind to put a deep cut below his left eye.

He survived—again.

Into the vale of years...and they're gone.

"You're alive," a voice came from behind.

He turned and saw Bricklander. "Still."

"NORM's going to take credit, but I think this was a miracle."

"That was an Apache, right?"

"Apache. The pilot's an old friend." Bricklander came closer. "Joab, listen, we lost a lot of people, but we don't have time to lick our wounds. There are still a whole lot of bad guys coming off that mountain."

Joab saw his men come into view. Bash, Pena, Hiram, and Vegas came out of the nursery. Coming through the opening in the rubble at the front of the church, Anspach sat down on the cement rail and began to weep.

"I saw Big Geoff go down," Joab said. "Where's everybody else?"

"Hutch bled out," Bash said. "I'm not sure about anybody else."

"The window frame gave way when the building shook, and Chang fell into them," Hiram said. "The helicopter got Frank and Hernandez."

Joab felt his stomach twist, and he knew what was coming next. It had to come. It had to remind him that he was the villain. Sometimes it was tardy, sometimes it teased it was dormant, but it always came to deny any relief to his soul.

"Joab, you going to be alright?" Bricklander said. "You with us?"

Don't look at me.

He couldn't be their leader, but as if caught in a riptide, he was being pulled into the role. Before speaking, he waited, hoping for another assignment or task to come and take him from this one.

"Jefe?" Bash said.

It was a consequence he couldn't avoid. When you were tagged, you were tagged. When you were called, you were called. As much as he fought it, he could never beat it.

"Is anyone critical?" he said. "Does anyone need to get to a hospital?"

"Jarvis is working on a few inside," Bricklander said. "But nothing we can't treat ourselves."

Taking in some of the suddenly clean air, Joab straightened, knowing it would come when it would come.

"We're not going to be enough to make a difference at San Quintana," Bricklander said. "All we can do is let them know when the next wave's coming."

"But that won't take all of us," he said.

"What are you saying, Jefe?" Vegas asked.

"I don't know how many devils are between them and us right now," Joab said. "But this was a miracle, and that Apache was the icing." He didn't know why, but his thoughts fired. "San Quintana needs to be armed with something more than guns, bad ministers, and NORM."

There was no protest, and there should have been protest. They should appreciate the miracle, get on the road, and enjoy the Lord's provision. That was the good brand of common sense he practiced before The Tilt.

"There's the mountain, and there's the desert," Joab said. "You choose for yourselves, but I'm going to San Quintana."

He saw Bricklander rub his mouth and reluctantly agree.

"Sergeant," he said. "I'm going to San Quintana, and one or two need to stay here with a radio, but you're going to Virginia."

For Joab, a measure of restoration had come, but the consequences —fighting devils, both living and dead—remained. This was clarity.

And there was no ping.

NOEL
(21)

The plywood, to her right, split, and a devil's hand reached for Noel. The shed rocked before another push forward came—its base cracked.

I would die for them. I am going to die.

The children huddled around her legs as she stood tall with the bat cocked. At least one of the devils was going to get it real bad.

"Sandoval's going to come," she whispered. "Larry or Big K...."

The back wall shattered. Hands pushed her down on the children. Noel covered them as everything collapsed. She could see the grass and the three trees in the distance. A man covered in mud and blood was unleashing a machete on the devils.

He screamed in rage as he dropped them one after another, in all directions. Splitting and smashing them before taking a final one to the grass and jackhammering his fist into it.

Noel kept a hand on the children for them to stay down but rose to her feet. Behind her, there were no devils except the dead ones. In front of the dining hall, they were dead. If there had been any others in the interior of The Garden, they were gone. Tables and chairs were on the ground. Through the busted windows of the dining hall, faces staring back at her were singing.

A clean wind shot over Noel as she was about to tag a name to the worship song when the man stood, pulled off his sweatshirt, and wiped his hands and face with it.

Throwing it down, Drew stared at Noel. He was cut, bruised, bit, filthy, and drenched in water, sweat, and blood. She couldn't describe what he was seeing because everything about her was cut, bruised, bit, and bleeding as well.

He came towards her, wasting no movement, taking no notice of anything else. Vaguely aware of people coming out of the dining hall, Drew stopped in front of her. Their eyes met, constricted in tears, and a small smile came to both of them. Without permission, he grabbed her by the waist, pulling her close.

Without permission, she closed the gap and kissed him.

The kiss, impossible to enjoy at first, was only his lips against her's. Then like a painkilling drug, the joy of it coursed through Noel's body, spangling down the length of her spine and rippling to the backs of her knees. Her arms went around his neck. The smells of evergreen came, and the odor of death evaporated.

Drew pulled his head back.

"Drew..." She smiled and touched a hand to his bare chest. "Drew..."

"I was so afraid," he said as his eyes consumed her. He raised a hand to her face. "I was afraid of you because I've loved you from the start."

Six Months Before

"...All our days as a country, as a people, we have fought the good fight, and we have prevailed. We've witnessed the collapse of empires, but we have survived. In this current crisis, we've known hardship as we have never known it before. We've experienced the pain of seeing a loved one turn into something we never believed possible. And we have survived as other nations have disappeared. This speaks to the resolve instilled in us as Americans. Keep faith, keep working, keep believing, dawn is coming, and like I learned in Sunday School as a boy growing up, joy comes in the morning. God Bless you, and God Bless the United States of America."

The President of the United States adjusted in his seat and removed his earpiece. A technician took it as the National Security Advisor approached.

"Excellent, Mr. President. You handled that very well."

"I didn't want to touch anywhere near the Jesus issue. Much better to just stick with God blessing us. We don't need any more fuel on this fire."

"You handled it very well, sir. Anything more would have been too much. The right tone is always struck by simply saying, 'God Bless America.' It's palatable for the ignorant and generic enough for the militant."

ABOUT THE AUTHOR

Joe Torosian has been a minister for 32 years, married for 30 years, a father for 27 years, and was a sportswriter for 21 years. He has written six books, two short stories, and 1,201 Fanview columns.

If you enjoyed this book, or have a question, drop Joe T. an email at jtbank1964@yahoo.com, follow him on Twitter @joet13b, and
checkout his website JoeTorosian.com

Also by Joe Torosian
available thru Amazon
& Kindle

Novels
Tangent Dreams: A High School Football Novel
The Dead Bug Tales
The Dark Norm
Temple City & The Company of The Ages
Sin Virus

Devotional
FaithViews for Storm Riders

Short Stories (Kindle)
Joy To The Langes: A Short Christmas Story

Breeze

Made in the USA
Las Vegas, NV
22 January 2022